More
Phylogenesis

"Foster does a fine job with his misfit heroes and even with his minor characters (such as the reptilian Aann). He shows his usual mastery of narrative pacing and slips in a great deal of wry wit. The novel will be a treat for those who have followed Foster's tales of the Humanx Commonwealth."
—*Publishers Weekly*

"One of the premier writers of fantasy and science fiction . . . Foster presents the reader with a science fiction spectacle that is a quest for both inspiration and redemption, beginning with the love of poetry and ending with the mutual respect and union of two worlds. Narrative threads of adventure and well-done characterization twine together to form a profound tale of conflict, interplanetary fellowship, and poetry's place in an always unpredictable and dangerous universe . . . A perfectly wrought and intriguing novel, with a multifaceted narrative vision that allows the reader a greater understanding of the magnitude of such sprawling, poignant, and soulful SF elements."
—*BarnesandNoble.com*

"The Thranx are a most appealing creation, and their interaction with humans provides seemingly countless opportunities for philosophizing and adventure . . . Reliable Foster fare that should stimulate high demand."
—*Booklist*

By Alan Dean Foster
Published by Ballantine Books:

PHYLOGENESIS

BOOK ONE OF
The Founding of the Commonwealth

ALAN DEAN FOSTER

A Del Rey® Book
THE BALLANTINE PUBLISHING GROUP • NEW YORK

A Del Rey® Book
Published by The Ballantine Publishing Group
Copyright © 1999 by Thranx, Inc.

All rights reserved under International and Pan-American Copyright Conventions. Published in the United States by The Ballantine Publishing Group, a division of Random House, Inc., New York, and simultaneously in Canada by Random House of Canada Limited, Toronto.

Del Rey is a registered trademark and the Del Rey colophon is a trademark of Random House, Inc.

http://www.randomhouse.com

Library of Congress Catalog Card Number: 00-190318

ISBN 0-345-41861-1

Manufactured in the United States of America

First Hardcover Edition: June 1999
First Mass Market Edition: July 2000

10   9   8   7

For Michael Goodwin and Robert Teague,
First citizens of the Commonwealth.

PROLOGUE

Things have a way of working out, if not always as planned. So it was with the Amalgamation that marked the establishment of the sociopolitical organization that came to be known as the Humanx Commonwealth. Contact having been established and maintained for some sixteen years, it was assumed by those advising both of the hesitant, uncertain species that procession to second-stage contact would take place within a predesignated time frame and would involve the implementation of carefully considered procedures, intricately designed programs, and closely scrutinized agendas.

That it did not happen this way was no fault of those charged with implementing the voluminously compiled and mutually agreed-upon contact strategy. All those involved, thranx and human alike, had done their work conscientiously and well. It was simply that, as history shows, there are times when events do not occur as planned. Physics included, the universe is not a perfectly predictable place. Action supercedes fabrication. Stars that are not supposed to go nova for a billion years do. Flowers that are expected to blossom die.

Anticipated ambassadors did not have the opportunity to exchange formal greetings. Innumerable carefully drawn covenants withered for lack of execution, made superfluous by unexpected realities. Formal protocols were rendered extraneous. Thus are the ways of virtuous diplomacy foully ambushed.

Chance chose a poet as its champion, while coarse circumstance on its behalf conscripted a murderer.

1

1

No one saw the attack coming. Probably someone, or several someones, ought to have been blamed. Certainly there was a convulsion of recriminations afterward. But since it is an unarguable fact that it is hard to apportion blame—or even to assign it—for something that is without precedent, nascent calls for castigation of those responsible withered for lack of suitable subjects. Those who felt, rightly or wrongly, that they bore a share of the responsibility for what happened punished themselves far more severely than any traditional queen's court or council of peers would have.

For more than a hundred years, ever since there had been contact between AAnn and thranx, animosity had festered between the two species. Given such a fertile ground and sufficiency of time, mutual enmity had evolved to take many forms. Manifesting themselves on a regular basis that varied greatly in degree, these were usually propagated by the AAnn. While a constant source of vexation to the ever-reasonable thranx, these provocations rarely exceeded the bounds of irritation. The AAnn would probe and threaten, advance and connive, until the thranx had had enough and were compelled to react. When forcefully confronted, the AAnn would invariably pull back, give ground, retreat. The spiral arm that was shared by both heat-loving, oxygen-breathing species was big enough and rich enough in stars so that direct conflict, unless actively sought, could be avoided.

Habitable worlds, however, were scarcer. Where one of these was involved positions hardened, accusations flew more sharply, meticulously worded phrases tended to bite rather than soothe. Even so, the swift exchange of space-minus communications was always sufficient to dampen a potentially explosive confrontation. Until Willow-Wane. Until Paszex.

Worvendapur bent his head and reached up with a truhand to clean his left eye. Out on the edge of the forest the wind tended to kick up dust. Lowering the transparent, protective shield over his face, he reflexively extended his antennae through the slots provided for that purpose and moved on, striding forward on all six legs. Occasionally he would arch his back and advance only on his four trulegs, not because he needed the additional manipulative capacity his versatile foothands could provide, but because it raised his body to its maximum standing height of slightly over a meter and a half and enabled him to see over the meter-high, lavender-tinted grass that comprised much of the surrounding vegetation.

Something quick and chittering scuttled through the sedge close to his right. Using the truhand and foothand on that side of his thorax, he drew the rifle that was slung across his back and aimed it at the source of the noise, tensing in readiness. The muzzle of the weapon came up sharply as half a dozen !ccoerk burst from the meadow. Letting out a whistle of fourth-degree relief, he let a digit slip from the trigger and reholstered the gun.

Their plump brown bodies shot through with purple streaks, the flock of feathered !ccoerk fluttered toward the satin-surfaced lake, cooing like plastic batons that had been charged with static electricity. Beneath a feathered, concave belly one trailed an egg sac nearly as big as herself. Idly, Worvendapur found himself wondering if the eggs were edible. While Willow-Wane had been settled for more than two hundred years, development had been slow and gradual, in the conservative, measured manner of the thranx. Colonization had also been largely confined to the continents of the northern hemisphere. The south was still a vast, mostly unknown wilderness, a raw if accommodating frontier where new discoveries were constantly being made and one never knew what small marvel might be encountered beneath the next hill.

Hence his rifle. While Willow-Wane was no Trix, a world that swarmed with dynamic, carnivorous life-forms, it was still home to an intimidating assortment of energetic native predators. A settler had to watch his steps, especially in the wild, uncivilized south.

Tall, flexible blue *sylux* fringed the shore of the lake, an impressive body of fresh water that dominated the landscape for a considerable distance to the north. Its tepid, prolific expanse separated the rain forest, beneath which the settlement had been established, from inhospitable desert that dropped southward from the equator. Founded forty years ago, the burgeoning, thriving colony hive of Paszex was already sponsoring outlying satellite communities. Worvendapur's family, the Ven, was prominent in one of these, the agri town of Pasjenji.

While rain forest drip was adequate to supply the settlement's present water needs, plans for future growth and expansion demanded a larger and more reliable supply. Rather than going to the trouble and expense of building a reservoir, the obvious suggestion had been made that the settlement tap the ample natural resource of the lake. As the possessor of a subspecialty in hydrology, Wor had been sent out to scout suitable treatment and pipeline sites. Ideally, he would find one as close to the lake as possible that was also geologically stable and capable of supporting the necessary engineering infrastructure, from pumping station to filtration plant to feeder lines.

He had been out in the field for more than a week now, taking and analyzing soundings, confirming aerial surveys, evaluating potential locations for the treatment plant and transmission routes for the water it would eventually supply. Like any thranx, he missed the conviviality of the hive, the press and sound and smell of his kind. Regrettably, another week of solitary stretched out before him. The local fauna helped to divert his thoughts from his isolation. He relished these always educational, sometimes engaging diversions, so long as one of them did not rise up and bite off his leg.

Seismic soundings could have been made from the air, or by a mechanical remote, but for something as critical to the community's future as a water facility it was felt that on-site inspection and evaluation by a specialist was required. Wor could hardly disagree. If it proved feasible, this same lake water would be used to slake the thirst of his own offspring. When the spouts opened inside the hive, he wanted their flow to come from a station that would not be subject to incessant breakdowns or microbial contamination.

Unlimbering his pack, he used all four hands to remove and set up the sounder. At the touch of a switch, its six slim, mechanical legs snapped into place. Setting the instrument down on the ground, he adjusted the controls until he was confident it was stationed in a precise and sturdy manner on the slightly boggy surface. Compared to many of the water-logged sites he had already visited and evaluated, the present location looked promising. It would not do to situate a water treatment plant on sodden, potentially temperamental ground.

Activating the sounder, he stepped back and let his compound gaze wander to a formation of *gentre!!m* gliding past overhead. A widespread native species familiar from numerous encounters in the long-settled north, they were migrating to the southern rain forests to escape the onset of the northern wet season and its accompanying monsoon rains. Their translucent, membranous wings shimmered in the haze-heavy sunshine of midday. Long, flexible snouts inflated and collapsed as individuals called tumescently to one another.

The sounder beeped softly, signifying the completion of the survey. While he had watched the wildlife soar past to vanish beyond the far horizon of the lake, the sounder had taken a sonic scan of the immediate vicinity to a depth of more than a hundred meters. From a study of such scans as well as a mass of other accumulating data, Worvendapur and his colleagues would choose a site for the filtration and pumping station.

While there was no need for him to perform an in-depth analysis of the actual readings in the field, he was always curious to see the unit's findings. Even more so than the average thranx, he was intensely interested in what the earth beneath his feet was like because he might have to live in it someday. The initial readouts that flashed on the screen were promising and devoid of surprise. As it had proven to be in every previous reading, the ground on which he stood was composed primarily of sedimentary rock, with the occasional ancient

igneous intrusion from a time when local tectonics were
more active. Though the area, and for that matter the ground
in which Paszex itself was located, was riddled with faults,
they appeared to be long quiescent and of no especial concern.

He dipped his head lower. Having only a transparent, nictitating membrane in place of opaque eyelids, he could not
squint, but his antennae dipped forward until the tips were almost brushing the screen. The sounder was reporting an
anomaly, virtually beneath his feet. A very peculiar anomaly.

It was so peculiar that he considered returning to the aircar and reporting what he had found. But while reliable,
sounders were not perfect. No instrument was. And neither
were those individuals charged with their operation. If he
called in his concern and it turned out to be baseless, he
would come off looking more than a little foolish in the eyes
of his peers. Thranx humor could be as sharp as a young
dancer's ovipositors. Uncertain how best to proceed, he carried the sounder toward the lake, repositioned it, and ran
a second scan. This time, instead of studying the wildlife,
he waited impatiently for the compact device to complete
its work.

The second scan, run from a different site, confirmed the
readings of its predecessor. Worvendapur pondered long and
hard. The unusual results he was getting could be due to a mechanical fault in the instrumentation, a consistent error in
the analysis program, a simple imperfection in the readout
system or screen itself, or any one of half a hundred other
possible reasons—any one of which would make more sense
than what he believed the instrument was telling him.

Breathing evenly through his spicules, he ran a detailed internal check on the sounder's systems. As near as he could tell
without taking it apart, something he was not qualified to do,
the device was working perfectly. He then examined himself,
and decided that he was working perfectly as well. Very well
then. He would leave it to a committee to debate and settle on
an interpretation of his inexplicable findings. But he would
not rely on one reading, or even two. Moving the sounder
again, he set about making the third of several dozen soundings of the immediate area, unaware that he was not doing so
in isolation.

His actions were being observed and subjected to the same
kind of rigorous analysis that he was applying to the ground
beneath his feet. The eyes that watched him were not compound, nor did they belong to representatives of the indigenous
wildlife.

"What is he doing?" Clad in color-shifting, pattern-
changing camouflage garb, the AAnn advance scout was
virtually invisible where she stood crouching within the wall
of weaving lakeside sylux. Together with her companion, she
watched the blue-carapaced intruder shift his six-legged device, wait, then move it again.

"I enjoy no personal familiarity with thranx scientific mecha-
nisms," the other scout confessed. "Perhaps he is taking weather
readings."

The slightly larger of the two females gestured third-
degree dissent and followed it with a hand movement indicating second-level impatience. "Why send a lone technician
out here with a single small device to analyze the weather?
Orbiters are far more efficient."

"That is so," her companion conceded testily. "I was simply
trying to suggest possibilities in the absence of information."

The concealed reptilian visage peered through the grace-
fully swaying, dark blue stems. Their constant motion made
detailed observation difficult. Furthermore, it was far too
humid out here on the surface for her liking. While the thranx
thrived in rain forest surroundings—the steamier the better—
the AAnn were most comfortable breathing air that was starved
of moisture.

"It takes readings of its surroundings. So *we* will take readings of it taking readings." Removing a small, tubular device
from her belt, she activated it and aimed the shiny, reflective
end at the thranx. It was a bit of a gamble, but so preoccupied
was the settler with his own work that he did not notice the
occasional brief, transitory light flashing from among the
dense, oscillating stand of sylux.

The results confirmed the worst fears of both scouts.

"He is making subsurface sonic readings."

Her companion was properly alarmed. "That cannot be
permitted!"

"Correction," her superior gestured. "The taking of readings

can be allowed. What must be prevented is the reporting of
those readings to his peers."

"Look!" Heedless of the fact that her sudden movement
might reveal their position in spite of the camouflage gear,
the other scout straightened and pointed.

The thranx was folding up his equipment. Turning, he
started resolutely back through the grass, making a straight
line for his waiting transportation. Keeping low, their suits
shifting pattern and hue to match grass instead of sylux, the
two scouts followed, steadily closing the distance between
themselves and the visitor. As they stalked him, they debated
how best to proceed.

"We should call this in," the smaller female decided.

"Cannot. By the time the seriousness of the situation is
realized and a decision handed down, the intruder will be
gone and it will be too late to halt the dissemination of the
information he has gathered. A broken tooth must be filed
down before it can spread infection."

"I dislike making a decision of such gravity without authority from above."

"So do I," her larger companion agreed, "but that is why
you and I are here, and most everyone else is not."

The second scout straightened to her full height, her scaly
tail switching nervously back and forth. "He is nearly to his
vehicle."

"I can see that," hissed her colleague. "The time in which
to debate how best to resolve this matter has passed." Powerful legs pumping, she broke into a sprint.

Worvendapur opened the storage compartment and carefully slid the folded sounder inside, making sure that the
cover sealed tightly before turning and heading for the board-
ing ramp. He would call a meeting of his work group as soon
as he returned to Paszex. The information contained in the
sounder was of sufficient import to justify an emergency
session. Even as he began mentally rehearsing his presenta-
tion, he fervently hoped that some mechanical glitch, some
other explanation he had overlooked, was responsible for the
controversial readings, and that he was not seeing what he
thought the sounder was seeing.

In light of the potential explosiveness of that information

he knew he ought to be more alert, but the peaceful, bucolic surroundings lulled him. Besides, in a minute or two he would be on his way back to the settlement, traveling at high speed just above the tops of the grass. There was nothing to worry about. Even when he glimpsed movement out of the side of one eye he felt no especial concern.

Then he saw the glint of light on something of artificial manufacture, and knew that what was approaching was at once larger and more lethal than anything he had encountered since commencing his survey.

Truhand and foothand reached down and back, all eight digits clutching at the rifle. Before it was halfway clear of its holster, a shaped sonic pulse struck the upper portion of Worvendapur's abdomen, stunning his nervous system and punching a hole in his blue-green exoskeleton. The force of the impact lifted him off the ground and threw him sideways against the idling aircar. Still trying to draw his weapon, he slammed off the gleaming, scored fuselage and collapsed to the ground.

As he finally managed to withdraw the rifle, a heavy sandaled foot came down on his truhand. Several of the delicate manipulative digits crumpled under the weight, but the wounded hydrologist was beyond feeling the pain. Despite the strong bracing of his chitinous internal structure, his insides were starting to leak out through the hole that had appeared just beneath his upper set of vestigial wing cases.

Consciousness and sight fading in tandem, he looked up to see a pair of homicidally alert eyes staring down at him. Then the piece of sky that framed the eyes shifted and he was able to discern the smooth outline of the skull, clad in camouflage suiting that was struggling to simulate a cloud. A second pair of eyes hovered nearby, glaring at him from behind a fluid mask of falsified brush. Words passed between the two figures. No linguist, Wor understood none of what they were saying in their clipped, sharp tones. He kept trying to reach his rifle with his foothand alone.

"What do we do now?" the smaller of the two assassins wondered aloud. "Take it in?"

"Of what use is a corpse?" Removing her foot from the

thranx's crushed truhand, the scout nudged the gaping, bleeding abdominal wound with the tip of her weapon. The helpless researcher cried out softly beneath her. "The shot was a lethal one." Moving the muzzle forward, she placed it against the side of the blue-green, valentine-shaped head. Her expression did not change as she pulled the trigger. The skull jerked once, twin antennae twitched violently, and then the body lay still. As the two scouts deliberated how best to proceed, the bands of red and gold that shone from the compound eyes of their victim gradually began to take on the blank brown tint of lifelessness.

The scouts were stolid but apprehensive when they were called before the tripartite board of inquiry. Following the conclusion of the usual terse formalities, questions were put to the female pair by their superiors, to which answers were unhesitatingly given.

"We felt we had no choice," the senior scout explained yet again. "The thranx was about to depart."

"We had to act," added her comrade by way of support.

The senior officer present scratched at an itch behind his head. His neck scales were dulled with age, and he was long overdue to shed and replace his skin. But his eyes were still bright, his mind sharp.

"You did the only thing you could." He emphasized his conclusion with a gesture indicative of second-degree conviction. "If the field researcher had returned to his settlement with the information he had gathered, our solitude would immediately have been compromised. That revelation must be prevented until our presence here is militarily secure."

"Then we were correct in our assumptions about his activities?" the senior scout inquired.

A junior officer gesticulated assent. "The information contained in the alien field instrumentation you recovered was extracted. It was substantially as damaging as you feared."

"The situation is to be regretted," added the third presiding officer, "but had you not acted as you did it would be much worse. That was quick thinking of you to place the body in the aircar, program it to retrace its course, and self-destruct after it had traveled a specified distance." He looked at his colleagues. "With luck, the locals will make the assumption that their researcher died as the result of a mechanical failure on the part of his equipment."

The senior officer gestured affirmatively. "These thranx are simple settlers. They are not sophisticated visitors from Hivehom. Our report will reflect these considerations." Slitted eyes met those of the two scouts who continued to stand stiffly at attention, their tails held motionless and straight out behind them. "It is fortunate you were in a position to effect this nullification. Appropriate commendations will be forthcoming."

The two scouts, who had entered the inquiry desiring simply to avoid condemnation for having precipitated the fatal confrontation, were silently overjoyed.

The hopes of their superiors, however, and of their superiors' superiors, were not to be fulfilled. Contrary to their overly sanguine predictions, the local thranx proved not to be as unresponsive as would have been wished. Puzzled by the circumstances in which the competent, well-liked hydrologist had perished, a pair of auditors was sent out from Paszex with orders to retrace the path of the deceased. When *they* failed to return, a larger search party was empowered. Following its equally inexplicable disappearance, the settlers requested and not long thereafter received an official commission of inquiry from the long-established northern government.

Covering the same conspicuously murderous ground as the thranx who had gone before them, they rediscovered what the by now long-demised Worvendapur had threatened to expose. In the ensuing violent confrontation, most of the heavily armed force was wiped out. But this time, the AAnn could not kill them all. Their retreat and flight covered by their rapidly falling comrades, a small contingent of thranx succeeded in reaching the settlement to report not only what they had found, but what had taken place subsequent to their discovery.

With serious escalation now appearing to be the only choice left to them, the AAnn proceeded to track the survivors in hopes of taking them out before they could file a formal report with the authorities in the northern hemisphere. Though the AAnn moved quickly, efficiently, and in strength, the thranx managed to hold Paszex and slip revelation of their situation past their assailants' attempts to impose a communications blackout on the settlement. At the same time, the AAnn noble in command was compelled to request that his position be bolstered by reinforcements from offworld.

Paszex was nearly taken by the time the first military transport arrived from the north. Startled by the strength of the attacking AAnn, the relieving thranx promptly called for reinforcements of their own. Analysis of sounding data revealed the presence of not merely an outpost, but an entire complex of AAnn settlements located beneath the innocent surface of the extensive lake. Excavating, quarrying, building, the AAnn had made a comprehensive and expensive effort to establish a permanent presence on Willow-Wane before the thranx became aware of their intent. The subsurface lines the late, lamented Worvendapur had detected and recorded on his instrumentation had been tunnels, not geologic faults.

Eventually, the AAnn were driven out of and away from Paszex. But their underground installation proved too extensive and well fortified to be taken. Diplomatic, if not military, attrition led to the AAnn being granted a portion of their claim to Willow-Wane, allowing them to maintain and expand the settlement in an area not seriously coveted by the thranx but forbidding them to establish any others. This compact was wildly unpopular on Willow-Wane itself, but larger factors were at work. Better to concede the existence of a single settlement, however far-ranging and illegal, than to risk war over a world already extensively settled and developed.

So the intruding AAnn were tolerated, the least of their specious claims accepted. Such are the workings of broad-scale diplomacy, in which assorted small murders are ingenuously subsumed into what professional diplomats euphemistically refer to as the "overall picture." In its inert and hypocritical shadow, the pain of those who have lost friends and relations is conveniently overlooked.

Revenge was not a prominent passion among the thranx, but there were more than a few feelings of loss and betrayal among the survivors of Paszex. Among these were what re-

mained of the family Ven. Comprising a sizable portion of the
settlement's population, they had nearly been wiped out in
the first assault. The survivors struggled to carry on the
family name, but ever thereafter not many were to be found
who could boast of the patronymic Ven among the hive Da
and the clan Pur. Acutely conscious of their loss and their
responsibility to keep the family line from dying out, these
few became more insular than was normal among their
kind. Their offspring were inevitably inculcated in these
same aberrant traits, and in turn passed them on to the next
generation.

To one in particular.

It had been a long day, and the members of the Grand Council
had retired, as was their custom, to the hot, steamy quiet of
the contemplation burrow deep beneath the council chamber,
there to relax and relieve the stress of governance. Solitude
was not sought, and conversation turned to more pleasant,
less weighty matters.

Except among two. Though aged by any standard, they
were among the youngest members of the council. Together
they discussed two recent events of import that appeared to
have no connection. It was in fact a connection they were
drawing.

"The AAnn grow bolder than usual."

"Yes," declared the male. "A terrible shame about Paszex."
As he spoke he inhaled perfumed steam from the herbal wrap
that covered half his breathing spicules. "Nothing to be done
about it. You cannot bring back the dead, nor can one in good
conscience vote to embark on an all-out war in memory of
the already deceased."

"The AAnn always count upon us to be reasonable and
logical in such matters. May their scales rot and their eggs
shrivel."

"*Sirri!!ch,* why not? We always are. But you are right. The
incursion onto Willow-Wane was unprecedented for its size.
But we can do nothing about it."

"I know," agreed the senior female. Her ovipositors lay flat
against the back of her abdomen, no longer capable of laying

eggs. "I am concerned about preventing a recurrence elsewhere in the future. We must strengthen ourselves."

The male tri-eint gestured second-degree ambivalence.
"What more can we do than what we have done? The AAnn
dare not make a blatant attack. They know it would invite an
overwhelming response."

"Today that is true. Tomorrow . . ." Her antennae fluttered
significantly. "Every day the AAnn work to strengthen and
enlarge their forces. What is needed is something to keep
them off guard, to divert them." Amid the steam, her gleaming compound eyes glittered softly. "Something perhaps not
as predictable as the thranx."

The male was intrigued. He shifted his position on the
resting bench. "You are not hypothesizing. You have something specific in mind."

"You know of the alien outpost on the high plateau?"

"The bipeds? The hu'mans?"

"Humans," she replied, correcting his pronunciation. Human words had no bite and were difficult to enunciate. Their
speech was soft, like their fleshy exteriors. "I have just read a
report. Progress there is good. So good that preparations are
being made to take the next step in deepening and developing
relations."

"With the humans?" The tone in the tri-eint's voice was
palpable and was accompanied by suitable gestures of disgust. "Why would we want to enhance relations with such
unpleasant creatures?"

"You do not deny their intelligence?" The female was
challenging him.

"Their morality and manners, perhaps, but their intelligence, no—not based on the secret reports I have seen." Sliding off the bench, he reached back to remove the herbal wrap.

"They have a conspicuous military capability."

"Which they are hardly about to put at the service of
such as ourselves." Antennae twitched. "I have seen those reports as well. The great majority of the human population
finds our appearance abhorrent. I must say that the feeling is
mutual. Mutual dislike is a shaky pedestal on which to raise
an alliance."

"Such things take time," she chided him as she used a foothand to rub scented polish across her exoskeleton. Combined with the steam that permeated the chamber, it imparted to the purplish blue chitin a semimetallic sheen. "And education."

The male councilor barked his antipathy. "You cannot educate without contact. Admittedly, from what little is released to us the project here goes well enough. But it is modest in size and scope, and does nothing to deal with the revulsion most humans seem to experience in our presence."

"That is so." Nictitating membranes flushed condensation from individual lenses. "But there is another project, larger in scope and more pointed."

Her counterpart looked up, uncertain. "I have not heard of another."

"It is being kept quiet until it has matured sufficiently for mutual revelation. Only a few know of it. A very few. It is considered absolutely crucial to the development of relations between our two species. Above all, the AAnn must not learn of it. As it is, they consider the humans a threat to their expansionist intentions. The thought of a human-thranx axis might drive them to do something . . . ill considered."

"What human-thranx axis? We hardly have relations with the bipeds."

"There is work afoot to change that," she assured him.

The male chirped skeptically. "Proper, formal relations between our two species I can envision. But a permanent alliance?" He executed the strongest possible gesture of negativity. "It will never happen. Neither side wants it."

"There are visionaries, admittedly few in number for now, who believe otherwise. Hence this second, most secret project." Her declaration of seriousness was leavened with just the barest hint of amusement. "You will never believe where it is." Moving close so that the other eints in the relaxation chamber could not possibly overhear, she touched antennae with him while whispering into the hearing organs on his b-thorax.

She was right. He didn't.

2

The thranx do not bury their dead: the deceased are lovingly recycled. Like so many components of thranx culture, this was a tradition that reached back to their primitive origins, when hives were ruled by pretech, egg-laying queens, and anything edible was deemed worthy of consumption, including the remains of a demised fellow citizen. Protein was protein, while nourishment and survival continued to take precedence over emerging notions of culture and civilization. The manner in which the traditional recycling was carried out was more decorous now, but the underlying canon remained the same.

Farewell giving was far more elaborate and formalized than it had been in the times before talking, however, though the one whose praises were presently being sung would doubtless have dubbed them overwrought. For a poet famous on not just Willow-Wane but all the thranx worlds, Wuuzelansem had been even more than conventionally modest.

Desvendapur remembered the last time he had sat with the master. Wuuzelansem's color had deepened from the healthy aquamarine of the young beyond the blue-green of maturity until in old age his exoskeleton had turned almost indigo. His head had swayed uncontrollably from side to side, the result of a nonfatal but incurable disease of the nervous system, and he but rarely rose up on only four legs, needing all six all the time to keep him from falling. But though they might flash less frequently with the fires of inspiration, the eyes still gleamed like burnished gold.

They had gone out into the rain forest, the great poet and his master class, to sit beneath a yellow-boled *cim!bu* tree that was a favorite of the teacher's. Possessed of its own

16

broad, dense canopy of yellow-gold, pink-striped leaves, this was the time of year of the cim!bu's flowering. Nectar-rich blossoms of enormous length saturated the air with their perfume, their dangling chimelike stamens thick with pollen. No insects hummed busily about those blooms; no flying creatures lapped at the dripping nectar. Attendants looked after the pollination of the cim!bu. They had to. It was an alien, a foreigner, an exotic outsider that was native to Hivehom, not Willow-Wane. A decorative transplant propagated by settlers. It thrived in the depths of the native forest, even though surrounded by strangers.

Beneath the cim!bu and the rest of the dense vegetation, Yeyll throve. The third-largest city on Willow-Wane, it was a hive of homes, factories, training institutes, recreational facilities, and larvae-nurturing chambers. Technologically advanced they had become, but when possible the thranx still preferred to dwell underground. Yeyll wore the preserved rain forest in which Wuuzelansem and his students strolled on its crown, like a hat. Though it exuded the scent of wildness, in reality it had been as thoroughly domesticated as any park.

There were benches beneath the cim!bu. Several of the students took advantage of them as they listened to the poet declaim on the sensuousness of certain lubricious pentameters, resting their bodies lengthwise along one of the narrow, rustic wooden platforms and taking the weight off their legs. Des preferred to remain standing, absorbing the lesson with one part of his mind while the other contemplated the lushness of the forest. The morning had dawned hot and humid: perfect weather. As he scanned the surface of a nearby tree, his antennae probed the bark, searching out the tiny vibrations of the creatures that lived both on and beneath its surface. Some were native insects, ancient relatives of his kind. They paid no attention to the declamations of the revered Wuuzelansem or the responses of his students, being interested only in eating and procreating and not in poetry.

"What do *you* think, Desvendapur?"

"What?" Dimly, it registered on his brain that his name had been invoked, together with the attached verbal baggage of a question. Turning from the tree, he saw that everyone was looking at him—including the master. Another student might

have been caught off guard, or left at a loss for words. Not
Des. He was never at a loss for words. He was simply sparing
with them. Contrary to what others might believe, he *had*
been listening.

"I think that much of what passes for poetry these days
is offal that rarely, if ever, rises to the exalted level of ten-
dentious mediocrity." Warming to the subject, he raised his
voice, emphasizing his words with rapid, overexpansive movements of his truhands. "Instead of composing we have com-
posting. Competitions are won by facile reciters of rote who
may be craftsmen but are not artists. It's not all their fault.
The world is too relaxed, life too predictable. Great poetry is born of crisis and calamity, not long hours whiled
away in front of popular entertainments or the convivial
company of friends." And just in case his audience felt that
he was utilizing the opportunity to answer the query in order
to grandstand before the master, he concluded with a choice,
especially coarse, expletive.

No one spoke, and fixed thranx countenances were capable of little in the way of facial expression, but rapid hand
movements showed that his response had elicited reactions
ranging from resentment to resignation. Desvendapur was
known to be habitually outrageous, a quality that would have
been more readily tolerated had he been a better poet. His
lack of demonstrated accomplishment mitigated against acceptance by his peers.

Oh, there were occasional bursts of rhetorical brilliance,
but they were as scattered as the *quereequi* puff-lions in the
trees. They manifested themselves just often enough to keep
him from being kicked out of the master classes. In many
ways he was the despair of the senior instructors, who saw
in him a promising, even singular talent that never quite
managed to rise above an all-consuming and very unthranx-
like preoccupation with morbid hopelessness. Still, he flashed
just enough ability just often enough to keep him in the
program.

Even those instructors bored with his disgraceful outbursts
were reluctant to dismiss him, knowing as they did his family
history. He was the last of the Ven save two, the progenitors
and inheritors of his family having been wiped out in the first

AAnn attack on Paszex more than eighty years earlier. This harsh hereditary baggage had traveled with him all the way north to Yeyll. Unlike the wrong word or an inept stanza, it was something he would never be able to redraft.

"Ven, Ven? I don't know that family," acquaintances would murmur. "Does it hail from near Hokanuck?"

"No, it hails from the afterlife," Desvendapur would muse miserably. It would have been better for him if he had come from offworld. At least then it would have been easier to keep his family history private. On Willow-Wane, where everyone knew the tragic history of Paszex, he could indulge in no such covertness.

Wuuzelansem did not appear upset by his comments. It was not the first time his most obstreperous student had expressed such sentiments. "You condemn, you criticize, you castigate, but what do you offer in return? Crude, angry platitudes of your own. Specious sensitivity, false fury, biased frenzy. 'The jarzarel soars and glides, dips to kiss the ground, and stumbles, perspiring passion: contact in a vacuum.' "

Softly modulated clicks of approval rose from the assembled at this typically florid display of words and whistles from the master. Desvendapur stood his physical and intellectual ground. Wuuzelansem made it seem so easy, the right words and sounds spilling prolifically from his jaws, the precisely correct movements of his hands and body accompanying and emphasizing them where others had to struggle for hours, days, weeks just to compose an original stanza or two. The war was particularly acute within Des, who never seemed quite able to find the terminology to frame the emotions that welled up from deep inside him. A simmering volcano, he emitted much steam and heat, without ever really erupting creatively. Artistically, something vital was missing. Aesthetically, there was a void.

He accepted the lyrical rebuke stolidly, but the way in which his antennae curled reflexively back over his head revealed how deeply he had been stung. It wasn't the first time, and he did not expect it to be the last. In this he was correct. Poetry could be a savage business, and the master's reputation did not extend to coddling his students.

Looking back, Des was not surprised that he had survived

the rigors of the curriculum. But despite being utterly convinced of his own brilliance, he was nonetheless surprised when he was graduated. He had expected dismissal with less than full ordination. Instead, he found himself armed with private blessings and official certification. Graduation had led to a boring but just barely tolerable position with a private company in the wholesale food distribution business, where he spent much time composing attractive jingles lauding the beauty and healthfulness of the concern's produce and products. While it provided for the maintenance of his physical upkeep (he certainly ate well), his emotional and artistic well-being languished. Day after day of waxing lyrical about the multifarious glories of fruits and vegetables left him feeling like he was ready to explode. He never did, with the result that one vast, overriding fear dominated his waking thoughts.

Would he ever?

Dozens of invited guests were arrayed in the traditional circle in the garden where the dead poet was to be recycled. Notables and dignitaries, former students both famous and obscure, representatives of clan and family, all listened politely to the respectful speeches and ennobling refrains extolling the virtues of the deceased that droned out on the steamy morning breeze. The ceremony had already gone on too long. Much longer than the humble Wuuzelansem would have liked. Had he been able to, Des reflected amusedly, the master would long since have excused himself from his own sepulture.

Wandering through the crowd as the sonorous liturgy wound down, he was surprised to espy Broudwelunced and Niowinhomek, two former colleagues. Both had gone on to successful careers, Broud in government and Nio with the military, which was always in need of energetic, invigorating poets. He wavered, his habitual penchant for privacy finally giving way to the inherent thranx proclivity for the company of others. Wandering over, he was privately pleased to find that they both recognized him immediately.

"Des!" Niowinhomek bent forward and practically wrapped her antennae around his. The shock of familiarity was more refreshing than Des would have cared to admit.

"A shame, this." Broud gestured with a foothand in the direction of the dais. "He will be missed."

" 'Rolling toward land, the wave pounds on the beach and contemplates its fate. Evaporation become destruction.' " Nio was quoting from the master's fourth collection, Des knew. His friends might have been surprised to know that the brooding, apparently indifferent Desvendapur could recite by rote everything Wuuzelansem had ever composed, including the extensive, famously uncompleted *Jor!k!k* fragments. But he was not in the mood.

"But what of you, Des?" As he spoke, Broud's truhands bobbed in a manner designed to indicate friendliness that bordered on affection. Why this should be so Des could not imagine. While attending class he had been no more considerate of his fellow students' feelings than anyone else's. It puzzled and even unnerved him a little.

"Not mated, are you?" Nio observed. "I have plans to be, within the six-month."

"No," Desvendapur replied. "I am not mated." Who would want to mate with him? he mused. An unremarkable poet languishing in an undistinguished job leading a life of untrammeled conventionality. One whose manner was anything but conducive to the ordinary pleasures of existence. Not that he was lacking in procreational drive. His urge to mate was as strong as that of any other male. But with his attitude and temperament he would be lucky to spur a female's ovipositors to so much as twitch in his direction.

"I don't think it's such a shame," he went on. "He had a notable career, he left behind a few stanzas that may well outlast him, and now he no longer is faced with the daily agony of having always to be brilliant. The desperate quest for originality is a stone that crushes every artist. It was good to see you both again." Dropping his foothands to the ground to return to a six-legged stance, he started to turn to go. The initial delight he had felt at once again encountering old friends was already wearing off.

"Wait!" Niowinhomek restrained him with a dip and weave of both antennae—though why she should want to he could not imagine. Most females found his presence irksome. Even his pheromones were deficient, he was convinced. Searching for a source of conversation that might hold him, she remembered something recently discussed at work. "What do you think about the rumors?"

Turning back, he gestured to indicate a lack of comprehension. Suddenly he wanted to get away, to flee, from memories as much as from former friends. "What rumors?"

"The stories from the Geswixt," she persisted. "The hearsay."

"*Chrrk,* that!" Broud chimed in with an exclamatory stridulation. "You're talking about the new project, aren't you?"

"New project?" Only indifferently interested, Des's irritation nevertheless deepened. "What 'new project'?"

"You haven't heard." Nio's antennae whipped and weaved, suggesting restrained excitement. "No, living this far from Geswixt I see that it is possible you would not have." Stepping closer, she lowered her voice. Des almost backed away. What sort of nonsense was this?

"You cannot get near the place," she whispered, her four mouthparts moving supplely against one another. "The whole area is fenced off."

"That's right." With a truhand and opposing foothand Broud confirmed her avowal. "With as little fanfare and announcement as possible, an entire district has been closed to casual travel. It is said that there are even regular aerial patrols in the area to seal off the airspace all the way out to orbital."

Mildly intrigued in spite of himself, Des was moved to comment. "Sounds to me like somebody wants to hide something."

Using four hands and all sixteen digits, Nio insinuated agreement. "A new biochemical facility doing radical research. That's the official explanation. But some of us have been hearing other stories. Stories that, in the fourteen years they've been being propagated, have become harder and harder to dismiss."

"I take it they don't have anything to do with biochemical research." Des desperately wanted to leave, to flee surroundings that had become suddenly oppressive.

Broud implied concord, but left it to his companion to continue with the explanation. "Maybe a little, but if so and if the stories are true, then such research is peripheral to the central purpose of the Geswixt facility."

"Which is to do what?" Des inquired impatiently.

She glanced briefly at Broudwelunced before replying. "To watch over the aliens and nurture a growing relationship with them."

"Aliens?" Des was taken aback. This was not what he had expected. "What sort of aliens? The Quillp?" Refusing to ally themselves with either thranx or AAnn, that race of tall, elegant, but enigmatic creatures had long been known to the thranx. And there were others. But they were well and widely familiar to the general populace. Why should any of them be part of some mysterious, secretive 'project'?

But then what did he, bard to fruits and vegetables, know of covert government undertakings?

"Not the Quillp," Nio was telling him. "Something even stranger." She edged closer, so that their antennae threatened to touch. "The intelligent mammals."

This time, Des had to pause before replying.

"You mean the humans? That's an absurd notion. That project was shifted in its entirety to Hivehom years ago, where the government could monitor it more closely. There are no humans left on Willow-Wane. No wonder it's the basis for rumor and speculation only."

Nio was clearly pleased at having taken the notoriously unflappable Desvendapur aback. "Bipedal, bisexual, tailless, alien mammals," she added for good measure. "Humans. The rumor has it that not only are they still around, they're being allowed to set up a colony right here on Willow-Wane. That's why the Council is keeping it quiet. That's why they were moved from the original project site to the isolated country around Geswixt."

He responded with a low whistle of incredulity. Mammals were small, furry creatures that flourished in deep rain forest. They were soft, fleshy, sometimes slimy things that wore their skeletons on the inside of their bodies. The idea that some might have developed intelligence was hardly to be credited. And bipedal? A biped without a tail to balance itself would be inherently unstable, a biomechanical impossibility. One might as well expect the delicate *hizhoz* to fly in space. But the humans were real enough. Reports on them appeared periodically. Formal contact was proceeding at a measured, studied pace, allowing each species ample time to get used to the existence of the fundamentally different other.

All such contact was still ceremonial and restricted, officially limited to one project facility on Hivehom and a humanoid counterpart on Centaurus Five. The idea that a race as bizarre as the humans might be granted permission to establish permanent habitation on a thranx world was outlandish. There were at least three different antihuman groups that would oppose such a development, perhaps violently. He said as much to his friends.

Nio refused to be dissuaded. "Nevertheless, that is what the rumors claim."

"Which is why they are rumors, and why stories imaginative travelers tell so often differ from the truth." For the second time he started to turn away. "It was pleasant to speak with you both."

"Des," Nio began, "I . . . we both have thought about you often, and wondered if . . . well, if there is ever anything either of us can do for you, if you ever need any help of any kind . . ."

He stopped, turning so suddenly that her antennae flicked back over her head, out of potential harm's way. It was an ancient reflex, one she was unable to arrest.

Preparing to leave, he had been struck by a thought pregnant with possibility. Bipedal, tailless, intelligent mammals were an oxymoron, but no one could deny that the humans existed. Tentative, restricted contacts between humankind and the thranx had been taking place for a number of years now. There were not supposed to be any humans on his world. Not since the project begun on Willow-Wane had been shifted to Hivehom. But what if it were true? What if such outrageous, fantastic creatures were engaged in building not a simple research station, but an actual colony right here, on one of the thranx's own colony worlds?

It was what the AAnn had sought to do by force, in their repeated attacks on the Paszex region. It was extraordinary to think that the Grand Council might actually have granted equivalent permission to another species, and to one so alien.

What possibilities might such an unprecedented situation present? What wonders, however inherently appalling, did it conceal? What promise would such an outlandish discovery hold?

The promise, just possibly, of the inspiration his muse and life had thus far been lacking? The thought simultaneously terrified and intrigued him.

"Broud," he said sharply, "you work for the government."

"Yes." The other young male wondered what had happened to transform his former colleague's manner so dramatically. "I am a third-level soother for a communications processing division."

"Near this Geswixt. Excellent." Desvendapur's thoughts were churning. "You just offered me help. I accept." Now it was his turn to lean forward, as the members of the commemorative funeral crowd began to disperse. "I am experiencing a sudden desire to change my living circumstances and go to work on a different part of the planet. You will recommend me to your superiors, in your best High Thranx, for work in the Geswixt area."

"You ascribe to me powers I don't possess," his age-counterpart stammered, truhands fluttering to indicate his distress. "Firstly, I don't live as near this Geswixt as you seem to think. Neither does Nio." He glanced at the female for support, and she gestured encouragingly. "Rumors may alert and influence, but they weigh little and travel without effort. Also, as I told you, I am only a third-level soother. Any recommendations I might make will be treated by my superiors with less than immediate attention." Antennae dipped curiously forward. "Why do you want to uproot your life, shift tunnels, and move nearer Geswixt?"

"Uproot my life? I am unmated, and you know how little family remains to me."

His friends gesticulated uncomfortably. Broud was beginning to wish Des had never come over to talk with them. His behavior was uncouth, his manner unrefined, and his motives obscure. They should have ignored him. But Nio had insisted. Now it was too late. To simply turn away and leave would have been an unforgivable breach of courtesy.

"As for the reason, I should think that's obvious," Des

continued. "I want to be nearer to these bizarre aliens—if there is any basis to these rumors and if there actually are any still living on Willow-Wane."

Nio was watching him uneasily. "What for, Des?"

"So I can compose about them." His eyes gleamed, the light reflecting gold from intricately interlocking lenses. "Wuu-zelansem did. He was a frequent contributor to the original project, composing for as well as about humans. I personally attended at least three performances during which they were mentioned." His antennae twitched at the remembrance. "Difficult as it may be to believe, he always claimed that despite the absence of appropriate cultural referents, they appreciated his poetry."

"What if there are no humans near Geswixt?" Broud felt compelled to point out. "What if the rumors of this implausible, unlikely, alien colony in the making are just that and nothing more? You will have embarked upon a radical change to your life for nothing."

Des turned to look at his colleague. "Then I will meditate on my impulsiveness and try to salvage illumination from the depths of quandary. Either way it will be an improvement over my present circumstances." He gestured with a truhand in the direction of the nearest tunnel entrance to the city below. "There is nothing for me here. Comfort, shelter, familiar surroundings, daily work, ritual compliments, intimacy with familiars. Nothing more."

Nio was openly shocked. Desvendapur was even more maladjusted than she had ever supposed. "Those things are what all thranx desire."

Des whistled sharply and clacked his mouthparts together in a particularly offensive manner. "They are the enemies of poetry. My mind embraces all, but with them my aesthetic is eternally at war."

"Poetry should reassure, and comfort, and soothe," Broud was moved to protest.

"Poetry should explode. Stanzas should burn. Word sounds should cut like knives."

Broud drew himself up on all four trulegs. "I see that we suffer from a serious difference of philosophy. I believe that my job as a poet is to make people feel better, about both themselves and their surroundings."

"And mine is to make them uncomfortable. What better source of inspiration than beings so grotesque they are scarcely to be believed? What rationale could the government possibly have for allowing them to set up a colony here?" He gestured emphatically with both truhands. "A small, official contact station to which access is severely restricted is one thing—but an actual colony of the creatures? If this is true, no wonder it is being carried out in secret. The hives would never stand for it."

Nio gestured uncertainly. The crowd was continuing to thin around them, the park emptying as attendees vanished down a handful of subsurface accessways. "If colonization is actually being carried out, there could be other reasons for the government wanting to keep things quiet. We are not privy to the rationale that underlies the Grand Council's inner decisions."

Des indicated understanding with a flip of his antennae. "What other reasons? They're afraid that hasty exposure of these aliens' intentions might enrage the populace, especially with the AAnn's repeated attempts to establish and enlarge their presence here by force. It would make sense to keep a second alien presence among us quiet for as long as possible." He stridulated wistfulness. "I have heard recordings of their voices. They can communicate, these mammals, but only with difficulty."

"I know nothing about them," Broud protested. "Remember, at this point their continued presence on Willow-Wane is only a rumor. Officially, they were all moved to Hivehom years ago. To find out if the rumor has any basis in fact you would have to speak with someone directly connected to this new project. If there *is* a new project."

Des pondered furiously. "That should be possible. Surely these colonizing humans, if they exist, must be supervised and attended by specialists of our own kind, if only to see that their activities remain unknown to the population at large. Aliens can be isolated, but not their supervisors. Every thranx needs the camaraderie of the hive."

Nio whistled amusement. "Why, Des, you hypocrite."

"Not at all," he shot back. "I need the hive around me as much as anyone. But not at all times, and not when I'm in search of inspiration." He looked up and past her, to the north. "I need to do something wonderful, something unique, something extraordinary, Nio. Not for me is the comfortable, easy life we usually aspire to. Something inside me pushes me to do more."

"Really?" Broud had had just about enough of their pretentious and probably unbalanced colleague. "What?"

Eyes full of reflected sunlight focused on his. "If I could explain it away, my friend, I would be assembling appliances and not words. I would be like a worker and not a poet."

Broud shifted uncomfortably. Without actually coming out and saying so, or directly denigrating Broud's profession, the other male had made him feel a bit like a lowly line worker himself. Des did not give him time to ponder the actuality of any deeper meaning hidden in his comment, however.

"Can you help me, Broud? *Will* you help me?"

Caught between Desvendapur's unwavering stare and Nio's curious one, Broud felt trapped into assenting. "As I've said, there is little I can do."

"Little is what I have here. Your help is more than I could hope for."

All four trulegs shifted beneath Broud's abdomen. "If it will make you happy . . ." he clicked lamely.

"I'm not sure that anything will make me happy, Broud. There are times when I would welcome death as an end to all this purposeless striving and futile activity in search of newness. But in lieu of an incipient demise—yes, it would make me less miserable."

"Then I'll see what I can do for you. I do not know how close I can get you to this mythical colony site. It is possible that I am already the nearest artist within our classification, and as you know, a little poetry goes a long way."

"Do the best you can." Advancing almost threateningly, Des dipped his antennae to entwine them tightly with the other male's. "After inspiration, hope is the best any poet can wish for."

"Just how close to these creatures are you hoping to get?" Nio asked him.

Desvendapur's tone, his whistles and clicks, were charged with excitement. "As close as possible. As close as you and I are now. I want to see them, to look upon their deformities, to smell their alien odor, if they have one. I want to peer into their eyes, run my truhands over their soft, pulpy skin, listen to the internal rumblings of their bodies. I will incorporate my reactions in a dramatic narrative suitable for distribution across all the thranx worlds!"

"What if, assuming any are present, they're simply too hideous, too alien to study at close range?" she challenged him. "I've seen the pictures of them, too, and while it is nice to think that we might have some new intelligent friends in this part of the Arm, I'm not sure I would want to spend any time in their actual company. That may be a matter best left to contact specialists." One foothand contorted in a gesture of mild distaste. "It is said that they have a vile odor."

"If specialists can sustain contact and survive, so can I. Believe me, Nio, there is little in reality that can exceed the warped imaginings of my mind."

"I have no doubt of that," Broud muttered. Already he was regretting his compliance, his offer to assist his colleague in his inexplicable efforts to get close to the aliens. Of course, it was very likely that there were no humans on Willow-Wane and that Desvendapur would be wasting time and energy looking for them. The thought made him feel better.

"If it exists, this is not only a secretive but highly sensitive government undertaking." Nio put a truhand on Des's thorax, just below the neck and above the first pair of breathing spicules. "You're not going to do anything antisocial, are you? I would hate for you to end up as a negative mention on the daily tidings."

"I don't care about that." She found his degree of indifference alarming. "But I will be careful, because if I break a law it will keep me from accomplishing what I hope to achieve. My own inner, personal goals—not the rules of society—will keep me honest."

"You need help." Broud's head was bobbing steadily, an indication of how seriously he viewed his colleague's intentions. "Urgent therapy."

"Perhaps the effort alone will be enough to divert me into

the tunnel of satisfaction. Perhaps the presence of humans is in fact no more than rumor. In either event, the change will relieve me of my boredom and help to alleviate my depression."

Broud was heartened by this assessment, if not entirely put at ease. "I will research possible openings near Geswixt. As soon as I have found the closest, I will recommend you for the position. It might be a lesser post than the one you enjoy now."

"That does not matter," Des assured him. "I will compose poetry for sanitation workers charged with disposing of hazardous wastes. I will sweep tunnels."

"Machines do that," Nio reminded him.

"Then I will write poetry for the machines. Whatever is necessary." Seeing the way in which they held themselves, he was compelled to comment further. "I can tell that you both think I'm crazy. Let me assure you that I am in possession of all my mental faculties and am perfectly sane. What I am is relentlessly driven."

"As a fellow poet, I know how small the difference is," Broud commented dryly. "You walk a thin line in this matter, Desvendapur. Have a care you don't fall off."

3

The image in the center of the room was notably unstable, flickering between two and three dimensions, the colors shifting more than the broadcast parameters ought to have allowed. But it was an old tridee projector, the best the backcountry establishment could afford. Nobody complained. Here in the depths of the Amistad rain forest, even the smallest comfort was appreciated.

Nor were the men and women whose blurred gazes occasionally turned to the image sufficiently sophisticated to complain about such details. Most appreciated the noise that emanated from the image more than the visuals. They were too engrossed in other matters to pay much attention to the broadcast, their serious interests lying in copious alcohol, swift-acting narcotics, cheap sex, expensive promises, and each other.

At the bar—a traditional affair of battered cocobolo wood, hard unupholstered seats, bottles of luminescent metal and glass and plastic, foul-mouthed conversation and unrealized dreams, overhead lighting, and a complaisant mixologist—the dented but still functional multiarmed automated blender was the only concession to modernity. A couple sat at one end, negotiating a price for services that had nothing to do with the surrounding rain forest and everything to do with the most basic mammalian needs. One man lay on the floor, snoring loudly in his own spittle, ignored by those around him.

Two others had turned in their seats to watch the tridee. Near them a third sat hunched over his drink, a pale green liquid concoction that whispered to him in soft, reassuring tones. The liquorish voice was not metaphorical: The drink actually spoke, its reassuring recording embedded in the

31

fizzing molecules within the glass. As the level was lowered by consumption, new sentences manifested themselves for the benefit of the drinker, like the layers of a drunken onion.

"Fat Buddha, would you look at that!" Shifting on his seat, whose aged and poorly maintained internal gyros struggled to keep the boisterous tridee-watching imbiber they supported from crashing to the floor, the speaker pointed at the image hovering in the center of the room. His clothes were thick with decomposing rain forest and he needed a shave.

"Man, I never seen anything so ugly!" agreed his companion. Turning slightly in his chair, he jabbed a finger hard into the side of his neighbor. "Hey, Cheelo, take a look at this, man!"

The false promises of his voluble drink lingering in his ears, the third drinker turned reluctantly to gaze at the tridee. The image presented therein, in unstable three dimensions, only barely impacted on his liquor-sedated consciousness.

His tormentor, an ostensible friend, poked him again. "Are they gruesome lookin', or what?" An unpleasant frown creased the man's dark face. "Hey, Cheelo—you getting any of this?"

"Look at his eyes," the heavyset drinker urged his companion. "He's right on the edge. Push him again and I bet you five credits he passes out. His chair ain't strong enough to hold him."

The words stung worse than the liquor. Cheelo Montoya sat a little straighter in his seat. It took a sustained effort, but he forced himself. "I ain't—I'm not going to pass out." He struggled to focus on the tridee image. "Yeah, I see 'em. So they're ugly. So what?" He looked sharply at his "friend." "You just have to look at 'em, not sleep with 'em."

This observation struck the two other men as uproariously funny. When the coughing and hooting had died down, the larger man wagged a fat finger at the diminutive Montoya.

"Sometimes I can't never figure you, Cheelo. Sometimes I think you're as stupid and ignorant as the rest of these sorry-ass poachers and *grampeiros* around here, and then you'll go and surprise me by saying something almost intelligent."

"Thanks," Montoya muttered dryly. He nodded in the direction of the tridee image. Feeling the familiar, irresistible glaze spreading over his eyes like heavy honey, he determinedly blinked it back. "What are they, anyway?"

The other men exchanged a look, and the one nearest Montoya replied. "You mean you don't know, man?"

"No," Cheelo mumbled. "I don't know. So shoot me."

"Waste of a bullet," the heavyset drinker husked, but too softly for Montoya to overhear.

"They're bugs, man. *Bugs.*" The speaker waved his arms wildly in front of Montoya, though the visual emphasis was unnecessary. "Giant, gross, filthy, stinking, alien bugs! And they're here! Right here on Earth, or at least at the two official contact locations."

Leaning back against the bar, the heavyset drinker gazed dully at the tridee. "Actually, I hear they smell kind of nice."

Visibly outraged, his lanky friend whirled on him. "What? Smell nice? They're *bugs*, man! Bugs don't smell nice. Especially alien ones." His tone fell threateningly, bursting with false courage. "I wish I had a size fifty shoe, so I could step on 'em and squish every one of 'em." Glancing down at the floor, he promptly slid off his seat and landed feet first on a large tropical roach. The insect tried to dodge, failed, and crunched audibly beneath the pair of heavily scored jungle boots. "*That's* how you treat bugs, man. I don't care if they do make speeches and build starships."

The bartender leaned slightly forward to peer over the bar. A look of mild distaste soured his expression as he evaluated the fresh black smear on the floor. "Did you have to do that, Andre?"

"Oh, right," the bug smasher replied sarcastically. "Like it seriously impacts the elegant décor of your fine establishment."

The eyebrows of the beefy individual behind the bar rose. He did not blink. "If you don't like it here anymore, there's always Maria's down the street."

The heavyset drinker choked melodramatically. "Maria's? This dive is Ambergris Cay compared to that hole. Hey, hey—" He prodded his friend. "—I bet if you paid enough you could get one of Maria's whores to sleep with a bug." He chuckled at his own debased humor. "They'll sleep with any*body*. Why not any*thing*?"

"Ay—they build starships?" Swaying slightly, Montoya struggled to focus on the tridee image.

"That's what they say." The man next to him resumed his explication. "First the lizards, now bugs. Me, I think we should keep to the solar system and forget about the rest of it."

"They're not lizards." His marginally more erudite associate did not hesitate to correct his drinking companion. "The AAnn are lizardlike. Just like the thranx are insectile, but not insects."

"Ahhhhh, go plug yourself, Morales. They're *bugs*." The other man's conviction was not to be denied, nor was he about to let awkward facts interfere with his ripening xenophobia. "If it was up to me, I'd call the nearest exterminator. Let 'em infest their own planet, but stay the hell away from ours. Keep Earth pure. We already got enough bugs of our own." He downed a long, corrosive swallow of biting blue brew, wiped his lips with the back of a hairy hand that was too conversant with manual labor, and remembered the smaller man on his other side.

"What about you, Cheelo?" Andre nodded at the tridee. "What do you think we should do about 'em? Let 'em hang around us or dust the lot of 'em? Me, I'd rather hang out with the lizards. Least they got the right number of legs. Cheelo? Hey, Montoya, you in there?"

"What?" Swaying on his seat, the smaller man's response was barely audible.

"I said, what would you do about the bugs, man?"

"Forget it," Morales said. He had turned away from the media image on the tridee and back to the bar. "You expecting a considered opinion on alien contact from *him*?" He tapped his glass, calling for a refill. "Might as well ask for his opinion on how to retire the world debt. He doesn't have an opinion on anything, and he's not going to do anything about anything." Small, porcine blue eyes glanced contemptuously in Montoya's direction. "Ever."

The words penetrated the dark, sweet mist that was slowly creeping through Cheelo's consciousness. "I am too going to do something." He coughed, hard, and the man seated next to him hastily backed out of the line of fire. "You'll see. One of these days I'll do something. Something *big*."

"Yeah, sure you will." The drinker next to him guffawed. "Like what, *qué*? C'mon, Cheelo, tell us what big thing you're gonna do."

There was no reply from the other seat because it was now vacant, its occupant having slid slowly out of the chair and down to the floor like a lump of diseased gelatin. Overwhelmed, the seat's internal gyros whirred back to vertical.

Peering over the barrier, the bartender grunted as he gestured to the other pair. "I don't give a good goddamn if he does something big, so long as he doesn't do it in my place." Reaching into a front pocket of his shirt, he removed a handful of small white pills and passed two of them to the heavyset man. "Take him outside and let him do his big thing there. If you're his friends, don't dump him in the street." He glanced at the ceiling. "Coming down pretty hard tonight, and you know it won't let up again till sunrise. Try and get these down him. It'll detox some of the alky radicals so maybe when he comes around he won't feel like his brain's trying to punch its way out of his skull. Poor bastard." Having done his duty, he turned back to his liquids and potions and other customers.

Thus co-opted, the two speakers reluctantly hauled Montoya's limp corpus outside. Tropical rain was plunging vertically into the earth, shattering the night with unrelenting moisture. Beyond the dark row of tumbledown buildings that marked the other side of the town's single street, rioting vegetation climbed a dark slope, the beginnings of the wild and empty Amistad.

Making ample show of his distaste, the heavyset man forced the pills into Montoya's mouth and roughly massaged his throat before rising.

"He get 'em?" the other drinker wondered. His gaze turned upward, to the deluge that formed a wet wall just beyond the dripping rim of the porch overhang.

"Who the hell cares?" Straightening, his companion nudged the limp form with one booted foot. "Let's toss him out in the rain. Either it'll sober him up or he'll drown. Either way he'll be better off."

Together, they lifted the pliant form off the prefab plastic sidewalk sheeting and, on the count of two, heaved it far out

into the downpour. It wasn't difficult. Montoya was not a big
man and did not weigh very much. Chuckling to themselves,
they returned to the warmth of the bar, the heavyset man
glancing backward toward the street and shaking his head.

"Never done anything, never will."

There was mud seeping into his open mouth, and the rain was
falling hard enough to hurt. Montoya tried to rise, failed, and
collapsed face first back into the muck that was running down
the imported plastic avenue. Standing up being out of the
question, he rolled over onto his side. The tepid rain coursed
down his face in miniature cascades.

"Will too do something," he muttered. "Something big.
Someday."

Got to get out of this place, he heard himself screaming.
Got to get away from here. Miners too tough to skrag; merchants too heavily armed to intimidate. Need money to get to
someplace decent, someplace worthwhile. Santo Domingo,
maybe. Or Belmopan. Yeah, that was the place. Plenty of tourists with wide eyes and fat credit accounts.

Something was crawling across his stomach. Sitting up
quickly, he saw a giant centipede making its many-legged
way across his body. Uttering the forlorn cry of a lost child,
he slapped and swung at himself until the enormous but
harmless arthropod had been knocked aside. It was a har-
binger, but he had no way of knowing that.

Then he turned once again face down to the street and
began to retch violently.

4

As time passed and contact was not resumed, Desvendapur could not keep from wondering if his friends had indicated their willingness to help him in his endeavor only to shut him up, and had forgotten all about his request as soon as they had returned to the comfort and familiarity of their own homes. But though it took a while to make things happen, the reluctant Broud eventually proved to be as good as his word.

There came a day when Des received a formal notification from the sub-bureau in charge of poets for his region, informing him that he had been assigned the post of fifth-degree soother to Honydrop. Hastily, he looked it up on his *scri!ber*. It was a tiny hive situated outside the main current of Willow-Wane life whose inhabitants worked at gathering and processing a few fields of imported, cultivated berries. Located high on a mountainous plateau, it suffered from weather sufficiently harsh to discourage most thranx from wanting to visit, much less immigrate. He would need protective clothing, a rarity among his kind, and a stolid disposition to endure the unforgiving climate. Furthermore, accepting the transfer would drop him two levels in status. He did not care. Nothing else was important.

What mattered was that the Honydrop hive was situated less than a day's journey from Geswixt.

There was no information to be had on a hypothetical, unacknowledged, and highly improbable human colony, of course. His personal scri!ber was a compact device capable of accessing every information storage dump on the planet, and he had long since given up hope of finding even the most oblique reference to such a development in its innards, no matter how clever or rigorous a search he assigned to it. There

37

was plenty of information on the humans—more than he could hope to digest in a lifetime—and some on the progress of the mature project on Hivehom. But there was nothing about a continued presence on Willow-Wane of bipedal, intelligent mammals. Despite his most probing efforts, it all remained nothing more than rumor.

Reaching Honydrop involved no less than four transfers, from a major tube line to, at the last, a place on one of the infrequent independently powered supply vehicles that served the isolated mountain communities of the plateau. He had never imagined so hostile an environment could exist on a world as long settled and developed as Willow-Wane.

Outside the transparent protective dome of the cargo craft in which he was riding, trees grew not only at absurd distances from one another, wasting the space and soil that lay between, but stood independent of mutual contact. No familiar vines or creepers draped in graceful arcs from one bole to its neighbor. No colorful blossoms added color to trunks that were drab and dark brown. The tiny leaves they sported seemed too insignificant to gather sufficient sunlight to keep the growths alive.

Still, many grew tall and straight. It was exactly the sort of landscape in which one might expect to encounter alien visitors. But the only movement came from animals that, while exotic to his lowland eyes, were quickly recognized by the transport's crew and were well documented in the biological history of the planet.

A glance at the cargo craft's instrument panel showed that the temperature outside was much nearer freezing than he had ever hoped to experience other than theoretically. He made sure his cumbersome leg wrappings were securely belted and that the thermal cloak that slipped over his abdomen was sealed tight. This left his head and thorax unavoidably exposed. A thranx had to be able to see and to breathe. Knowing that he would tend to lose the majority of his body heat through his soft under-abdomen, he felt as confident as one could be in his special apparel.

The two drivers were similarly clad, though in contrast to his their suits displayed evidence of long wear and hard use. They ignored the single passenger seated behind them as they

concentrated on their driving and on the softly glowing readouts that hovered above the instrument panel. The vehicle
sped along over a crude path pocked with muddy patches and
small boulders. These did not impact on its progress because
the bulky cargo craft traveled on a cushion of air that carried it along well above such potentially irritating natural ob-
structions. Outlying communities like Honydrop and Geswixt
were too small and isolated to rate a loop on the network of
magnetic repulsion lines that bound together Willow-Wane's
larger hives. They had to be supplied by suborbital fliers or
individual vehicles like the one on which he managed to secure transport.

One of the drivers, an older female with one prosthetic
antenna, swiveled her head completely around to look back
at him. "Cold yet?" He gestured in the negative. "You will
be." Her mandibles clicked curtly as she turned back to her
controls.

The paucity of vegetation compared to what he was used to
was more than a little unnerving. It suggested an environment
hostile beyond anything he had ever experienced. Yet, thranx
lived up here, even at this daunting altitude and in these hor-
rific conditions. Thranx, and if the Willow-Wane Project was
more than just rumor, something else—something the tri-
eints who made the decisions that affected all thranx wanted
to keep from the eyes of their fellow citizens.

Other than an orbiting station, they couldn't have chosen a
better place, Des mused as the cargo vehicle sped along below the granitic ramparts of the high mountains that framed
the plateau. This was not terrain where thranx would casually
wander or vacation. The AAnn would find the thinner air and
infinitely colder temperatures equally uninviting. Glancing
out the dome, he saw that the upper slopes of the peaks whose
gaze they were passing beneath were clad in white. He knew
what *rilth* was, of course. But that did not mean he had any
desire to see it up close or to touch it. His body shivered
slightly at the thought. There were certain kinds of inspiration he could do without.

Hardship, however, was not among them. Even if there was
no colony, or if there was some other kind of clandestine government project involving subject matter that did not include

bipedal intelligent mammals, the harsh surroundings had already suggested more than a few couplets and compositions to him. Any poet worthy of the designation was an open spigot. He could no more turn off the thoughts and words that cascaded through his head or the relevant twitches and tics that convulsed his arms and upper body than he could cease breathing.

There was little to see when they arrived. Unlike more established thranx communities in more salubrious climes, Honydrop was situated almost entirely below ground. Normally the surface would be covered with vehicular docking alcoves, a forest of power air intakes and exhausts, bulk storage facilities, and parks—lots of parks. But except for places where the brush and some of the peculiar local trees had been cut down, the terrain the cargo carrier embraced late that afternoon had been left in a more or less natural condition.

He had been expecting too much. Honydrop, after all, was only a very small community on the fringe of what was still the ongoing settlement of Willow-Wane. Three hundred and sixty-odd years was a long time in the settlement of a continent, but with an entire world to develop and civilize, there was still space to accommodate little-visited, empty places. The vast plateau on which Honydrop, Geswixt, and a few other minuscule outposts had been established was one locale where frontier still prevailed.

The transport slipped smoothly into a weather-battered shelter. Immediately, double doors labored to close behind it. To Des's surprise, the two drivers did not wait for the interior temperature to be raised to a comfortable level. They cracked the dome soon after shutting down the vehicle's engines.

The blast of cold air that struck the poet made him gasp. Shocked spicules caused his entire thorax to contract in reaction. Using all four hands he hurried to tighten the unfamiliar, constricting clothing around his unacclimated limbs and abdomen.

At least the interior of the warehouse reflected traditional thranx values. Everything was organized and in its place, although he had expected to see more in the way of supplies. An isolated community like Honydrop would require more support than a hive of similar size set in an equitable climate.

Perhaps there were other storage facilities elsewhere. Disembarking from the cargo carrier, he took further stock of his surroundings. Power suits and mechanical assistants at the ready, a stevedore crew appeared. Working in tandem with the drivers, they began to unload the big bulk carrier. Des waited impatiently for his baggage, buried unceremoniously among the rest of the cargo.

A foothand prodded him from behind. Turning clumsily in the cold-weather gear, he saw a middle-term male staring back at him. Seeing that the local was encumbered by even more clothing than himself made Desvendapur feel a little bit better. The people who lived up here were not superthranx, inured to temperatures that would stiffen the antennae of any normal individual. They were subject to the same climatic vagaries as he.

"Greetings. You are the soother who has been assigned from the lowlands?"

"I am," Des replied simply.

"Wellbeing to you." The salutation was curt, the touch of antenna to antenna brief. "I am Ouwetvosen. I'll take you to your quarters." Pivoting on four trulegs, he turned to lead the way. When Des hesitated, his host added, "Don't worry about your things: They will be brought. Honydrop is not a big enough place in which to lose anything. When can you be ready to recite?"

Apparently, traditional protocol and courtesy were as alien to his new home as was the climate. A bit dazed, Des followed his guide. "I've only just arrived. I thought—I thought I might accustom myself to my new surroundings first."

"Shouldn't take you long," Ouwetvosen declared bluffly. "The people here are starved for therapeutic entertainment. Recordings and projections are all very well in their way, but they're not the same as a live performance."

"You don't have to tell me." Des followed his host into a lift. When the doors closed, the temperature within approached something closer to normal. His body relaxed. It was as if he had stepped into a larval nursery. Aware that Ouwetvosen was watching him closely, he straightened his antennae and shifted from six legs back onto four.

"Chilled?"

"I'm fine," Des lied.

His guide's attitude seemed to soften slightly. "It takes some getting used to. Be thankful you're not an agricultural worker. You don't have to spend time on the outside if you don't want to. Myself, I'm a fourth-level administrator. I don't go to the surface unless somebody orders me."

Desvendapur felt emboldened. "It can't be that bad." He indicated his cold-weather gear. "Equipped like this, I think I could stand it for a workday."

The administrator eyed him thoughtfully. "After a while, you probably could. That's how the agri folk dress. Except when the rilth is precipitating out of the atmosphere, of course. Then they require full environmental suits." His mandibles clicked sharply. "One might as well be working in space."

Des had not made it to the administrator's sarcasm. "You are subject to falling rilth? Here, at Honydrop? I saw some compacted on the high peaks, of course—but it actually *falls* here?"

"Toward the end of the wet season, yes. It does sometimes grow cold enough to freeze precipitation and make it fall to the ground. You can walk on it—if you dare. I've seen experienced, long-term agri workers do it barefoot. Not for more than a few moments," he added quickly.

Des tried to imagine walking barefoot in rilth, the icy frozen moisture burning the underside of his unprotected foot-claws, numbing nerves and crawling up his legs. Who would voluntarily subject themselves to such hell? That kind of cold would penetrate right through the chitin of a person's protective exoskeleton to threaten the moist, warm fluids and muscles and nerve endings within. Did he dare?

"One question, Ouwetvosen: Why did they name a hive situated in country like this, in a climate like this, Honydrop?"

His host glanced back at him and gestured with a truhand. "Someone had a sense of humor. What kind of sense, I'd just as soon not say."

Desvendapur's private quarters turned out to be of modest dimensions and were equipped with comfortable appointments. Once settled within, he prepared to address the matter of the individual climate control. His mouthparts parted con-

templatively, then hesitated. It was his state of mind that
was chilled, not his body. Here below the surface, within the
Honydrop hive, the temperature was set at thranx norm and
the internal humidity was raised to the appropriate 90 percent. Stop thinking about conditions on the surface, he admonished himself, and the rest of your body will follow your
mind's lead.

Already he had composed and discarded a good ten minutes' worth of material. Inspired by what he had seen, it had
been full of portentous references to the searing cold and
barren mountains. Reviewing the stanzas, he realized that
these were not what the locals would want to hear about. They
wanted to be soothed, to be transported by his words and
sounds and hand gestures; not reminded of the harshness of
their surroundings. So he threw out everything he had contrived and began anew.

His inaugural recitation was well attended. Anything fresh
was a novelty in Honydrop, and that included a recently
arrived therapist like himself. Having full confidence in
his abilities, he did not force his performance, and it went
"soothly." Following his well-thought-out coda, more than a
few females and males walked to the center of the small community amphitheater to congratulate him and to chat amiably.
After the stark, tense journey up from the lowlands, it felt
good to be back among a swarm, the warmth and smell of
many unclothed thranx pressing close around him. He accepted their thanks and comments readily, grateful for the
attention. Veiled promises of possible mating opportunities
were appreciatively noted.

Reassured and exhausted, he retired to his quarters at the
appropriate hour, reviewing in his mind all that he had seen
and experienced since arriving. The isolation, the ruggedness
of his surroundings, should make for inspired composing. In
a few days he felt he would be mentally secure enough to join
the agricultural workers on one of their daily forays to the
berry fields, to watch them at work and experience more of
this exotic, little-visited corner of Willow-Wane.

He knew he would be watched while his work was being
evaluated. It would not do to inquire too quickly into rumors
about a nearby mysterious project, or to ask frequently about

clandestine government operations in the area. Honydrop was located a respectable distance away from and on the opposite side of a high, sharp mountain ridge from Geswixt, the hive that would be the support base for any eccentric outworld operations. Somehow he would have to find a way to pay the place a visit without arousing any suspicions. Honydrop was a typical agricultural community, albeit a markedly isolated one. Its inhabitants went about their business free of immoderate surveillance. Geswixt could be different.

If it wasn't, then he had come all this way and gone to all this trouble—not to mention sacrificing two levels in status—for nothing.

As the weeks passed he found himself settling in among his fellow workers. They were a hardy lot, the thranx of Honydrop. They appreciated every word of his poetry, every mannered gesture, dip of head, and spiral of antennae. Even the less inspired of his workmanlike refrains drew praise. His success, he felt, was due more to the ardor he emanated while performing than to any brilliance of invention. As a soother, he was inescapably impassioned. This additional emotional warmth was gratefully embraced by the citizens. Unsolicited commendations piled up in his record. There was talk of recommending him for an embedded shoulder star.

At any time, he could have requested a transfer to a larger, more rewarding venue. Promotion within his calling also beckoned. He made no effort to procure either.

What he did do was strive to make friends with anyone engaged in transportation, be it the operator of one of the loaders that gathered the plump fruit from the scattered fields, the drivers of internal individual transports, or the occasional visiting cargo pilot. A check of maps showed that it would be futile to attempt to walk overland to Geswixt or anywhere in its vicinity. Without a full environment suit he would never get across the intervening ridge, and there was no viable reason why a poet should need to requisition that kind of extreme-weather gear. It left him no choice but to try and hitch a ride some day.

The difficulty was that despite their geographic proximity, there was little interchange between Honydrop and Geswixt. The produce harvested by Honydrop hive went directly out of the mountains and down to processing plants in the nearest city. Nothing was shipped from Honydrop to Geswixt, and all necessary supplies came straight up from the lowlands. For all the formal intercourse that took place between the two hives they might as well have been on opposite sides of the planet.

He was sitting in one of the two community parks, surrounded by supplementary humidity, dense tropical growth, and edible fungi, basking in the artificial light that filtered hazily down from the ceiling, when he was approached by Heulmilsuwir. A logistics operator who, like many, admired his work, she had become a good if casual friend.

"Sweet tidings to you, Desvendapur."

He set his scri!ber aside, mildly irritated at having been interrupted in midcomposition. "Good day, Heul. Are you on off-time?"

"For a little while." She settled herself on the bench next to his, straddling it with her abdomen, her trulegs splayed out to either side. "You're still working, even here?"

"The curse of creativity." He made a soft, humorous gesture to take the edge off his tone. "Even a soother needs soothing. I find that in all of Honydrop, this place does that for me."

"Only this place?" Reaching out with a truhand, she stroked his slick, blue-green thorax just below the breathing spicules.

Idly, he mused on the slenderness of her ovipositors, curled up over her lower abdomen. "There are others," he conceded with grudging warmth.

They made inconsequential but diverting chatter for a while. Then her tone changed. "Am I wrong, or in the intervals when we were talking days ago did you mention that you would like to visit Geswixt?"

He fought to suppress his initial reaction. While his face was inflexible, his limbs were not. He felt he largely succeeded in hiding from this female what he was feeling. "A change of scenery, however transitory, is always a welcome diversion."

She indicated disagreement and clicked her mandibles sharply for emphasis. "Not if it means going outside. Personally, I can't imagine why anyone would want to go to the trouble of visiting Geswixt. Everything I've heard about the place suggests that it's a grim, spare little mining station, with nothing in the way of amenities." She gestured with a tru-hand. "Less so even than Honydrop."

"What do they mine there?" he asked absently. "What kind of ore?"

She gestured uncertainty. "I do not know. I think I re-member hearing something about an ongoing dig for nonfer-rous materials, but I don't believe they've actually hit an ore body yet. They're still searching."

"And tunneling a lot, I imagine. A mine would mean many tunnels. A great deal of earth and rock would have to be moved."

She eyed him curiously. "Why, yes, I suppose so." Light flashed off the multifarious golden mirrors that were her eyes. "Anyway, if you really want to go there and have a look around, I've found someone who might take you."

His hearts pounded a little faster. "That is interesting. Would I know this person?"

"Perhaps. Her name is Melnibicon. She's a driver." When Des indicated his ignorance, Heulmilsuwir elaborated. "We've met a number of times, in the course of checking her mani-fests. It seems that there is a need for a certain medicine in Geswixt. A small quantity of a little-used enzymatic catalyst. Rather than wait to have it shipped from Ciccikalk, our de-partment is sending some over the mountains to Geswixt. A quick courtesy run. Melnibicon is taking it. Since her trans-port will be pretty much empty except for a single package of medication, I thought she might have room for a passenger."

"You asked her on my behalf?" Had he not made a con-scious effort to suppress it, Desvendapur might have been moved to affection.

"I knew you were interested, and I have enjoyed your reci-tals so much—and your company."

"I thought travel was prohibited between Honydrop and Geswixt." He watched closely for any reaction.

"Restricted. Not prohibited. Otherwise, clearing the requi-site bureaucratic strictures would prevent Melnibicon from making the trip. Officially, casual travel is not supposed to take place. But now and again, people do make the journey."

Leaning forward, she reached into a beautifully embroidered, hand-woven abdominal pouch and handed him an embossed plastic rectangle.

"This is where you will find her. She's leaving mid-midday so she can make it back before dark. It is better to do these things on the cusp of the moment. Too much planning can lead to exposure. Are you going to meet with her and try to do this?"

Gathering all four trulegs beneath him, he slid off the bench. "I don't know," he lied. "I'll have to think about it. If I am found out, it could mean trouble for me."

"I won't tell." The logistics officer flexed her ovipositors coquettishly. "You will get there, have your little look around and visit, and be back before anyone in a position to object realizes that you've gone. Where is the harm in that?"

No harm indeed. Eventualities cascaded through his mind like logs swept before a spring monsoon. "I will be back tonight," he declared flatly.

"Of course you will." She abandoned her own bench to stand alongside him. "And I will be waiting to greet you, to hear all about your furtive visit to exotic Geswixt." She gestured amusement.

He started to leave, composing the necessary preparations in his mind. Then he hesitated and looked over at her. "Heul, why this interest in me? Why the persistence on my behalf?"

"You're a poet, Des. You conform so differently." With that she was gone, scampering off in the direction of one of the south tunnels. He watched her depart, then headed for his modest quarters. There were several small items he wanted to be sure and take along with him—just in case.

If he was lucky, the opportunity might arise not to come back.

Melnibicon was an older, taciturn thranx whose ovipositors had long since lost their resilience and collapsed against her wing cases. After assuring herself that Desvendapur had come alone and had not been followed, she directed him into the back of the cargo lifter's cramped cockpit. No one saw him board, the rest of the warehouse facility's crew being fully occupied with tasks of their own.

Granted clearance, the lifter trundled out through the weather-tight double doors onto a small, spotless landing area. Des was jolted when the craft took off straight up, rising to a height of several hundred feet before leveling off and accelerating eastward.

"Sorry about that." Melnibicon grunted a terse apology as she kept a careful watch on her instrumentation, occasionally glancing up to take in the daunting view forward. "I'm used to hauling cargo and produce, not sightseers."

"It's all right." Settling himself onto the narrow, empty bench alongside her, he studied the view outside. Rugged peaks and jagged ridges saddled with rilth separated the fertile but cold valley beneath which Honydrop lay from the higher vale that was home to Geswixt. Once again, he saw that attempting to cross between the two on foot in anything less than full environmental gear would have brought a quick death to the hardiest thranx. In contrast, the lifter would make the trip in less than an hour.

He felt some sort of thanks was in order. "This is very good of you."

A reply that was more grunt than whistle assailed his ears. "This job is boring enough. A little risk is worth it for a little company. Talk to me, poet. Tell me about yourself, and the world beyond this cold hell. How goes life in Ciccikalk?"

"Why ask me? You have pictures, images."

"That's not the same as hearing it from someone who's recently been places. Use flowery language, poet. I like being soothed in High Thranx."

He complied as best he was able, resorting to improvisation when knowledge and experience failed, and all the while doing his best not to look outside. Doing so reminded him of the cold death that awaited below.

In spite of his nervousness he found that the time passed quickly. When Melnibicon indicated that they had crossed the ridge and were descending into Geswixt, he forced aside his unease and pressed his face and antennae to the port.

The view was less than instructive. Not having any idea what to expect, he was still disappointed. The panorama was less than inspiring. Certainly it dispensed no revelations.

Below them, a long, narrow valley stretched from the impossibly inhospitable high mountains that lay to the north off in the direction of the distant sea. A fast-flowing river ran down the center of the valley. Unlike the country above and around Honydrop, the land showed no signs of cultivation. Only the rubble-free disc of the landing platform indicated the presence in the valley of intelligent inhabitants. They were flying over one of the most remote regions on Willow-Wane. Geswixt, like Honydrop and every other thranx hive built in a less than ideal climatic zone, would of course be located entirely underground.

What did you expect? he admonished himself as the lifter hummed through a pass between two rilth-clad crags. Hordes of humans dashing about in all directions, or genuflecting at the approach of every craft making an arrival? The absence of any visible indication that the bipedal mammals were present was hardly conclusive proof of their absence.

Neither, however, was it encouraging.

After an uneventful descent, Melnibicon set the lifter down gently on the landing disc and taxied forward until they were once more within a sheltering enclosure and surrounded by other vehicles. The assortment of battered, weather-scoured craft parked in the Geswixt terminal betrayed no hidden uses. The terminal looked exactly like the one in Honydrop, only larger. Cargo was being unloaded from one aircar while a small lifter was being filled with an assortment of crates and barrels from a pair of container transports. There was no evidence of unusual activity or exceptional security.

If it was after all nothing but rumor, he thought disappointedly, then he had wasted not just an afternoon but the past several seasons of his life on a quixotic, futile quest.

The muted hum of the lifter's engine died. Slipping free of the pilot's bench and gear, Melnibicon turned to look back at him. "Welcome to Geswixt. Is it what you expected?"

He gestured noncommittally. "I haven't seen anything yet."

She generated the high-pitched whistle that was thranx laughter. "Have a look around. I need to make delivery of that medication. They're waiting for it, so it shouldn't take long. Then I am going to take a little break for myself, chat with some fliers I know here." She spoke to the lifter and it replied with the correct time. "Be back in four time-parts. I'd rather not fly through these mountains after dark, even if the lifter does most of the flying itself. Just because the route is prepro-grammed doesn't mean I don't want to be able to see where we are going."

Disembarking, he found himself alone in the spacious ter-minal. With no specific destination in mind, he wandered from craft to craft, observing handlers at work and asking what he hoped were innocuously phrased questions that would give the impression he knew about something that might or might not actually exist. The replies he received varied from the bemused to the straightforwardly indeterminate. In this manner he passed most of the remainder of the afternoon, at the end of which period he was no more enlightened than he had been prior to leaving Honydrop.

One young male in particular was having a difficult time shifting a stack of six-sided containers from an off-loading platform onto the back of a small transport vehicle. The ma-chinery he was using to perform the work was balky and un-cooperative. It was a rare example of thranx patience wearing thin. Having nothing else to do and already resigned to re-turning to Honydrop devoid of the edification he sought, Des wandered over and offered his help. If there was nothing here to stimulate his mind, at least he could exercise his body.

The youth accepted the stranger's offer gratefully. With the two of them working in tandem the process of shifting the containers accelerated noticeably. The open back of the little vehicle began to fill.

"What is in these?" Only mildly interested, Desvendapur glanced down at the container cradled in his four arms. The information embossed on the side of the gray repository was less than descriptive.

"Food," the other male informed him. "Ingredients. I am a food-preparation assistant, third level." There was no false pride in his voice. "Graduated at the top of my classification several years ago. That is how I secured this position."

"You make it sound like it's something special." Never known for his tact, Desvendapur was not about to open a new wing case now. He passed another container to the waiting male. "This is Geswixt, not Ciccikalk." In what had become a rote comment, he fished automatically. "Of course, if the humans were here, it would be different."

"Here?" The hardworking preparator whistled amusedly. "Why would there be any humans here, in Geswixt?"

"Why indeed? An absurd notion." A practiced Des displayed neither discouragement nor excitement.

His new acquaintance barely paused to catch his breath. "It really is. They are all up-valley, in their own quarters." He indicated the rapidly growing stack of containers. "This is food for them. I'm learning how to prepare sustenance not for our kind, but for humans."

5

Having by now more or less come to the depressing conclusion that the presence of humans in Geswixt was a myth, Desvendapur made the fastest mental adjustment of his life. With admirable lack of hesitation, he responded, "Yes, I know."

"You know?" The preparator hesitated uncertainly. "How do you know that?"

"By the markings on the containers," the poet replied without hesitation, supple prevarication being close kin to the white heat of creation. The only difference was that he was creating for the sake of convenience and not for posterity.

His new acquaintance clicked dubiously. "Every shipment is coded. How do you come to know the codes?"

Self-immersed in semantic mud and unable to see a way clear to extricating himself, Des blithely burrowed in deeper. "Because I'm here to cross-check you. I am also in food preparation, just assigned here as a general kitchen assistant." He tapped the repository he was cradling with all four digits of one truhand. "How are your skills? Current? Up-to-date? Tell me what this contains."

Distracted, the preparator glanced at the embossing. "Powdered milk. A natural mammalian bodily extract that is used as an ingredient in many meals."

"Very good!" Des complimented him slavishly even as he wondered what 'powdered milk' might be. "This one's trickier." He singled out a cylinder with a larger embossed identification area than its predecessor. "How about this?"

The younger male hesitated only briefly. "Soya patties, various nut extracts, dehydrated fish, assorted fruits and vegetables. I don't know all the individual names yet."

"Go on, try," Des urged him. "I'm going to catch you out yet before we're finished here."

"Nothing was said to me about another assistant being assigned to my section," the preparator murmured, still uncertain.

"That's what I thought." Des moved to stack the container without letting the other have a look at its index. "This one is too alien for you."

"No content listing is too alien for me. At least, I don't think it is." Antennae gyrated pridefully. "I complete all my assignments and receive notable ratings."

They continued in this fashion until the last of the containers had been transferred and its contents elucidated. "Where are your quarters?"

"They have not been designated yet." Des continued to improvise, a skill at which poet-soothers excelled. "I came up early. I'm not supposed to present myself until next day next."

The preparator considered. "There is not much to see here in Geswixt proper. Why don't you come with me? You can share my room until you have been assigned."

"Many thanks, Ulunegjeprok."

His new friend glanced around. "Where is your personal gear?"

"It missed the transport because I decided to come up early," Des explained. "Don't worry about me. It will work its way through the system in a couple of days."

"You can borrow some of mine if you need anything. I see you've already got cold-climate gear." He indicated the special protective attire that covered most of Desvendapur's body. "I need to see if there is any other cargo here for the kitchen. If not, we can leave in half a time-part."

"I will meet you right here," Des assured him.

Leaving the preparator, the poet rushed from one part of the terminal to the next in search of Melnibicon. When he found her, she was conversing amiably with a pair of older thranx. Fighting to conceal his excitement, he drew her aside.

"What's going on?" She eyed him warily. "Your spicules are dilated."

"I have . . . met someone," he hastened to explain. "An old friend. He has invited me to stay with him for a while."

"What's that? You can't do that." The senior flier looked around uncomfortably. "I took a chance just in bringing you over here for the afternoon. I can't leave you here. Your absence will be questioned."

"I'll take care of it. I will not involve you in any way, Melnibicon."

She took a step back from him, fending him off with both foothands. "Blood parasites, you won't! I am already involved. You came *with* me, soother, and you are coming back with me."

"It is only for a day or two," he pleaded with her. "I won't be missed."

"What about your regular daily recitals, your rounds?"

"Tell anyone who asks that I'm not feeling well, that I am suffering from an internal upset and am self-medicating myself. Have Heul activate the privacy lock on my quarters."

"So you would involve her in your subterfuge as well. I will not be a party to this, Desvendapur. If you want to spend time here, place an application through the proper channels."

"It will not be approved," he argued. "You know it won't. Geswixt is a restricted destination."

"Exactly why you're coming back with me." She started to turn away. "Now if you will excuse me, *soother,* I am not finished talking with my friends."

He stood motionless, thoughts churning and anger rising as she persisted in ignoring him. It was impolite of him to remain standing there, but she remained adamant. Since she did not acknowledge his presence, her friends did not feel compelled to, either. Hiding his mounting frustration and his fury, he turned and started back across the broad, flat surface of the terminal. He would meet his new friend Ulu at the designated pickup point and at the appointed time, but first he had to make a stop at the lifter that had brought him here from Honydrop.

Walking gave him time to ponder what he was about to do. Though his mind was clear, his intentions firm, a part of him remained hesitant. What he contemplated was unlike him, unlike anything he had ever done before. But wasn't that the source of true artistic inspiration: the naked plunge, the embarkation into regions never before visited, the effort to break

free of convention and restraint? He argued with himself all
the way back to the lifter, while he was on it, and after he left
it behind. But having set his mind, he solidified his decision
as he approached the meeting place. He took considerable
pride in not looking back over his shoulder, not even when he
boarded the small truck and drove off in the company of chattering Ulunegjeprok.

Melnibicon would look for him, he knew. She would ask
who had seen him. He doubted she would receive much in the
way of response. Everyone in the terminal was busy, intent
on his or her own business. No one would have noticed one
more thranx striding purposefully through their field of vision.
Eventually she would give up, cursing all the while, and re-
board the lifter for the return flight to Honydrop. It was not
her fault if he missed the departure. Upon her return she
would report him as absent, accept whatever chiding was due
for taking an unauthorized passenger to Geswixt, and go on
about her business.

It troubled Desvendapur, but not to the point of preventing
him from engaging in conversation with Ulu. They spoke
about alien foodstuffs and their sometimes eccentric preparation, Des giving the impression he knew a great deal while in
reality he was utterly ignorant on the subject. But the more
Ulu talked, the more Des 'tested' and 'checked' him, the
greater grew the poet's rapidly burgeoning store of knowledge. By the time they reached the checkpoint, he felt he
could have carried on a limited conversation on the subject.
Certainly he now knew more about it than any nonspecialist.

It was rare to see a hive tunnel blocked or guarded. Desvendapur supposed that access to military installations was
similarly restricted, as was that leading to sensitive scientific
installations, but this was the first time in his life he had
actually encountered an armed guard. One of the pair recognized Ulunegjeprok immediately. Des tensed when the no-
nonsense sentry turned his attention to the truck's passenger.
But it was late in the day and the guard was tired. When Ulu
cheerily explained that his passenger was another newly arrived worker assigned to his own section, the body-armored
thranx accepted the explanation readily. There was no reason not to. Why would anyone not ordered to do so want to

willingly place himself in close proximity to a bunch of soft-
bodied, pinch-featured, antenna-less, malodorous mammals?
The truck was waved through.

They entered a much longer tunnel, featureless except for
periodic electronic checkpoints. Their progress was being
monitored, Des realized. The amount of security was daunting. How long he would be able to continue to brazen his way
through he did not know. Long enough to gain inspiration for
a small volume of stanzas, he hoped. Phrases, at last, that
would be underlain with real meaning and significance. After
what he had gone through to get this far, he had better accomplish at least that much.

Would Melnibicon notice that the lifter's navigation system had been accessed? Would it occur to her to recheck a
preprogrammed course that the craft had followed faultlessly
many times before? If she did, then he would have only hours
of freedom in which to seek inspiration. If she did not, and relaxed on board as she had on the flight over, then he might
have a day or two in which to interact with the aliens and the
storm of exotic sights and sounds they hopefully represented
before Security caught up with him. As for Melnibicon, her
hastily reprogrammed lifter would set her down automatically among the rilthy peaks, whereupon if he had done his
work properly the flight instrumentation would then freeze
up and compel her to call for rescue.

It never occurred to him while he had been entering his
irate, hasty adjustments that the disoriented craft might simply
run into the side of a mountain.

For a service tunnel, the corridor they were speeding down
seemed to go on forever. Locked into the passageway's guide
strip, Ulunegjeprok abandoned the controls to let the truck do
its own driving. He would return to manual when necessary.

"So, where did you study?" he inquired innocently of his
newly arrived counterfeit colleague.

Nothing if not voluble, Des spun an elaborate story woven
around what he knew of Hivehom. Since Ulu was a native of
Willow-Wane and had never been offworld, he could hardly
catch Des in any mistakes. By the time the truck finally began
to slow as they approached another floor-to-ceiling barrier,

the poet had half convinced himself of his own skill at food preparation.

He held his breath, but the facility on the other side of the seal was disappointingly ordinary. Certainly there was nothing to indicate the presence of aliens. He was reluctant to press Ulu for details lest he appear too eager. Besides, the less he opened his mouthparts, the better. Silence was the best way of hiding ignorance.

Turning down a subsidiary corridor, Ulunegjeprok eventually parked the truck in a vacant unloading slot. Wordlessly, acting as though he knew exactly what he was doing and that he belonged, Des proceeded to help him unload. The kitchen facilities were extensive, spotless, and more or less familiar, though he did espy several devices whose purpose was foreign to him. That did not necessarily mean they were intended for the preparation of mammalian food, he reminded himself. He was a poet, not a cook, and the only food preparation equipment he was familiar with was the individual kind that he had made use of personally.

Encountering and finding himself introduced to a couple of Ulu's coworkers, he was delighted to discover that he could pass himself off as a colleague with a certain aplomb. They in turn were able to present him to still others, with the result that by nightfall he was an accepted member of the staff. Thus accredited through personal contact, his presence was not further remarked upon. He even assisted in the preparation of the nighttime meal, noting that for this purpose the staff responsible for the preparation of the alien food had the extensive facility entirely to themselves.

To his surprise he discovered among the courses a number that were familiar to him. He did not comment on this revelation lest he expose his ignorance. But it was fascinating to learn that the humans could eat thranx food.

"Not all of it, of course," Ulu remarked in the course of their work, "but then you know that already. Fortunately, they don't ask us to assist in the treatment of meat."

"Meat?" Desvendapur was not sure he had heard the preparator correctly.

"That's right, joke about it," Ulu whistled. "I cannot imagine it myself. They warned us when we were taking the special courses, but still, the idea of intelligent creatures consuming the flesh of others of their own immediate family was more than a little terrifying. Didn't you find it so?"

"Oh, absolutely." Desvendapur was quick to improvise. "Meat eaters! The proclivity seems utterly incompatible with true intelligence."

"I have not seen them do it myself. I do remember asking, early on in the first seminar, why they did not just do all their own food preparation, but as you know the idea is to encourage them to become as comfortable as possible here. That means learning to eat food that we prepare." He whistled a soft chuckle. "What the media would not give to know that the only contact project isn't on Hivehom." Light flashed from his compound eyes as he looked over at Des, who was whitened up to his foothands in something called flour. "Wouldn't it be funny if you were a correspondent who had slipped in here under cover, and not a preparator assistant?"

Desvendapur laughed in what he fervently hoped was an unforced manner. "What an amusing notion, Ulu! Naturally, I am as sworn to secrecy as everyone else who has been chosen to work with the aliens."

"Naturally." Ulunegjeprok was forming the flour into loaves. Watching and learning something new and useful every minute, Des imitated him with rapidly accelerating skill. Alien food formed the basis for a nice quatrain or two, but where were the aliens themselves? Where? Would he have the opportunity not simply to prepare their food but to see them eat? To observe their flexible mouthparts in motion and see the long pink tongue thing that resided, like some symbiotic slug, within their mouths? That would provide inspiration for more than a few stanzas! Horror was always an efficacious stimulus.

He did not get his wish. The food was taken from them for final treatment and delivery, leaving the prep staff alone in the kitchen to clean up before retiring. Desvendapur followed Ulu to his quarters, memorizing sights and routes, learning something new and useful with every step.

"I have to present myself and my credentials in the morning, so I will be late to work," he told Ulu as they were preparing to retire. "Meanwhile, thank you for all that you have done, and for your hospitality tonight."

"Glad to be of help," the preparator replied guilelessly. "All kitchen assistance gratefully welcomed. You're good at your work."

"I had excellent instruction." By now Desvendapur had come to believe it himself. As of this moment he was not only an amateur poet, but a professional food preparator, one specializing in alien cuisine, who was and always had been a denizen of large, professional kitchens.

The death of Melnibicon, when he learned of it the following morning, threatened to shatter his resolve as much as his confidence. He had never intended for her to die, only to be delayed a day or so while he penetrated the secrets of Geswixt. But he was forced to set aside the overwhelming sense of guilt as he considered the ramifications of the corollary knowledge that in addition to her passing, the crash of the lifter had also resulted in the death of one Desvendapur, poet and soother, whom she had illegally transported to Geswixt for an afternoon. It seemed that neither body had been recoverable from the incinerated crash site.

He had become an instant nonperson. Desvendapur the soother no longer existed. His family and clan would grieve. So might Heul, for a short while. Then all would go on with their lives. As for himself, he had a chance to begin a new one—as a simple, hardworking, lowly food preparator for humans.

But first he needed a place to sleep, not to mention an identity.

There were a number of empty living cubicles. Settling on one located as far from the nearest inhabited space as possible, he moved himself in. The dearth of personal possessions within might puzzle a visitor, but he did not expect to have much in the way of company. His personal credit having perished along with his former identity, he would have to establish a new one with the fiscal facilities in Geswixt.

Altering a personal identity chit was a serious crime, but such ethical considerations no longer weighed heavily on Des. Not after having committed, however inadvertently, a killing. Artists died for their art, he rationalized. Melnibicon had died for his. He would compose a suitable, grand memorial to her in dance verse. It would be more honor than someone like herself was due or would normally rate. She should be grateful. Certainly her clan and family would be. Meanwhile, he had more important things to do than mourn the passing of someone who was, after all, practically a complete stranger, and an individual of indisputably little importance.

With the aid of the electronics in the cubicle it turned out to be surprisingly easy to forge a new identity. It helped that he was not attempting to have his new self classified as a specialist in military weaponry, or a communications expert, or a financial facilitator. Who would want to assume a false identity as a bottom-level food preparator? With a few delicate cybernetic twitches, his name became Desvenbapur, a change sufficiently significant to render him wholly separate and apart from the dead poet, but not radical enough to make a mess of his original identity chit.

He waited tensely while the hive network processed his work. Because he had a position, because he was there, because he could now rely on the confirmation of others to support his new self, it was accepted, showing a credit balance of zero. Because he had been acknowledged by the system, no one thought to question his presence. With each succeeding day, Desvenbapur the assistant food preparator became a more familiar and well-liked figure around the complex. With each succeeding week, applying himself intensely to a job classification for which he was seriously overqualified, he grew more and more adept at its practice.

A day came when a newly arrived sanitation tech appeared, luggage in tow, to claim his previously unassigned cubicle. Finding someone already living within, both thranx referred the situation to the official in charge of housing. Preoccupied with more serious matters, she acknowledged that it was clear some degree of oversight had been at work. With Ulunegjeprok and other coworkers vouching for the amiable Des, she simply reassigned the newcomer to a different vacant cubicle, at which point the shelter the poet had earlier appropriated was officially entered into the hive records as his.

With an official residence, an accepted line of credit into

which seasonal income was placed—as soon as the hive financial officer was informed by Des's friends that he was not being paid, the oversight was hastily corrected—and an occupation, Desvendapur's reinvention as Desvenbapur was complete. The chance of exposure still existed, but with each succeeding day it became less and less likely. Finding himself gifted with another highly efficient and willing assistant who seemed to have materialized out of nowhere, the food division supervisor was more than happy to have the additional, to all intents and purposes legitimate, help. Des's name began to creep, by default, into the official records of daily life at the complex. Desvenbapur the food preparator came into conclusive existence through the inherited process of bureaucratic osmosis.

He learned that anyone associating in any capacity, however distant, with the visiting humans was encouraged to learn more about them. Des was quick to take advantage of these free educational facilities. His off-duty hours were spent poring over the history of thranx-human contact, the official records of the ongoing project on Hivehom, and the hesitant but ongoing attempts to broaden contact between the two radically different, cautious species. There was nothing in the official records about another project at Geswixt. As far as publicly available history went, the complex did not exist.

He was afraid to be promoted, but commendations came his way in spite of his efforts to avoid them. The alternative was to work less diligently, to slack off on the job, but that might attract even more attention, and of an unwanted sort. So while striving to endear himself to his coworkers, he struggled to do that work which was assigned to him and little more, seeking safety in anonymity.

Already more knowledgeable about human food intake than all but the biochemists and other specialists, Desvendapur absorbed what knowledge was available about everything from the bipeds' appearance to their tastes in art and amusement to their mating habits. That a great deal was marked *unknown* did not surprise him. Though improving, contact between the species was still tentative and infrequent, proceeding officially only at the single recognized project site on Hivehom.

The reason for the clandestine complex at Geswixt was obvious: Both sides wanted to speed the pace of contact, to increase the opportunities for an exchange of views, and to stimulate learning. But it had to be done in such a way as not to alarm the general populace. Even after some fourteen years, each side was still far from confident they could trust the other. The thranx had more experience than they wished with duplicitous, deceitful intelligences, among whom the AAnn stood foremost. Sure, these soft-skinned mammals seemed sociable enough, but what if it were all a ruse, a ploy, an attempt to lull the hives into a fatal relaxation of their guard? No one wanted to see another Paszex happen on Hivehom, or anywhere else.

Among the humans there existed an equal if not greater number of concerns. With insects constituting a hereditary racial antagonist, the idea of becoming close friends with their giant, albeit distant alien cousins, the thranx, was difficult for many to stomach. Objections and concerns emerged less often intellectually than they did viscerally.

So each species continued to feel the other out, to study and to learn, and as they did so to keep a wary eye on the activities of the AAnn as well as the other known intelligences. The covert complex north of Geswixt was an attempt by the thranx to broaden and accelerate those contacts.

Though he experienced a delicious shudder of instinctive revulsion every time he called forth in his cubicle a three-dimensional projection of a human, Desvendapur relieved the nausea by composing a new set of sonnets, complete with appropriate accompanying choreography. These files he encrypted and secured with great care lest someone stumble upon them accidentally and wonder at the extraordinary aesthetic skills of a simple food preparator. The lines he devised were facile, the inventions clever, but they lacked the fire he sought. Where was the explosion of brilliance that would gain his work universal recognition? How was he to fabricate lyrical phrases so glorious that they would leave listeners stunned?

In his off hours he threw himself into a study of the humans' principal language, after first dismissing as a hidden joke the revelation that they still practiced dozens of different tongues. That was an absurd notion, even for creatures as alien as humans. Different dialects could exist, to be sure, but different languages? Dozens of them? How could a civilization arise out of such a counterproductive babble? Deciding that the first linguists to make contact were having a little fun at the expense of those who came after, he ignored the assertion as he concentrated on the language of contact.

Recordings of their speech yielded a brutal, guttural mode of communication that made Low Thranx sound like a clear stream running over water-polished stones. It was not unpronounceable, but it was unwieldy. And where were the whistles and clicks that gave civilized speech so much of its color and variety? Not to mention the modulated stridulations that humans seemed utterly incapable of duplicating. Though it was difficult to countenance, the records indicated that some human linguists had succeeded in mastering portions of both High and Low Thranx. Furthermore, they had the ability, like the AAnn, to take in air through their mouths instead of through designated, specialized breathing orifices as did the thranx and others. Like the AAnn, their air intakes were located on their faces, resulting in a severe crowding of important sensory organs in the same place. And there were only two air intakes. The thranx had eight, four on each side of the thorax. Given such a deprived physiological architecture, Des thought it something of a minor miracle that the humans were able to take in enough air to supply their blood with sufficient oxygen.

With no one to practice on, he learned by means of repeating human phrases in the solitude of his cubicle. As he studied, he composed, waiting for the time when blinding inspiration would strike. What would help, what he wished for more than anything else, was to meet an actual alien. He knew their food, or at least the thranx food they could digest. Now he wanted to know them.

He had been at the complex for more than a year, long enough to experience the first feelings of despair, when the opportunity finally came.

6

Golfito wasn't much of a city. Located in a fine natural harbor, it existed only to service the cruise ships and other tourist vessels that stopped to give their passengers a quick taste of the Corcovado rain forest. After making a wild flurry of purchases and embedding tridee cues into their home units like crazy, they reboarded the giant, luxurious hydrofoils and zeps and floated or flew onward, heading for more glamorous destinations to the north, the south, or across the isthmus. In their wake they left memories of foolish behavior, hasty sexual assignations with Golfito's enterprising exotics, and much-appreciated credits.

Montoya had tried his best to attach himself to some of the thousands of credits that spilled from the bulging cred-cards of the laughing, wide-eyed visitors, but despite his most strenuous efforts he never seemed quite able to cement any valuable contacts. He was always a little too slow, a step behind, left fumbling for the right word or phrase, like the fisherman who never manages to pick the right lure to attract the fish that surround him on all sides.

But if he had failed to cash in on the bounty offered up by the regular loads of visitors, he had succeeded in making a few potentially useful contacts among the less reputable denizens of Golfito's waterfront and rain forest suburbs. Among these sometimes agreeable, sometimes surly specimens was one who dangled promises in front of the struggling immigrant like sugarcease before a diabetic.

Surprisingly, the ever-hopeful but always realistic Montoya had received word that one of those promises might actually be on the verge of being fulfilled.

Ehrenhardt's place hugged one of the steep rain forest–

covered hillsides that rose above the town. As he rode the silent electric lift up to the gated enclosure, Montoya gazed down at the exquisite blue of the bay and the dark Pacific beyond. Monkeys, jaguars, quetzals, and all manner of exotic creatures inhabited the carefully preserved lands on both sides of the city. They interested him only to the extent of their cash value. Not that he would dare to compete with one of the known poacher consortiums. He knew better. Try, and he'd end up a skin at the bottom of somebody else's trophy case.

A lanky Indian with a prominent sidearm and expressionless eyes met him at the top. Beckoning for the intimidated guest to follow, he escorted Cheelo out onto the porch that overlooked the sultry panorama below. Rudolf Ehrenhardt did not rise, but he did offer Montoya a drink from the iced pitcher sitting on the lovingly polished purpleheart table before him. He did not, however, gesture for his visitor to take a seat, and so Montoya remained standing, drink awkwardly in hand.

"Cheelo, my friend." The fixer squinted behind his polarizing glasses, eyes completely hidden. It was like conversing with a machine, Montoya thought. "You really should invest in some nose work."

Montoya flinched inwardly. It was not his fault that over the course of a difficult life that distinctive protuberance had been broken and reset more times than he cared to remember. "If I could afford it, Mr. Ehrenhardt, sir, I'd certainly consider it."

The older man nodded approvingly. It was a good reply. "What if I were to tell you that the opportunity to afford that, and many other good things, has finally arrived for you?"

His guest put the already empty glass back down on the table. He had been unable to identify any of the contents beyond wonderful. "Ay, you know me, sir. I'll do whatever is necessary."

Ehrenhardt chuckled, enjoying himself, drawing out the suspense even though he was quite aware that his guest was in an agony of expectation. A harpy eagle soared past below, skimming the treetops in search of somnolent monkeys. Somewhere an indolent pet macaw screamed.

"You've always told me that you wanted to do something big."

"Just the opportunity, Mr. Ehrenhardt, sir. All I want is for someone to give me a chance. That's all I've ever wanted."

The fixer smiled condescendingly. "There is an opening in Monterrey that has come about through . . . let us say *attrition*." Ehrenhardt did not add the word *natural* before attrition, and Montoya did not question him as to the reason for the omission. "I have been asked to recommend someone suitable to take over the franchise. It is exceptionally lucrative, but it requires the attention of someone with drive, intelligence, and desire. Also someone who knows the meaning of loyalty, of when to speak and when to keep his mouth shut."

"You know me, Mr. Ehrenhardt, sir." Cheelo drew himself up to his full, if unprepossessing, height.

"No, I do not know you." The older man was staring hard, hard into Montoya's eyes. "But I am learning more each time we meet. I placed your name before the involved parties, and I am happy to say it has been accepted. Conditionally, of course."

"Thank you, sir! Thank you!" At last, Montoya thought. The chance to fulfill all his dreams! He would show them all. Everyone who had ever mocked him, looked down on him, spit on his intentions. Here at last was the opportunity to prove himself to all of them, to each and every one of the sarcastic, heartless bastards. In particular, there was a worthless little town up in the Amistad . . .

Something Ehrenhardt had said made him hesitate. "Conditionally, sir? Conditional on what?"

"Well, my ambitious friend, surely you know that such opportunities do not come along every day, and those special things that do not come along every day are not for free. A franchise is what it is because it must be paid for. A minimal sum, provided as a guarantor of the prospective franchisee's good faith."

Montoya swallowed and maintained his self-control. "How much?" So nervous was he that he forgot to say *sir*.

Either Ehrenhardt did not notice or chose magnanimously to ignore the oversight. Smiling, he pushed a piece of embossed plastic across the table in the direction of his apprehensive guest. Montoya picked it up.

He breathed a little easier. The amount was daunting, but not impossible. The date . . .

"I have until this day of the indicated month to raise the required fee?"

Ehrenhardt nodded paternally. "If it is not forthcoming by then, the franchise must by mutual agreement of the parties involved be awarded to another. That is the way of things. Tell me: Can you be in compliance?"

"Yes, sir! I know that I can do it." The time allowed was generous. But he had none to waste, to linger on the beaches and ogle the ladies in the bars and restaurants.

"That is what I told the others." The smile faded. "I know the extent of your financial condition, Cheelo. It is not one to inspire confidence."

He did his best to shrug off the criticism. "That's because I enjoy myself, sir. I spend credit as I acquire it. But if you know my status, then you know that it is not always so insignificant."

To Montoya's relief, the fixer's smile returned. "Another good answer. Keep giving the right answers, Cheelo, and come up with the necessary fee by the indicated date, and you will have your chance to do something big. Take advantage of this opportunity, work hard, and you can become a wealthy and important person, just like myself. I need not tell you that such a chance comes along but rarely in a man's lifetime. For most, it never comes at all."

"I won't fail it, sir—or you."

Ehrenhardt waved diffidently. "This has nothing to do with me, Cheelo. It has everything to do with you. Remember that." He sipped contemplatively at the pale liquid maintained at just above the freezing point by the thermotic tumbler. Somewhere within the rambling white stucco building that idiot macaw refused to shut up. It was making Montoya nervous. "Tell me, Cheelo—what do you think of these aliens that are so much in the news these days?"

"Aliens, Mr. Ehrenhardt?"

"These insectile creatures who persist in trying to further relations with us. What do you think is their real purpose?"

"I really don't know, sir. I don't think much about such things."

"You should." Adjusting his dark glasses, the fixer gazed out across the bay to the open ocean beyond. "This is a surprisingly crowded corner of the galaxy, Cheelo. It behooves every one of us to consider what is taking place here. We can no longer go about our business here on Earth indifferent to what happens on other worlds, as we could in the days before the invention of the drive. Take these reptilian AAnn, for example. The thranx insist they are incorrigible, aggressive expansionists. The AAnn deny it. Whom are we humans to believe?"

"Ay—I really couldn't say, sir."

"No, of course you couldn't." Ehrenhardt sighed deeply. "And it's wrong of me to expect it of someone like yourself. But living here, I am inescapably surrounded by those of limited vision." Rising abruptly, he took the startled Montoya's hand and grasped it with a firmness that belied his age.

"Deliver the fee by the indicated date and the franchise is yours, Cheelo. The franchise, and the prestige and everything else that goes with it. One thing more: The credit transfer must be made in front of me. I am required by those others involved in the business to witness it in person. There are many traditionalists among us who do not trust long-distance electronics. So I *will* see you before the indicated date?" Montoya nodded, and the hand moved to the jittery younger man's shoulder. "Then you can do your 'big things.' " He sat back down. The interview was at an end.

Cheelo rode the lift back down to the city in a haze of euphoria. His chance at last! By all the gods of his forefathers and all the gonads of those who had ever kicked, beaten, or insulted him, he would raise the necessary money somehow. It shouldn't be too hard. He had ample experience in such matters.

But he could not do it in Golfito. Because of the prevalence of the tourist ships and zeps there were simply too many police about. They were alert to the activities of denizens such as himself. He was too well known to them. He would have to go to work elsewhere.

He knew just the place.

7

Ulunegjeprok's voice was flat, betraying no hint of the excitement he felt. "Instead of preparing foodstuff basics for humans," he asked his friend and fellow worker, "how would you like to deliver some?"

Desvendapur did not look up from where he was cleaning a large quantity of pale pink *vekind* root. "Do not joke with me, Ulu. What are you talking about?"

"Hamet and Quovin, the senior biochemists in charge of final checkout and delivery, are both down sick. It has fallen to Shemon to carry out the transfer of this week's produce. I spoke to her earlier. She has never done this before and is apprehensive about doing it alone."

"Why?" Des wondered. "You know the procedure as well as I. It is not complicated."

"It isn't procedure that concerns her. She has never dealt with the humans in person, only via communicator, and she is not sure how she will react. So she asked for subsidiary personnel to accompany her." His antennae straightened. "I volunteered. Knowing of your interest in the aliens, I also volunteered you." He extended a foothand. "I hope you are not disappointed in me. If you want to withdraw your services for this afternoon . . ."

"Withdraw?" Desvendapur could hardly believe his good fortune. At last, after all he had suffered—physically, mentally, and emotionally—he was going to encounter the bipeds in person instead of via research team projections and odorless images. Already mellifluous phrases and biting stanzas were bubbling in his brain. "This afternoon? How soon?"

Ulunegjeprok whistled amusedly. "Clean your eyes. We have several time-parts yet."

69

Des did his best to concentrate on his work, but everything he managed to accomplish subsequent to his friend's revelation he did by rote. His mind was spinning. He would take a scri!ber with him so that he could compose on the spot, to ensure that nothing was lost and every advantage taken from the forthcoming confrontation. There was no telling how long his superiors' illnesses or Shemon's aversion would last. It might be some time before the opportunity arose again.

"What are you doing?" As he labored at his own station, Ulu eyed his weaving, bobbing coworker curiously.

"Composing poetry."

"You? Poetry?" Ulunegjeprok whistled long and hard. "You're an assistant food service preparator. What makes you think you can compose poetry?"

"It is just a hobby. Something to occupy my recreational time."

"Good thing Hamet and Quovin are both out sick and Shemon is busy inventorying the week's consignment. They wouldn't look upon this as recreational time. Well, as long as you're making the effort, I'll give it a try. For friendship's sake, even though it will be painful. Go on, I'm braced— recite something."

"No, never mind." Aware that in his excitement he was skirting potentially dangerous territory, Desvendapur turned back to his work, stripping the thorny casing from oblong *cazzi!!s* fruit. "I'm not very good at it."

"That goes without saying, but I would still like to hear something." Ulu would not be put off.

Cornered, Des complied, trilling and clicking as inconsequential and unsophisticated a brace of stanzas as he could manage, a feeble collage of words and sounds guaranteed to get him whistled down at any semiprofessional gathering of qualified soothers.

Ulu's reaction was wonderfully predictable. "That was awful. You had better stick to making *hequenl* buns. You're good at that."

"Thank you," Des told him, and he meant it.

Systems idling, the small transport truck in the warehousing chamber hovered an arm's length off the floor. Des and Ulu saw to the transfer of assorted crates and containers while the venerable Shemon accounted for each one as it was loaded. It was evident from her attitude as well as her words that she did not want to be doing this, that she dearly wished the absent Hamet or Quovin were present instead, and that the sooner they had concluded the delivery and returned, the better she would like it.

There was barely enough room in the vehicle's enclosed cab for three. As she adjusted the guide controls and the truck started silently forward down a well-lit corridor, Desvendapur checked to make certain his scri!bers were nestled snugly in the abdominal pouch slung over his left side. He had brought two, in case one should fail.

"Why do you need us to come along anyway?" Ulu was asking her. At these words, Des wanted to reach out and smother him. "Are these creatures so physically feeble that they cannot unload their own supplies?"

"The ones that are present are engaged in more important tasks. They are scientists and researchers, not manual laborers. Easier for us to do such work." She looked over at him. "Why? Do you want to go back?"

Desvendapur hardly dared to breathe.

"No. I was just wondering," the unimaginative Ulu concluded.

The corridor was blocked by another guard station. Here they were waved through without an identification check, the contents of the transport being sufficient to establish their legitimacy and purpose. As the vehicle accelerated, Des looked for any sign of a change, for anything exotic or alien, and saw nothing. They might as well still be traveling through the thranx portion of the complex.

Eventually they pulled into a storage chamber scarcely different from the one they had left. Easing the truck into a receiving dock, Shemon shut off the power to the engine and slipped off the driver's bench. Ulu and Des followed her around to the back of the conveyance.

Under her direction, they began unloading the foodstuffs they had brought. Save for small robot handlers and cleaners, the chamber remained empty. He tried not to panic. Where were the humans? Where were the aliens he had sacrificed his career, more than a year of his life, and the life of another to see? Unable to stand it any longer, he asked as much.

Shemon gestured indifferently. It was evident that she was well pleased with the turn of events. "Who knows? It is not necessary for them to be here for the unloading."

"But don't they have to acknowledge receipt? Don't they need to check the delivery to make sure everything's here?" Desvendapur was moving as slowly as he possibly could without appearing to be deliberately inhibiting the unloading process.

"What for? They have been notified that the weekly delivery was on its way. If anything is missing, or out of the ordinary, our department will be notified and the omission corrected." Her relief was palpable. "At least *we* won't have to deal with it personally."

But that was precisely what Des wanted, needed to do: to deal with things personally. Despite his best efforts to bring about an inconspicuous slowdown, the quantity of cargo in the back of the transport was diminishing at an alarming rate. At this pace they would be done and gone within half a time-part. He invented and discarded dozens of scenarios. He could fake an injury, but Shemon and Ulu would only load him into the rear of the transport and hurry him back to the infirmary in the thranx sector. He could try overpowering the two of them, but while Shemon might prove a less than challenging adversary, Ulunegjeprok was young and fit and might be difficult to surprise. Besides, Des was a poet, not a soldier. And while such a hostile action might gain him a few time-parts of independence, the reverberations of such a gesture would undoubtedly result in his expulsion from the Geswixt hive and the loss of any further opportunity to encounter the aliens.

There was nothing he could do. He was trapped in a web of inexorably contracting time. His abdomen twitched, reminding him that his thoughts did not operate independent of his body.

Revelation congealed like a ripe pudding. Perhaps that was enough.

Passing a self-hovering cylindrical container twice his size to the waiting Ulu, he glanced in Shemon's direction. "I have to relieve myself."

She did not even look up from the readout on which she was tallying inventory. Truhand and foothand pointed. "Over there, through that second door. Don't you recognize the markings?"

Desvendapur looked in the indicated direction. "Those are indicators for a human facility."

"It is a joint facility, or so the instruction manual claims. But you didn't see my instructions; you only saw yours, so I suppose your ignorance is understandable. Be quick, and do not linger." There was unease in her voice. "I want to leave this place as soon as possible."

He gestured assent leavened with understanding as he hurried off in the indicated direction, all six legs working. The doorway yielded to his touch and granted entry, whereupon he found himself confronted with as exotic a panoply of devices as if he had stepped into the cockpit of a starship—although their functions were far more down to earth, in more ways than one.

In addition to the familiar sonic cleanser and slitted receptacles in the floor, there were a number of what appeared to be hollow seats attached to a far wall. He would have liked to inspect them more closely, but he was here to try to encounter aliens, not their artifacts. Desperately he searched the waste chamber for another exit, only to find none.

Refusing to give up and return to the unloading dock, he eased the door to the service chamber open and peered out, folding his antennae flat back against his smooth skull to create as small a profile as possible. Shemon was focused on her readout while Ulu was preoccupied with the remainder of the unloading. Waiting until his coworker was busy in the back of the vehicle, Desvendapur bolted to his right, hugging the wall of the storage chamber while hunting desperately for another way out. He had to try three sealed portals before he found one that was not locked.

Entering and closing the door behind him, he noted that it was of human design, being narrower and higher than that intended solely for thranx. Ahead lay a ramp leading upward. Advancing with determination, he took in a plethora of alien artifacts around him: contact switches of human design in a raised box; a railing of some kind attached to the wall head-high, too elevated to be useful to a thranx; a transparent door behind which was mounted equipment whose pattern and purpose he did not recognize; and more. Though the ramp was oddly ribbed instead of pebbled as was normal, it still provided excellent purchase for his anxious feet.

A second, larger door loomed in front of him. From its center bulged a recognizable activation panel dotted with unfamiliar controls. Touching the wrong one, or the wrong sequence, might set off an alarm, but at this point he didn't care. Even if that proved to be the ultimate result of his intrusion, at least there was an outside chance aliens might respond to the alert. Without hesitating, he pressed two of the four digits of his left truhand against a green translucency. From his studies he knew that humans were as fond of the color green as were the thranx.

The door buzzed softly and swung back. Without waiting for it to open all the way, he dashed through as soon as the opening was large enough to allow his abdomen to pass. There was a temperature curtain ahead, and he hurried right through it as well. Then he came to a stop, stunned physically as well as mentally. He was outside. On the surface.

In the mountains.

His feet sank into drifted rilth, and incredible iciness raced up his legs like fire. The shock was magnified by the fact that he was not wearing cold-weather gear, but only a couple of carrying pouches. There was no need for special protective attire in the hive below. Looking around, he saw whiteness everywhere—the whiteness of newly fallen rilth.

Turning, he took a step back toward the portal. The intense cold was already numbing his nerves, making it difficult to feel his legs. It struck him forcefully that no one knew he was out here. Ulu and Shemon would not begin to wonder at his continued absence for another several minutes at least. When they did, they would start by searching for him in the unloading area. By the time anyone thought to look for him outside, he would be dead, his respiration stilled, his limbs frozen solid.

He tried to take another step, but even with all six legs

working, the cold had reduced his pace to a bare shuffle. Fresh rilth, frozen white precipitation, began to sift down around him, spilling from a leaden sky. I'm going to die out here, he thought. The irony was unspeakable. His death would provide excellent fodder for some bard in search of inspiration. The tragic demise of the poet aspirant. No, he corrected himself. Of a stupid assistant food preparator. Even his motives would be misascribed.

"Hey over there! Are you all right?"

He found that he could still turn his head, though the effort made the muscles in his neck shriek. The salutation had come from a figure a full head taller than himself—from a biped, a human.

From his studies Des knew that humans rarely went without protective attire, even when indoors and out of the weather. This one was clad in a single pouch of loose gray clothing that covered it from neck to ankle. The leggings fit neatly into short gray boots of some synthetic material. Astonishingly, its head and hands were unprotected, directly exposed to the falling rilth. Though it evinced no sign of an integrated heating unit, it moved freely and easily through the accumulated rilth that came up to just below the tops of its footwear.

Though it was far from the circumstances under which Desvendapur had first hoped to try out his store of meticulously memorized human phrases, he was not shy about responding. The vocal modulations sounded unnaturally harsh to his ears, and he hoped he was not overemphasizing the guttural nature of the mammalian speech.

Evidently he was not, because the human responded immediately, hurrying toward him. It was astonishing to observe it lifting first one foot and then the other, plunging one uncaringly downward into the rilth, raising the other, and bringing it forward. How it managed to stand upright, much less advance on only two limbs, and without a counterbalancing tail like the AAnn or the Quillp, was something to behold.

"What are you doing out here like this?" Up close, the biped's odor even in the clear outside mountain air was all but overpowering. Desvendapur's antennae flinched away. Performed in front of another thranx, the reaction would have constituted a grave insult. Either the human was unaware of its meaning or did not care. "You guys hate the cold."

"You—" Desvendapur continued to hesitate over the words even though it was clear that the human understood him. "—You don't mind it?"

"It's not bad out today, and I'm dressed for it." With a soft, fleshy hand that boasted five flexible digits the human began brushing accumulated rilth from the errant thranx's head and thorax.

"But your face, and your hands—they're exposed."

The creature had only two opposing mouthparts instead of the usual four. These parted to reveal teeth as white as the falling rilth. Des did not have teeth, but he knew what they were. He struggled to recall the library information that dealt with the utterly alien aspect of human facial expressions. While the bipeds could and did gesture with their limbs, they preferred to use their obscenely flexible faces to convey meaning and emotion. In this ability they exceeded even the AAnn, whose visages were also flexible but because of the scaly nature of their skin, far more stiff and restricted.

As the human continued to brush rilth from the thranx's numbed body, seemingly oblivious to the dangerous damp coldness melting against its hands, Des marveled at the exposed flesh. Why the rippling pink stuff simply did not slough off the internal skeleton was another of nature's marvels. There was nothing to protect it: no exoskeleton, no scales, not even any fur except for a small amount that covered the top of the skull. The creature was as barren of natural cover as the muscles that were barely concealed within. The poet shuddered, and not entirely from the cold. Here was the stuff of nightmares indeed—and of shocking inspiration. Animals could exist so, but something sapient? He found it hard to believe the evidence of his eyes.

"We've got to get you inside. Hang on."

If Des had wondered at the biped's ability to ambulate on only two limbs without toppling sideways at every third or fourth step, he was positively stunned when it bent at the middle lower joints, reached beneath his abdomen, and lifted. He felt himself rising, the lethal cold of the drifted rilth sliding away from his exposed feet, the heat of the creature reaching out even through its protective clothing. Then he was being carried. That the biped, heavily burdened with its load, did not immediately fall over backward was scarce to be believed.

Not only did it not collapse or lose its balance, it carried Des all the way back through the temperature curtain. Warm moist air enveloped them like a blanket. Feeling began to return to Desvendapur's limbs, and the creeping stiffness started to recede.

"Can you stand by yourself?"

"Yes, I think so."

Once they were through the main door the human set him down, keeping a steadying hand on his thorax. Despite the absence of a supportive exoskeleton, the digits were surprisingly strong. The sensation was one no library spool could convey.

"Thank you." He gazed up into the single-lensed human eyes, trying to fathom their depths.

"What the hell were you doing outside like that? If I hadn't come along you'd be in a bad way."

"I would not be in a bad way. I would be dead. I intend to compose a sequence of heroic couplets about the experience. The sensation of the cold alone should be worth several inspiring stanzas."

"Oh, you're a poet?" Absently, the human checked a numerical readout attached to his wrist. Desvendapur had decided the creature was a male due to the presence of certain secondary sexual characteristics and the absence of others, though given the thickness of the voluminous protective clothing it was difficult to be absolutely certain.

"No," Des hastily corrected himself. "That is, I am an assistant food preparator. Composition is a hobby, nothing more." To try to change the subject he added, "If you have sampled thranx fare, I have probably worked on the initial stages of its preparation."

"I'm sure that I have. We eat your stuff all the time. No way we could import enough to keep everybody fed and still maintain our privacy here. Willow-Wane fruits and vegetables and grains are a welcome change from concentrates and rehydrates. What's your name?"

"Desvenbapur." He whistled internally as the human gamely assayed a comical but passable imitation of the requisite clicks and whistles that comprised the poet's cognomen. "And you?"

"Niles Hendriksen. I'm part of the construction team working with your people to expand our facility here."

Expand, Des thought. Then the human presence on Willow-Wane likely *did* consist of more than just a small scientific station. Still, that did not make it a colony. He needed to learn more. But how? Already the human was exhibiting signs of impatience. It wanted to resume its own schedule, Des suspected. Furthermore, perspiration was pouring down its exposed face. Even deprived of every last piece of attire, Desvendapur knew, it would find the heat and humidity within the unloading area acutely uncomfortable.

"I would like to see you again, Niles. Just to talk."

The human's smile was not as wide this time. "You know that's not allowed, Desvenbapur. We're breaking a couple of pages of stipulations and restrictions right now by just standing here conversing. But I'll be damned if I was going to walk on by and let you freeze to death." He started to back up, still without falling down. "Maybe we'll see each other again. Why don't you apply to come work in our sector?"

"There is such a position?" Des hardly dared to hope.

"I think so. There are always a couple of thranx working with our own food people. But I think they must be master preparators, not assistants. Still, with the installation expanding and all, maybe they can use some lower-level help." With that he turned and headed back up the ramp, closing the door at the top behind him.

Thoughts churning, Desvendapur made his way back to the central dock and the waiting truck. A distraught Ulu and an angry Shemon were waiting for him, having long since completed the unloading.

"Where were you?" Shemon inquired immediately.

"I needed to relieve myself. I told you." Desvendapur met her gaze evenly, his antennae held defiantly erect.

"You're lying. Ulu went to check on you. You were not in the facility."

"I was having digestive convulsions so I took a walk, thinking that it might ease the discomfort."

She was having none of it. Her antennae dipped forward. "What more appropriate place to deal with intestinal convulsions than the hygienic facility you were already inside?"

"I wasn't thinking straight. I am sorry if I caused you to worry."

Ulunegjeprok stepped forward and spoke up in his co-worker's defense. "There is no need to torment him. Look at his eyes. Can't you see that he is not feeling well?" He reached out to lay a reassuring hand on Des's thorax.

Desvendapur quickly stepped back. His friend gestured surprise, and Des hastened to concoct an explanation. "I am sorry, Ulu. It's nothing personal, but I do not want to be touched just now. I am afraid it might irritate my insides, and they do not need any more stimulation." The real reason was that his chitin was still chilled from his sojourn on the surface, a phenomenon that would not be so easily explained away as his extended absence.

"Yes, I can see that." His colleague gestured concern. "You should report to the infirmary immediately upon our return."

"I intend to," a relieved Des replied.

Little was said on the return journey down the access tunnel. Desvendapur kept, physically and verbally, largely to himself. Believing him ill, neither Ulu nor the still silently fuming Shemon intruded on his personal privacy.

Once back in the complex, the poet excused himself. He went not to the infirmary but to the preparation area. There he searched until he found a suitable bin of spoiled *hime* root and ripely decomposing *coprul* leaves. From this he fashioned a suitably noxious meal and forced himself to eat every last leaf and stem. Within half a time-part he was able to present himself outside the complex's medical facilities with a genuine, full-blown case of severe gastrointestinal upset, for which he was tenderly treated.

By the next day he was feeling much better. He could hardly wait for his work shift to end, whereupon he retired to his cubicle, set a flagon of thin *!eld* by the side of his resting bench, lowered the lights, activated his scri!ber, and in the carefully crafted privacy of his quarters, prepared to compose. And then a strange thing happened.

Nothing happened.

When he struggled to find the words and sounds to describe his encounter with the human, nothing suitable manifested itself. Oh, there were sounds and phrases at his disposal: an ocean of suitable components wanting only inspiration to lock them tightly together. He assembled several stanzas—and erased them. Attempting to mime the sound of the human voice while utilizing thranx terminology, he constructed an edifice of hoarse clicks—and tore it apart.

What was wrong? The words were there, the sounds—but something was missing. The consecution lacked fire, the framework elegance. Everything had happened so fast he had only been able to react, when what he really needed was time to absorb, to study, to contemplate. Concentrating on survival, he had not had time to open himself to inspiration.

The only explanation, the only solution, was obvious. More input was needed. More of everything. More contact, more conversation, more drama—though next time, not of the life-threatening variety. He remembered the words of the human Niles. But how could he apply for a professional position in the human sector that might not even exist? Or if it did, how could he ingratiate himself with the necessary authority without revealing information he was not supposed to know?

He would find a way. He was good with invention, with words. Not inspired, perhaps. Not yet. But he did not need to be inspired to proceed. He needed only to be clever.

Would the human speak of their encounter to his own superiors or coworkers? And if he did, would word of the unauthorized contact reach the thranx authorities who administered the indigenous half of the complex? Desvendapur waited many days before he was convinced that the human had kept the details of the confrontation and rescue to himself. Either that, or his coworkers did not feel the incident worthy of mention to their hosts. Only when Des felt halfway confident that news of the occasion had not been disseminated did he risk probing possibilities.

*   *   *

"I do not understand." Rulag, Des's immediate superior, was gazing at the readout on her screen. "It says here that you are to report for service to the human sector tomorrow morning at sunrise. You have been assigned to the inner detail."

Somehow Desvendapur managed to contain himself. This was what he had been waiting for. "I have repeatedly applied for any opening in food preparation in the human sector, in the hopes that they might expand our presence there."

"You know very well that they have been doing so, albeit slowly and carefully. But that's not what puzzles me." With two digits of a truhand she indicated the readout, which was positioned out of Des's line of sight. "It says here that you are to bring all your belongings with you. Apparently you are not only to work in the human sector; you are also to reside there." She looked up at him. "To my knowledge, all thranx who work with the bipeds have their quarters here, on the border of Geswixt proper."

He shifted edgily on all four feet. "Obviously there has been a change in policy. Or perhaps it is part of some new experiment."

Her interest as she studied him was genuine. "This doesn't bother you? You are prepared to go and live among the humans?"

"I will be with others of my own kind." He genuflected confidence. "Surely I'm not the only one to be so assigned. The humans would not request only a lowly assistant food preparator to come live and work among them."

"No, there have been others. You are right about that. Only you from our division, but I have talked with other level-nine supervisors. One from meteorology has been similarly assigned, another from engineering—you will have company." She gestured brusque negativity. "*I* couldn't do it."

"You don't have a sufficiently open or exploratory nature," Desvendapur replied gently. It was not a criticism.

"Yes I do, but only where innovative food preparation is concerned." Rising from the desk, she dipped her antennae toward him. "I will miss you, Desvenbapur. Not particularly on a personal basis, but in the kitchen. You are a good worker. In fact, I don't believe I have ever seen such dedication in so prosaic a classification. It is almost as if you have the capability to achieve much more."

"As you say, I like to work hard," he replied evasively, refusing to bite on the bait of the compliment. "At first light, you said?"

"Yes." She turned away. "Report to the transition chamber, dock six. I am told there are three others who are going at the same time, so your first encounter with the humans will not be a solitary one."

He had already had a first encounter, but that was and would always remain a private matter. "It will not take me long to gather my things."

"No, from all that I've been told you are not an accumulator. I suppose that under the circumstances that's all for the best. Farewell, Desvenbapur. I hope you find your stay among these creatures enlightening, or at least not too frightening."

She would not have understood if he had told her that he hoped to be frightened—also amazed, overwhelmed, terrified, awed, and subject to every other strong emotion possible. It was only from such extremes of feeling that true art arose. But he could not tell her that. He could not tell anyone. What emotions he experienced, as first assistant food preparator Desvenbapur, were only supposed to arise from intimate contact with vegetables.

8

He was the first of the four adventurous ones to present himself at the designated assembly point. The others arrived soon after. The meteorologist was there, as was a senior structural engineer. The third member of the group was a young female sanitation worker who went by the dulcet patronymic of Jhywinhuran. Forcing himself to ignore the more interesting conversation of the two high-level researchers, he gravitated toward the only one of the group with whom he might naturally be expected to bond.

He would much rather have discussed their situation and prospects with the two scientists, but joining in an ongoing discussion with two such cerebral heavyweights was just the sort of misstep that could call his carefully constructed false identity into question. As it turned out, he was only mildly disappointed. Jhywinhuran was lively, personable, far more attractive than either of the two senior techs, and did not rank his job classification. It did not take much of an effort on his part to settle readily onto the bench alongside hers.

"This is so exciting!" Light from overhead sparkled in her eyes. He observed that the red bands that streaked the predominant gold of her multiple lenses shaded delicately to pink. "Ever since the existence of the bipeds was acknowledged by the government I've dreamed of working closely with them. That's why I applied for a position here. But I never imagined I would ever have the opportunity of actually living among them as well."

"Why?"

She gestured uncertainty. "Why what?"

"Why do you want to work and live among them?" Beneath them, the transport shifted slightly as it backed out of the loading bay and moved toward a tunnel whose terminus he knew from a previous visit.

"I've always liked new things," she replied. "Anything new. When I heard about this, it seemed like the newest thing there could be."

He looked away from her, scrutinizing the tunnel ahead. "You sound like you should be an artist."

"Oh, no!" She seemed shocked at the notion. "For that you need a constructive imagination. Mine is purely deductive. I have no aesthetic discipline at all. But I'm very good at what I do."

"You must be," he told her, "or you would not have been chosen for this transfer."

"I know." She stridulated personal pride. "I'm proud of my skills, even if my position is a lowly one."

"Not at all," he chided her. "Mine is lower still. In essence we are both laborers in the same discipline: biology. I work one end, and you the other."

To make the mild witticism work he was forced to employ a couple of whistles in High Thranx. It took her several moments for comprehension to dawn, but when it did her gesture of amusement was highly appreciative. As always, he knew that he would have to be careful not to reveal too much of his erudition. Assistant food preparators rarely made use of High Thranx, which was not a dialect but a second language whose use was largely reserved for the learned.

The journey through the tunnel seemed to go on forever. Certainly he did not remember it taking half so long on his previous visit. When questioned, the transport driver could only say that he was taking them to the destination decreed on his manifest. What would happen to them after they arrived at their destination he did not know.

After what felt like an interminable junket the transport pulled into a dock unlike any Des had seen before. All thranx facilities were spotless, but this one gleamed as if it was scoured down every other time-part. Security was noticeably prominent. The travelers were escorted off the transport, equal attention being paid to scientists and support workers. Ushered into a clean room, their bodies and personal luggage were minutely inspected, scanned, probed, and analyzed. Des-

vendapur would have been uneasy had he not observed that
Jhy was even more nervous. Was she too the manufacturer
and possessor of a false identity?

No, that was absurd, he told himself. As ever, he needed to
be wary of slipping into paranoia. The four of them were
going to be working in close quarters with humans. What
more natural than that they should be profoundly screened?

Still, the procedures being followed struck him as excessive. After all, he had experienced close contact with one of
the bipeds without any prescreening whatsoever, to the detri-
ment of neither. But that contact had been unofficial.

He had anticipated the inspection and review would last a
few time-parts at most. It occupied the better part of three
days, during which time the four assignees were kept isolated
not only from humans but from all other thranx except those
immediately involved in their examination. At the end of that
period they were directed to board another transport. Des
noted that it was not independently powered, but instead was
mounted on magnetic repulsion strips. That suggested a high-
speed journey, and a much longer one than he had expected.

He was moved to query the official marching alongside
him. She had a silver star and two subsidiary bursts embedded in the chitin of her right upper shoulder. "Where are
we going? Why the rapid transport?" He gestured with a truhand. "The human sector is right over there somewhere."

"The Geswixt sector is," the escort agreed. "But you
four have not been assigned to Geswixt. You're going to the
project."

"The project!" Striding along just behind the poet, Jhywinhuran was listening intently. "The project on Hivehom. They
didn't tell us."

"No point in keeping it a secret now. I envy you," the escort murmured. "You will have the opportunity to meet and
interact with the famous first-contact supervisor, the Eint
Ryozenzuzex. Quite an honor."

"I've never been offworld." Desvendapur's mind was spinning. Space-plus travel itself—the experience of journeying
between different star systems—should provide marvelous
fodder for composition. And then there was the opportunity
to live and work with members of the original project, set

up soon after the first tentative thranx-human contact was established.

"Neither have I." The escort gestured appropriately as they reached the portal that provided entrance to the transport. "Nor is it likely I will ever be. But I am grateful for the opportunity to work here and contribute to interspecies understanding."

"How many humans have you met?" Des asked as he stepped into the waiting vehicle. "How many have you dealt with?"

"None." The escort stood stiffly to one side as they boarded, all four arms upraised in salute. "I am with Security. Our job is to keep the wandering curious away from the humans, not to interact with them. But there is still the satisfaction of contributing. Sweet traveling to you."

Anticipation surged through Desvendapur as he settled his abdomen over a vacant bench, straddling it expectantly. Very soon thereafter, the transport began to move, picking up speed as it rose above the strip and raced toward an unknown destination. No, not entirely unknown, he told himself. There would be a ship waiting, a shuttle to lift them into orbit. There they would board a starship for the journey through space-plus to Hivehom, the thranx homeworld and the location of the project.

For someone who had hoped only to meet another human or two in their own environment, events were moving along encouragingly indeed.

There were no signs to identify the station where they eventually disembarked, and no crowds to query. Insignia and attitude indicated that they had arrived at a military as opposed to a commercial facility, a supposition that further inspection and scrutiny confirmed.

Everything was going so well that Desvendapur was unprepared when the processor standing on the other side of the railing looked up from his readout to declare calmly but firmly, "Desvenbapur? There's no Desvenbapur in this file."

The poet's blood went colder than it had on the day he had stumbled inadvertently outside the Geswixt hive and into the accumulated rilth above. The new identity he had worked so long and hard to construct seemed to evaporate like a puff

of perfumed *pleorin*, leaving him standing exposed and revealed to every set of compound eyes in the facility. But no
one was looking in his direction; no one was staring at him
accusingly. Yet.

"There must be a mistake. I made a proper application and
have been passed on through to this point without any difficulty." He struggled to keep his antennae from twitching,
fought to conceal the fear that was raging through him.

The processor was not impressed. He was a senior, his
chitin shading heavily to purple, but he was still alert and in
full possession of his faculties. He replied without looking up
from the readout.

"That is why a hive has multiple layers of security. What
slips past one can be caught by another."

There was nothing Desvendapur could do but stand and
wait. Having passed on to the next station, a puzzled Jhy
walked back to see what was taking so long. When Des explained, she became irate.

"What nonsense is this? Of course this male belongs. He is
one of four assigned to this duty. No—*honored* by this duty."

"Really, Jhy." He did his best to quiet her, looking around
uneasily. Drawn to the commotion, the two scientists who
had already been cleared had paused at the top of the landing
to look back. The one thing Des did not seek in his present in-
carnation was attention. "I'm sure it will sort itself out."

She gazed at him out of eyes that were a flaxen composite of shattered mirrors. "You shouldn't let him treat you
like this, Des. You are special now. All four of us are." She
eyed the processor sternly. "Regardless of our individual job
classifications."

The elderly drone remained unperturbed. "Procedures must
be followed. Otherwise you do not have a hive: you have an-
archy. If he is not in the file, then it admits of an irregularity.
Irregularities must be resolved."

"I am sure this one will be." The poet made short, swooping, soothing gestures with both truhands. "It has to be some
sort of administrative error."

"No." The processor was adamant. "There is no Desvenbapur registered here." A truhand reached toward a communicator. "I will have to summon a superior—and Security."

Tussling with a couple of warriors with oversized mandibles would not get him a cubicle on the waiting starship, Des knew. There was nothing he could do but stand and wait. Wait, he feared, for the inevitable—for that which he had succeeded in putting off for more than a year.

"I do not understand." If Desvendapur was distressed, Jhywinhuran was openly baffled. "He has been working at Geswixt hive for some time. That is a security-sensitive area, and there has been no difficulty. Why should there be a confusion now? It's not as if he is laboring for military intelligence or energy research. He works in food processing."

"It does not matter," declared the processor with finality. "A security breach is a security breach, no matter what the status of the . . ." He halted in midapprobation. "Food preparation?"

"Eighth-level assistant," Desvendapur supplied quickly.

The processor clicked sharply, his mandibles grinding together just so. "The file lists you as a food *synthesizer*. That is a much more illustrious designation."

"I completely agree," Des told him, "but it is not one that applies to me. I am only an assistant preparator." Leaning forward, he tried to steal a glimpse of the readout, and failed. It was attuned only to the eyes of the processor.

Digits moved and the readout changed. Desvendapur reminded himself to breathe.

"*Aht,* here it is." The drone's tone did not change. "Desvenbapur. Assistant food preparator, level eight. You may proceed to the next checkpoint."

"That's it?" The challenge emerged of its own accord. "After all that?"

"After all what?" The processor eyed him curiously. "It was a simple filing error. I was doing my job."

He would have to learn to accept such things in stride, a relieved Desvendapur told himself. His identity had not been compromised—only momentarily misplaced. With Jhy leading the way, he advanced to the next station, ready now for whatever challenge it might present.

He need not have concerned himself. At each successive checkpoint his presence was acknowledged and his legitimacy confirmed. If he had been at all worried about the integrity of his newly wrought identity, two days of processing did much to lay his concerns to rest.

They were housed together until the following morning, when they were due to lift off via atmospheric shuttle. Waiting in high orbit was the space-plus transport *Zenruloim*. No one had officially told them they were going to Hivehom, and no one had to: That was where the project was located.

He tried to prepare himself mentally for the voyage ahead. His first journey offworld should be good for a folio at least. Then would come the descent to an entirely new planet, the ancestral homeworld of the thranx. Finally there would be, at long last, extended and intimate contact with the extraordinary bipedal mammals called humans. His sleeping chamber was comfortable enough, but he hardly slept at all.

Morning brought with it an excitement that was as difficult to contain as it was to quantify. He was pleased to note that the two scientists, far from being intellectually or emotionally above such simple emotions, were as visibly excited as food preparator and sanitation worker.

They boarded the shuttle via a long access ramp. At no time were they exposed to the outside, but that was perfectly natural. Very little of a hive beyond parks and recreational sites was located on the surface. The atmospheric shuttle itself was of modest dimensions, long and low. Brief prelift instruction was given; no one materialized to offer good-byes or farewells; and before he really had time to inspect his surroundings, Desvendapur found himself airborne and thundering toward orbit.

Offworld. There were no ports on the government transport, but by utilizing the seat controls he was able to call up a three-dimensional projection of the external view in any direction. He saw Willow-Wane receding below him and the firmament of stars and worlds and other species—primitive and intelligent, familiar and alien—drawing infinitesimally closer. Within him fresh inspiration simmered but did not boil. That would come with consistent contact, he felt. When he was surrounded by alien bipeds, by humans dwelling in their own facilities, that was when the river of enlightenment would wash over him to cleanse him of the puerile, classical heritage of traditional thranx rhythmic narrative.

He had studied hard, had prepared for this his whole life. What it was permitted to know, he had absorbed, from available records and reports. He knew how humans lived, but that was not the same as living with and among them. He knew how they were supposed to smell, but that was not the same as smelling them. He knew how they moved, how their peculiarly restricted speech patterns sounded, how they viewed the universe out of undersized single-lensed eyes, how their digestive systems worked to process not only normal food but dead animal products as well. All these things he knew, but studying them in recordings and reading about them in second- and third-hand reports was not the same thing as experiencing them for himself.

Furthermore, almost all of it was knowledge that had been gained under controlled conditions. From the standpoint of an artist as opposed to a scientist, he valued his single, brief, dangerous encounter with the lone human in the rilth above Geswixt more than all the recorded lore he had assimilated. How he was going to duplicate and expand upon that under the controlled conditions of the project he did not know. He only knew that it was necessary, even vital, to the maturation of his art. Somehow he would make it happen.

But first they had to get there.

When the *Zen* made the jump from normal space to space-plus he was sufficiently disoriented to contrive the sounds for what he believed to be a modestly successful tripartite stanza. Realizing that it undoubtedly duplicated, in spirit if not in actual phraseology, a hundred similar initial deep-space experiences, he promptly discarded the entire minor opus. He had not come this far, had not lied and invented and lowered himself and abandoned the patrimony of his hive, to grind out pale imitations of the work of others who had gone before him. He sought the unique, the new, the distinctive. That would not be found in duplicating the obvious experiences of predecessors.

As the journey through distorted space-time progressed he came to know his fellow travelers better. Though he focused his attentions on Jhywinhuran and the two scientists who had also been assigned to the project, he did not neglect the other passengers or those members of the crew who found time to

spend with an inquisitive lower-level passenger. He partook
of everything. A true artist disdained nothing, never knowing from where true inspiration might arise. So he acquired
and stored away information on topics as diverse as hydro-
logical engineering and starship maintenance, not neglecting
the area of food preparation, in which he could boast some
expertise.

They were two eight-days out and he was sleeping soundly
in his private cubicle when he heard the noise. It was a
muffled creaking, repeated at regular intervals. Since the
components of a thranx vessel fit together seamlessly, it was
difficult to imagine what might be causing noise sufficient to
wake him. As he regained consciousness, lying in the dark on
the low sleeping bench, he listened intently to the soft, unsettling sounds. He did not have to open his eyes because they
were always open. He had only to struggle to pull together the
constituent bits and pieces of his consciousness.

The subtle shushing was produced by the movement of
clothing against the body of its wearer. But it was not the
slick rush of thranx protective attire against smooth, hard
chitin. The noise that had awakened him was more subtle, almost as if cloth were being dragged across water.

Looking up, he saw the shape looming over him. In the
twilight that filled the cubicle it was enormous and unarguably human. From his studies Des knew that specific bipeds varied considerably in size, as opposed to other sapient
species like the thranx or the AAnn whose individual physical dimensions were relatively consistent. This one was at
least twice as big as the solitary male he had encountered in
the exposed air of Geswixt. An enormous waterfall of tangled
black fur sprouted from its face and head to hang down
over the upper portion of its chest and shoulders. Its eyes
were black and protruding. Its immense five-digited hands, of
which the creature had only two, gripped a shiny length of
projection-studded metal that was vaguely ominous in outline. The creature wore a heavy jacket of some dun-colored
material and matching pants, and its single pair of feet were
shod in calf-high black boots fashioned from some muted,
reflective material.

Towering above his bed, it glared down at him, showing

the even, white teeth that served the same function as normal
mandibles. Its entire aspect was quietly intimidating. No em-
pathetic "Are you all right?" greeted the awakening of the
single sleeper. From head to foot the massive figure was the
perfect embodiment of alien nightmare.

Despite the insulation, he could hear some commotion
outside the door to his cubicle. There were high-pitched
whistles that passed for screams, followed by the muted
whisper of running feet and loud, anxious conversation.
Querulous mandibular clicks filtered into his quarters from
the corridor outside as if it had been invaded and was being assaulted by a horde of migrating carnivorous *metractia*
from Trix.

Raising his upper body off the sleeping bench he whispered in the direction of the cubicle's scri!ber. The aural
pickup winked to life. "Projective intrusion noted. Presumed
unscheduled emotional stability test acknowledged. Returning to sleep." When no further vocals were forthcoming from
the sleepy occupant of the room, the scri!ber winked off,
having duly made note of Desvendapur's terse report.

Glancing to his right, he saw that the forbidding figure had
vanished. The projection really had been well done, he mused
as he drifted back toward unconsciousness. Had he been confronted with it the previous year he undoubtedly would have
joined the others who had been assailed with the same nocturnal visitation in scrambling in panic for the corridor outside his cubicle. But he was not the same individual he had
been then. He knew more now—a great deal more. That acquired knowledge was reflected in the calm with which he
had confronted the figure, and in his ability to return readily
to a state of uninvolved repose.

Following the daybreak meal the four fellow travelers were
called away from the other passengers to a private, secured
conspectus session in a spacious meeting chamber. Warm
earth tones dominated the décor, and the walls exuded the familiar fragrance of rammed earth and decomposing vegetation. The two senior researchers who debriefed them were
especially intrigued with Desvendapur's laconic reaction to
the finely rendered three-dimensional imaging of the previous night.

"You did not panic when confronted with the human visualization," the elder, a female, declared almost accusingly. "To greater and lesser extent, your colleagues did."

Des was aware that this time not only Jhy but the two scientists were watching him curiously. Had he stepped too boldly outside his carefully constructed identity? Should he, too, have run out into the hall whistling in fear and panic? But he had been awakened from a sound sleep and had reacted, not as a false persona, but as himself, bringing into play all the knowledge he had acquired in the past year. He could only hope that it would not mark him so singularly as to prompt a probe from which this time he might not emerge unscathed.

Realizing that the longer he delayed responding the greater the likelihood of suspicion germinating in the minds of his interrogators, he replied succinctly, "I saw no immediate reason for alarm."

A slightly younger male questioner spoke up sharply. Desvendapur wondered if in addition to being recorded, this encounter was also being broadcast to and studied by an unknown number of other suspicious professionals.

"An armed alien of considerable size and menacing aspect appears without warning in your sleeping quarters in the middle of the night, waking you from a deep rest, and instead of panicking you immediately recognize the intrusion as specious, react accordingly, and go back to sleep. How many thranx do you think would react in such a fashion?" Awaiting his response, every antenna in the chamber was inclined in his direction. He hoped he was not emitting a strong odor of concern.

"Probably very few."

"Probably not more than a handful." The female's tone was sharp, incisive but without overtones of anger. "An assistant food preparator from Willow-Wane would not generally be accounted a member of that group."

Subdued light glinted off the curve of the male's eyes. "How did you recognize so quickly that the intruder was a projection, and therefore posed no threat to you?"

"From his clothing." This time Des replied promptly and without hesitation.

The interrogators exchanged a glance and passing antenna

contact. "Every effort was made to ensure the verisimilitude of the human's appearance. What was wrong with its clothing?"

"There was nothing wrong with it. At least," the poet hastened to add, "nothing that I, based on my own private studies of humans and their habits and accouterments, could see."

"Then why did you react so calmly?" the male pressed him. "What about the appearance of the simulacrum's attire told you that it could not be real?"

"There was too much of it." Des felt safe in indicating mild amusement. "Humans thrive in a climate of considerably less heat and one-third the humidity that thranx enjoy. They can *endure* what we consider optimum living conditions, but they are not comfortable in them. And what we would regard as an excessive but tolerable climate could prove fatal to even well-adapted humans." Feeling more confident, he shifted easily on the resting bench.

"The temperature in my quarters was, if anything, set slightly warmer and moister than usual to accommodate my personal sleeping preferences. The bipedal figure wore not less than two layers of *heavy* human clothing. According to my studies, no human—no matter how well acclimated to Willow-Wane or Hivehom or any thranx world—would voluntarily wear a fourth as much apparel. Its system could not tolerate it for more than a time-part or so without suffering serious overheating. Yet the figure that woke me from my sleep did not appear even slightly inconvenienced by the microclimate in my room. The characteristic cooling condensation known as sweat was not present on its skin at all." He looked from his interrogators to his colleagues. "That's how I knew it couldn't be a real human."

The examiners looked briefly to their scri!bers before the female replied. With a truhand she indicated not suspicion or accusation, but admiration. "You are observant beyond your station, Desvenbapur. It is no wonder you were chosen to participate in as significant an undertaking as this."

He hastened to demur. "I have always tried to learn everything possible about any task I was involved with, whether it concerned food preparation or anything else. The simulacrum *could* have fooled me. It just happened that I was studying that section provided to us that deals with human physiology only last eight-day, and remembered it right away. It was at the front of my memory."

"A fine memory," she complimented him. "I would let you prepare my food anytime." Indicating that their involvement in the meeting was concluded, she and her companion rose and left the room. Their place was taken by four new officials, one of whom had two full stars inset into her right shoulder.

Desvendapur leaned toward Jhy and whispered. "I wonder what we have done to deserve the attention of so much rank."

"I don't know." She was grooming an antenna, bending it forward and down with her left truhand and running the sensory organ delicately through her mandibles. "You certainly elevated yourself in the project's estimation with your actions last night."

"I was lucky." Using a surreptitious foothand, he stroked her upper abdomen. Her ovipositors reacted with a slight quiver. "Easy enough to be nonchalant in the presence of a projected simulacrum. Next time I will probably be the one who runs screaming."

"Somehow I don't think so." She would have said more, but the first of the newly arrived ranking elders was speaking to them.

"You four will be joining and participating in what many eints have dubbed the most important social experiment in thranx history. As you know from your studies, ever since contact was first made we have found these bipedal mammals to be at once fascinating and frightening, refreshing and appalling, useful and dangerous. They are an aggressive, inventive species that exhibits a disturbing tendency to act before thinking. More often than you might expect, this produces results that are not to their benefit. Yet they will plunge blindly on, sometimes even when they are aware that what they are doing is detrimental to their own cause. It has been theorized that they have too much energy for their own good.

"Based on our initial contacts with them they are, I am pleased to report, not fond of our old friends the AAnn. But neither are they openly antagonistic toward them. Their attitude toward *us* is characterized by an unreasonable, irrational fear of the innumerable small arthropods that inhabit their own world, against which they have been waging a war not merely for dominance but for survival since they acquired the first stirrings of sapience. Our physical appearance was therefore something of a shock to them, from which only the most intelligent and responsive of their kind have managed to recover. Progress in advancing relations has therefore been much slower than either government would like. Yet to rush matters risks alienating the more conservative among our own kind while simultaneously activating the latent xenophobia that is regrettably endemic among the vast majority of humans.

"Overall, their present attitude toward us might best be characterized as a suspicious ambivalence. It is hoped that this will correct itself with time. In the interim, various proposals have been put forth, by both sides, for different means of accelerating the process of contact."

"The project," the meteorologist pointed out.

"Yes." It was the two-star who responded. "Everyone who wants to be or needs to be—human as well as thranx—is familiar with the project and its estimable goals." Her great golden eyes lingered individually on each of the four designates. "What is not known except among the highest representatives of both governments is that a similar project has been established elsewhere."

"The need for secrecy is absolute," a third supervisor commented tersely. "As suspicious and mistrustful as the humans are of us, it is believed they would react in a manner most unfriendly to the revelation that not simply a contact post, but the beginnings of a real colony were being established in their midst."

Desvendapur was not sure he had heard correctly. The thranx had begun establishing colonies on habitable worlds generations ago, but to the best of his knowledge they had never tried to situate one on a world already inhabited by another intelligent species. The idea of establishing a full-blown hive on a human-occupied world was more than daring. Many would call it foolhardy.

Yet he sensed this was not a test, as the simulacrum of the previous night had been. The supervisors were as serious as a pregnant female about to lay.

"Which world?" the engineer asked. "Centaurus Five, or one of the other Centaurian spheres?"

"None of those." The two-star was speaking again. If possible, her manner was more serious than before. "It is to this colony that you have been assigned. It is there that you will be working, often in closer quarters with humans than any thranx anywhere else. Nothing of this kind has ever been attempted before. You will be part of a pioneering interspecies social experiment." Lifting a scri!ber, she flicked a control on the panel. A fully featured three-dimensional globe appeared in the air between supervisors and incipient colonists.

"The great majority of humans are unaware of it, and if everything goes according to plan they will remain so for quite some time, but there is even as we speak an expanding thranx presence here, growing and thriving with the help of a few dedicated, farseeing humans."

As she spoke the global image rotated before them, the view zooming in and out at the whim of the controller. It was a beautiful world, Desvendapur thought, swimming beneath its sea of thin white clouds. Not as beautiful as Hivehom, or even Willow-Wane, but except for the prevalence of large oceans, an inviting planet nonetheless. He wondered which of the human-colonized worlds they were seeing, wondered what the name of their destination might be.

The one supervisor who had not spoken yet now stood back on all four trulegs and proceeded to enlighten, elucidate, and explain.

"Burrowers, fellow hive pioneers, future colonists, here is your destination. I extend to you all an early welcome— to Earth." Turning, he gesticulated somberness mixed with humor. "After all, if the humans can be allowed to have a colony on Hivehom, why should we not have reciprocal privileges on their homeworld?"

9

They looked like a prosperous couple. Too staid to be romantic, walking side by side without touching or holding hands, they had probably gone for a stroll in the tropical downpour so they would be able to tell their friends back home that they had done it. Anyone with any sense would have stayed inside a nice dry hotel until the clouds closed back up. That was what the permanent residents of San José were doing. That was what the great majority of tourists were doing.

But not these two. Since they were wearing matching electrostatic repulsion rain gear, only their hands were getting wet, and these only when they emerged from large, accommodating pockets. The tepid water struck the invisible protective fields and slid off, leaving the strollers and the expensive clothing they wore underneath comfortable and dry.

Montoya followed them at a discreet distance. There were a few others out walking or running through the heavy rain. In the hilly downtown historical district there were always people making deliveries or pickups. There were plenty of other tourists out and about besides the couple he had targeted, but they were sensibly holed up in gift shops, restaurants, or hotel lobbies, waiting for the storm to piss itself out.

Hold-ups were not Cheelo's preferred mode of personal enrichment. He disliked confrontations. Like narcotics, mugging was a bad habit that could all too easily become addictive. He'd seen it happen to acquaintances. He would have seen it happen to friends, if he'd had any. Given a choice, he would have preferred to rifle a hotel room or two, or pick a plump pocket, or lift a purse. No such opportunity had presented itself for days. Now he was growing anxious.

One more good score, just one more, and he would have all the good-faith money he needed to present to Ehrenhardt to secure the franchise. Well ahead of the deadline that had been set, too. Ehrenhardt and his people would be suitably impressed—which was Montoya's intention.

This would not be the first time he had mugged. Unlike a number of younger compatriots he derived no thrill from it, got no adrenaline rush from seeing the look of fear on the faces of his intended victims. With him it was all business, in the tradition of professional highwaymen going back to archaic times. To fulfill his dream he needed a few hundred credits more. These negligent travelers would provide it.

He continued to track the couple, pausing when they paused, turning to peer into a store window whenever they chanced to look in his direction. For the most part he remained invisible, another tourist like themselves out for a lazy afternoon's stroll in the rain. Only unlike them, he was unable to afford expensive water-repulsion rain gear. Already he was damp and uncomfortable beneath his old-fashioned maroon slicker.

In a sense he *was* a tourist, having come up from Golfito specifically to make the money necessary to buy the franchise. He had learned early in life that it was better to keep one's place of business separate from one's current home. Avoiding the authorities was difficult enough without living in the same city as the ones who would be most interested in finding him. Besides, there were far more opportunities to accumulate the requisite credit in bustling San José than in the smaller, sleepier city on the coast.

He tensed slightly, preparing his thoughts and muscles, and began to walk a little faster, closing the gap between himself and the perambulating couple. They had turned down one of the city's quaint alleys, a narrow street with scoured cobblestone sidewalks.

He was reaching inside his coat when they unexpectedly stepped into a store specializing in the distinctive woodwork for which the city was famed. Forced to continue on past, he glanced surreptitiously at the paduk and cocobolo handicrafts on display in the window. The next store was closed. Beyond, a serviceway barely wide enough to admit

one person at a time split the line of old buildings as it penetrated to the heart of the block. Ducking inside, he found
some shelter from the rain.

He waited there, biding his time, occasionally leaning out
to look back up the hill. The sodden stones were deserted.
Rain staccatoed off the pavement, fleeing in small distinct
rivulets into the nearest storm drain. If the couple chose to retrace their steps instead of extending their excursion, he
would have no choice but to continue following them, like
a caiman marking the progress of a tentative tapir grazing
along a riverbank.

Before long he heard the subdued murmur of casual chatter: three voices—those of the couple and that of the store
owner. Then footsteps, splashing in the rain, growing louder
instead of more distant. Reaching into his coat, his fingers
closed around the grip of the tiny pistol.

Timing his appearance, he stepped right out in front of
them, trying to make himself look larger than he was. The
stunned expressions on their faces showed that his surprise
was complete.

Quickly now, he told himself. Before they have time to
think or time to react. He extended his other hand, palm
upward.

"Wallet!" he snapped curtly. When the man, who was despite his age large and fit looking, hesitated, Cheelo barked as
threateningly as he could, "Now—or I'll skrag you and take
it anyway!"

"Martin, give it to him!" the wife pleaded. "Everything's
insured." Ah, traveler's insurance, Cheelo mused. The casual
thief's best friend.

"Slowly—so I can see it as you bring it out." He couched
the warning in his most intimidating manner.

Glaring down at him, the well-dressed pedestrian removed
a soft plastic pouch from beneath his coat and handed it over.
Cheelo took possession gingerly, never taking his eyes off the
man. Slipping the prize into his own inner shirt pocket, he
turned his attention to the woman. Above and below them,
the narrow street remained deserted. A couple of vehicles
hummed past on the main avenue above, their occupants

oblivious to the pitiful drama that was being played out beyond their windows.

"Purse," he ordered her. "And jewelry."

Trembling fingers passed over the handbag of woven metal, then reluctantly followed it with a ring and two bracelets. Nervously eying the front of the store from which they had recently emerged, he gestured imperatively at her left hand. "Come on, come on—the rest of it."

The woman covered the remaining exposed ring with her other hand. Her expression and tone were imploring. "Please—it's my wedding ring. I've given you everything else." He knew the droplets that were starting to run down her cheeks were tears because her face was protected from the rain by the wide brim of her stylish water-repelling hat.

He hesitated. Enough time had been spent standing out in the street. He had wallet, purse, and jewelry. The woman's anguish *seemed* genuine. He had seen enough of it faked by those attempting to protect expensive but impersonal possessions. Wearing the same expression he had presented when he had first stepped out of the alley, he started to turn away from them.

"Sure, why not? Look, I'm sorry about this, but I've got a big deal pending—the opportunity of a lifetime—and I just need a few more credits to . . ."

That was when the husband jumped him.

It was a stupid move, a foolish move, the kind propounded by middle-aged men who think a little regular exercise and a lifetime of watching action tridees equips them with the wherewithal to handle sinewy professionals. He was a lot bigger than Cheelo, which made him bold, and a lot stronger, which made him overconfident. In fact, he superceded Cheelo in every aspect of fighting ability except the most important one: desperation.

As the man's large hand, fingers aligned in a karate chop, came down on Cheelo's flinching arm, the impact caused his finger to contract on the trigger. The compact weapon spat a small, silent blue flash. Instantly, the delivered charge interrupted the flow of electrical impulses running through the millions of neurons in the man's body. A shocked look on his face, he collapsed onto the sidewalk, falling over sideways so that his shoulders and then his head struck the pavement. The skull took a visible bounce. Hovering over him, pistol in hand, Cheelo was no less shocked than the woman, who immediately dropped to her asinine husband's side. His eyes were wide open.

When it had gone off, the muzzle of the pistol had been aimed right at his chest. His heart had momentarily been paralyzed. That was not necessarily a lethal proposition—except that the man's heart had not been an especially sound one to begin with. The problem was not that it had stopped; the problem was that it did not start beating again. Cheelo had seen death before, though it had not been propitiated by his own hands. He saw it now, in the gaping frozen face that was filling with rain where it lay upturned to the sky on the cobblestone sidewalk.

Heedless of her own circumstance, the woman began screaming. Cheelo raised the pistol, then lowered it. He had not meant to shoot the poor dumb grandstanding bastard. He had certainly not meant to kill him. He doubted the admission would carry sufficient weight with the authorities. Clutching the purse close to his chest beneath the raincoat, he turned and ran, shoving the weapon back into his pocket. Behind him, the woman's screams were swallowed up by the gray torrent that fortuitously continued to spill from the clouds. He was more grateful than ever for the rain. For a little while at least, it would keep the shopkeeper from hearing her wails.

Breathing hard, he threw himself onto the first public transport that presented itself. Surrounded by preoccupied, indifferent *ticos* and *ticas*, he pulled the collar of his raincoat higher around his neck and head and strove to make himself as inconspicuous as possible. *Now* what the hell was he supposed to do? Self-defense made a bad defense for a known brigand. At the very least he would be sentenced to a selective mindwipe, the extent of which would depend on how tolerant a court he found himself in. The truth machine could possibly support his claim that he had not intended to kill, but his state of mind at the time might appear as a gray area on the device's readout.

It didn't matter. He had no intention of being incarcerated or of letting the authorities erase any part of him.

He did not go back to the cheap hotel room that was his address when he stayed in San José. Instead, he transferred to public transport traveling in the opposite direction. By the time he reached the airport the rain was diminishing, the sky becoming merely sentimental instead of sorrowful.

The nearest shuttleport where he could secure offworld transport was in Chiapas. Even if he could somehow make it that far without being picked up, he couldn't be sure his efforts of the past month had accumulated enough credit to purchase passage. Not that it mattered. The first thing the local authorities would do would be to run a report on the incident, complete to a police molder's rendering of the attacker based on the woman's eyewitness account. As soon as he stepped off a down shuttle on, say, one of the Centaurus colonies, a grim-faced welcoming committee would be there to greet him. Besides, he had no intention of traveling offworld. Not when he had important business on this one.

What he needed was to get as far away as possible as quickly as possible, but not so far that he couldn't get back to see Ehrenhardt before the deadline that had been set for payment. At least for the moment, returning to Golfito was out of the question. Ehrenhardt would not take kindly to a personal visit from a man wanted by authorities for murder. As a known antisoc, his home and businesses would be watched.

Paying with credit from his personal account, Cheelo locked himself in a shower room at the airport while he renegotiated the unfortunate husband's credcard. In minutes, using the room's public terminal, he had succeeded in draining the credit and switching it into his own account. Colorless and untraceable, it would provide him with a means of flight. He was grimly gratified to see that with the addition of the latest sum, even after the purchase of a ticket to somewhere else, enough remained for him to pay Ehrenhardt what was required. The transaction would simply have to be delayed for a while. There was no reason to panic. He had plenty of time.

The woman would remember what he had been wearing. With considerable reluctance, he discarded the raincoat, shoving the crumpled bundle of fabric into a disposal chute where, hopefully, it would be compacted and then incinerated. Underneath, he wore attire that was simple but clean

and untattered. Adopting as best he could the air and attitude
of a small businessman, he approached one of the automated
ticket dispensers and logged in.

"Where is it you wish to go today, sir?" The device's syn-
thesized voice was brisk and feminine. He tried not to be too
obvious as he looked sideways, backward, down, anywhere
but directly into the visual pickup. Frequently, he passed a
hand over his face as if wiping rain from his eyes. He kept his
voice at the lower limits of audibility as he shoved his illegally recharged credcard into the accept slot.

"As far as this will take me on the next flight out and still
leave twenty thousand in the account. No, make that twenty-
two thousand." If his estimate was off he could always cancel
the request and make a new one.

"Could you be a little more specific, sir? Random, spon-
taneous vacationing is a joyous adventure, but it would be
helpful to me if you could at least pick a direction."

"South," he mumbled without thinking. His choices were
simple. West or east would send him out over one of two
oceans. North would find him very, very cold.

The dispenser hummed softly. Seconds later a small plastic
strip emerged from a slot. Cheelo stood ready to bolt if the
device's internal alarms went off, but his credcard popped out
normally alongside the ticket a moment later. Taking the strip,
he placed it on his card, to which it promptly adhered.

"Thank you for your patronage, sir," the dispenser told
him. He turned to go, then halted and spoke without looking
anywhere in the direction of the unit's visual pickup.

"Where am I going?"

"Lima, sir. Via suborbital, gate twenty-two. Enjoy your
flight."

He did not offer thanks as he strode purposefully in the direction of the requisite concourse. A glance at a monitor
showed that he would have to hurry if he was to make the departure. His expression set; he was inwardly pleased. The last
thing he wanted to do was to have to linger in the vicinity of
the airport.

No one challenged him as he approached the gate. The
ticket processor did not eat his card, passing it through to him

on the other side of the entryway. The man and woman seated
next to him ignored him as they chattered inconsequentially.

Even so, he did not allow himself to react until the plane
was in the air, gaining altitude to climb above the tropical
weather while accelerating rapidly to supersonic speed. He
had to try to relax. He had a couple of hours before the next
crisis, when the time would come to disembark. It was futile
to agonize. If the police traced him to the flight, they would
be waiting for him when he stepped off the plane. There
would be nowhere to run. He would be promptly put on a return flight and extradited back to San José.

As he leaned back in the seat he remembered the face of
the lurching husband, the sharp pain of his big hand coming
down on Cheelo's arm. He did not even recall pulling the
trigger. Then the man collapsing, his life imploding like a
mud wall under assault from a rain forest downpour. His wife
falling to her knees next to him, disbelief seizing control of
her throat and vocal cords. He shuddered slightly. Though he
had administered his share of beatings, he had never killed
anyone before. He still felt the same. The pistol had done the
killing, not him. The man had set if off himself, as a consequence of his own idiotic actions. Why couldn't he have
just stood there for another lousy couple of minutes? Why
couldn't he have played out his role of victim? A lot of good
his insurance did him now.

Lima. Cheelo had never been to Lima, had in fact never
been south of Balboa. Whenever he accumulated a little credit
he usually went to Cancun or Kingston for a while, until he
was broke again. He tried to recall what little he knew of
planetary topography. Lima was near the Andes, but was it in
them? He was dressed for the subtropical clime of San José,
not high mountains.

Well, he would find out when they landed. Assuming the
ticket dispenser had abided by his instructions and that his
transfer of credit from the dead man's account was not compromised, he would have the additional wherewithal beyond
the franchise price to purchase clothes as well as food and
shelter. And transport. He could not afford to linger long in
Lima, or in any big city boasting competent police technology. He began to feel a little better about his randomly

selected choice of destination. Mountains were a good place
to hide. He knew nothing of the region, but he would learn
quickly. As soon as he landed he would purchase a guidebook
or two and have them transferred into his card where he could
peruse the information at leisure.

Somehow, he would manage to lose himself. He had done
it before, though not under the impetus of such urgency. A
new identity, a new look, and he would be safe. He was thirty-
five years old and for twenty of that had lived off his wits and
illicit activities. He was not about to let himself in for even a
partial mindwiping. Hell, no! Not when the answer to all his
dreams lay virtually within his grasp.

Just let me get off the plane and out into the city, he thought
tightly. Just that one moment of freedom and from then on I'll
be able to make my way in silence and safety.

He was shaking when the plane slowed to a stop at the
disembarkation gate. When one of the flight attendants remarked on his evident distress he managed to reply in a calm
and unaffected voice that he was just a little cold, and he even
thanked her for her solicitude. Shuffling off the aircraft, he
kept his gaze fixed resolutely straight ahead. As the passenger
load thinned around him—businessmen striding toward connection gates or baggage pickup, families reunited joyfully—
he kept walking without any real destination in mind. When
he was halfway through the terminal and it was apparent
that no officials were waiting to intercept and detain him, he
lengthened his stride.

Public transport into the city was readily available in various familiar forms. Avoiding both the cheaper bulk carriers
and the more expensive private vehicles with drivers, he
chose an automatic. It answered his questions as readily
as any human escort and without propounding inquiries of
its own.

Once downtown he immediately felt better about his situation. New clothing, a meal, the purchase of a guidebook, and
a dose of depilatory to remove his attractive but too distinctive beard improved his outlook considerably. All he had to
do was to disappear for a while. It was much too soon after
the incident to search out a surgery where he could have
his appearance permanently altered. When the furor over the

killing had been pushed off the front page of police screens he could return to Golfito and conclude the transaction with Ehrenhardt.

Lima was not in the Andes, he discovered, and at this time of year it was subject to heavy fog, a development that delighted him. The less visible he was at all times, the better. But, like any large metropolitan center, the city boasted an unobtrusive yet sophisticated police center and an appropriate number of active response sites. Enough stolen credit remained in his account to get him out of the city and away from public scanners without impacting on the twenty thousand he needed to keep for Ehrenhardt. The only question was where to go. It would have to be someplace where the police presence was slight to nonexistent, someplace where he could walk without having to worry about keeping his face turned away from pole-mounted scanners.

The guidebook suggested several possibilities. To the north lay a largely uninhabited region of rolling hills and flat plains. But the area was thick with important archeological sites that were periodically swarmed with tourists. That wouldn't do. The mountains were a suitably forgotten fastness, except that the habitable valleys were full of neat vegetable farms and ranches that echoed to the hoofbeats of alpaca, llama, and cattle genetically engineered to thrive at altitude. The higher elevations were sufficiently inhospitable to discourage settlement. Similarly, the low temperatures and thin air were more than enough to discourage him.

More promising was the strip of southern coastal desert. Behind the beaches, with their resorts and desalinization plants, few people lived who did not work in one of the numerous mines gouged from the arid landscape. There was still room for a person to lose himself, but not enough room— not for the kind of near-total disappearance Cheelo had in mind.

That left the enormous Reserva Amazonia. The most biologically diverse stretch of rain forest wilderness left on the planet, it had seen its last indigenous inhabitants resettled elsewhere more than a hundred years earlier. Since then it had been abandoned to its great profusion of plants and wildlife, save only for scheduled incursions by tourists and scientists. The dense canopy would hide him from prying overhead eyes, and the presence of so many other forms of life would mask his heat signature from patrolling remotes.

According to the information he read on his card, the most primitive and isolated part of the park lay at and encompassed the eastern foothills of the Andes. There, where cloud forest met lowland rain forest, there had never been a need to remove and resettle traditional inhabitants because there had never been any. The region was as inhospitable to man as it was lush, a place where some of the rarest creatures left in the wild roamed free. Yet even there, isolated tourist facilities could be found that catered to the most adventurous, to those seeking a true wilderness experience.

Having spent some time in the rain forest himself, plucking tourists instead of tropical fruit, he enjoyed a certain familiarity with such country. The miserable months he had spent drunk and diseased in Amistad came back to him in a rush. It wouldn't be very comfortable—he would be hot and sweaty all the time, and there would be bugs—but the same conditions that would make it unpleasant for him would also discourage extended examination by officers of the law. If stopped and challenged, he could pass himself off as just another tourist. If anyone thought to probe further, he could vanish into the immense forest while they were running a background check on him.

He was unable to outfit himself to his satisfaction in Lima, but Cuzco boasted a number of shops where he was able to obtain his modest requirements. The lightweight, rip-proof pack he purchased filled rapidly with a good supply of basic emergency concentrates and vitamins, a permanent water filter and purifier, insect-proof bedroll and tent, fuel-cell cooker, and mapping ware for his card. The live clerk assured him that his new clothes would repel everything from army ants to a rainy season downpour.

Thus equipped, he booked passage on a slow lift to Sintuya, the only community permitted within the boundaries of the southwestern portion of the Reserva. It existed solely to serve the needs of tourists and researchers. Since he could hardly pass himself off as the latter, he assumed the identity of the former. At the same time, he had as little intercourse with his fellow sightseers as possible, though he made a con-

scious effort to be polite rather than taciturn. Anything to
render himself as bland and forgettable as possible.

The flight over the Andes from Cuzco was spectacular, an
unfolding panorama of ancient Inca terraces—now groomed
and tended by machines—irrigated ranches, and tiny, quaint
Quechua alpine communities that made a good living from
crafts and tourism. Then the peaks gave way to mist-swathed
cloud forest. The slow lifter descended, following the steep
eastern slopes, occasionally blowing mist and cloud aside to
give those aboard a glimpse of the thick vegetation beneath.
Once, a family of spectacled bears ambled into momentary
view, and recorders whispered as the travelers imaged the
moment for replay back home in London and Cairo, Delhi
and Surabaya.

Cheelo Montoya took no pictures, though he made a show
of oohing and aahing over the scenery as energetically as
those around him. A tourist who failed to tour would stand
out in the minds of his fellow travelers, something he intended to avoid. The absence of a recorder did not have to be
explained. Not everyone spent their vacation gazing fixedly
into a color imager.

Sintuya proved to be even smaller than he had expected. A
few restaurants served meals of exotic rain forest produce,
everything from starfruit mousse to caiman fritters. Aware
that it might be the last meal he would enjoy for some time
that he would not have to prepare himself, he splurged on
a ragout made with agouti, yuca, assorted vegetables, and
blanched Brazil nuts. A couple of hostels, a flurry of handi-
craft and gift shops, the usual traveler's aid stations, and an
outlying scientific complex comprised the rest of the town.
Though the air-conditioned, dehumidified hostels beckoned,
he resolutely ignored their civilized blandishments. Except
for the purchase of one meal, he would leave no record behind of his presence in the remote community.

Idling away the rest of the day among the town's minor
amusements, he waited until well after nightfall to steal a
boat. It was a small, silent tour lifter that could carry up to
four persons. There were half a dozen of the sleek little craft
bobbing at the dock. He set all of them free, shepherding the
others out into the middle of the current and watching as they

drifted off downstream. Theft might be suspected in the disappearance of one boat. The flight of all six would be interpreted as a consequence of bad luck, vandalism, or a youthful
prank gone awry. When only five of the errant craft were recovered it would be assumed that the other had sunk or that it
would be found washed up in some overgrown bend of the
river or stream mouth.

The silent engine whisked him upstream at high speed, the
boat's built-in sensors automatically avoiding any obstacles
in its path. An aircar would have offered greater speed and
more flexibility, but unless he wanted to skim along above the
canopy it would have been as useless as an ancient ground-
bound vehicle. Also, it would have run out of power in a few
days. The boat's energy cell ought to last for a couple of
weeks, at least. By keeping to the main river and hugging
close to its lush, overgrown banks, he ought to be able to
make his way deep into the Reserva without much risk of detection. Once he turned up a tributary, there was no reason to
suppose anyone would come looking for him at all. Runaway
boats did not head themselves up the current.

He would find a suitable site, perhaps an old abandoned
tourist blind, and settle in until his supplies began to run low.
Supplementing his stores with living off the land, he should
be able to exist quite tolerably, if not entirely comfortably, for
a number of months. By that time the urgency attending the
death of one unfortunate traveler in distant San José would
have faded, and he would still have several weeks in which to
make his meeting with Ehrenhardt. Emerging from the rain
forest, he would solidify his credit balance, arrange to have
his physical appearance altered, and start afresh as master
of a lucrative, semilegal franchise. He would finally, at last,
be someone important. He would finally have done something *big*.

Setting the boat on automatic after programming it to
follow the course he had predetermined, he settled back
within his bedroll and watched the stars slide past in a
pristine, uncontaminated sky. A typical criminal would have
sought refuge in the depths of one of the great cities. That
was where the authorities would be looking for him now—
running scans, posting electronic flyers, querying informants.

He was reasonably certain he had escaped San José unnoticed, was more confident his arrival in Lima would pass unremarked upon, and was sure he had transited Cuzco without being scanned. Let them hunt for him in Golfito, ransack his tiny one-room apartment. Out here, in the depths of the great wild park, there was nothing and no one to take notice of him. Even the rangers who monitored the Reserva were concentrated in the areas of highest tourist density. He had deliberately chosen a section famed for the ferocity of its insect life. In return for physical anonymity he would gladly sacrifice some skin and blood.

Feeling pretty good about himself and his resourcefulness, he rolled over and let the near-silent hum of the boat's engine lullaby him to sleep.

10

The world outside the port matched precisely the projection Desvendapur and the others had been studying for days: an impressive globe of cloud and earth all but submerged by a disproportionate volume of water. It seemed impossible that intelligent life could have arisen and matured on such a scattering of isolated landmasses, but such was indisputably the case. Then the time for study was over, and a senior official was delivering their last briefing.

"Because of the need for secrecy, transport to the surface must be carried out clandestinely." The large male gestured for emphasis. "Since we and our human associates established the colony a routine has been devised whereby this can be accomplished with some degree of safety and assurance. That isn't to say that some risk is not involved." He eyed each of them in turn. The four new colonists-to-be waved truhands and twitched antennae to indicate that they understood the gravity of the situation.

"If by some chance the drop is intercepted, you four know nothing. You are workers on your way to the official contact site at a place called Lombok." To Desvendapur it sounded as if the official's spicules must be underwater and that he was in the first stage of drowning, but in spite of linguistic difficulties he managed to pronounce the human word clearly. "If questioned, you may describe your respective specialties. There is nothing in them to indicate that you are bound for a covert colony as opposed to the officially recognized site.

"Collect your personal gear and report to the disembarkation chamber in two time-parts." He gestured a mixture of caution and admiration. "You are to be part of a great experiment. In twenty or so years, when it is time to reveal the exis-

tence of the colony, it is expected that humans will be sufficiently used to our presence among them so that they will not
only accept it but be amused at their own initial uncertainty. It
will also show that we are capable of sharing one of their
worlds as opposed to one of our own without adversely impacting their society or environment. There are other important social questions that the colony will answer, but it is not
necessary to go into the details now. You will be thoroughly
briefed about your sojourn among these creatures by those
living and working on-site."

The meteorologist gesticulated a question. "What about
you? Have you spent much time among them?"

"Some," the official admitted.

"How do you find them? Our own contact to this point has
so far been limited."

"Frustrating. Friendly but hesitant. Impulsive to the point
of nonsapience. Vastly amusing. Threatening. Liquid of movement, clumsy of hand. You will see for yourselves. They are a
bumbling, stumbling, wondrous medley of contradictions.
And I am speaking of the best of their kind, those within their
government who have helped to establish the colony project
by deceiving their own people. The general human population, which this experiment is designed to help win over, is a
surging, unpredictable, cacophonous sea of barely controlled
chaos. One moves among humans the way one would among
an arsenal on the cusp of detonation. Each individual is a
bomb waiting to go off. Collectively, they make one want to
flee their presence as rapidly as possible. Personally, I do not
like them. But it has been decreed by the Grand Council that
we are to try and make them our allies. Myself, I would prefer
the Quillp." He moved forward.

"But I am bound by my instructions. I admit that they are
undeniably clever and intelligent. It is claimed that in spite of
individual dislikes we must work to make them our friends,
and us theirs, lest the AAnn or some other equally unpleasant
species gain the low ground with them. That will be part and
parcel of your work. You are all specialists, some in advanced
fields of research, others in support, but each of you is an am-
bassador. Never, never, forget that."

They were dismissed to return to their quarters to collect

their belongings and their thoughts. Des did not know what
was racing through the minds of his three companions, but
as for himself he could hardly contain his excitement. This
was what he had worked for for so long. This was what he
had lied and deceived and falsified to attain: inspiration wild
and fresh, of a kind that was denied to every other poet on all
the thranx worlds.

A sudden thought clouded the dream. What if there was already a poet within the secret colony? Surely it would boast
among its complement an official soother or two. He decided
he could not worry about that. If they existed they would
be occupied with official duties, with performing for their
fellow colonists. He labored under no such obligation. When
not carrying out his rote, lowly duties in the kitchen he would
be free to compose, locking his inventions away from prying
eyes in the secure section of his scri!ber. They would be revealed only when he was back on Willow-Wane, only when it
was time to retire Desvenbapur the assistant food preparator
and resurrect Desvendapur the poet.

In time, he cautioned himself. In good time. Stimulation
and enlightenment first, then revelation.

To all outward appearances there was nothing to distin-
guish the thranx shuttle from the dozens that had preceded it.
A sleek multiwinged shape designed for atmospheric as well
as orbital travel, it emerged from the side of the *Zenruloim*
like a *vlereq* voiding its egg. There was nothing in its external
configuration to suggest to observant eyes either in orbit or
on the planet below that there was more to it than what was
immediately visible.

Receiving final clearance from planetary authorities, it
drifted away from the starship on secondary thrusters before
engaging its main engine at a safe distance. Braking against
orbit, it began to fall not only behind but below its parent
craft.

Along with that of his companions, Desvendapur's attention was fixed on the screen before him as they drifted clear
of the queen vessel's gravity field. It showed a portion of the
cloud-bedecked globe filling the field of view. They fell past
a human orbiting station, a massive assemblage of rotating
interlocking discs that swarmed with smaller craft. A pair of

starships were docked at one end. To the poet's untrained eye
they appeared to be about equal in size and mass to the *Zenruloim*. It was an impressive sight, but hardly an overawing
one. Certain aspects of human design were quite similar to
those of the thranx while others were radically, even incom-
prehensibly, different. It seemed impossible that the laws of
physics could be bent to identical ends by engineering that
differed so startlingly.

Then the shuttle was below and beyond the busy station.
An intensely blue ocean loomed below. From his studies Des
knew there were three such primary bodies of water on the
human homeworld, the least of which was larger than the
most extensive sea on either Willow-Wane or Hivehom.
Though he knew there was no reason to worry, the sight
chilled him more than he would have cared to admit. With its
breathing spicules located on its thorax, a thranx could stand
upright with its head and all its principal sensory organs held
well above water—and it would quietly drown. A hard exoskeleton and slim legs made swimming difficult.

Humans, he had learned, not only swam efficiently but
were naturally buoyant. Put representatives of both species
side by side and a human would turn on its back and float
whereas a thranx would, after suitable panicky thrashing,
sink to the bottom of whatever body of water it had been
unfortunate enough to stumble into. Conversely, no human
could match an active thranx, with eight limbs at its disposal,
for stability. Nor were the bipeds as dexterous, their two
hands and ten manipulative digits unable to equal the finesse
of the thranx four and sixteen.

When they wished to be, however, humans could be much
louder. Whether this was a particularly useful trait was the
subject of debate.

As the shuttle entered atmosphere, weight began to return,
dragging Des's abdomen down against the thickly padded
flight bench he straddled. The view on the screen shifted
wildly between impenetrable ramparts of cloud and flickering
glimpses of surface. The colors of the latter varied considerably, as did those of any world that supported indigenous life.
He heard Jhywinhuran calling out to ask how he was doing,

and he replied absently. His attention was wholly focused on the alien world that was rushing up toward them.

Calm and collected flight commands echoed over the chamber speakers. Then there was a sharp lurch as the secondary shuttle that was mounted within the belly of the larger dropped away. Its plunge toward the surface was precipitous, masked and electronically warped to avoid detection by planetary instrumentation. It helped that they were descending over a swath of unbroken rain forest that boasted one of the lowest population densities anywhere on the planet.

At the low altitude at which separation occurred and given the velocity and angle of the drop, there was absolutely no room for error. Too conservative an approach and the shuttle would overshoot its target, appearing unannounced and uninvited above a populated area. Too extreme, and it would be unable to brake in time, resulting in tragedy as well as accusation. But the pilots of the tiny craft had performed the requisite difficult maneuvers before. The g-forces that piled up against Des and his companions pressed their antennae back against their skulls and kept them pinned to the flight benches. It did not worry him. They had been briefed to expect it, and in the cramped confines of the downsized sub-shuttle there was nowhere for them to walk anyway.

Oversized braking thrusters rocked the craft, and his mandibles clamped tightly together. The viewscreen darkened as they dove into heavy weather. It rained frequently in the region chosen for the site of the secret colony—a warm, wet reminder of home. Familiar with such conditions, the rain forest downpour posed no unexpected difficulties for the pilots.

Through dark gray cloud and mist he had a glimpse of a vast, unbroken forest full of unfamiliar shapes. Then he felt impact and a jarring, wrenching slide as the shuttle disappeared into a heavily camouflaged opening. The noise level within the chamber rose appallingly as the shuttle slowed, finally coming to a halt within a sealed corridor. As his respiration returned to normal and he began to release himself from the landing harness, Desvendapur saw small service vehicles, mechanicals, and several heavily laden six-legged figures advancing swiftly and efficiently toward the craft.

He and his companions emerged into a landing chamber that except for its exceptionally compact dimensions was little different from one they might have encountered on Willow-Wane. The same equipment, the identical facilities, were much in evidence although greatly reduced in mass. A single young female was waiting with transportation and greetings to welcome them when they disembarked. Assured that their belongings would follow, they climbed onto a stripped-down surface transport and were promptly whisked away from the shuttle chamber.

Nothing unfamiliar assailed their senses. Strong, light-weight composites had been sprayed on the walls of the excavation to form a solid seal against intrusion from outside. Familiar fixtures and markings indicated the location of side corridors, specific facilities, water, and utility conduits. It looked exactly like the hive facilities they had just left. To all outward intents and appearances, they might as readily be back on Willow-Wane.

He had a horrible thought. What if this and they were part of some extraordinary, extreme social experiment? What if they had indeed traveled through space-plus, but only to make a looping curve back to Willow-Wane, or to journey on to Hivehom itself? What if they were gullible volunteers in an experiment to see how humans and thranx would get along in close quarters—in a physical and mental environment faked to resemble the humans' homeworld? The view out starship and shuttle windows could be simulated. What if they had simply landed on a thranx world? It was impossible to tell. Everything was the same; nothing was different.

Except for the air.

It stank of exoticism, of alien vegetation and musk. Even purified and cleansed before being drawn into the colony it was still ripe with the fragrance of the utterly foreign. Of course, an atmosphere could be falsified as easily as images. All manner of smells and stinks could be artificially introduced into a closed environment. If so, he thought, someone was doing a superb job.

Because of his unique personal circumstances he was inherently more distrustful than any of his companions. Aware

of this he chose not to reveal his suspicions. He hoped they
would be proved wrong.

If the gravity differed from that of Willow-Wane, the difference was negligible. He didn't know whether to be uneasy
or delighted at the realization. The transport turned down a
second corridor and began to slow. That was when many, if
not all, of his suspicions were laid to rest.

A trio of specialists were strolling down one side of the
tunnel, chatting amiably among themselves, their antennae
bobbing and weaving animatedly. They wore no special attire, nothing to mark their surroundings as unusual. Two humans were walking and talking with them, gesturing with
their forelimbs. Compared to the lone human Desvendapur had encountered on the surface of Willow-Wane, these
two wore virtually nothing. Their fleshy, multihued epidermi
were blatantly exposed for all to see. Recalling his studies,
Des decided that both were male. It was neither their presence nor their lack of clothing that particularly intrigued the
poet, however. It was their nonthranx companions.

The pair of small quadrupeds that gamboled around both
human and thranx legs were covered with a bristly sub-
stance that he managed to identify as fur before the transport
hummed on past. One had covering that differed significantly
from that of its counterpart. It was also considerably larger,
though neither would have come up to the underside of the
poet's abdomen. They had long faces, intelligent eyes, and
jaws that resembled those of the AAnn more than they did
those of their human associates.

He fought to recall the details of human society. As he remembered it, the bipeds not only consumed the butchered
flesh of other creatures, they kept representatives of certain
species in their own homes, as if the company of their own
kind was insufficient to sate their need for companionship.
In this regard, certain subspecies were more privileged than
others. Among the latter were dogs, of which the two furry
quadrupeds accompanying the strollers appeared to be legitimate representatives. What was especially fascinating was
that despite their lack of sapience, the dogs appeared to be
paying as much attention to the three thranx as to the two
humans.

To the best of his admittedly restricted knowledge, no such creatures had been imported to Willow-Wane. They did not occupy space reserved for humans on Hivehom. Support facilities were designed to provide for humans, not their domesticated animal companions. It was costly enough to properly care for the bipeds. On the human homeworld no such restrictions would apply. The presence of the dogs had not entirely erased his concerns, but they had made it much easier for him to be convinced. The domesticated furry quadrupeds had appeared far too comfortable in the company of the three thranx to have been recently imported to a project site.

The transport slowed to a stop, settling to the floor with a whine. They were met by a pair of females wearing a type of insignia Desvendapur had never seen before. While the two scientists were whisked off to a separate destination, Des and Jhy were given a quick tour of the facilities where they would be working before being escorted to their new quarters. The two of them made arrangements to meet and share the nightfall meal along with the rest of the day's experiences.

Waiting for his belongings to arrive, the poet inspected the double cubicle that would serve as his new home for an indeterminate period. Nothing was unfamiliar; little differed from the living chamber he had occupied at Geswixt. Everything appeared to be of thranx manufacture. Given the professed secretive nature of the nascent colony, he would have expected nothing else. The bipeds who were surreptitiously helping the thranx to establish a foothold on their own homeworld could hardly place an order with one of their local manufacturers for a load of thorax massagers.

He halted. Something rising from the equipment stand at the foot of the sleeping bench caught his eye. As he turned toward it, an odor as pleasant as it was subtle tickled his antennae. The small, carefully arranged cluster of flowers was unlike anything he had ever seen, with spreading white petals that shaded to deep purple at the base of the stamens. Bending close, he dipped his antennae forward to sample the essence of the bouquet. The stems rested in a fluted afterthought of tinted glass. If it had been grown on Willow-Wane or Hivehom, there was a group of botanists who deserved whatever compensation they had been allotted. But it did not smell of either of those thranx worlds. The amputated blossoms reeked of the here and now.

He looked forward to learning his way around the kitchen facility, but that pleasure was denied him until tomorrow. No one was expected to step off a shuttle after completing an interstellar journey and get right to work. If it was all part of a script to convince them they were on Earth when in fact they had never left home, it showed an attention to detail he could only admire. But with each passing time-part he became more and more convinced of the reality of the interstellar trek, and that they had truly arrived at a furtive colony-to-be hidden on the most hallowed of all human worlds.

He had hoped to encounter some of the bipeds, but the nightfall meal was attended only by fellow thranx. A number smelled strongly of *outside*, and of a moist, pungent, alien outside at that. He consoled himself with the knowledge that he would probably have the opportunity to interact with humans tomorrow or the next day. Had he not seen two of them walking casually in the company of three of his own kind on the way in? He had been patient this long; he could wait a while longer.

But as the days went by without even a glimpse of a human, he found himself growing uneasy. He had not traveled all this way, had not forged a false identity, to toil at the preparation of food for the rest of his life. Though he had mastered the limited demands of his new vocation, he was anxious to shed it and resume the mantle of full-time poet. In order to do that it was necessary for him to immerse himself in his chosen source of new inspiration. But that source remained as elusive as ever.

Where were the humans? Save for the pair he had passed on the day he and his fellow assignees arrived, the bipeds had been conspicuous by their absence. It was absurd to think that he might have less contact with the bipeds on their own world than on his. Yet for all the contact, inspirational or casual, that he had experienced so far he might as well have stayed on Willow-Wane. His frustration gave rise to several robust, acidic stanzas, but while well crafted and original they did not burn with the fervor of discovery he so desperately sought.

Any attempt to probe further would require great caution on his part. An assistant food preparator who was both persistent and inquisitive about subjects that were far removed from his official duties might well draw unwanted attention to himself. Any queries would have to be carefully framed and delivered in an offhand, almost indifferent manner. His coworkers in food preparation were notable for their lack of enlightenment.

Jhywinhuran was only marginally more helpful. Despite his intentions to keep his distance, he found himself drawn to her. Though her hive ranking was no lower than his, it was clear that she regarded him as her intellectual superior and looked up to him in matters outside their respective specialties. It was not a matter of flattery for ulterior motives or extraneous personal ends. Her attention and admiration were genuine. In her presence he relaxed far more than he intended. Constantly on guard, ever alert to the possibility of discovery, he luxuriated in the companionship of another of his kind who was openly fond of him no matter how mysterious his origins or how unforthcoming he was when certain subjects were broached.

In response to his query she informed him that she had actually seen humans on two occasions, but at a distance. There had been no personal contact. There was no reason for it to occur at her level. No doubt the rogue humans had to consort with their thranx friends on matters that reached beyond the boundaries of the colony. In matters of Jhywinhuran's field of sanitation, outside advice and help would be necessary unless the incipient colony was designed to act as a completely closed system. That was possible, but only up to a point. That it was not the case was clear from the limited interaction that had taken place between human and thranx specialists on the two occasions that Jhy had observed.

But there was no reason for humans to come into the kitchens. Desvendapur and his coworkers needed no assistance in preparing the basics of the colony's meals. That there was another feeding station he already knew from contact between the two. It was no consolation to him to learn that his counterparts in the other facility had no more interaction with humans than he did.

He had to find some way to reach out to them, to immerse himself in the strange culture of these creatures and their world. While personally satisfying, advancement in his adopted specialty promised nothing in the way of additional contact while exposing him to additional personal scrutiny he did not want. Given the extremely sensitive nature of the secret installation, like everyone else in the subterranean colony his movements were restricted. He was allowed to wander freely within the food service area and to roam the communal recreational and social intercourse areas, but everything else was strictly off-limits. This included the heavily camouflaged shuttle bay and all hive departments with access to the outside, of which there were very few.

The location of these exits, the majority of which had been established for categorical emergency purposes only, were well known. Keeping them secret would only have obviated their purpose. No thranx, however curious, would brazenly defy restrictions by attempting to make unauthorized use of any such egress. Not only would it violate strict hive procedure, there was no reason to do so. Within the colony all was comfortable and familiar. Outside—outside lay an unknown alien world swarming with exotic fauna and dominated by an unstable intelligence. Who would *want* to go outside? Any sensible thranx who expressed a desire to do so would immediately find himself branded as unbalanced, marginally mad, or outright insane.

As a poet, Desvendapur qualified on multiple counts.

If he had spent all his time dwelling on his frustrations, he might well have ended up in the hospital. Aware of the dangers, he forced himself to concentrate on his work. It was much worse at night, when he had nothing to occupy his hands or mind, when he was free to meander both physically and mentally. Unable to fathom a reason for the agitation that sometimes bubbled to the surface of Desvendapur's personality, Jhywinhuran did her best to comfort him. He responded as best he was able, but there were times when she could do nothing. How could she understand the nature of the creative fury that seethed within him, a raging torrent dammed and held back by stricture and circumstance?

It was a state of affairs that could not go on, he knew. Sooner or later his mounting frustration would overwhelm his good judgment and common sense. He would do something stupid and end up exposing himself. Then he would be removed from his duties, taken into custody, and shipped offworld for treatment and, inevitably, castigation. If his link to the death of the transport pilot Melnibicon was discovered, he would be subjected to worse than that. Any chance for a notable creative career, of course, would be permanently dashed.

How to inquire about matters outside his area of expertise without appearing too curious? After careful consideration of possible alternatives, he decided that a bold approach to one person offered fewer risks than dozens of furtive queries put to many different individuals.

He settled on a junior transport operator named Termilkulis who periodically delivered supplies to the kitchen facility. Cultivating friendship, slipping the active and efficient young male leftover delicacies from food storage, Des gradually drew him out until the operator felt completely comfortable in the assistant food preparator's company.

It was early one morning, after preparations for the morning meal had been concluded and the results turned over to the division masters for final tinkering, that he encountered Termilkulis concluding a delivery. Remarking that he was about to take time for a rest, Desvendapur was gratified when the operator responded agreeably to the suggestion that they do so together. They retired to a back corner of the facility, near the narrow unloading dock, and assumed resting stances on all four trulegs and both foothands.

Following an indeterminate number of minutes spent in lazy contemplation of the morning that were interrupted only by inconsequential remarks, Des ventured casually, "It seems strange to me that, finding ourselves on the human homeworld, we do not see more of the natives."

"Well, I don't imagine that you would, working in the department that you do." Wholly at ease, Termilkulis's antennae drooped listlessly over his forehead.

Desvendapur indicated assent, careful to keep his gestures moderated and brief. "I suppose that's true. What about you?" he asked with apparent indifference. "How many have you seen?"

The transport operator did not appear to find the question in any way out of the ordinary. "One or two."

"But I would think that in the course of making deliveries throughout the colony you would surely have the opportunity to see many of the bipeds."

"Not really. You know, for a while after I was first assigned here I wondered about the same thing myself." The poet tensed, but it was evident from the operator's attitude that the food preparator had not triggered any latent suspicion in the young driver. "So I inquired about the seeming discrepancy, and what I was told made perfect sense."

"Did it?" responded Desvendapur casually. "Did it really?"

Termilkulis turned toward him. "This is a thranx colony, a thranx hive. Only a few humans, working for an enlightened but covert division of their government, know of its existence. It is designed to show that we can live among them, in sizable numbers, without adversely impacting their civilization. When the time comes, when the xenosociologists on both sides think it is all right, our existence will be revealed and will hopefully have a salutary effect on the bipeds' opinion of us.

"But there is no reason for more than a very few of them to visit the hive. This is a thranx colony. As such, it is populated by thranx." A foothand rose to gesture. "By such as you and me."

It made damning, frustrating sense, Desvendapur knew. Why should any hive, even one located on the human homeworld, require the presence of humans? While the respective projects on Willow-Wane and Hivehom had been designed from the start to explore the ramifications of intimate human-thranx interaction, this colony was different. It was surreptitious, officially unacknowledged by both governments. It was designed to show that thranx could thrive on a human-dominated world. Open interaction here would come later, when both species had become acclimatized to the presence of the other, when humans did not find thranx abhorrent and vice versa.

This much he could understand. He also found many aspects of humankind distasteful. The difference between him and his fellow thranx was that for him, abhorrence was an excellent source of inspiration.

But how to immerse himself in that and its related emotional states if he was denied interaction with its progenitors, in all their billions? He would gladly settle for contact with a dozen or so, but it appeared that even that was to be denied him. He could not wait indefinitely for something to happen, for circumstances to change. His term of service was finite. More than that, he was too impatient to wait around and react. Fatalistic resignation was not a component of his character.

What to do? If he happened to see another human in the distance, walking the fringe of a sector off-limits to him, he could ignore restraint and brazenly confront the visitor. That might work—for a minute or two, until Security forestalled extensive interaction by hauling him away. Too much risk for too little potential reward. Or he could try to isolate a visiting biped, keep it to himself for a while, but even the suggestion of the use of force within the colony would find him shipped offworld faster than he could pack his meager belongings. With his access to vehicular transport, Termilkulis might be of real help—until he became aware of his new friend's intentions. That would doubtless result in immediate termination of their relationship and the reporting of the food preparator's eccentric behavior to hive authority.

No, whatever he did, Desvendapur decided quietly, he would have to do it on his own. His choices were decidedly limited. Or at least, the sensible, rational ones were. There remained the option of the insensible and the irrational. These were not available to the average thranx. Had there been anything average about Desvendapur, he would not even have been contemplating them.

The solution was as obvious as it was insane. If he could not find humans to interact with within the hive, then he would have to find a way to encounter them without.

11

As had quickly become his routine, Cheelo was awakened by the gothic choir of howler monkeys greeting the return of the sun. Lying on his back beneath the thin tropical blanket, he gazed up through the dense, featherweight material of the tent. This close to the Earth's waist, the sun rose and set with equal alacrity. "Lingering twilight" was terminology that belonged to the temperate zone and had no place in the equatorial rain forest.

Yawning, he reached up to scratch an itch—and sat up fast, yelping. Looking down, he saw a rushing river of red-tinged brown flowing across his stomach from left to right. The river entered through a hole in the left side of his tent and exited through a gap of correspondingly tiny dimensions on his right. It went over, around, or through anything and everything in its path. It might have gone through him as well if he had not been tucked into the tough, inedible blanket.

He had gone to sleep without activating the electronic insect repeller in his backpack.

The army ants had eaten through his tent because it was in their path. Able to surmount his sleeping form, they had chosen to go over him. This was fortunate, though he did not think so until later, when he had time to reflect on the closeness of his call. At the moment he was standing and screaming, slapping at the soldier ant that had sunk its mandibles deep into the flesh of his right thumb. Had he known more of army ants and their ways he would have reacted in a more circumspect fashion.

Detecting the release of alarm pheromones from their smashed colleague, a subsection of the living brown stream detached and attacked. Flailing wildly as if afflicted with

some aberrant disorder of the nervous system, Cheelo hopped
and stumbled out of the tent and the trees, across the open, intervening beach, and into the river. Even submerged, the ants
hung on tenaciously. Since it was not the dry season and
ample customary prey was available, the resident piranhas ignored this violent intrusion into their world. The four-meter
long black caiman on the far bank did not, slipping silently
into the water, its dragon's tail cleaving the rippling, mirrored
surface as it sinuously advanced to investigate. By the time
it arrived, a fully awake and much chastened Montoya had
slogged back onto the beach. Disappointed, the caiman sank
back beneath the surface, its intended quarry as ignorant as
ever of its majestic, carnivorous presence.

Muttering a steady stream of gutter curses, Cheelo made
his way back to his tent. Reaching inside, he checked his pack
carefully before picking it up. A pouch within yielded oint-
ment to treat the red welts left behind by the jaws of the
soldiers. A pair of tweezers were necessary to remove the
mandibles and attached heads of those ants that had refused
to release their grip, even after having been drowned and
dismembered.

There was not much he could do then except wait for the
column to finish moving through. Fortunately, all of his foodstuffs and concentrates were vacuum sealed. This was critical not only to prevent spoilage in the dank depths of the
rain forest but to keep edibles from detection by marauding
scavengers no matter what their size.

It was late afternoon before the rear guard moved through
the hole in his tent and out the other side. After carrying out a
visual inspection to ensure that no stragglers remained, he
broke down the shelter and its contents and placed them once
more in the boat. Normally before loading his gear he would
have first checked everything for those dangerous lovers of
dark places who inhabited the rain forest: scorpions, spiders,
kissing bugs, and their ilk. Subsequent to the column's passage he knew that would not be necessary. As efficiently as if
they had intentionally been making amends, the ants would
have scoured clean his tent and belongings. In the wake of
their passage, nothing lived.

He vowed that from now on he would be more careful in

his choice of campsites. In the rain forest no locality was perfect, however. Bushes concealed dangers of their own; trees were home to voracious insects of other species; and sleeping in the boat, where he could not erect his tent, would expose him to predation by mosquitoes and worse, such as disgusting parasites like the human botfly. Despite his unfortunate experience, he continued to favor open ground within the forest itself for sleeping. He carried a patch kit for the tent, and the holes the insectile multitude had gnawed could be repaired.

Perversely, he was grateful for the presence of everything that stung, bit, chewed, or parasitized. All contributed to conditions the average tourist found uninviting. The worse the climate, the more rapacious the fauna, the less likelihood there was of him running into a tour supervised by a querulous escort. Despite the area's isolation, a guide or even a tourist equipped with a communicator could quickly call a skimmer full of rangers down on him. With the unfortunate encounter in distant San José still a recent item on police call sheets throughout the hemisphere, that was a confrontation Cheelo desired devoutly to avoid. By the time he was ready to return to Golfito, the furor surrounding his unfortunate encounter ought to have died down.

So far he had been successful. What was proving more difficult than evading the attention of the authorities was living off the land. He had succeeded in catching plenty of fish: The river was awash with them, and they bit at the first hint of bait. But he discovered that there were far fewer edible fruits and nuts than he had hoped to find, and he had been beaten to most of those by the park's thirteen species of monkey or dozens of parrots and macaws before he could so much as find a ripening tree. The fish were plentiful and tasty and kept him sated, but after a couple of weeks, even a steady diet of piranha and catfish grew boring.

The craving for variety in both taste and nutrients forced him to draw down his stock of concentrates to a point where he began to grow uneasy. Having worked so hard to isolate himself, he was extremely reluctant to make his way to Maldonado, the nearest town, to replenish his supplies. He did find some yuca root that he cleaned and fried. That restored his confidence in his back-country abilities, learned if not polished during his youth in Gatun and its own tropical environs. He knew he was being too hard on himself. Nothing could really prepare one for living beyond the limits of civilization, in the greatest surviving rain forest on Earth, in the place known as the lungs of the planet.

When he found the grove of fruit trees, planted long ago by vanished villagers and now gone wild, he was euphoric. Not yet decimated by monkeys, the fruit was a welcome and refreshing addition to his food stores. His success cheered him mentally as well as physically. That evening he caught a thirty-kilo catfish on his compact line and streamer, enough meat to fill the preserver compartment in his pack to bursting.

Cruising upriver, he lay back in the boat and let the onboard navigator take control. It would keep him from running into the banks, or any floating logs or embedded snags. Beneath him, the electric motor hummed almost silently, its batteries recharged by the amorphous solar cells that lined the sides and top of the boat. For a fugitive, he was exceptionally relaxed.

Until the boat struck something unseen.

A cry of distress, a pained yelp, came from near the bow. Sitting up quickly, Cheelo looked over the side just in time to see the injured pup floating on the surface. Blood streamed from the side of its head and flank. Preoccupied with chasing fish in the murky water, it had failed to react to the boat's presence in time. Now it limped along the surface, yipping piteously.

Swarming to its aid, the rest of the pack instantly focused on the assumed attacker. Nearly two meters long and weighing in at more than thirty kilos, the adult river wolves swarmed the boat, barking angrily.

"Ay, it was an accident!" Cheelo found himself yelling as he scrambled frantically to unholster his pistol. "The kid ran into me!"

The dozen or so giant otters did not understand him. Even if they had, it was conceivable they would not have been swayed in their course of action. Two leaped into the boat and began nipping at his feet, taking bite-sized bits out of his jungle boots. Their canines were as long as his thumb. Jaws powerful enough to crunch bone snapped at his calves while bright black eyes glared furiously.

It took an eternity to free the gun, but he couldn't use it lest he risk holing the boat. Instead, he fired over the heads of his attackers. Barking and squeaking in panic, they dove back over the side, but not before one practically ran up his leg to take a bloody chunk out of his left biceps. By the time the cursing, fulminating fugitive could bring the weapon to bear, the otters had vanished into the depths of the river.

Setting the pistol aside, he grumbled aloud as he sought to bind up the wound. With all the poisonous insects, lethal snakes, giant crocodilians, burrowing parasites, and voracious rodents in the rain forest, leave it to him to be grievously assaulted by otters. Dousing the open wound with disinfectant, he sprayed sealer over the injury and wrapped it in a thin layer of transparent artificial skin. The tape immediately contracted and began to bond with his own flesh. Once healing had concluded beneath, the artificial epidermis would dry, crack, and flake off, leaving the restored flesh exposed. Finishing up the first aid, he restowed the emergency kit and cleared some vegetation from the autobailer so it could more efficiently remove from the bottom of the boat the water the otters had brought in with them.

That was when one of them, apparently deciding that the intruder had not been punished enough, jumped out of the water and onto his back.

As its teeth and claws tore into his shoulders, a screaming, cursing Cheelo flailed wildly at his back in an attempt to pull it off. Twisting violently, locked together, man and otter overbalanced the narrow craft and tumbled into the river. As he fell, the flailing fingers of Cheelo's free hand contacted his backpack and instinctively grabbed hold. The safety strap connecting it to the side of the boat gave way beneath his weight and followed him into the water. Automatically righted by its internal gyro, the swift craft promptly resumed its course upstream—carrying with it Cheelo Montoya's tent, sleep sack, and all of his supplies that were not contained in the pack.

Perhaps the impact dislodged the river wolf as well as discouraging it. Or possibly it had finally slaked its need for revenge. Regardless of the reason, the meter-and-a-half-long otter released its bloody grasp on Cheelo's shoulders and swam off, occasionally popping its head out of the water to look back long enough to sputter a few final insulting chirps and barks at the intruding human. Treading water, Cheelo had no time to respond to the insults of his fellow mammal. Clutching tightly to the backpack with one hand and his pistol with the other, he struck out for the shore opposite the one favored by the otter clan, occasionally glancing upstream to track his boat as it blithely powered on out of sight minus its absent passenger.

He shouldn't have been such a lazy sailor, he reflected in dismay. With its autonav activated the craft would continue to make steady progress until halted by impassable rapids or some other obstacle it had not been designed to cope with. Then it would stop and wait for instructions from its absent owner.

Thoroughly drenched, he hauled himself out on the nearest beach. Smooth-shelled turtles watched him from a nearby log, butterflies fluttering about their snouts in search of ex-truded salts. Wading birds accelerated their stride to give him additional room. Checking his pants for worms, candiru, and other potentially dangerous hangers-on, he contemplated his options.

Recharging by day, the boat would not run out of power. Programmed to proceed upstream, it would not pause for rest or sleep. It was gone, and along with it much that he had brought to sustain him in the rain forest. By great good fortune he had shoved the compact fishing kit into the backpack after the last time he had used it. That was helpful, but still left him with little choice. No longer could he gambol care-lessly through the forest. In order to make his critical ap-pointment with Ehrenhardt, he had to find his way to a town, an isolated farm, even a tourist encampment, and he had to start now. Anyplace would do so long as it was not home to official authority. A convincing liar, he felt that he could suc-cessfully pass himself off to a group of adventurous tourists as a kindred spirit. It would take very little to render wholly believable the story of falling out of a boat set on autonav and not being able to catch back up to it.

With luck he would find assistance in returning to civilization. There he could access his credcard and without further ado, book the sequence of flights necessary to take him back to Golfito. Because he was on foot he would have to move a little faster now, that was all. He still had ample time to make the deadline.

But first he had to find those hypothetical charitable tourists, and avoid the attention of park rangers while doing so.

Two days later he felt he was closer to the nearest town but no nearer fellow sightseers. So preoccupied was he with searching for food to supplement the small stock of concentrates that remained in his pack that he almost overlooked the probe. Disguised as a split-tailed eagle, the drone came gliding down the river at treetop level. It was not the smoothness of its flight that caught Cheelo's attention and caused him to duck deeper into the woods, but the fact that the too-perfect raptor did not flap its wings—not even once. Superb glider that it was, even a large eagle needed the intercession of an occasional wingbeat to keep it aloft.

Tracking its progress from behind the buttress roots of a rain forest hardwood, he watched as the drone circled a spot on the far bank, descended to a height of several meters, and proceeded to hover. Eagles could hover, he knew, but only on strong, warm updrafts. There was no updraft a couple of meters above the riverbank, certainly not one forceful enough to support even a medium-sized hawk, much less the eagle. The cameras that were its eyes were doubtless taking pictures and relaying them back to one of the distant ranger stations that ringed the perimeter of the immense Reserva. Monitoring the health of the forest and its fauna without disturbing any of the inhabitants was a task best carried out by such disguised mechanicals.

Surely they couldn't be looking for him, he thought. Even if the authorities had somehow managed to track him and trace his flight from San José to Lima, there was next to nothing to lead them to the middle of the rain forest. He thanked whatever deities looked after such as him that he had grabbed his pack while falling out of the boat: It contained all his identification. Then it occurred to him that they might not be looking for him, Cheelo Montoya, wanted for murder, but for the missing occupant of a runaway boat. Proceeding mindlessly on its way upriver, it was not unreasonable to assume that the intruding craft had caught the attention of one of the Reserva's robotic monitors. Rangers and administrators could be expected to wonder at the presence of an unoccupied craft, packed with supplies, cruising blithely northward devoid of passengers. It would be percipient for them to assume that a small disaster might have occurred and to go looking for the owner of the wayward craft.

That was fine, except that he did not want to be rescued. It was his intention in coming to the Reserva to get himself good and lost. He did not want to be found, no matter how well-intentioned his would-be saviors were. Despite his reluctance to abandon the only landmark he knew, he had no choice but to move away from the main river and deeper into the forest. Searchers, human or mechanical, would assume that stranded travelers would keep to the shoreline and the beaches where they could easily be spotted. He had taken care to acquire a boat that could not be traced, so if scanned it would not lead back to him. With luck, it would sink and break up before inquisitive rangers could haul it ashore and check its contents.

Meanwhile he plunged deeper into the forest, knowing that it would conceal him like a hot, green blanket. The profusion of life in the canopy and on the ground would make it next to impossible to isolate his heat signature from the air, even if a properly equipped drone knew exactly where to search. He made slow but steady progress. Unlike thicket or jungle, virgin rain forest permitted relatively easy hiking. Large trees grew well apart, and the canopy harvested the sunlight before it could hit the ground, restricting the density of the undergrowth.

Not only was the solid overstory reassuring, it was also beautiful—diverse with epiphytes and flowers. Monkeys rattled their way through the arboreal highways, and the bell-like warbling of the oropendula punctuated his footsteps. He was careful to shuffle his feet as he walked. Making as much noise and vibration as possible would keep the local serpents out of his path. Avoiding the authorities would not help him if he accidentally stepped on a bushmaster or fer-de-lance.

After making a careful check for ants, he settled down between the buttress roots of a sprawling tree and prepared to spend the night. His tent was still on the boat, but his pack yielded a light, strong emergency blanket. One root curved sideways and out, creating a swooping overhang that when combined with the blanket served to protect him from the evening rain. It was a good thing he had not come in the wet season, he mused. Without his boat he would be helpless, trapped by flooded rivers and lakes, unable to cross ground churned to mud. That he was going to get wet despite the lightweight raincoat he could extract from the pack was a fact he could not avoid: He was, after all, deliberately lost in Earth's greatest rain forest. But he would not drown and, so long as he could fish, he would not starve. He did not care to think what he would have done had the folding fishing kit been lost along with the boat.

He had no difficulty the following morning pulling several small fish from a sizable pond. Using his belt knife, he gutted and filleted them. His camp stove was on the wayward boat, and making a fire was out of the question. Even if he could find sufficiently dry wood in the waterlogged forest, it would most likely be too soft to burn for long, or already so rotted it would fall apart in his hands. Nor could he risk giving away his location by producing smoke.

As he ate the fish raw he wished for a few limes or lemons. They were not available, so the tang of ceviche would have to wait until he found himself once more in a town. But the fish would give him strength. With the small remaining stock of supplements contained in the pack's emergency kit, he ought to be able to keep going for some time. At least, he thought with a grim smile, he would not be slowed down by the weight of supplies.

Settling the pack on his shoulders and back, he struck off into the trees, keeping to the highest ground that presented itself. His feet stayed warm and dry, as the surrounding mud and muck was repelled by the permanent static charge in his jungle boots. He was glad that when he had made his purchases he had not stinted on appropriate clothing. It would have been nice, however, to have the tent.

On the other hand, he might have grabbed something be-

sides the pack when tumbling out of the boat. He did not care
to think about what his situation might be like without it. He
would have had no choice but to risk rescue by the Reserva
rangers and to hope that no one connected his face to the one
that was by now no doubt splashed across police wanted files
all across the planet.

The repeller in the pack kept the swarms of ravenous
insects at bay. He could see them, could hear them hum-
ming and clicking and chittering as they flew and crawled all
around, unable to enter the restricted sphere of electronic dis-
location that had at its core a warm, pulsating, blood-filled
figure. They wanted to nibble on his flesh and drink his blood.
Mosquitoes and flies, beetles and ants, all gave way as the
precisely modulated stridulations of the repeller urged them
aside like a drifting iceberg parting the sea. Without the compact device, he knew, his skin would by now have taken
on the reddened, uneven contours of a strenuously abused
golf ball.

The birds kept him company, and the monkeys. While easy
to hear, the latter were difficult to see. The natives who had
once inhabited this region had been fond of monkey, but the
thought of consuming a simian was not one that appealed to
Cheelo. Anyway, he had only a single-bladed knife and could
not have used a bow and arrow had heaven provided them.

The following morning a skimmer flashed by overhead,
traveling slowly at treetop level. Alerted to its approach by
the startled screeches of a family of squirrel monkeys, he
had taken shelter beneath a dense cluster of dieffenbachia.
Thick, spatulate leaves shielded him completely from above.
Peeping out as the skimmer thrummed past, he saw that it was
camouflaged visually as well as aurally. If not for the panic
that had arisen among the monkeys he would never have noticed it until it was right on top of him. Despite the cover provided by the trees, he might have been spotted.

The forest is my friend, he thought, waiting beneath the
concealing leaves until he was sure the patrolling vehicle
was gone. When he resumed his march, his confidence was
shaken by unexpected uncertainty.

Come to think of it, why would Reserva rangers need to
camouflage their patrol craft? True, the soft whine a skimmer

generated might disturb the native fauna, but it was hardly loud enough to be flagrantly unsettling. Masking the sound of an engine was an expensive procedure that hardly seemed justified by the limited disruption it might cause.

He could understand disguising drone probes as eagles and other birds. They could move more freely among the forest creatures, taking surveys and monitoring their health. But it seemed a waste of money to camouflage a skimmer. Its size and unfamiliar shape would instantly identify it to the creatures of the forest as an unknown and possibly hostile intruder. His confusion deepened.

If the skimmer was not disguised to conceal it from the denizens of the rain forest, then from whom? Wouldn't it be more likely that an official Reserva vehicle would be boldly emblazoned with identifying marks and colors? A scientific expedition might opt for anonymity, but not for expensive camouflage. In the event of an emergency, they would want to make certain their craft could be spotted from the air by a search party. The same would be true for a tourist vehicle.

That left open to speculation the possibility that there were others in the rain forest who did not wish their presence advertised. Biochemical companies, for one, extracted enormously valuable and useful derivatives from rain forest plants. Most of these took the form of legal, government-approved, exhaustively tested products. A few did not. Their scarcity and novelty value enhanced their price.

If botanical pirates were active in this part of the forest, they might—once he had the chance to explain himself—accept him as a kindred spirit and take him in. That would obviate his need to find his way into a town, thereby risking exposure to the local authorities. On the other hand, such illicit organizations did not usually take kindly to the appearance of uninvited outsiders, no matter what their social standing. Depending on the frame of mind of the people in charge of such a hypothetical illegal operation, they might as readily decide to punch a hole in his chest and dump him in the nearest river for the caimans and the piranhas to clean up as invite him to share their camp.

He would have to tread carefully. He might already have tripped hidden sensors, resulting in the appearance of the patrolling skimmer. If he had strayed inside some undefined perimeter, the possibility of automated traps could not be discounted. From now on he would have to pay even more attention than usual to where he put his feet. But, he reminded himself, any assault by the authorities on a clandestine rain forest operation would come from the air. He would be cautious anyway. He did not know what he was dealing with, and until he did, he would continue to treat his immediate surroundings with heightened suspicion.

Another skimmer flew over later that day, forcing him to take shelter a second time. He knew it was a different vehicle from its size and silhouette. It only reinforced his conviction that it was someone other than the local authorities who was searching for him. If it was the police and they suspected a fugitive was afoot in the area, they would have called for him to surrender himself. If it was the as-yet-unidentified owner of the wayward boat who was being sought, they would have advertised the opportunity for rescue rather than gone to expensive lengths to conceal its presence.

That left him with his suspicions of a criminal operation hidden somewhere in the depths of the rain forest, its operators as eager as he to avoid the attention of the authorities. They would be people who might as readily kill him as welcome him, even if he invoked Ehrenhardt's name. The choices thus presented were not easy ones. He decided that until he knew more he would maintain his privacy. Meanwhile let them search for him. He had avoided the authorities all the way from San José to the Reserva. No manufacturers of illicit pharmaceuticals were going to find him if he did not want to be found.

Whoever they were, he reflected as he stepped over a fallen log lush with fungi, they had money. Camouflaging a skimmer's appearance was one thing, but muting its engine called for expensive technological expertise. This remote corner of the vast rain forest was not being guarded by a handful of amateurs working out of a few thatched huts. The presence of not one but two such costly disguised skimmers hinted at a level of sophistication outside his experience.

Maybe he could do more than merely survive here, he thought. Maybe there was a chance to make some contacts—

big, important contacts. If the opportunity presented itself to fall in with a group of well-connected felons, he would take it. Or he might learn all he could about them and then turn in their operation to the nearest authorities, using his knowledge to bargain for the dropping of the charges that would have arisen from the incident in San José. That had been an accident, after all. No one could claim premeditation. Either way, he had options. What he needed now was to supplement them with knowledge, as much as he could gather without being discovered.

It struck him that the drone that had been disguised as an eagle might be owned and maintained not by the Reserva authority but by these same people. Monitoring a buffer area outside their immediate zone of operations, it could watch for patrolling rangers and unwitting tourists without drawing attention to itself. He whistled softly to himself, impressed by the implications. Everything he had seen so far suggested the existence of an illegitimate operation on an imposing scale. That was assuming he was right in his assumptions and that it was not the local authorities who were conducting the flyovers.

For a moment he worried that the electronic repeller might give him away. Then he relaxed, secure in the knowledge that if it was going to, it already would have. Its output must be infinitesimal, he decided. Anyone close enough to pick it up would be able to see and identify its owner. Even so, he considered turning it off. The continued presence of the active insect multitude that had helped to keep this portion of the Reserva pristine for hundreds of years forestalled him. He was uncomfortable enough already. He would not add to his discomfort by exposing his flesh to the attentions of a million marauding mandibles, stingers, and probing proboscises. Aside from the potential for loss of blood and the acquisition of disease, he flat-out hated and always had despised bugs.

Trying to make as little noise as possible as he advanced, he kept his eyes alert for the glint of metal and plastic and composite, and his ears attuned to the harmonic discord of the surrounding forest. If the monkeys failed to warn him next time, the birds might do so. He was not alone here; he had allies, however unconventional. He had escaped confine-

ment and mindwipe by never letting down his guard and by
trusting no one. Early in his life he had chosen to swap companionship for freedom. It was a philosophy that had served
him well, and he saw no reason to tamper with it now.

Overhead, a pair of scarlet macaws were screeching with
pleasure as they attacked a cluster of ripe figs. A pair of the
juicy green fruits fell to earth not far from where Cheelo was
standing. Bending, he picked them up and, after checking for
ants, shoved them in a pocket. Later, when his stomach was
feeling more adventurous, he might try a bite. Raising a
hand, he saluted his rain forest confederates with a grin before moving on.

It did not matter who was looking for him, he decided with
satisfaction. Police or traffickers, rangers or poachers—he
would avoid them all until he and he alone decided it was
time for Cheelo Montoya to leave the Reserva. They kept the
rain forest at arm's length: He embraced it. The trees and the
animals and the insects were his friends, his shield. All he had
to do was find out what was going on here, in this empty, isolated place, and figure out the best way to profit from that
knowledge before he left.

While taking care, of course, to make sure that his friends
and his shield did not poison, infect, dismember, eviscerate,
or otherwise impede him.

12

Sustenance would not be a problem, at least not in the short term. Desvendapur had readier access to food than anyone else in the colony, far more than he would be able to carry. Besides, it was his intention to live as much as possible off the alien land. Just as the bipeds had been able to derive nourishment from many of the native foodstuffs available on Willow-Wane, so the residents of the hidden colony on the human homeworld found that their digestive systems could tolerate a significant variety of the local plant products. This greatly facilitated settlement and the perpetuation of secrecy, since suspiciously large quantities of food did not have to be brought down from orbit.

Certain vital minerals and vitamins not found in terrestrial vegetation, or available only in insufficient quantity or incorrect proportion, were supplied to the colonists in the form of supplements, and it was these that Desvendapur was careful to stockpile for his pending enterprise. As a food preparator he was as familiar as the senior botanists and biochemists with those local growths that provided the bulk of the colony's provender. Once outside, he would know exactly what to look for in its raw form and how best to prepare it. Provided he could get outside, of course.

He spent a good deal of his leisure time surreptitiously studying and evaluating potential egresses. There was only one main exit to the surface: The shuttle dock where he had first arrived. On those occasions when it was necessary for them to pay a visit, the colony's human friends and facilitators entered via the same portal.

There were in addition a number of artfully concealed emergency exits, to be used only in the event of disaster.

Their design and construction was familiar to him. Every hive boasted similar "shoot" tunnels equipped with automatic, individually powered lifts to the surface. Utilizing one in the accustomed manner was out of the question, as its activation would set off all manner of alarms.

At least he would not have to deal with guards, armed or otherwise. The forest that grew above the colony was undisturbed and empty save for those remote monitors that had been designed jointly by humans and thranx to keep watch for unforeseen intruders. Since the establishment of the colony there had been none. This portion of the planet was not only vast and untouched, it was guarded by the humans themselves against unauthorized entry. The monitors were a calculated afterthought, a precaution whose presence was very likely unnecessary. Nevertheless, they existed, and he would have to deal with them.

But no one guarded the exits. There was no reason, no need for sentinels. Bold and audacious as the colonists were, no thranx in its right mind would think of taking a solo, unsanctioned jaunt on the actual surface, exposed to thousands of exotic alien life-forms. Additionally, it could get uncomfortably cool outside, especially at night. There was also hostile fauna with which the colonists were utterly unfamiliar, and they wanted to keep it that way.

All except Desvendapur. Hostility was fertilization for tragedy, and tragedy was the foundation for many a noble epic. As for the climate, he would cope. Of all the places on Earth, the colony had been established in the one most copacetic to his kind. If he could not persevere on the surface above the colony, it was highly unlikely he would be able to do so anywhere else on the world.

It took him some time and much careful calibrating to forge the necessary internal directives. Anyone who chanced across them would discover that he had been temporarily transferred to the colony's other food preparation facility. Anyone who happened to check personnel records would note that he was still hard at work in the colony. With his work location temporarily blurred, no one should miss him at either location. He would be free to wander, to absorb and learn, to discover and explore. When he was finished he would return to his old station, there being a good likelihood of his never having been missed. He would resume work while devoting the majority of his time to the tailoring of his rough notes.

When they were revised to his satisfaction he would submit them to the appropriate sources on Willow-Wane for criticism and publication. That they would cement his celebrity he had no doubt. Then he would gladly submit to the public revelation and exposure of his true self, in the process reclaiming his identity. If this connected him with the death of the transport driver Melnibicon, he would deal with the consequent ramifications as required. What happened after that did not matter. His fame would be assured. The honor and renown he would bring to his much-reduced family, to his clan and his birth hive, would blaze forth no matter what his eventual disposition at the hands of the authorities. There was even a good chance he would escape punishment. Great art traditionally excused a multitude of sins, as well it should. He did not dwell long on the morality of this conviction.

But his compositions would have to be exceptional indeed.

It was with growing confidence that he made ready. The thrill of preparing to do something as illicit as it was extraordinary inspired him to fire off half a dozen scrolls filled with screaming hot stanzas. Reviewing them, he decided that they represented his best work to date. And they only anticipated the sights he expected to see, the experiences he proposed to have. He could foresee that any creative difficulties that might develop were not going to arise from insufficient inspiration, but from a need to channel and guide a surfeit of illumination.

And then, falling upon him as heavily and abruptly as a collapsing tunnel, the chosen day was at hand. He bade temporary farewell to Jhywinhuran and his friends and co-workers within the food preparation section, assuring them that he would return from his temporary reassignment to their quadrant of the colony within a single moon cycle. Returning to his quarters, he made certain that everything was in order and that, should anyone come calling and enter uninvited, they would find a chamber in a state reflecting the continued residence of its occupant. He had arranged everything just so, even to programming his favorite relaxation music and visuals to power up at appropriate times of the day.

There was only so much he could do. If someone should post a watch on his living quarters they would quickly discover that the cubicle was not in use. But why would anyone do that? As jointly devised by humans and thranx, colony security was designed to keep a lookout for wandering strangers on the surface. It was intended to keep outsiders sealed out, not residents locked in.

The supplies he had so patiently and laboriously accumulated were packed within a waterproof commodities sack appropriated from food preparation. Anyone observing him in transit would think he was making a delivery. The fact that he would be traveling outside the usual food freighting routes was unlikely to give rise to a great deal of comment. It was not as if he were transporting a bomb.

Strapping the sack onto his back, he used a reflective surface to make sure that it was properly balanced against the long, narrow sweep of his abdomen. The fact that he had not been mated and still retained his vestigial wing cases helped, since the additional layer of hard chitin served to shoulder some of the weight. Slipping a carry pouch over his thorax found him heavily burdened, but not intolerably so. Taking a last look around the comfortable chamber that had been his home ever since he had touched down on the world of the bipeds, he walked out, closing and securing the entrance behind him with his personal code.

He had deliberately chosen the hour of early morning when hive shifts were in flux. With half the colony's workers retiring and the other half rising to their assignments, there was a lot of traffic in the corridors. Everyone walked who could. The fewer vehicles the colony utilized, the less the chance that an accumulation of stray vibrations might be picked up by unknowing travelers on the surface above. Given the isolation of the colony's site within the immense protected rain forest, that was extremely unlikely, but every precaution that could be taken to ensure secrecy had been fully implemented.

No one confronted him or greeted him as he made his way westward through the hive. General anonymity was one of the benefits of working in food preparation, and he had deliberately done nothing since his arrival to cultivate conviviality or friendship among his fellow thranx outside his department. Jhywinhuran was the one exception. He tried not to think of how she might react to the revelation of his true identity. Seeing her perfect vee-shaped face, her golden eyes that seemed to glow within, the elegantly sensuous sweep of her ovipositors and the gleam of soft light off her brilliant bluegreen exoskeleton made him uncomfortable. He forced the images from his mind. A poet on the hunt was not permitted to indulge in the balm of soothing reminiscence.

As he traveled farther from the centers of operation and into zones designed for general maintenance he encountered fewer and fewer residents. Machines held sway here, muffled and muted to emit as little in the way of vibration and telltale impulses as possible. Every technological blanket available had been thrown over the colony to screen it from prying eyes.

But in addition to basic foodstuffs imported from orbit and water from the colony's own wells, there was one other component vital to the continued health of the facility: air.

Filtered and purified, the alien atmosphere was drawn into the hive by means of a series of all-but-silent vacuum pumps. Narrow of diameter, camouflaged to look like tree stumps, they dotted the floor of the rain forest above, inconspicuous and immobile. When he entered via a servicing and maintenance hatch the one he had singled out, Desvendapur struggled against the pull from below. If he lost his grip, if he fell helplessly, arms and legs flailing, he would find himself trapped at the bottom of the shaft. If he was lucky, someone would detect the reduction in the flow of air and come to see what was causing the obstruction. If not, he would lie there until his food ran out and until—despite the presence of biological inhibitors—he began to rot.

Bracing all four legs, both foothands, and both truhands against the sides of the vertical cylindrical shaft, he stepped through the opening, using his truhands to carefully close the service hatch behind him. Even with eight limbs to brace himself against the dark composite walls, it was a struggle to ascend against the powerful downdraft. The untreated atmosphere being sucked down into the hive was ripe with a pervasion of exotic odors that threatened to overwhelm him. He persisted in his ascent. As expected, the air was cooler than he would have preferred, but adequately impregnated with moisture. He might get cold, but he would not dry out.

Once, he slipped, a rear leg losing its grip, threatening to send him hurling down the shaft. His other legs stiffened to take up the slack, and he quickly reasserted his stance, resuming the full brace. The supply sack strapped to the back of his abdomen now felt as if it were filled not with food and medication and survival gear but with bars of unrefined metal. The place where his thorax met his upper abdomen rubbed painfully together with each upward step, threatening to crack and expose his semiopen circulatory system. If that happened and the break was serious, he could easily bleed to death before he reached the surface.

Though always in view, the upper terminus of the shaft seemed impossibly far away. He elected not to look at it lest the distance he still had to climb discourage him. From the trembling in his legs he knew that he had already passed the point of no return. The top of the shaft was closer than the service hatch through which he had entered. Since it required almost the same energy to rise as to retreat, he clasped his mandibles tightly together and continued his ascent. His thorax pulsed with his hard breathing.

The higher he rose, the stronger became the alien stench from outside. Just when he thought his legs could no longer support him, his head slammed into something unyielding. The pain that raced down his unprotected antennae was intense. Only the shock kept him from losing his grip on the walls of the shaft entirely and plunging to the bottom. If that happened at this height he would not have to worry about rescue. Drawn inward by the suction from below, alien air entering through screened, eye-sized gaps blasted his face and exposed eyes. Ignoring the dust and grit, he reached up with both truhands to feel along the inner edge of the rim. There should be a single latch. In the near darkness he could see very little, and he was constantly having to look down to protect his eyes from the barrage of minuscule debris that threatened to rip the shielding nictitating membranes.

If he failed to locate the latch, or if it refused to open, he would have no choice but to try and work his way all the way back down the shaft to the service hatch. Given how his legs were shaking, he doubted very seriously if he would be able to make it.

He had studied the design of the air shafts closely, but perusing a schematic in the comfort of his quarters was very different from hunting for a tiny component part, trembling and exhausted, while braced only by his legs at the top of a lethally high duct full of incoming air that seemed determined to break his grip and send him hurtling downward. The delicate digits of his left truhand skimmed the place where the upper rim met the top of the shaft. They encountered an immovable obstruction. Raising his head, Desvendapur fought to see clearly in the poor light and softly moaning air. It was the latch. It *had* to be. Using all four digits, he pressed and twisted according to the schematic he had memorized.

The latch did not respond.

Regulating his breathing as best he could, he tried again. The latch might as well have been welded shut. Refusing to concede, unable to do anything else, he readied himself for a third attempt. But he needed more leverage—or more strength.

Sending his last surge of energy and determination into his lower body, he released his grip on the shaft walls with his upper limbs. Braced now only by his four trulegs, he grasped the latch with all sixteen digits of his foothands and truhands while pressing and twisting. Something unyielding complained. The latch gave.

He was not sure whether his legs lost their brace before he pulled himself out or at the same time. All he knew was that he was hanging on with his upper limbs for what seemed like an eternity before he was able to finally kick, pull, and drag himself out of the shaft. He lay on the ground, breathing hard, his vision unfocused, alongside what looked like the stump of a dead diderocarpus. The last thing he had done before collapsing was to close the top of the shaft. It had snapped shut, automatically resealing.

He was committed now. He could not reopen the shaft and regain access to the hive from outside. He was trapped on the surface of an alien world, the world of the bipeds. Right where he wanted to be.

It had not been difficult to learn where the few fixed monitors were located, or when the mobile scanners passed over their respective sections of the site. Colony-based security was necessarily limited lest it attract the attention of the local human authorities. Of necessity, the majority of it was left to those renegade humans who had assisted in the establishment of the colony, and even they had to keep a low profile. Those few who had infiltrated the park authority were the most useful, but even they could not linger in the colony's vicinity. It would be difficult to explain the attraction of a patch of rain forest that, literally on the surface, was no different from the thousands of square kilometers surrounding it. So while he remained attuned and alert to the possibility, he believed that any chance of imminent discovery remained slight.

His excitement at having made it this far was muted by his exhaustion. Every joint in his exoskeleton ached. He lay on his lower abdomen, his legs folded beneath him, slowly regaining his strength. Gradually it returned, and with it, the ability to marvel at his outlandish surroundings.

The trees were all the wrong color: gray or grayish-green where they should have been dark brown. Leaves tended to be broad and spatulate, which was normal, but with their veins all too visible. It was a relief to observe distant ancestor types crawling and flying through the forest. The screech of primitive mammals, the predecessors of the dominant planetary species, pierced the sodden air. Any less humidity and Desvendapur would have been distinctly uncomfortable, but the near-normal moisture content helped to mitigate the cool temperature. He might feel a slight chill now and then, especially at night, but otherwise he anticipated no difficulty surviving.

Having devoted himself in his spare time to the study of the biology of the surface in the immediate vicinity of the colony, he was able to locate not one but several edible plants. None of them were palatable to humans, whose ability to consume and digest plant matter was notably inferior to that of the thranx. Rising, he hefted his pack and started off into the woods, choosing an easterly heading. He ignored the edible vegetation. At the moment he was not hungry, and there would be plenty to choose from in the course of his journey. Nor did he wish to leave behind any evidence of his passing.

With that in mind he was careful to step only in very wet or very dry places so as not to leave footprints, to avoid the breaking off of leaves or branches, and to disturb as little of the forest litter as possible, even though there were other large animals in the forest and any such damage would likely be ascribed to them. Even a human specialist would find it hard to tell whether a branch had been snapped off by a thranx or a tapir.

As he traveled farther from the site of the colony and deeper into the untouched terrestrial rain forest his elation increased. This was what he had come for, what he had struggled so long to achieve—exposure to something utterly new and different. Already, long lines of continuous verse were scampering unbidden through his brain so voluminously that he had to halt from time to time to recite them into his scri!ber. Every tree, every flower and insect, peeping amphibian or raucous bird, inspired him to compose. He could no more stop himself from doing so than he could halt his breathing. It slowed his progress but raised his spirits.

A fruiting tree was ablaze with cacophonous color, not from flowers but from the flock of scarlet macaws busily gorging themselves in its upper branches. Pausing below, Desvendapur assembled an entire sonnet, complete to rhythm and accompanying stridulation. Following a creative lull of many cycles, the explosion of artistry left him giddy. And this was only the first morning of the first day! What inspirational wonders awaited him in the cycles to come? He resolved to maintain his freedom for as long as possible, or at least until the last of his strategic supplements gave out.

It did indeed grow decidedly chilly when the sun set, but the personal covering and tubular shelter he had brought with him proved sufficient to ward off the cold. A human would have spent the night sweating in the nocturnal heat and humidity, but the comfort level of a thranx demanded more of both. Within the solitary six-legged sightseer, excitement and elation battled exhaustion. To Desvendapur's benefit, exhaustion won. He slept soundly and well into morning.

Rising, he repacked his gear and resumed his march eastward. Surrounded by a profusion of exotic edibles, he did not hesitate to try one after another, but only if he was certain of his identification. Many terrestrial growths contained toxins to discourage the attention of predacious herbivores. Some of these were deadly to humans but harmless to thranx, and vice versa. Strong botanical alkaloids that would have sickened or disabled a biped, for example, the thranx considered piquant and spicy.

Ambling along between the trees, the poet ate as he walked. Truhands reached out to pluck leaves from surrounding bushes or hanging branches. Many things a human would have considered fair game the vegetarian thranx ignored, including the abundance of insects. For Desvendapur to have consumed a plump, protein-rich grub would have been akin to a biped eating a baby monkey.

Water was everywhere, eliminating the need for him to carry a supply. Obstacles that would have given a human pause proved no impediment to a six-legged thranx. His only fear was that there might not be room enough in his scri!ber to hold all of the endless stream of invention that poured from his mandibles.

Carefully picking his way through a jumble of small fallen trees that had been washed up in one place by the annual wet-season flood, he felt something strike his middle left leg forcefully. Looking down, he was intrigued to see the three-meter long bundle of lethal curves known to the humans as a fer-de-lance drawing warily away from him. With a soft hiss it turned to slink off into the rotting litter. Its method of locomotion greatly intrigued him. Nothing half so large lived on Willow-Wane that was capable of rapid movement over land without legs. He observed its departure with interest. A glance at the limb that had absorbed the impact revealed a pair of shallow dimples in the faintly metallic blue-green chitin where the elapid's fangs had struck. When they had failed to penetrate, the aggressive and slightly bewildered snake had turned to slink off into the darkness of the forest understory.

Having paid close attention to his studies, Desvendapur had been able to identify the snake instantly. Had it bit the soft, unprotected leg of a human, pain and paralysis would have rapidly ensued and—without the prompt application of the appropriate antivenin—death. Unless struck in the eye, the soft underside of the abdomen, or between joints, an armored adult thranx ran no such risk.

Not every threat manifested by the wild rain forest could be so easily dismissed. Knowing this, Desvendapur was alert to its many dangers. A large constrictor like a boa or an anaconda could kill a thranx as readily as an unwary human. So could a startled spectacled bear or an angry caiman. By virtue of his hard exoskeleton the poet was, however, virtually immune to the attentions of the omnipresent hordes of biting, stinging, blood-sucking insects.

Despite the wonderful excess of exotic tastes freely available on the trees and bushes growing all around him, he was careful not to overindulge. It would be foolish to survive the forest only to succumb to a self-inflicted stomach upset. There would be plenty of time later to try everything.

The narrow, shallow rain forest streams were a source of constant wonder and delight, but the first sizable tributary he encountered gave him pause. It was less than five meters across, no more than half a meter deep, and devoid of visible current. Any human child could have plunged in and crossed it easily. Not so Desvendapur or any other thranx. No matter how hard they thrashed and kicked, even with all eight limbs they were feeble swimmers. Their bodies had simply not been designed with buoyancy in mind. And while members of both sapient species could keep their heads above water while they swam, humans breathed through double openings set in the center of their faces. A thranx utilized eight breathing spicules, four to each side, located on the thorax. Following immersion, these invariably found themselves situated below the surface.

Turning upstream, the poet kept alert for a place to cross. A large fallen mahogany tree trapped among rocks provided a bridge. It was shakier than he would have liked, but in the absence of alternatives he felt he had no choice but to trust it.

He wanted to put as much distance as possible between himself and the colony as rapidly as he could.

The log held steady beneath his weight, and with all six legs securing his footing he was able to accomplish the potentially lethal transit without difficulty. Besides, there was nothing like tempting death to stimulate the creative muse within. Composing as he walked, the scri!ber held comfortably in one truhand, he plunged gleefully into the dense rain forest on the far shore.

In this manner he passed a number of days, camping in a different place every night, sampling the local vegetation, composing relentlessly, crossing intervening streams with an abandon that began to border on recklessness. He was drunk with delight at the sights he encountered, knowing that few if any of his kind had ever seen half as much of the world of the bipeds as he was seeing now. Via recordings, yes, but that was not the same as and could not compare with trudging through the deliciously decomposing muck of the rain forest floor, catching the flash of light from a flitting morpho or dragonfly, listening to the squawk and screech of birds arguing with tree-dwelling simians, or pausing to ingest and sample the taste of yet another exotic leaf or flower.

It was worth everything he had gone through to get here, he told himself with satisfaction. It was worth anything the authorities might do to him if he was caught. He had composed more and better in the past few days than in his entire previous lifetime. For a true artist, that made any and all consequences worthwhile.

He marveled at the miniature jewels comprising the family Dendrobatidae, the poison arrow frogs. When he encountered a sloth lumbering lugubriously between trees, he sat for hours watching it. Reaching a stream whose bottom was clearly visible through the transparent water, he chose to wade it instead of hunting for a bridge or a way around. The meter-deep water covered his legs and submerged his abdomen, coming right up to the base of his thorax. All four trulegs were underwater, a condition designed to make any sensible, right-thinking thranx exceedingly nervous. What if he stepped into a hole and went under? What if the appearance of the streambed was deceptively deeper than it appeared, or gave way beneath his feet?

Holding his breath, he deliberately lowered himself until the stream rose to his mandibles. With his spicules submerged, only his head remained above water. He could still see with his eyes, hear with his ears, taste with his antennae, but he could not breathe. He held the unnatural position for as long as his lungs would allow before finally straightening. Water trickled off his exoskeleton as he emerged onto the far bank. The experience had been empowering as well as exhilarating.

Raising the overworked scri!ber to his mandibles, he poured a stream of florid composition into the integrated pickup. As he walked and dictated, he strode into a patch of low swamp seething with voracious, newly hatched leeches. They swarmed onto his legs and promptly dropped off, unable to penetrate his exoskeleton. Those that persisted he picked off and flung aside. They tried to cling to his digits but were unable to secure a grip on the hard, smooth surface.

There were sizable native predators on Willow-Wane, and in prehistoric times primitive social thranx on Hivehom had suffered predation at the claws of rampaging *colowact* or the ferocious burrowing *bejajek*. Large meat-eaters tended to make a good deal of noise prior to attacking, however. So it was with more than a little surprise that Desvendapur, who thought himself by now comparatively well attuned to the movements and the rhythms of the terrestrial forest, stepped through a clump of deep green calathia and found himself confronting a round, speculative face deep of eye and carnivorous of aspect.

More than a little surprised itself, but equally intrigued, the jaguar inclined its head upward and sniffed curiously. Recognizing the quadruped from his studies, the poet halted where he was standing. One foothand reached up and back to remove the kitchen cutting tool he had appropriated from the food preparation section. It was the nearest thing to a weapon Desvendapur had been able to expropriate and bring along. Food preparators did not have access to stunners or projectile devices. Not that it mattered. Even if he had been allowed open and free access to the colony's stores he doubted if such

appliances were extant. Even the rogue humans who had assisted in helping the colony to get started might balk at the
unregulated importation of alien weaponry.

Taking care not to make any sudden movements that might
agitate the big carnivore, Des transferred the cutting tool
from his foothand to a truhand. The foothand was stronger,
but the truhand was more dexterous and agile. Also, it could
reach high enough to protect his face. Thranx and jaguar
stared, each one utterly foreign to the other.

When the big cat took a deliberate step forward, the poet
fought down the urge to turn and run. Thranx were not noted
for their sprinting ability, and he didn't doubt for a moment
that the terrestrial predator could overtake him with little
effort. Approaching, the jaguar lowered its head and commenced a thorough olfactory inspection of this unprecedented prowler, beginning at the excessive number of limbs
and working its way upward. The scent it was inhaling was
not unpleasant, but neither did it correlate with anything in
the jaguar's experience. Ears inclined sharply forward, it
worked its way along the length of the thranx's body.

Was this peculiar creature alive? Was it something good to
eat? A thick pink tongue emerged to take a lick of Desvendapur's hind left leg. Finding this foray inconclusive, the
jaguar employed the only sampling means left at its disposal.
Opening massive jaws, it placed them around the poet's leg
just above the middle joint and bit down.

Desvendapur winced at the pain and lashed out with the
cutting tool. It was not the resultant shallow incision that
caused the jaguar to leap up and backward, however, but the
reflex stridulation generated by the wing cases on the thranx's
back. Sharp, piercing, and unprecedented in the big cat's experience, the reflexive distress cry hurt its sensitive ears. With
the alien vibration ringing in its head, it landed on all fours,
whirled, and disappeared into the forest.

Breathing hard, Desvendapur hung onto the cutting tool
with one truhand while he used the truhand and foothand on
his other side to explore the injury. Though oozing blood and
body fluids, the wound was not deep. Unpacking his improvised medical kit, he disinfected and then patched the hole,
filling it with quick-drying synthetic chitin. Fortunately, the

jaguar had not bit down with its full strength, or it might have cracked the limb. That would have posed serious problems indeed, though less so for a six-legged thranx than for a two-legged human. He could have rigged a splint, but it was just as well that the attack had not been more serious.

He could not really call it an attack, he decided. The bite had been more in the nature of a tasting. But for purposes of dramatic composition, he would remember and render it otherwise. Exaggeration was as much a tool of the poet as accent and cadence. Like everything else he had experienced since escaping the hive, the encounter with the big cat would be turned to creative profit. Unlike nearly everything else, it was one experience he had no desire to repeat.

The next large predator might decide to see if the eight-limbed alien was edible by taking a bite out of his head instead of a leg.

13

Increasingly confident of his ability to elude the attentions of whoever was probing this portion of the rain forest, Cheelo finished the last of his supper and prepared to retire for the night. The enormous branch that protruded from the lower portion of the trunk of the diderocarpus would not have been easy for a city dweller to reach, but in his time Cheelo had been forced to do more than his share of scrambling over, around, and through obstacles to avoid the attentions of security guards, alerted authorities, and violated merchants. The modest ascent caused him no difficulty.

In minutes he had his pack snugged deep in a crook formed by two tributary branches and his thin emergency blanket spread out on a flattened portion of the largest. Safer than usual from those forest inhabitants who chose to do their marauding after dark, he settled down to a meal of fruit supplemented with vitamin pills and dehydrates. The latter responded gratifyingly to his experienced ministrations and the application of a little water.

The sun did not so much set as silently evaporate behind the clouds and trees, so he could not watch it drop below a vaporous horizon. But seated silently in his temporary aerie he was able to observe the performance of parrots and macaws, of monkeys and lizards, and to hear the ever-present thrum of hyperactive insects. For company he had a brace of black-and-yellow frogs, each of which was no bigger than his thumb. The rain forest was an unending, round-the-clock carnival in which one never knew what act was going to present itself next.

That did not mean he retained his composure when the

meter-and-a-half tall bug wandered out of the woods in the direction of his tree.

At first he thought he was hallucinating, a not-uncommon occurrence in the deep tropics. As opposed to the giant insect, however, everything else looked, smelled, felt, and sounded unceremoniously real. Hallucinations usually involved more than one element of perception. Excluding the outlandish apparition, nothing—not even the clouds, not even the explosion of green growth—appeared abnormal.

As it came closer he saw that while it was insectlike, it was not an insect. It had eight limbs instead of the compulsory six, but neither did that make it a spider. Other details marked it as significantly different. Each of the upper four limbs terminated not in hooks or claws, but in four manipulative digits of equal length. Cheelo could not avoid thinking of them as fingers. Not while one delicately gripped a device of some kind and another casually held a stick.

As he stared, the blue-green, hard-shelled specter halted. It looked down at the device it was carrying, up and around at its immediate surroundings, and again at the device before reaching back to place it in a pocket or slot in the sack slung across its body. The sack was fashioned from a synthetic material Cheelo did not recognize. Unable to reach the pouch with the smaller limb that had held the device up for inspection, the creature was forced to transfer the object to a second set of arms in order to complete the transfer.

Raising itself up onto its four hind limbs, it looked around before resuming its approach. Unless it deviated from its present course, it would pass directly beneath the branch on which Cheelo had chosen to make his bed. Flattening himself out, he fumbled apprehensively for the pistol in his backpack. He could see nothing like a weapon hanging from or attached to the bug or its gear.

That was when he recognized the creature from a hazy remembrance of an old media report. As he recalled, it was his mind that had been hazy at the time, not the report. He had been very, very drunk; he recalled the moment as one of the low points in his life, of which he had suffered many. If he remembered correctly, this creature was a representative of one of the several intelligent, space-traversing species mankind had encountered subsequent to the development of the posi-gravity, or KK-drive, that had made other-than-light travel possible. He tried to remember the species' name: cranks or drinks or—thranx. That was it. Never one to care about or much keep up with planetary, much less extrasolar, news, he had overheard and filed the information in that corner of his mind where he stored data that was unlikely to immediately impact his personal social and financial standing.

Explorers might contact and encounter a dozen new spe-cies or a hundred: It meant nothing to him if he was unable to somehow profit from it. Nor was he alone in his reaction. Convinced that all matter, existence, and the universe re-volved around each of them individually, the bulk of hu-manity paid little attention to that which did not affect their lives directly. The far-reaching, far-ranging vision that the species possessed as a whole tended to dissolve into its bil-lions of self-serving individual components when redacted to the petty concerns of one person at a time.

Well, he was damn well concerned now. Tense and wary, he observed the alien's approach, marveling at the fluid yet jerky motion of the four hind limbs that propelled it forward. What the hell was one of these buglike thranx things doing here, in the empty reaches of Earth's largest rain forest preserve? Shouldn't it be quarantined on an orbiting station, or at the very least confined to a well-established diplomatic site like Geneva or Lombok?

Anxiously scanning the trees behind the creature revealed no other signs of movement. Though it would be premature to make the assumption, as far as his senses could tell him, the alien was alone. As he stared, it stopped again to take stock of its surroundings. The valentine-shaped head, about the size of his own, turned almost a hundred and eighty degrees to look back the way it had come. In striking contrast to the blue-green exoskeleton, the oversized compound eyes were a muted gold marked by latitudinal streaks of red. Like an extra pair of fingers, the two antennae would incline first one way, then another, and sometimes in opposite directions, as they investigated their immediate surroundings.

Individuals of a different and more advanced intellectual bent would have reacted to the intrusion with curiosity and interest. A nervous, edgy Cheelo just wanted the stiff-legged monstrosity to go away. He had spent too much time in the company of cockroaches, had been stung too often by scorpions, had been bitten too many times in his life by spiders and ants and aggressive tropical beetles, to want this gigantic if distant relation to tarry in his vicinity. Even though he knew it was intelligent and not an insect in the accepted terrestrial sense, he just wanted it to go away. If it did not, if it caused him the slightest bit of trouble, if it reacted in any way, shape, or form that might be construed as hostile—his fingers were firm and unyielding on the butt and trigger of the compact pistol.

That killing the intruder might precipitate some kind of interstellar diplomatic incident never crossed his mind. Interstellar diplomacy and interspecies relations had no immediate impact on the lifestyle of one Cheelo Montoya and therefore did not concern him. If there was trouble of that kind it was up to the government to sort out. All that concerned him was *his* freedom of movement, *his* health, and the fluctuating status of *his* bank account. He did not see how the shooting of one overlarge, out-of-place, alien bug would adversely affect any of that.

Hopefully, he would not have to deal with any such exotic ramifications. Preferably, the extraordinary creature would keep right on walking—through the forest, under his branch, and off in a westerly direction, intent on pursuits or destinations that would remain forever a blissful mystery to the uninterested Cheelo. As it drew nearer still he noted the size of the second, larger sack strapped to the alien's back and wondered what it contained besides small lumpy devices of unknown purpose. It was preparing to pass beneath his bough now, and he edged a little farther back, the tough bark scraping against his legs, belly, and chest.

Dislodged by his actions, one of the fruits he had scavenged tumbled backward, off the branch, and plunged to the ground directly in front of the extraterrestrial visitor. It halted immediately, gazing down at the green orb where it had landed among the leaf litter. Cheelo held his breath. There was no reason for the creature to look up. In the fecund rain forest, fruit fell from the canopy all the time.

But it did look up—directly at him. Though it had no pupils on which he could focus, he could not escape the feeling that it was staring directly at him. It was an unnerving sensation, an unsettling feeling, as if all the bugs he had ever stomped, sprayed, squashed, or swatted had been rolled up together into one measureless, accusatory, all-encompassing insectoid stare. Even though he knew it was his own memories and guilt that were gazing back up at him, the realization did nothing to alleviate the unease in his mind or the pounding of his heart. Bringing up the hand that held the pistol, he started to point it at the silent specter standing beneath the branch. While he knew nothing about alien physiology or vulnerability, he was willing to chance that it could not take a burst to the skull at close range. He lowered the muzzle so that it was pointed right between the two bulging, reflective eyes. His finger started to tighten on the trigger.

The accent was soft to the point of being incomprehensible, but slight and wispy as it was, there was no mistaking the conjoined syllables of Universal Terranglo.

"Hello," the big bug said. "I hope you will not expose me."

Expose me? Had he expected the outrageous apparition to say anything at all, that was not what Cheelo would have predicted. "Greetings, man," perhaps, or maybe "Can you tell me how to contact the nearest authorities?" not "I hope you will not expose me." It had also, he noted, not reacted either visibly or verbally to the presence of the lethal weapon that the nervous human was pointing directly at its head. Cheelo hesitated.

Could the soft voice and gentle words be a ploy to relax him and put him off his guard before it attacked and sucked out his innards? Simply by looking at it he could not tell if it could climb. Was it trying to lure him down to the ground where it could set upon him with all eight limbs? It was shorter and looked like it weighed less, but knowing as he did nothing about the species he had no idea how strong it might be. Crabs were smaller than humans, too, but they had jointed chitinous limbs that could effortlessly amputate a man's fingers.

"Can you talk?" it inquired in a manner that could only be described as curiously polite. "I spent a great deal of time studying recordings of your language until I thought myself fluent. Of course, mimicry is not the same as competency."

"Yeah." Cheelo found himself responding reflexively. "Yeah, I can talk." As for competency, the thranx's Terranglo was more cultivated than his own. Montoya's speech reflected its origin in small villages and mean streets, not fancy recordings or educational programming. "You're a thranx, aren't you?"

"I am thranx." The creature gestured elaborately with its set of small upper limbs and their eight digits. "I am individually, in the sounding of your speech, called Desvenbapur."

Cheelo nodded absently. Was there any harm in telling this alien his name? Was there anything to be lost or gained by it? If they were going to continue this conversation—and the bug showed no signs of being in a hurry to move on—it would need to call him something. He gave a mental shrug. Whatever else the thranx might represent, he doubted it worked for the local police.

"Cheelo Montoya."

He smiled at the thranx's initial attempts to pronounce his name. Maybe its speech wasn't all that cultivated after all. It was, however, sufficiently inquisitive to cause Cheelo to tense all over again.

"What are you doing out here in this empty place?" Desvendapur inquired innocently. It took a step backward, away from the branch and the tree. "Are you a ranger on patrol?"

At the mention of the word *ranger* Cheelo started to bring the pistol up again—only to relax, not a little confused, when he saw that the alien suddenly appeared to be more nervous than he was himself. It was looking around with rapid, twitchy movements and had drawn its forelimbs up against its—well, whatever passed for its chest. Being utterly ignorant of alien gesture and motivation, Cheelo could only interpret what he was seeing based on that which he knew, and it looked to him as if the creature was ready to bolt.

"No," he responded cautiously. "I'm not a ranger. I'm not an official of any kind. I'm . . . a tourist. An amateur naturalist, studying the forest."

Sure enough, the two withdrawn forelimbs resumed their previous relaxed position and the searching, rotating, head twisting ceased as the creature focused once more solely on the man in the tree. "You must be a confident one. This is supposed to be an exceptionally remote, uninhabited area."

"That's right." Cheelo nodded agreeably, then found himself frowning. He had drawn the pistol aside, but he did not put it down. "How do you know that? And what are *you* doing here, anyway?"

Desvendapur hesitated. Unable to interpret human gesture or the extraordinary range of expression their flexible faces were capable of producing, he had no way of determining the biped's true intent. As such, he had to rely entirely on his knowledge of their language. For a thranx, used to employing and translating gesture as organically as sound, the absence of interpretable gesticulation was akin to hearing only every other word of a conversation. He would have to fill in the gaps by inference, as best he could.

As near as he could tell based on what he thought he knew, the human struck him as curious rather than hostile, though the poet could not help but wonder about the function of the small device it had previously been pointing at him. That it was no longer doing so was a relief. But how to respond to the coarse, guttural inquiry? Of course, if he had simply stumbled into the lair of a wandering naturalist, then there was nothing to fear. He doubted that the human counterpart to a thranx researcher would be much of a threat. Students of science, regardless of species, tended to be reflective rather than violent.

That did not mean it would hesitate, if provoked, to give him away. He could do nothing, could not determine on a course of further action, until he knew what means of communication the human maintained with the outside world. At least, he decided, it had not immediately drawn forth a communicator of some kind to announce the encounter. As a naturalist, it might well be as curious about Desvendapur as the poet was about him.

In any event, benefits from the confrontation were already manifesting themselves. A rush of suggestive stanzas raced through Desvendapur's freshly stimulated brain. Reaching back with a foothand, he searched for his scri!ber.

The sudden movement alarmed the suspicious biped. "Hey,

what are you doing there?" Again, the small pointed device the mammal was holding made an appearance on the rim of the bough.

Maybe it's got a gun, Cheelo found himself thinking nervously. And if it did, would he be able to recognize an alien weapon if it was pointed in his direction? Maybe he should just shoot it, right now. But what if it was not alone? What if it was a member of some larger exploration party? What if it was working in concert with people, with human scientists? Painfully aware of his ignorance, he realized that until he knew more it would be prudent to react cautiously. He had not survived worse than the rain forest and come as close to realizing his lifelong dream as he had by acting impetuously. Observe, analyze, think, plan, then act: the ancient lessons of the street.

Besides, the stiff-legged alien didn't look particularly fast, and it gave no indication of wanting to run away. He could always shoot it later.

Not wanting to upset the biped further, Desvendapur brought the scri!ber out very slowly. "This is a harmless recording device."

"I don't give a shit what it is." Cheelo gestured with the pistol. "Don't point it at me." He did not want his picture taken, either.

"As you wish." Exhilarated by the tension and the unexpectedness of the contact, Desvendapur proceeded to deliver a stream of clicks, whistles, and sibilant syllables to the scri!ber, together with breathless suggestions for appropriate accompanying gestures. Throughout the euphonious discursive, the human continued to gaze down at him from its perch up in the tree. Such a primitive stare! the poet thought. So straightforward and unvarying, heightened by the directness of a single lens. Human eyes were very vulnerable, Desvendapur knew. A thranx could lose part of an eye, dozens of individual lenses, and still be able to see, albeit with a reduced field of vision and focus. Should a human lose its lens, the ocular function of the entire orb would be largely lost. The realization transformed part of his discomfiture into sympathy.

When he was finished he attached the scri!ber to the pouch hanging from his thorax, where it could be accessed quickly.

The human responded by lowering the unidentified mechanism it had been clutching so tightly in one hand.

"You still haven't answered my questions. I told you who I am and what I'm doing here. I'm still waiting to hear your story."

Desvendapur knew he would have to summon all the creative inventiveness at his command. It was vital to prevent the human from notifying the authorities. If that happened, not only would the poet's presence be revealed to the outside world, so would that of the colony. He could hardly explain that he had found his way to the forest preserve from the official, highly restricted contact sites halfway around the planet. Officially, few thranx had even set foot on the human homeworld.

The biped claimed to be an amateur naturalist. But unless he was concealing his equipment, he appeared to Des to be traveling exceptionally light even for a casually interested nonprofessional. For that matter, why was he even bothering to have this conversation? Any human encountering an unannounced alien could be expected to immediately contact a higher authority. Instead, this Cheelo individual seemed content, at least for the moment, to perform his own interrogation. Something was not as it seemed, but Desvendapur knew it was far too early for him to render judgments. He needed more information—a great deal more. After all, what did he know of human scientific procedures? Perhaps this self-proclaimed naturalist's gear was stored or buried nearby.

Irrespective of the actual explanation, the delay was greatly to the poet's liking. The longer the encounter lasted before it was terminated due to contact with the planetary authorities, the greater the opportunities to set down new and exciting poesy.

"I am a food preparations specialist." He spoke slowly to make certain he was being understood.

He was being understood, all right. Utterly ignorant of thranx dining deportment, Cheelo did not much like the sound of "food preparations specialist."

"Who do you prepare food for?" He looked past the bug, scrutinizing the rain forest from which it had emerged. "Not just yourself, surely? There must be more of you."

"There are," Desvendapur explained creatively, "but they are, *crrrk,* carrying out limited studies of their own far, far from here. I am on a solitary expedition of my own."

"To do what?" Suspicious to a fault, Cheelo kept searching the woods for any hints of closing ambush. "Gather herbs and spices?" He lowered his gaze. "Or maybe you'd like to catch me off guard so you could kill and eat *me*?"

Utterly unanticipated, the sickening speculative accusation caught Desvendapur completely off guard. He had thought that his surreptitious research and studies adequately prepared him for just this kind of contact, but he was wrong. Unwilled and unbidden, an image formed in his mind: the human, stripped of clothing and nude, its pulpy, fleshy pink form stretched out over a fire; raw animal fat dripping from its scorched limbs, oozing into the flames and sizzling; the smell of carbonizing meat . . .

Reeling, he promptly regurgitated the undigested portion of the day's meal that had been quietly fermenting in his upper stomach. He had turned away not out of embarrassment but to avoid retching into the space between himself and the human. That would have constituted a serious breach of manners, though without further knowledge of human habits he was unsure how the biped would have reacted to it.

As it was, the lone male's tone rose in volume. Based on his studies, a retching Desvendapur thought it sounded slightly alarmed.

"Ay—what're you doing? Are you all right?" It looked like the alien was throwing up, but for all Cheelo knew it might have been seeding the ground with its spores, planting more of its kind deep in the rain forest soil. As the creature explained when it finally recovered its equilibrium, Cheelo's initial assumption had been the correct one.

"I am apologizing." As it spoke, the bug was cleaning its four opposing mandibles with the back of a leaf it plucked from a nearby plant. "Your insinuation conjured up a most unpleasant picture. Thranx do not eat"—his voice quavered— "do not eat . . . other creatures."

"Ay—vegetarians, eh?" Cheelo grunted. "Okay, so you're a cook or something. That still doesn't explain what you're doing out here all by your lonesome."

Desvendapur plunged ahead. He had nothing to lose now, less so by revealing himself to this representative of another species. "I am also an amateur poet. I was transmuting my impressions of my alien surroundings into art."

"No shit? You don't say?"

Desvendapur was unsure if he had heard correctly. "Yes I do say," he responded hopefully.

A poet. That sounded about as unthreatening as anything Cheelo could imagine. "So when you were speaking into that recording device of yours, you were composing poetry?"

"A portion of it. Much of the artistry lies in the delivery. You humans use gesture as a supplement to language. For thranx, how we move is as important a part of communication as what we say and how we say it."

Cheelo nodded slowly. "I can see that. If I had four arms, waving them around would probably be twice as important to me, too." While he still did not trust the alien, neither did it appear as threatening as it had at first appearance. Nevertheless, a giant bug was still a giant bug, even if taxonomically it wasn't a bug at all. He kept the pistol drawn as he rose from his crouch and scrambled down the trunk of the tree.

Desvendapur watched in awe. While adept at traversing rocky slopes or narrow ledges, a thranx had difficulty with verticalities. A certain sinuosity of self was required that their inflexible exoskeletons did not permit. To thranx eyes, the actions of a climbing human were as fluid as those of a snake.

Leaping the last meter to the ground, Cheelo found himself confronting the outlandish visitor. Inclined back on its four hind legs with thorax, neck, and head stretched as high as possible, the creature's face came about to Cheelo's chest. He estimated its weight at fifty kilos or so, perhaps slightly less. When erected, the twin feathery antennae added another thirty centimeters to its height.

"So," Cheelo continued, "this expedition of yours? It's authorized by the authorities? I thought all aliens were restricted to contact on orbiting stations, with only a few high-ranking diplomatic types allowed to actually set foot on Earth."

Desvendapur falsified rapidly. "A special waiver was granted to my group. They are being supervised by representatives of your own kind." Years of practice had given him the ability to lie with great facility and skill.

"Then you'll be rejoining them soon?"

How best to answer so as neither to make the biped suspicious nor activate its defensive instincts? "No. They will be continuing their work for," he fumbled for the appropriate human time referents, "another of your months."

"Uh-huh." The human's head bobbed up and down several times. From his studies Desvendapur recognized the gesture as a "nod," an indication of general concurrence. It was one the thranx could easily mimic. Though he normally would have used his truhands to suggest agreement, the poet duplicated the motion in so natural and relaxed a fashion that the biped did not think to question its unlikely origin.

For a self-proclaimed naturalist, Desvendapur reflected, the human's queries seemed to troll far from the realms of science.

"So this special group of yours is here kind of secretly, so it can do its work without alerting the media or even the locals?"

For a second time Desvendapur "nodded," finding the movement natural if overly simplistic, as were the majority of human gestures.

Cheelo was more than merely relieved. For a disquieting time he had been forced to deal with the prospect of dozens of reporters swarming the site of the first thranx expedition to pastoral Earth. Wandering media types might well have trailed an adventurer like this Desvenbapur, anyway. That was all Cheelo needed—half a dozen tridee pickups shoved in his face as their manipulators asked the rain forest hiker for comments. Following broadcast, one of the automated fugitive matchers that monitored the media would set off alarms in half the police centers in this part of the world, and that would be the end of his freedom and anonymity, not to mention any chance of delivering his fee to the waiting Ehrenhardt in time to secure the precious franchise.

But if he was reading the situation correctly, then this small group of thranx this Desvenbapur was talking about were as anxious to keep their presence hidden from the rest of the

world as was he. He and this cook-poet were symbiotes in secrecy. Unless . . .

"Okay, I accept that you are what you claim to be. But what
are you doing out here by yourself?" He gestured expan-
sively without stopping to wonder if the sweeping movement
of his arm would be interpreted correctly, or indeed if it
would mean anything at all to the alien. "This is one of the
most isolated, primitive places on the planet. There are dangerous animals here."

"I know." With its inflexible face the thranx could not
smile, but its upper limbs moved expressively. "I have met
several of them. As you can see, I am still unharmed."

"Defended yourself, huh?" Cheelo squinted as he tried to
identify the purpose of the visible bulges in the creature's
backpack. Amiably as they were conversing, he still did not
trust the alien as far as he could throw it.

"Not really. Some I avoided, while others proved not as
dangerous to me as I believe they are to your kind." With the
middle digits of his left truhand Desvendapur tapped the
center of his thorax. "Unlike you, my people wear their supportive skeletons on the outside. We are more resistant to
punctures and cuts. However, because of the nature of our respective circulatory systems, if epidermally compromised,
we bleed more easily."

"Then you're not armed?" Cheelo tried to peer deep into
the alien's eyes but was unsure where to focus.

"I did not say that. Should it prove needful, I can protect
myself." The biped was being agreeable, but it would not do
to let it know how helpless Desvendapur really was. Capabilities unrevealed are capabilities held in reserve.

"Glad to hear it." Cheelo was mildly disappointed. Not that
the alien had acted in any way hostile.

"Actually," it continued in its soft, melodious rendering of
Terranglo, "I am lying. I am actually part of a large complement of warriors scouting sites for the invasion."

Cheelo's expression dropped, and he started to bring up
the hand holding the pistol. Then he hesitated. The bug was
emitting a vibrant, high-pitched whistle, and the feathers of
its antennae were quivering.

"Chinga—that was a joke, wasn't it? A goddamn up-front

right-out-there joke! Bugs with a sense of humor. Who woulda thought it?" Carefully, he holstered the pistol, though he kept the safety off.

"You see, despite your unavoidably hideous appearance we have many things in common." The valentine-shaped head inclined slightly to one side, momentarily giving the alien the appearance of a querulous canine. "You will not reveal my presence here to the local authorities? To do so would be to put an end to my gathering of raw material for my artistry—and to the work of my fellow expedition members as well."

"Naw, I won't give you away. Tell you what—I won't mention your presence here, and you don't mention mine to your coworkers when you rejoin them."

"I am pleased with the arrangement, but why do you wish your presence here to remain unknown? Surely secrecy is not a necessary component to the work of a naturalist?"

Cheelo did not think as fast as the poet, but he managed to improvise a reply before Desvendapur could grow uneasy.

Lowering his voice, he moved a little nearer. As the lanky bipedal form loomed over him, Des took a step backward, then forced himself to halt. Was this not, after all, what he had come for? The decreasing distance that separated them would have been easier to deal with if the human had not smelled so bad. The climate of the humid rain forest served to magnify the pungency of its body odor, which unavoidably reeked of previously ingested flesh.

"To tell you the truth, I'm sort of here illegally myself. Access to this part of the Reserva is restricted. Not everyone can get a permit to do work in the Manu. And I needed to be here." Oh, how I needed to be here, he thought. "So I just kind of slipped in, quietly and on my own. It's not hard to do, if you know how to go about it. The Manu is big, and ranger outposts hereabouts are isolated and lightly staffed." He drew himself up proudly.

"Not many people would think of exploring this region on their own, much less actually try to do so. You might say that I'm an exceptional person."

"Yes, I can sense that." Were humans, too, vulnerable to praise and flattery? It was another similitude, but this time one that Desvendapur chose not to expound upon. Such knowledge could prove valuable in the days ahead.

"Well, this has been fascinating, really fascinating, but I have to get on with my work, and I'm sure you feel the same about your own." Demonstrating astonishing balance, the biped pivoted and turned to leave. In so doing, Desvendapur saw the wrenching, intense inspiration he had worked so long and hard to access disappearing with it.

By taking several steps forward, he induced the human to turn back once again. Rather abruptly, the poet came to a decision. "Your pardon." He fought down the churning in his stomachs that was induced by proximity to the creature. "But if you would not object, I would just as soon adapt my route so that it coincides with yours."

14

Words had never been Cheelo Montoya's forte. Needing some to cope with an unexpected moment deep in the rain forest was no exception. He found himself fumbling for an appropriate response.

The last thing he wanted was company. The more alone he was, the better his chances of avoiding the attention of local authorities. He saw no advantage to having his tracks shadowed by a curious artist, be it human or alien.

Unable to think of an all-inclusive reply, he stalled. "Why would you want to tag along with me?"

"I am—I have been interested in your kind ever since I learned of the inaugural project that was set up on Willow-Wane to try and facilitate communication and understanding between our species. Long ago I resolved to thrust myself, with only my studies and my wits, into direct confrontation with your kind, seeking in it a source of inspiration as new to me as it was forbidden to my brethren."

Cheelo could not help but respond with a short, derisive snort. "If it's inspiration you're looking for, you won't find it in my company."

"Allow me to be the judge of that."

Formal sort of bug, Cheelo found himself thinking. He wondered if they were all like this. "I travel alone." He indicated the surrounding rain forest. "Isn't this enough alien inspiration for you? A whole new world to explore?"

"It is wonderful," Desvendapur agreed, "but better I see it through your eyes, peculiar as they are, than only through mine. Don't you see? In your company I experience everything twice: as I apperceive it, and as you do."

"Well, you're going to have to damn well apperceive it by

170

your lonesome. I don't like company." For the second time he turned away.

"If you do not allow me to travel with you, I will expose you to the local human authorities," the poet declared rapidly.

This time Cheelo grinned wolfishly. "No you won't. Because you're not supposed to be here, either. Your little research expedition is poking its antennae way, way outside established perimeters for alien visitors. Even I know that much. You don't belong here. In fact, I ought to be the one threatening to expose you!"

Desvendapur deliberated. "Then why don't you?"

"You already know. Because to do so would mean revealing my own unauthorized presence here. I don't belong, and neither do you. So neither guy can risk exposing the other. But that doesn't mean I have to let you follow me around."

"I would rather have your cooperation." The thranx's antennae were never entirely still, Cheelo noticed. "But if necessary, I will follow and observe you and your interactions with the environment at a distance."

"No you won't." The lanky human patted his holster. "Because if you do, I'll splatter your bug guts all over the forest."

The valentine-shaped head dipped slightly to allow compound eyes to focus on the weapon. "That is a very belligerent attitude for a professed naturalist to take."

"We all have our little character flaws." Cheelo's lips were set in a thin, tight line.

The human's expression had no effect on the contemplative Desvendapur, but his words did. Did he realize how deep the truth of his observation ran? The poet suspected the biped did not.

"You won't shoot me. If I do not report in according to a prearranged schedule, my hive companions will come looking for me. When they see how I died, they will come looking for *you*."

"I'll take my chances." Cheelo's fingers twitched in the vicinity of the holster. "If your compadres can identify your remains after the caimans and the piranhas have finished with them, then they're better forensic pathologists than any I've ever heard about."

Desvendapur did not have to ask for elucidation. From his

studies he was familiar with both varieties of local predators. "What makes you think your native carnivores will find my body palatable? They will ignore me. My corpse will drift until it is found. Then those who will come looking for me will react in a relentless and savage fashion."

They would do no such thing, he knew. Their only concern would be to remove the body lest it be found by other humans, thereby giving rise to awkward inquiries. But the biped did not know that. All he knew of the thranx, Desvendapur suspected, was what the poet chose to tell him.

Man and thranx regarded one another speculatively, each as ignorant as to the true motives of the other as they were to those of their respective kind. Neither had any training in interspecies contact. Operating from mutual nescience, they were making it up as they went along.

"All right." Cheelo's fingers reluctantly drifted away from the gun. "So maybe I won't shoot you. But that still doesn't mean I want you following me."

"Why not? If you choose, I will not intrude on your solitude. You may continue to conduct your research as if I was not there. I only wish to observe, and record, and compose."

My *research*, Cheelo thought. All he was doing was researching a way to keep one step ahead of the police. He did not see how an eight-limbed insectile alien could assist in that end.

Yet despite his otherwordly origins, the hard-shelled poet seemed to know a great deal about their surroundings. It had spoken of studying the area. If not an advantage, maybe it at least wouldn't be a burden. Come to think of it, if the police did manage to track him down, Cheelo could always claim— after first blowing the bug's head off, of course, so it couldn't contradict his story—that he had uncovered an illicit alien outpost. If he could not get rid of it, either by threat or inducement, he would have to find a way to turn the creature's persistence into an advantage. That was something Cheelo Montoya had always been good at.

"You're right, as far as it goes," he snapped. "I can't keep you from following me, and even though I'm not sure I believe all your chatter about your buggy friends coming looking for revenge, I'm not going to risk it by killing you. Not right away, anyhow. Just stay out of my way and do your recording, or composing, or whatever the hell it is that you're doing, quietly."

"I will become a veritable nonentity," a pleased and much relieved Desvendapur assured him.

Too bad you couldn't become a real one, Cheelo mused. Maybe the alien would drown in a river or break a couple of legs and fall behind. Then no one could be blamed for the consequences. Given the right place and time, he might even be able to hurry the process along. If not, well, hadn't the bug said that he only had a month to do his work? Before then Cheelo would be ready to quit the forest himself in order to make the journey back to Golfito.

How fast was a thranx? How durable? After a day or two of trying to follow and keep up with the agile, hardened thief, the many-limbed poet might decide that it was a good idea to seek inspiration from less wearisome sources. Cheelo would lead him a chase, all right!

"Come on, then." Turning, he gestured with a hand— and paused. Head back, expression reflecting uncertainty, he found himself sniffing the air. To Desvendapur, who sensed odors through his antennae, it was a fascinating display worthy of several original and elaborately bizarre stanzas.

"What is it? What are you doing?"

"Smelling. Can't you see that?" Noting the absence on the alien's face, or for that matter anywhere else on its body, of anything resembling nostrils, Cheelo added tersely, "No, I suppose you can't. I'm sampling the air for odors. For one particular odor, actually."

The feathers that lined Desvendapur's antennae flexed to allow as much air as possible to pass between them. "What particular odor?"

Turning, Cheelo found himself inexorably drawn to the exotic exoskeletoned alien. There was no longer any doubt as to the source of the subtle, suggestive aroma. "Yours."

The thranx regarded the tall biped warily. "And what does mine remind you of?"

As Cheelo sniffed, Desvendapur watched the pair of openings in the middle of the human's face expand and contract obscenely. "Roses. Or maybe gardenia. I'm not sure. Could be frangipani. Or bougainvillea."

"What are these things?" None of the names the human was reciting were familiar to Des from his studies.

"Flowers. You smell like flowers. It's a strong fragrance, but not overpowering. It's not . . . it's not what I expected."

Desvendapur remained on guard. "Is this a good thing?"

"Yes." The human smiled, though his attitude suggested that the expression was dragged forth involuntarily. "It's a good thing. If I seem surprised, it's because I am. Bugs aren't supposed to smell like flowers. They never smell like flowers. They stink."

"I am not a 'bug,' which I believe is a generic colloquial human term for insects. Thranx and terrestrial insects are an example of convergent evolution. Yes, there are many similarities, but there are significant differences as well. Carbon-based life forms that have evolved on planets with similar gravity and within stable atmospheric and temperature parameters frequently display many recognizable characteristics of form. But do not mistake body shape for species relationship."

Cheelo's gaze narrowed slightly. "You know, for a cook's helper, or whatever the hell it is exactly that you do, you seem awfully smart."

Desvendapur could not give himself away with a startled expression, and the human was untutored in the subtle meanings of thranx hand movements. "The position I occupy requires more intelligence than you might suspect. All members of my expedition were chosen from the elite within their respective categories of expertise."

"Yeah, right." Cheelo was unconvinced. He had known the alien for only a short while, but unless the nature of thranx-kind differed greatly from that of humans (a possibility that could not be discounted), he almost felt as if the bug was hiding something.

He sniffed again. Orchids this time—or was it hibiscus? The distinctive scent seemed to change with each successive sampling, as if the alien's shiny blue-green body was emitting not one but a complex, ever-changing bouquet of fragrances. He was surprised it was not being swarmed by rain forest nectar eaters, from hummingbirds to bees. But while it exuded a strong natural perfume, it did not look very much like a cluster of blossoms. Also, birds and bees were more sensitive to odors than any human. It was likely that they could detect subtle alien overtones to the thranx's body scent that his cruder sense of smell missed completely.

What other surprises did the bug have in store? "What about me?" he asked curiously. "How do I smell to you? You *can* smell, can't you?"

Desvendapur dipped his antennae forward, but not before compacting their sensitive feathering to shutter his perception of the biped's odor as much as possible. "I can. You are . . . pungent."

" 'Pungent,' " Cheelo repeated. "Sure, okay." Turning, he climbed back up into the tree to get his pack. Desvendapur observed the process with fascination, composing avidly as he watched. Not even the most gymnastic of thranx could match the flexibility of the human's body and limbs. Nor would they want to, he reflected. His reaction was similar to what a human would feel watching an octopus unscrew the lid of a sealed jar to get at food left inside.

Cheelo started to toss his pack down, considered, and then called out, "Here, make yourself useful. Catch this." He held the tough, lightweight material out over the branch.

It was not a significant drop, but Desvendapur knew nothing of the bag's contents. Still, based on what he knew of human physiology he did not think it could be dangerously heavy. Obediently advancing until he was beneath the branch, he extended both foothands, taking care to ensure that his smaller, more delicate truhands were folded tight against his body and out of the way.

"Ready? Catch." Cheelo let the pack fall.

The thranx caught it easily in both outstretched foothands, then used all four manipulative limbs to place it gently on the ground. Satisfied, Cheelo rolled up his blanket and tossed it over next, then climbed down to join his implausible companion. Desvendapur watched silently as the human bundled his equipment together, straightened, and slipped the pack-and-strap arrangement onto his back. It was difficult to understand how and why the additional weight did not cause the biped to fall over backward. Though smaller and lighter, with a minimum of four legs and a maximum of six to support its slim body, an adult thranx could carry more than even a very large human. This knowledge led him to make an offer that was in the nature of a painless gamble.

"Want me to carry that for you? It has to hurt your upper body, trying to support it that way."

Cheelo eyed the shorter creature in surprise. "What's the matter? Aren't you packing enough gear of your own?"

"I can manage the extra mass easily. If we are going to travel together we should each make use of the other's natural strengths. I could not climb into that tree without help, as you did, but I can carry a good deal of weight. Your pack would not inconvenience me."

Cheelo found himself grinning. "That's real nice of you." He started to reach up and around to slide the pack off his back. Abruptly, his smile faded. "No, on second thought, I think I'll hang onto my own stuff for a while longer. But thanks for the offer."

Desvendapur automatically gestured an appropriate response. The rapid hand and finger movements meant nothing to the human. "As you wish."

It might have been an honest offer, Cheelo thought as he turned and strode off into the trees. But what did he know of alien motivation? Suppose the thranx was operating from ulterior motives. At an opportune moment it might decide to take off with a nice, prepacked grab bag full of terrestrial souvenirs, graciously supplied by one trusting, half-witted Cheelo Montoya. He knew next to nothing about the big bugs, including how fast they could run. It had confessed to being a poor climber, but it didn't look clumsy or lumbering. He was willing to bet that when it utilized all six legs it could move over the ground at a respectable clip.

The thought of allowing someone else to haul his gear through the hot, steamy rain forest was a tempting one. His back and legs were wholly in favor of the notion, but his brain vetoed it outright. Surviving alone in the vast rain forest was hard enough. Trying to do so without blanket, electronic insect repeller, food supplements, water purifier, and other gear might prove well nigh impossible. So he would suffer on.

Time enough to figure out if he could trust something with eight limbs, twin antennae, and eyes like shattered mirrors.

It sure did smell good, though.

That night he had the opportunity to see how a thranx not only ate, but slept. As it sipped liquids from a narrow-spouted utensil and chewed compacted food with its four opposing mandibles, he wondered what it thought of his own dining habits. The fact that it kept its distance could be considered significant. Cheelo took some of the fish he had caught the previous day out of his pack. The thranx studied the process of consuming with obvious interest, chattering and whistling into its recording device without pause.

Finally Cheelo could stand it no longer. "I'm just having supper. No big deal. Where's the poetry in that?"

"There is verse in everything you do, because it is all exotic to me. Presently I am much taken with the contrast between your exceedingly civilized behavior and your lingering barbarism."

"Excuse me?" Breaking off a small fillet, Cheelo scaled it with his fingernails before shoving it into his mouth and biting off a piece. He chewed slowly.

"You utilize the tools and knowledge of a contemporary civilization to eat the flesh of another creature."

"Yeah, that's right. Are you guys all vegetarians?" He held out the pungent fistful. "This is just a fish."

"A water-dwelling animal. It has a heart, lungs, nervous system. A brain."

Cheelo squinted through the gathering darkness. "What are you trying to tell me? That a fish thinks?"

"If it has a brain, it thinks."

"Not much it don't." He chuckled and bit off another chunk.

"Thought is an absolute, not a matter of degree. It is a question of morality."

The human gestured back the way they had come. "How'd you like to go find your creative inspiration elsewhere? So now I'm immoral?"

"Not by your own standards. I would not presume to judge a member of another species by standards that were developed to apply to my kind."

"Smart boy." Cheelo hesitated with the remaining fish halfway to his mouth. "What kind of poetic inspiration are you getting out of me eating a fish, anyhow?"

"Crude. Powerful. Alien." The thranx continued chattering into its scri!ber.

"Shocking?" Cheelo inquired thoughtfully.

"I would hope so. I did not come all this way and go through a great deal of trouble to find inspiration of a cloying, puerile kind. I came in search of something radical and extreme, something dangerous and unsafe. Ugly, even."

"All that from a guy eating a fish," Cheelo murmured. "I'm not much on poetry myself, but I wouldn't mind hearing some of what you've written. As your source of inspiration, I think I have that right."

"I would be glad to perform it for you, but I am afraid much of the subtlety and nuance will be lost. You don't have the necessary cultural references to understand, and there are concepts that simply cannot, given its innate restrictions, be rendered in your language."

"Is that so?" Taking a long swig from his purifier, Cheelo leaned back against a tree, knees apart, and gestured commandingly at the oversized arthropod. "Try me."

"Try you?" Confusion impregnated the thranx's response.

"Let me hear what you've done," Cheelo clarified impatiently.

"Very well. I dislike performing without proper rehearsal, but since you are not going to understand very much of it anyway, I suppose that doesn't matter. I cannot translate into your language and properly follow through, but I hope that you will get some sense of what I am trying to accomplish."

"Wait. Wait a minute." Rummaging through his pack, Cheelo produced a compact flashlight. A glance at the canopy showed that they were reasonably well hidden from above. No low-flying scanner blocked out the few visible stars, and clouds would conceal their presence from anything higher. Flicking the light to life, he placed it on the ground so that its soft beam illuminated the thranx. In the darkness the alien's stiff limbs, bobbing antennae, and reflective compound eyes were components of an atavistic nightmare shape—but it was hard to be afraid of something that exuded the aroma of a Paris perfume boutique.

"I am afraid that the title of my latest exposition is not translatable."

"That's okay." Cheelo waved grandly. "I'll think of it as 'Human Eating Fish.' " Scarfing down the rest of his supper, he leaned back and began licking grease and bits of white flake from his fingers. Suppressing his distaste, Desvendapur began.

In the tropical night, surrounded by the sounds of the rain forest's emerging nocturnal inhabitants, words mingled with whistles sharp and soft, with clicks that varied in volume and intensity from that of tiny tappings to a rhythmic booming that might have been generated by muffled drums. Accompanying this stately carillon were intricate dancelike gestures, weavings in the air executed by four limbs and sixteen digits. Antennae twisted and curled, dipped and bobbed, as the insectile alien body swayed and contorted.

At first the sight was somewhat frightening, but as Cheelo grew more comfortable with the thranx's appearance he found himself starting to think of it not as a giant bug but as a sensitive visitor from a distant star system. The scent of fresh flowers that emanated from the hard-shelled body certainly played a large part in effecting his change in perception—not to mention attitude. As for the performance, even though Desvendapur was right and Cheelo understood little of what was being imparted, it was undeniably *art* of a complex, sophisticated order. Poetic, even. While he understood nothing of what the creature was saying, the confluence of sound and movement conveyed a grace and elegance the likes of which he had never encountered before.

Growing up poor and forever on the fringe of society, Cheelo Montoya had never had much of an opportunity to sample anything other than the crudest kinds of art: violent tridee recordings, raucous popular music, unsophisticated pornography, cheap stims, and low-level hallucinogens. He was aware that what he was hearing and witnessing now, alien though its origins might be, comprised creation of a much higher order. At first amusedly contemptuous, the longer and more intricate the thranx's interweavings of movement and sound became, the quieter and more solemn Cheelo's expression grew. When a quietly triumphant Desvendapur finally concluded the performance, the sun had set completely.

"Well," he prompted when no response was forthcoming from the silent, seated human, "what did you think? Did you get anything out of it, or was it all nothing more than alien mumblings and twitches?"

Cheelo swallowed—hard. Something crawled over his left hand without biting, and he ignored it. In the nearly complete darkness the light from the flashlight was stark on the thranx's blue-green exterior.

"I . . . I didn't understand a goddamn word of it, and I think it was one of the most beautiful things I've ever seen."

Desvendapur was taken aback. It was not the reaction he had anticipated. A polite gesture of courtesy, perhaps, or a mumbled word of mild appreciation—but not praise. Not from a human.

"But you say you didn't understand." Taking a chance, presuming on an acquaintance that was still untested, he moved forward, out of the throw of the flashlight and into proximate darkness.

The human did not shy away. The scent of fresh-picked posies was very close now. In the shadow of night his absurdly tiny but nevertheless sharp eyes searched those of the thranx. "Not your speech, no. Not a word of it. But the sounds you made, like music, and the way all four of your hands and the rest of your body moved together with it—that was wonderful." He shook his head from side to side, and Desvendapur struggled to interpret the meaning of it.

"I don't know anything about it, of course," Cheelo continued, "but it seems to me that you're very good at your hobby. People—humans—would pay to watch it."

"You really think so? As I said earlier, I am only an amateur."

"I know they would. I may not know much, but I know that. I . . . would pay. And if you could figure out a way to translate your speech into Terranglo without sacrificing anything of the performance . . . Well, it would *have* to contribute to understanding and good relations between our species. Doesn't anyone do performances like that at the project on your world—what's it called?"

"Willow-Wane," Desvendapur murmured softly. "I suppose they must, but I do not really know. I don't know any more about what goes on within the project than what the Grand Council chooses to disseminate. They might have soothers there, or they might not."

"Is that what it's called? Soothing?" In the poor light, Cheelo nodded thoughtfully. "Listen, I know I'm not much of an audience—not knowledgeable or anything like that—and I can't exactly return the favor with constructive criticism, but anytime you want to practice a new piece or a part of one, I'd be real pleased to look at and listen to it."

"You *did* actually enjoy it, didn't you?" Desvendapur stared at the biped.

"Damn right I did. Tell you what. Tomorrow night I'll eat something different, just to give you fresh inspiration. Maybe I'll try and kill an agouti or something."

Desvendapur gagged, and his antennae flinched reflexively. "Please do not cannibalize a living creature on my behalf."

"I thought you wanted radical, extreme stimulation."

"My mind does. My digestive system is a different matter."

Cheelo crossed his legs and grinned. "Okay. We'll build up the inspiration gradually." Leaning over and reaching into his pack, he extracted a stimstick and unwrapped the vacuum tip. On contact with the air, it flashed alight.

Desvendapur watched the human place one end of the burning shaft between its lips and inhale. This was more than he could have hoped for. Every moment spent in the biped's company was a source of unprecedented enlightenment. What whimsical pleasure the creature gained from placing combusting organic matter in its mouth the thranx could not imagine, but the inscrutable activity proved to be the source of not one but two complete, condensed compositions before the evening bored its way into night and they were compelled to retire.

15

It was not the howlers that woke Cheelo the following morning. A sharp, cawing call caused him to roll over and sit up, the lightweight blanket falling away from his neck and chest and down to his hips. The bird that was pecking at some fallen, rotting fruit nearby was grotesque in the extreme. Out-sized red eyes peered from a narrow, blue-skinned face that was lined and surmounted by a crest of stiff, yellow-black feathers. His rising startled the creature and it flew, awk-wardly and with undisguised effort, into a nearby tree. The size of a small turkey, it rocked on a branch while contemp-lating the odd duo resting on the ground below.

As he rubbed at his eyes and climbed to his feet, Cheelo tried to remember names from the guideware he had bought in Cuzco and installed in his card. The bird was big enough to be a raptor, but its short beak and small claws, not to mention its awkwardness in the air, marked it as belonging to some other family. Still blinking away sleep, he opened his pack and took out the card. A few adjustments called forth the guidebook and the section on birds.

The clumsy flier with the prehistoric mien was a hoatzin. If there ever was a bird that looked like a dinosaur, he thought, here it was. His attention shifted from the red-eyed forest dweller to the far more alien figure slumbering nearby.

Having found a suitable fallen log, the thranx had straddled it. Three legs hung on one side, three on the other, with the first set of arms tucked neatly up against the insectoid's chest, if that's what the forward-facing portion of its anatomy could be called. Since it had no opaque eyelids, but only a very thin, transparent membrane that sometimes slid down to protect those golden orbs, it was impossible to tell by looking at it

whether it was awake or asleep. The absence of any movement or reaction as Cheelo cautiously approached, coupled
with the steady bellows-like pumping of its thorax, was enough
to convince him it continued to occupy whatever unimagin-
able region such creatures visited when they turned off their
consciousness for the night.

What kind of dreams did aliens dream? he wondered. For
the first time, he found himself within touching distance of
the creature. Up close, the ambrosial fragrance of its body
odor was even stronger. Bending over, he was able to see himself reflected dozens of times in the multiple lenses of one
golden eye. A line of small openings in the blue-green chitin
of the thorax pulsed rhythmically, showing where the creature siphoned air. The sensitive, feathery antennae described
twin limp, forward-facing arcs on the otherwise smooth curve
of the skull.

Reaching out, he ran fingertips along the glistening exoskeleton of one wing case. It was hard, smooth, and slightly
cool to the touch, like plastic or some highly polished building material. Letting his hand drift downward he felt of a leg,
unable to escape the feeling that he was exploring a machine
and not a living creature. That perception vanished the instant
the thranx woke up.

Startled by the unexpected human touch, Desvendapur let
out a shrill stridulation and kicked out reflexively with all six
legs. One caught Cheelo in the thigh and sent him stumbling
backward. Scrambling frantically, shocked into wakefulness,
the poet slid off the makeshift bed and promptly fell over
on his side onto the moist, leaf-strewn earth. He recovered
quickly to stand facing the human across the log.

"What are you doing?"

"Take it easy," Cheelo admonished his otherworldly companion. "Nothing weird."

"How can I be sure of that? Humans are noted for their peculiar habits." As he spoke, Desvendapur was checking the
length of his body. Everything appeared to be undamaged
and where it belonged.

The human snorted derisively. "Look, it was hard enough
for me just to touch you."

"Then why did you?" Desvendapur shot back accusingly.

"To make sure that I could. Don't worry—I won't be doing it again." Cheelo rubbed his fingers together, as if trying to remove dirt or grease from beneath the nails. "It was like rubbing a piece of old furniture."

The poet walked over to his pack and checked the seal. It was undisturbed, but he could not be absolutely sure until he checked the contents. "Better than making contact with flesh that flexes beneath one's fingers." His antennae quivered. "All that soft, pulpy meat held in check only by a thin layer of flexible epidermis, full of blood and muscle, just waiting to be exposed to the air. It's indecent. I cannot imagine what nature was thinking when she designed such animal forms and then built them from the inside out."

"You're the one who's inside out." Walking back to where he had laid his own gear, Cheelo crouched and pondered breakfast. "Walking around with your skeleton on the outside."

"And it is not bad enough that all your support is internal," Desvendapur continued, "you come in a bewildering variety of colors. There is no harmony, no consistency at all. Our color deepens naturally as we age, a reflection of the natural progression of time. Yours only changes when diseased, some of which you induce voluntarily. And it shrivels." Truhands were in continual motion as the thranx spoke. Cheelo had no idea what the bug was saying with its eloquent limbs, but he could make inferences from the tenor of its comments.

"Because of these flaws, which are the unavoidable consequence of defective genetics, I feel an instinctive sympathy for you."

"Gee, thanks." As he prepared his simple morning meal Cheelo wondered if the bug could detect sarcasm and decided it probably could not. "Not that it means anything, or matters, but why?"

This time a truhand and a foothand on the same side of the smooth body gestured in tandem. "Your epidermis is so incredibly fragile, so easily cut or compromised, that it is outright wondrous you have survived as a species. One would think that mere incidental contact with the world around you would result in the incurring of an unavoidable succession of incapacitating wounds."

"Our outside's tougher than it looks." By way of demonstration, Cheelo pinched up a fold of skin on the back of his hand. Simultaneously fascinated and repelled, Desvendapur could not turn away from the incredible sight. It was at once ghastly and captivating to behold. Grossly descriptive, the burgeoning verses that hurtled through his mind skittered on the very edge of possible censorship.

"Here." Walking toward the thranx, Cheelo rolled up one sleeve and held his naked arm out to the alien. "Try it yourself."

"No." The boldness that had brought Desvendapur this far wavered at the sight of the exposed, almost transparent skin, with its components of deeply tanned muscle, tendon, and blood clearly visible beneath. Mushy and resilient, the soft mammalian flesh would deform beneath his fingers, he knew. Envisioning this threatened to bring up what remained un-processed of his previous meal.

Steeling himself, he forced a halt to his mental flight. If it was safe, unthreatening inspiration he wanted, he should have stayed on Willow-Wane, ascended through the custo-mary methods of promotion, and accepted a conventional academic post. Instead, he was here, on the homeworld of the humans, illegal and alone. Raising a truhand, he reached out.

All four of the delicate manipulative digits came together. They were of equal length and shorter than a human thumb. Making contact with the exposed flesh, Desvendapur felt the heat rising from within. No wonder humans had to eat so much, he thought. Without a proper exoskeleton to provide insulation, they must lose enormous quantities of energy in the form of heat to the surrounding air. How they spent as much time in water as they did without instantly freezing was one of those exotic physiological mysteries best left to the xenobiologists.

When the skin and flesh of the human's arm compacted and rose between his fingers, he nearly gagged. The compres-sion did not seem to hurt or harm the biped at all, though surely if pressure was increased it would ultimately do so. Utilized for extraordinarily delicate manipulation, a truhand was incapable of exerting that kind of force. A foothand could do so, but the poet had no desire to put the hypothesis to the test.

When the human deliberately moved his arm slightly, the flesh and skin in the thranx's grasp flexed with the motion but did not tear. Cheelo grinned, enjoying the alien's discomfort. When it released its grip, he rolled his sleeve back down.

"See? No harm done. We're *flexible*. It's a much better physical design."

"That is an assertion very much open to debate." Dipping his head, Desvendapur searched the surrounding ground until he found a small rock with an edge. Holding it in one truhand, he extended a foothand and, to Cheelo's surprise, deliberately drew the sharp edge of the stone across the upper portion of the smaller limb. A pale white line appeared in its wake. "Try this on your 'better design.'" He chucked the rock.

Cheelo caught it reflexively. The ragged, splintered stone edge was sharp enough to slice easily through skin, leaving exposed flesh raw and bleeding. Tight lipped, he let the stone fall from his fingers. He didn't like being shown up, never had, whether it was by some street punk or a sassy well-dressed citizen or a visiting alien.

"Okay, shell-butt. So you made a point. It doesn't make you any less ugly. You smell nice, sure, and I guess you're sort of smart, but to me you're still nothing but a big, bloated, overgrown bug with brains. My people have been stepping on your kind since we could walk."

Open hostility! Where virtually any other thranx would have been dismayed and appalled by the grimy human's response, Desvendapur was elated. Such primal social interaction was all but unheard-of among the thranx, whose close-quarter, underground society was necessarily founded upon an elaborate hierarchy of courtesy and manners. Here was inspiration indeed! Drawing forth his scri!ber, he directed a rapid-fire stream of clicks, whistles, and wordings at its pickup.

Cheelo frowned. "What are you jabbering about now?"

"I am just trying to capture the moment. Outright anger is rare among my kind. Please, sustain that tone of voice and those urgent syllables."

"Sustain . . . ? What the hell do you think I am, some kind of archetype for you to capture in verse?" His voice rose.

"D'you think I was put here just for your stinking benefit, to give you something to compose about?"

"Wonderful, marvelous!" the thranx breathed in his whispery Terranglo. "Don't stop!"

Cheelo folded his arms over his chest and set his jaw. Seeing that the human had finished, or at least terminated his current rant, a disappointed Desvendapur paused the scri!ber. Might there be some way he could induce the biped to resume? Proceeding against nature, in direct contravention of everything he had been brought up to believe in and act upon, he unhesitatingly hostiled back. The larval adolescent within him rebelled violently at his tone, but there was no one else around to overhear or to be shocked.

"I am not your tiny, primitive insect pest. Try stepping on me, and you'll slide off. Or I will throw you into the nearest river."

Cheelo's gaze narrowed. "You and what bug army? If there's any throwing to be done, I'll do it."

"Come on, then." Astonished at his audacity, his mind storming with inspired verse that burned and crackled, Desvendapur turned to face the taller, heavier human head-on. He adopted a defensive posture; truhands folded back, stronger foothands extended, eight digits splayed in grasping position, antennae erect and alert. The thranx might be excessively polite, but they were not helpless. "Let's see you try."

The pistol weighed heavily as Cheelo Montoya mulled the challenge. He was bigger and heavier than the bug, but outlimbed eight to four. Since all its musculature was internal, hidden beneath the chitinous exoskeleton, he could not get an idea of its strength from looking at it. He knew that small insects like ants and fleas could lift many times their own weight, but that did not mean such physical ability would scale up proportionally to something the size of a thranx. In their brief time together he had not seen it throw any logs around or push trees out of its way.

Slowly, he slid the pack off his back. A small stream flowed through the woods nearby. It was no river, but it did spread out to form a sizable pool. For purposes of demonstration it would have to do.

As Cheelo approached, the thranx began weaving slowly

from side to side, up and down, forcing the human to deal
with a moving target. When he tried to circle around and get
behind it, it pivoted on its four legs to keep facing him. Ex-
perimentally, he struck out with his right hand, grabbing for
one of the extended foothands. It drew back, and the other
foothand came down sharply on his wrist. The blow stung
more sharply than he expected, and he reflexively jerked his
arm back.

"Come on." Desvendapur chided the human even as he
tried to store as many new stanzas in his head as possible.
This was extraordinary! The possibility that the confrontation might end in injury did not enter his mind. "I thought you
were going to throw me in the river."

Cheelo continued to circle the alien, searching for an opening. With eight limbs blocking his reach, he saw that it wasn't
going to be easy. "You're quick, I'll give you that. You can
block a grab, and probably a punch—but what can you do
about this?"

Arms outstretched, he rushed forward. When the thranx
tried to feint, Cheelo swerved in response. He'd survived too
many breathless fights in too many dark alleys and deserted
buildings to be easily fooled. As his arms wrapped around the
alien's lower thorax, he tucked his head low and out of reach.

Perfume exploded in his face. His upper body blocked the
weaker truhands from extending and getting a grip, while the
foothands clutched at his back and tried to pull him off. They
were insistent, but not strong enough. Bending his knees,
he lifted the alien off the damp ground and started walking
toward the stream.

He'd taken two steps when all four feet slammed into
his belly, knocking the air out of him. Losing his grip, he
stumbled backward, tripped, and sat down hard on his back-
side, curled over and clutching at his stomach. When he released the thranx, it fell on its side. All four legs churning, it
scrambled back onto its feet and came toward him. This time
all four hands were extended.

He waited until they grabbed his shirt. Reaching up, he
wrapped his fingers around the foothands, the unyielding
chitin smooth and slick beneath his fingers. Bringing up his
right foot, he planted it in the middle of the alien's abdomen

and rolled backward, pushing with his leg as he did so. The thranx went flying over his head to land hard on its back.

Rolling, breathing hard, he staggered to his feet. Lying on its back and kicking with all eight limbs, the alien's resemblance to an upturned crab or spider was unnerving. Finally succeeding in getting a couple of legs under its body, it pushed, straightened, and once more stood confronting him. A truhand reached up to groom flexible antennae. It did not look like it was hurt, but it was hard to tell. Rigid chitin did not bruise in the manner of soft flesh.

"Had—had enough?" Cheelo gasped, bending over and bracing one hand against his right thigh.

Though quite familiar from training with the techniques of hand-to-hand combat, Desvendapur was unfamiliar with the consequences. Execution and practice in a polite, scholastic setting was one thing; being thrown around on hard, unyielding, alien ground was quite something else. He was sore from head to foot. But if the transliteration of the extraordinary experience from reality to exposition did not win him a major prize in composition, then he truly might as well give up trying to be an innovative poet and remain a food preparator for the rest of his life. The experience was exhilarating, rousing, and yes, inspiring.

"A time-part fraction, if you will. Please. I have to get this down!" Removing the scri!ber from its padded pouch, the poet once again spewed a stream of elegantly embellished alien rhetoric into its pickup.

"Sure," Cheelo responded graciously. "Take your time." Approaching cautiously, he gave the device a curious once-over before bending to wrap both arms quickly and tightly around the alien body and lifting it for a second time off the ground—but this time from behind.

Flailing arms and legs could not reach him. The thranx was not flexible enough to reach behind its back. The head, however, could swivel almost a hundred and eighty degrees. The face was expressionless as always, but the rapid movement of mandibles coupled with the anxious writhings of all eight limbs succeeded in conveying the creature's distress.

"Kick me in the gut *now*, why don't you?" Cheelo was not a big man, and the bug was as much of a load as he could handle, but he was determined to fulfill his earlier threat. Bending slightly backward to manage the weight, he staggered toward the stream.

Despite his helpless position in the human's grasp, Desvendapur continued to compose until they stood at the water's edge. The stream meandered rather than flowed into a pool and was no more than a meter or so deep.

"You have proven your point," he declared as he slipped the scri!ber back into its pouch. "I accept that you can throw me into this unpretentious river. Now you may put me down."

"Put you down?" Cheelo echoed stiffly. "Sure, I'll put you down." Swinging both arms, he flung the thranx forward. All eight legs kicking in surprise and alarm, it landed noisily in the water—in the center of the pool.

It resurfaced immediately, flailing violently. A grinning Cheelo watched from shore. At any moment, the creature would come staggering out onto dry land, dripping water and weeds, its dignity more bruised than its body. It would glare up at him but acknowledge the human as its physical superior. He wondered if it would drip-dry or shake like a dog.

His smug expression faded to uncertainty. The fluttering of blue-green limbs was slowing. It was almost as if the alien was in some kind of trouble. But how could it be in difficulty, with its head and neck well above water? And if it was hurting, why didn't it cry out, in its own singular combination of clicks and whistles and words if not in Terranglo?

It could not cry out, he realized, because its lungs were filling with water. Even as he met its resilient, reflective gaze, it was drowning before his eyes. The thorax, he remembered. The damn things breathe through holes in their thorax—and all eight of those vital openings were submerged beneath the surface of the pond.

Leaping forward, he plunged into the water. At its deepest point, the pond came up to his neck. No wonder the alien was having trouble. Unlike many of its smaller terrestrial cousins, it had negative buoyancy. It might not sink like a stone, he reflected, but sink it obviously would.

He half carried, half dragged it out of the pool. Once safely back on land he stepped back and watched as it convulsed in great heaves, exuding water through a spasming thorax that expanded and contracted like a blue-green bellows. When the last drop had been expunged from the anguished lungs, it stumbled sideways until it found support against the buttress roots of a nearby strangler fig. The bulbous, red-streaked, golden eyes turned to face him.

"That lethal a demonstration was not necessary. I would not have done the same to you." A hacking cough convulsed the aquamarine-hued body, emerging from the sides of the thorax and not the alien's mouth.

"You couldn't do the same to me," Cheelo could not resist sneering.

"Don't be so sure. My kind learn quickly." A truhand gestured at the human's lower limbs. "That was a clever trick, that earlier move with the leg. I think I could do it. After all, I have four or six to your two. It would not work on me a second time."

Cheelo shrugged. He'd gone *mano a mano* with his share of street punks and thugs, though never before with an alien. Maybe he was the first, he thought. "Doesn't matter. I know more than one trick." He stared unblinkingly at the contentious thranx. "Maybe next time I won't pull you out." An edgy, mildly contemptuous snicker born of hard life on the streets emerged from his lips as he nodded at the still convulsing body. "Eight limbs and you bugs still can't swim?"

"Regrettably, no. We tend to sink. Not immediately, but all too soon. And no thranx can kick hard enough to hold its entire upper body out of the water. So we drown. Thank you for pulling me out."

"I'm beginning to wonder if that was such a good idea." As he mumbled the rest of a reply, Cheelo saw that the alien neither drip-dried nor shook. Instead, it inclined its head downward and used its mandibles to squeegee water from its body and limbs. Its large supply pack lay on the ground nearby, but the thorax pouch had gone into the pond with it. He wondered if it was watertight. It contained everything the insectoid had composed since their fractious first encounter.

"Look," he proposed condescendingly, "if you want to write about me, or compose, or whatever the hell it is that you're doing, go ahead. Just don't provoke me for the sake of your art, okay? You want to tag along, fine, but keep out of my way. I can be—I have a temper, and I've been known to lose control of myself on occasion, see? Next time I might not be able to get to you in time—or want to. Or I might hit hard enough to break one of your limbs."

The head paused in its grooming to look up at him. "That I do not think you can do. You would be more likely to damage your own appendage. You may be more flexible, but I am physically tougher."

"Says who? Maybe we should just . . ." Hearing his own words, Cheelo calmed himself. "This is stupid shit, what's going on here. It doesn't matter who's stronger, or tougher, or whatever. What am I—in a competition here with another species? So, educate me: If I'm ever in a life-or-death struggle with a thranx, what do I aim for?"

"Why would I tell you that?"

Why indeed? Cheelo mused. Not that the information was vital. The aliens might have particularly vulnerable points that were not obvious, but he could see that in a fight it would be best to strike at anything soft and unprotected by chitinous body armor. The eyes, for example, or the soft under-abdomen. A tug on one of those feathery antennae would probably make an attacker let go, too. Not that he was anticipating a fight, but it was always better to be prepared for one. That was how it was on the streets of Gatun and Balboa and San José. Why should it be any different in the jungle?

All he knew about the thranx was the little, the very little, he had picked up while absently listening to media. This one, this Desvenbapur, might be friendly, might be harmless, might be merely suspicious and sarcastic, or it might be some kind of giant arthropod alien schizo, agreeable one moment and eager to cut his throat and suck out his organs the next. Hope for the former and plan for the latter had always been Cheelo's motto. Proof of its efficacy was that he was still alive and, except for a few scars and a couple of missing teeth, reasonably intact.

"Okay. You've got a tough outside, and you smell good. Those I'll grant you." His mouth split in a nasty grin. "But you're still ugly."

"Ugly?" The vee-shaped head cocked sideways as compound eyes studied the human. "What a profound observation coming from a representative of a species whose bodies are raised up out of jelly. Not only do you all wobble when you walk, you can practically see through the thinner patches of your skin. You look at the world out of a single lens which, if damaged, practically renders that organ blind. Your sense of smell is primitive and relies on olfactory organs set in the middle of your face, where they have to strain to detect even a hint of a scent." By way of illustrating the superiority of thranx design, feathery antennae wagged back and forth.

"You have only four limbs instead of a much more sensible eight, and those four are restricted in their function." Foot-hands rose from the ground in a demonstration of how the second set of thranx appendages could be utilized either as feet or hands. "Your skin is exceedingly vulnerable to even the slightest cut or puncture, you can't make any music worthy of the designation by rubbing any of your limbs together, and you're not even properly symmetrical."

"Who's not symmetrical?" Using the fingers of his right hand, Cheelo pointed to the appropriate portions of his anatomy. "Two eyes, two ears, two arms and legs. Where's the asymmetry in that?"

"Look at your hands." Desvendapur nodded in their direction. "Are the number of digits divisible by two? No. There should be six fingers—or four, like mine. Additionally, you need to look deeper."

"Deeper?" Shifting his pack higher on his shoulders, Cheelo frowned uncomprehendingly.

"Within your pitiful self. How many hearts do you have? One, shoved off to one side. The same is true for all other major human organs, except your lungs, of which you have, by what mysterious quirk of nature I cannot fathom, the proper division." A foothand ran down the front of the poet's thorax to his abdomen. "Two hearts, two livers, two stomachs, and so forth. A proper body design for an advanced species, symmetrical and serene. Whereas yours is a mess of internal nonsense, with lonely, vulnerable organs struggling for space and pushed all out of proper position."

Out-argued, not to mention a bit overwhelmed, Cheelo could only mumble, "So you're saying that you guys have two of everything inside you?"

Finding the equivalent, appropriate human gesture amenable, Desvendapur nodded. "Not only is such an arrangement aesthetically pleasing, it makes us more durable. Thranx can lose any major organ secure in the knowledge that another just like it will keep them alive. Humans have no such luxury. You must live every day of your existence in fear of organ failure."

"If you've got two or more of everything," Cheelo replied thoughtfully as he started off into the forest with the thranx following close behind, "and your bodies run smaller than ours, then everything that's inside must also be smaller—heart, lungs, everything. Our organs are bigger."

"Better to have backup than size," Desvendapur argued.

They ambled along in that fashion, debating the merits of their respective anatomies, until Cheelo's train of thought was interrupted by a germinating uncertainty. "For a cook, or cook's assistant, or whatever it is you are, you sure know a lot about humans."

Though the biped could not interpret his reflexive gestures, Desvendapur instinctively tried to mute them nonetheless. "Those of us who were assigned to this information-gathering expedition were well prepared."

"Ay, you told me that." Still dubious, Cheelo was watching the bug closely. Its body language might be throwing off all kinds of suggestive signals, but he wouldn't know it. The thranx's complex hand and head movements held less meaning for him than the antics of the monkeys in the canopy overhead. Fellow primates he could relate to: a pontificating alien bug he could not.

The thranx had the advantage. It had been prepared for contact with humans, whereas he knew next to nothing about the eight-limbed aliens. But he was learning. Cheelo Montoya was nothing if not a fast learner.

"Also," his otherworldly companion added by way of a delayed afterthought, "you stink."

"I can see why they put you in food preparation instead of the diplomatic corps." However, Cheelo had no comeback for the thranx's latest imputation. While it continued to exude an ever-changing panoply of aromatic perfumes, he pushed on through the brush, grime-soaked and sweaty, reeking of mammalian ooze.

As for appearance, he had to admit that the more often the bug strayed into his range of vision, the less alien and more pleasing to the eye it became. There was much to admire in the graceful flow of multiple limbs; the glint of light shining off smooth blue-green chitin that was one moment the color of dark tsavorite, the next that of Paraiba tourmaline; the delicate rustling of twin antennae; and the splintering of sunshine by the bulging, gold-tinted compound eyes. While not the dreamed-of exotic dancer from Rio or Panama City, neither did it make him anymore want to raise a leg and stomp it.

With a bit of a shock, he realized that in appearance it was not so very different from its distant, terrestrial cousins. Did mere intelligence, then, count for so much in altering one's perception? If ants could talk, would people still find them so disagreeable?

People would if they persisted in trying to eat a person out of house and home, he decided. It's not a bug, he kept telling himself. It's not a spider. It's a recently contacted alien species, intelligent and sensitive. He had some success convincing himself of that—but only some. Ancient, atavistic sentiments died hard. Easier to think of the thranx as an equal and not something to be stepped on when he kept his eyes closed. You couldn't do that very often in the rain forest. There was too much to trip over or step into.

Perfunctory insults aside, he found himself wondering what the alien really thought about him.

16

The court of the Emperor MUUNIINAA III was designed to impress and overawe, from its profusion of bejeweled robotics and whisper-silent electronic attendants to the luxuriousness of its furnishings. The fact that everything in the throne room was functional as well as decorative was wholly indicative of the AAnn mind-set. While the AAnn were fond of ceremony, it was never allowed to get in the way of operational efficiency. This extended from the lowliest sand monitor to the highest levels of government.

The emperor, of course, had not possessed absolute powers since ancient times. It was an elective position, as were those of lord and baron and the lesser nobles who ruled beneath them. It was simply that the AAnn could not let go of tradition, so they adapted it to fit a contemporary, star traversing cluster of systems and worlds. Though it rang of history and ancient regimes, it was in reality about as feudal in nature as the programming of the latest massive parallel quantum computers that navigated the ships that darted and plunged through space-plus.

So while Lord Huudra Ap and Baron Keekil YN wore the ceremonial robes of high office, each noble's elegant attire and gem-studded investitures powered individual defensive screens and a full suite of communications gear to keep them in constant touch with both immediate underlings and detached constituencies. Standing with bowed heads and lowered tails as the Emperor retired from the chamber to deal with the mountainous and decidedly unglamorous paperwork of office, they exchanged a glance that signified a mutual need to talk.

Other groups broke away from the assembly to chat infor-

mally or to discuss matters of serious import. For Huudra and
Keekil it was a matter of both.

Heads bobbed in greeting, and finely manicured claws
were courteously sheathed. In addition to their repertoire of
other skills, both nobles were masters of manners. Together
with several other nobles, they formed one of the dozen or so
organized cliques that dominated the politics of the assembly.
The matter that Keekil wished to discuss with Huudra, however, had nothing to do with imminent business of state. It
was more a matter for mutual speculation that both had made
a specialty of theirs. Aware that everyone from the opposition
parties to the emperor himself relied on them for the most
current information on the matter, they had made it their
business to keep in constant communication with those far-
flung representatives of the Empire who were in a position to
be knowledgeable.

It was in this spirit of curiosity and need that Huudra
greeted his friend and ally, whom he would not hesitate to
undermine to advance his own status and position. Keekil
hissed a warm greeting, quite aware of what his associate was
thinking. He was thinking the same thing. There was no
animosity involved. It was the natural order of things. Such
constant competition strengthened the assembly, and by inference, the Empire.

"It is all sso very peculiar." Keekil favored blue in his
robes, in all its most sallow permutations. Even the communicator that hovered patiently several centimeters to the left
of his mouth was plated in gleaming pale blue metal. "Thiss
business of the thranx attempting to make alliess of the
mammalss."

Huudra excused himself long enough to answer a priority
call and suggest several alternatives to a disagreeable situation to the technocrat on the other end. "Apologiess, honored
Keekil. Then you think the inssectiles are sserious about it?"

The baron gestured assent, adding a supportive hiss.
"Yess, I do. The quesstion iss, are these humanss?"

Overhead, hoverators hummed back and forth, scanning
for intruders, petitioners, and possible assassins. The temperature in the room was high, the humidity a tolerable 6 percent.

Both nobles' personal communicator suites hummed for attention. For the moment, they were ignored.

"My own ressearchess indicate an inherent reluctance on the part of the human population, both on their homeworld and their coloniess. More than that, they sseem to have a vissceral fear of the thranx sshape." He hissed his amusement. "Can you imagine it? Deciding intersstellar politicss on the basiss of sshape? They are an immature sspeciess!"

"There iss nothing immature about their technology," Keekil reminded his aristocratic colleague. "Their weaponry iss the equal of the besst of the Empire's—or of the thranx. Their communicationss are ssuperb. Their sshipss . . ." The baron gesticulated admiration mixed with paranoia, a difficult gesture for any but the most accomplished orator to execute eloquently. "Their sshipss are elegant."

Huudra drew back his upper lip to reveal even, sharp teeth set in a long jaw. "I have sseen ssome of the preliminary reportss. There iss ssome dissagreement as to whether they are better than ourss."

"If they do indeed exceed the capabilitiess of ourss, then they are better as well than anything flown by the thranx." Irritated, Keekil waved a ringed hand across his waist. The persistent hum of communications demanding response promptly died.

"That would be reasson enough to sseek them as alliess." Huudra scratched at a loose scale on the side of his neck. Sparkling in the bright artificial light of the throne room, it fell to the floor and was promptly vacuumed away by an unobtrusive remote cleaner built to resemble a four-legged *kerpk*. "Our interesstss would be better sserved by convincing them to become confederatess of the Empire."

"You know our envoyss have had little ssuccess in perssuading the humanss of the many advantagess that would lie in aligning themsselvess with our interesstss." Raising a hand, Keekil had to wait less than a minute for a drifting sustainer to place a filled drinking utensil between his fingers.

"Yess." Huudra was not thirsty. Idly, he wondered if Keekil's drink might be poisoned. It was a natural thought, as was the corollary that the baron would not be so readily consuming the contents of the container if they had not been thoroughly tested by an independent machine prior to arrival. "These mammalss value their independence."

"That will have to change. I am persuaded by our pssych sspecialisstss that the humanss *can* be convinced. We already know that they are resisstant to pressure. Nor have rational arguments ssucceeded in sswaying them."

Huudra indicated his irritation. He ranked Keekil, but not by enough to intimidate the other noble. "Then what are we to do?"

"Have patience, I am told. The most convinced human iss one that hass convinced itsself. Wait for them to entreat *uss*. When that happenss, it will make for a sstronger alliance between uss, as well as one in which we remain the dominant component." The baron sipped at his refreshment. "There iss only one problem: otherss who have the ssame hope."

"The benighted, dirt-loving insectiles." Huudra added a general curse notable for its grace of understatement.

"Truth. They have had only the most modesst ssuccess thuss far in overcoming the humanss' natural antipathy toward them. For that matter, a great many thranx find the appearance, habitss, and activitiess of humanss detestable. Thiss mutual abhorrence iss of coursse greatly to our benefit."

"Then nothing hass changed." Huudra prepared to depart. The administration of his own fief awaited, and decisions waited on no AAnn.

"That iss not entirely true, honored friend, if certain reportss are to be believed."

Huudra hesitated. "What reportss? I have heard nothing to indicate that the relationsship between human and thranx hass changed. Certainly not for the better."

Keekil gestured apology mixed with slyness. "Perhapss that iss becausse my ssources are more penetrating than yourss." He was unable to resist the dig.

Huundra scowled. "I will grant you the ssmall triumph of esspionage—if you have ssomething worth hearing."

"There iss ssomething very ssecret afoot. Information sspeakss to a great rissk the thranx are taking, in concert with a few sselect human alliess."

The lord of the Southern Fief spat his disbelief. "The thranx do not gamble. They are cautiouss, calculating, and predictable. They do not take 'risskss,' esspecially on matterss of ssuch importance."

Keekil refused to be put off. "Nevertheless, the report iss there, for any who care to read it. It claimss that the inssectiless have embarked on a rissky coursse of action that, if ssuccessful, would greatly accelerate the improvement of their relationss with the humanss."

Huudra's instinctive inclination led him to shrug off this outrageous claim. The thranx did not gamble, and any attempt to rush humans into a decision, as experience had already shown, usually had the opposite effect. The insectiles knew this as well as the AAnn, and whatever else the eight-limbed might be, they were not stupid.

"I would deign to perusse ssuch a report," he replied absently, thus presenting a formal request to see the analysis in question. "I do not dissmiss it out of hand. I ssimply find it difficult to countenance."

"As do I." Finishing the last of his drink, Keekil held the utensil high over his head. A cleaner swooped down to pluck it painlessly from his fingers. "Yet to ignore it sshould the information it containss mature to fruition could prove perilouss."

It was a diplomatic way of saying that their titles, not to mention their tails, might be at stake. Buried as he was in administrative work, Huudra knew he could not ignore any report that commented upon human-thranx relations, no matter how seemingly ludicrous. Not when he and Keekil had been charged with keeping the emperor's council informed of the matter. He hissed soft resignation.

"I will read it through, of coursse. Tell me, honored colleague: Sshould the leasst of it prove to have a basiss in fact, iss there anything we can do about it?" The thought of frustrating the aims of the pedantic but indomitable thranx raised his spirits.

Keekil blinked slyly. "Jusst possibly, honored associate. Jusst possibly. The thranx are not the only sspeciess capable of ssubtle interference in the affairss of other sspeciess of ssignificance. It iss amazing how with a little imagination and careful planning, one ssecret can be turned againsst another."

Caucusing quietly, they exited the room as the rest of the

assembly trickled out behind them. The more Huudra heard of Keekil's intentions, the greater his professional admiration for his colleague. In the shifting sands where cunning slithered, none traveled more subtlely than the AAnn.

17

Cheelo knew he probably should have seen the anaconda. What such a big snake was doing in so small a stream he could not imagine, but the serpent's motivation was not important. What mattered was that it was there, that it had been aroused by their passage, and that it struck.

Not him, but his unwary companion.

When the snake hit, the thranx emitted a loud, startled stridulation, the wing cases on its back vibrating like cellos. The blunt, reptilian head grabbed a middle leg, biting down hard, the small, sharp teeth gaining an immediate purchase without completely penetrating the chitin. Coil after coil emerged from beneath the cola-colored, tannin-stained water to wrap around the thranx's rear legs and abdomen. It struggled, antennae and upper limbs flailing wildly, but it could no more break that steel-cable grasp than its vestigial wings could carry it aloft.

The mass of writhing alien limbs and constrictor coils went down in a heap. A loud, distinct crack split the humid, still air and the alien screamed a sharp, high-pitched whistle. Cheelo stood off to one side, wary and watching.

Doesn't look like a very superior body now, he found himself thinking.

The alien was going to die. That much was clear. Whether the anaconda was capable of swallowing it was another matter, but it would quickly suffocate the thranx no matter how many lungs it had. The huge constrictor would continue to tighten its grip until its prey could no longer exhale. Cheelo wondered if the brilliant compound eyes would dim in death.

"Do something!" the alien was gasping. "Get it . . . off. Help me!"

Did he want to do that? Montoya mused. He had lived a long time without knowledge of or the company of aliens of any kind. He could certainly continue to exist in that same fashion. If he got too close, the snake might decide to forsake its present cumbersome, hard-shelled prey for something softer and more familiar. Why take the chance? He owed this garrulous representative of a race from a distant world absolutely nothing. *It* had intruded on *his* privacy, and he had graciously consented to allow it to accompany him. That did not imply in any way that he took any kind of responsibility for it. Besides, he had an appointment to keep.

If they happened to stumble across its indigestible, extruded remains, no searchers, human or thranx, could connect Cheelo Montoya to the fatality. More likely than not, the bug's own people would come to the conclusion that their wayward associate had received exactly what he deserved for wandering off on his own. Its death meant nothing to Cheelo, meant less to him than the passing of a bird or monkey. Besides, if their situation was reversed, there was no reason to assume that the alien would do anything for him.

"Ah, *shit*," he muttered as he reached into his pocket holster for the compact pistol.

Edging closer to the combatants, one of whom was tiring rapidly, he tried to draw a bead on the snake's blunt, shovel-shaped skull. Initially impossible, it became easier to aim as the thranx's struggles steadily weakened. Sensing the imminence of its prey's demise, the serpent began to relax. Though he wasn't sure he had a clean shot, Cheelo's finger tightened on the trigger. It wouldn't do any good to wait until the snake stopped moving completely, because by then the thranx would be dead.

When the full charge struck, the constrictor's head jerked sharply. The tiny anacondan eyes made it hard to tell how effective the shot had been. Risking contact, Cheelo put the pistol as close to the snake's skull as he could and fired a second time. This time the resultant spasmodic twitch was purely reflexive.

Pocketing his weapon, he began struggling with the weighty mass. It took more than a few minutes to unwind several hundred pounds of solid, limp serpent from the thranx's body.

"How're you doing?" he queried the alien. "Talk to me, bug. Let me know I'm not wasting my time here."

"You're not." The Terranglo was more heavily accented than usual as the injured thranx strained to mouth the humanoid phrases. "I am alive, but I'm afraid that one of my legs is broken."

"Ay, I heard it snap." With a grunt, Cheelo heaved a center length of snake aside. "You hurting?"

"Of course I am hurting!" Freed from the imprisoning coils, a shaken Desvendapur turned to look back at the human who had saved him. "Do you think I'm made of metal?"

"No, I think you're made of crab shell and bug guts. Pardon me for asking."

Aware that his artless declaration of fact might have been misinterpreted by his savior, a grateful Desvendapur hastened to soothe any misconceptions. "I meant no scorn. It is just that I would think it obvious to anyone that a broken leg would be found to be painful."

"I don't know bullcrap about your internal makeup, or how your nervous system works." Under Cheelo's strong fingers, a last span of solid muscle sloughed away from the thranx's upper abdomen.

"Then listen and learn: We feel pain as surely as do you."

"But not in the same places, or to the same degree." Kneeling, Cheelo examined the section of leg where the anaconda's jaws remained locked, even in death, on the chitin of one foreleg. "If you did, this would have you screaming in pain." He glanced up, meeting compound eyes, and with both hands wrenched sharply on the snake's neck. "That hurt?"

"Only slightly. Few nerves run through our outer covering. We are not as tactilely sensitive as you."

"I'm not sure if that's a good thing or bad. In this case, though, it's for sure good. Stay there."

With a truhand and a foothand Desvendapur gestured down at himself. "I have a broken leg. Where would I go?"

"Beats me. A while ago you were boasting about having four or six legs as opposed to my lousy, inadequate two and how much better the arrangement was for getting you around."

Sliding his pack off his back he searched inside until he

found the multitool. Returning to the alien's side, he deployed a pliers configuration to remove the great constrictor's teeth, one by one, from the thranx's foreleg. Only when the last tooth had been forcibly extracted did the dead snake's head finally slide away from its would-be prey.

Though he was ready to apply disinfectant and appropriate follow-ups, Cheelo saw that the wound was beyond his simple knowledge of first aid. The chitin was bleeding profusely. A double line of small holes showed where the snake's teeth had sought and found a grip.

"Can we do anything with this?" he asked curiously.

"With time and the proper dietary supplements, yes." Looking back and down, Desvendapur examined the wounds. "Though they testify to impressive jaw strength, the punctures are fortunately not too deep."

"What about applying a sterile covering or spray?"

"The necessary materials for sealing the wounds are in my pack. Once treated, the internal perforations will heal on their own." His abdomen shifted. "The break is another matter."

Cheelo sighed. Why he didn't just offer a final salute and farewell and return to the solitary depths of the rain forest on his own he didn't know. Perhaps it was because it was beginning to occur to him that there might, just might, be a way to realize some profit from his unexpected encounter. Experience had taught him that there was always money to be made from the new and the different, and if the alien wasn't new and different, why then, nothing qualified.

"Let's have a look."

It was the lower portion of the middle right limb that had been snapped. Blood poured from the split more freely than it would have from any human. Under Desvendapur's direction, Cheelo applied sealants and dressings from the thranx's kit to freeze and close the wound, binding it shut with a pastelike composite that would set the fracture firmly. Derived from a synthetic chitin, it would become as much a part of the alien's body as his natural limbs.

It did not set instantaneously, however. They would need to move slowly for several days. Additionally, the broken limb required supplementary support. Demonstrating a dexterity that surprised the poet, Cheelo fashioned a makeshift double splint from available wood, securing it to the mended limb with multiple twists of tough vine.

"That should do you." He stepped back to admire his handiwork.

"It will suffice very well," the thranx agreed. "But then, it's only natural that someone who spends his time working alone in vast tracts of jungle should have mastered such necessary survival skills."

"That's right." Cheelo did not go on to explain that the jungle whose survival skills he had mastered consisted of dark streets and back alleys, shadowy business enterprises and their glowering associates. On reflection, it was not surprising how many of the abilities that allowed someone like himself to survive the threats and dangers of the urban jungle were applicable to survival in the natural world as well.

In lieu of a suitable couch, Desvendapur settled himself across a broken stump padded with thriving fungi, resting as much of his abdomen as possible on the wooden brace. "Now that immediate problems have been dealt with, I was wondering if you could answer a question or two for me?" His human companion was not surprised to see that the alien's scri!ber was out and activated.

More in an endless succession of queries about humankind, Cheelo grumbled silently. For someone who had developed a healthy dislike of questions, he found himself answering an awful lot of them lately.

"Okay, as long as we don't waste the rest of the day playing Who's Got the Answer. I'm working on a schedule. What do you want to know this time? How our 'hives' are organized? What our hobbies are? Why we keep other animals as pets? Details of our mating habits?" His face broke into a wide smirk. "Ay, yeah —let's talk about mating habits. Only this time, for every one of your questions I answer, I get to ask one of my own."

"For the moment I would prefer not to delve into matters so intimate, though in a way my first question might be considered even more personal." The thranx was staring at him. Leastwise, Cheelo thought it was staring at him. Given the amorphousness of those multiple compound lenses, it was hard to tell.

"Like what, for instance?" The human was still grinning. It pleased him to think that his directness might have unsettled the alien.

"Like, for instance, why have you been lying to me?"

Cheelo tensed. There was no reason for him to do so, not with the only other intelligent creature for kilometers around an alien—and one that was reduced to hobbling on a busted wheel to boot. His reaction was pure reflex.

"Lying to you? *Who's* been lying to you? Not me. What makes you say that?" He was watching the insectoid closely. "What are you—telepathic or something?"

"I am nothing of the kind. There is no such thing as telepathy. At least, its existence has not yet been formally verified. I don't need to be able to read your mind, Cheelo-person, to know that you have been lying."

"You've got some nerve, bug. I save your life and fix up your leg real good, and the first thing you can think of to say to me afterward isn't 'Thank you very much, man, for saving my life,' it's 'Why have you been lying to me?' "

"Thranx are very forthright—and you are being deliberately evasive."

Cheelo shrugged diffidently. "I got nothing to hide. So if I'm lying, give me an example. Catch me out with one." Sneering, he leaned forward and made beckoning motions with both hands. "Come on, big-eyes. Hand me back one of my own lies."

"Very well. You are not a naturalist."

Cheelo looked up sharply. Why was he wasting his time on this nonsense? "You're new to this planet, I'm the first native you've spent any time with, and already you can tell when a human is telling the truth or not? Sorry, but I don't think you're that smart."

"It is merely a matter of analyzing causal observations made during the time we have spent together." Desvendapur was neither intimidated nor angered by the human's attitude. "We have shared each other's company for a number of days now. In all that time I have not seen you perform a single act of scrutiny that might justify your presumed appellation. You have examined nothing, identified nothing, collected nothing. You have utterly ignored the 'natural' world around you except when it threatened to impede your progress or complicate your movements.

"While I am willing, indeed am forced, to assume the existence of significant differences in our cultures, science is not nearly so variable. Body shape, size, and perceptive abilities may vary, but certain things remain constant throughout the galaxy.

"One is that all science is based on observation. In the time I have spent in your company, you have made none. Not one. Nor have you taken notes, or made visual recordings, or done anything else to indicate that you are in the profession of gathering and analyzing information."

"See these? These are my cameras!" Using forked fingers, Cheelo indicated his eyes. "And these are my scri!bers—my recorders." He pointed to his ears. "I've got a good memory, and I remember everything I see."

Desvendapur gestured comprehension, then remembered to follow it with a head nod so that the human would understand. "Do you? Yesterday a flock of most interesting avians flew past overhead, visible through a fortuitous gap in the forest canopy. Both of us remarked on their appearance. Can you tell me what color they were?"

Cheelo fought to remember. "Blue!" he announced finally. "They were bright blue, with touches of yellow." He smirked triumphantly at the multilimbed alien. "How's that for an example of a naturalist's memory at work?"

"More than sufficient to diminish his standing, if he were thranx. They were green, not blue, and their beaks were red."

"Not true!" Cheelo objected strenuously. "Blue with yellow, and you can't prove otherwise!"

"But I can." Holding out his scri!ber, Desvendapur gestured with the instrument. "I do not only record my compositions; where possible I also record their sources of inspiration. Would you like to see the flock in question? I can play it back for you, together with my notes for the stanzas I composed to accompany the flight."

Caught. Cheelo snarled at the compact alien instrument. "Okay, so I *can't* remember everything. So what? That proves nothing."

"It proves that you are either the most extraordinary naturalist of your species, or the most indifferent. Any thranx claiming to hold such a position would carry instruments designed to take measurements, carry out analyses, and make records. I have not seen you utilize a single such device." A truhand indicated the human's pack. "Show them to me. Show me one. Now."

Yet again, Cheelo found himself wondering why he was tolerating this aggravating alien's company. Use the pistol, dump the body in the river, and be done with it, he thought. Still, he could not escape the feeling that there was money to be made here, and that the quantity would be greatly augmented if the subject of potential recompense was preserved in an animate as opposed to a defunct condition.

Besides, what was the thranx going to do? Report him to the nearest branch of the Global Association for the Advancement of Science? If he and his absent multilimbed companions were carrying out their observations under the umbrella of a special scientific dispensation, he could hardly go shooting off his mandibles about the status of a human who claimed to be doing essentially the same thing.

"Well, hoorah for you. You've found me out. So what? It means nothing."

"On the contrary, it means a great deal." The thranx was staring at him now, Cheelo was sure of it. "It means that if you are not a naturalist, as you have claimed, then you are something else." Painfully, using foot- and truhand, he manually repositioned his injured leg.

"The question then becomes, What are you?"

18

Electric with the realization that the colony was in the forefront of developing human-thranx relations, the terrestrial hive was an exhilarating place to work. The knowledge that it was also illicit, an operation whose very existence was unknown to all but a few enlightened members of the human government and scientific establishment, only added to the excitement. Rising to work every shift, one never knew when the operation might be discovered. Having been as thoroughly briefed on humankind and its peculiarities and distinctive foibles as was possible before their journey to the colony, every assigned thranx had been made fully aware of the inherent irrationality built into each individual human. If anything went wrong and they were subject to unforeseen exposure, there was no telling how the great mass of seething humanity might react to the presence of an unauthorized alien colony in its midst. Consequently, even as they went about their commonplace, everyday tasks, the colonists had to be ever vigilant and prepared for anything.

As weeks and months passed without discovery, a modest sense of security invariably settled over the colony. If even the apprehensive rogue humans who had cooperated and conspired in the secret establishment of the hive could relax, then certainly their thranx associates could do no less.

So it was that Jhywinhuran's thoughts were far from such matters as she busied herself at the end of the day's work, running a final check and chemical disbursement before signing off her station to her shift replacement. Instead of concentrating on the admittedly rote toil at hand, her mind strayed to remembrances of the time spent in the company of a particularly distinctive male. Somewhat to her chagrin, her thoughts had been repeatedly drawn in that direction for several days now.

Why she should have found an assistant food preparator so fascinating she could not quite explain. Certainly her attraction had nothing to do with his vocation, which was even more prosaic and mundane than her own. Within the bustling colony there were many unmated males who found her attractive, stridulating softly in her presence in an attempt to attract more than polite attention. Some she spent time with, chatting and disporting, but always her thoughts returned to a certain singular food preparator.

What it was about him that she found so distinctive proved elusive, no matter how often she tried to define it. Something in his manner, perhaps, or in the way he modulated communication: not only his vocalizations but the attendant clicks and whistles that were as much a part of thranx speech as strings of individual words. Maybe it was the way that when he became excited, exquisitely inflected snippets of High Thranx slipped into his conversation; something not to be expected from an assistant food preparator. There were other distinctions: the way he spoke of the alien world above, the animation that overwhelmed his gesturing when they attended a less-than-proficient performance by one of the colony's official soothers, the indifference with which he acknowledged both praise and criticism of his own work.

There was something not quite right about the food preparator Desvenbapur, something simultaneously irresistibly enticing and edgily off-putting. Try as she might, she could not get him out of her mind. She considered visiting a senior matriarch for counseling but decided that her condition had not yet advanced from the merely affected to the obsessive. Until that line was crossed she would deal with the situation herself.

One way to do so would be to go and visit the object of her anxiety. As in any hive, the colonists had been assigned not only labor but living quarters and sectors. While with certain specific exceptions the length and breadth of the hive was open to all who dwelled within and no permit or permission was required to wander beyond those sections that had been individually apportioned subsequent to arrival, it was infrequently done. There was no reason to explore beyond one's assigned territory. Everything a colonist needed could be found within an individually prescribed zone. It was a system that was traditional and efficient and that contributed mightily to the efficiency of every hive, whether on Hivehom, Willow-Wane, or the alien world known to its dominant inhabitants as Earth.

Humans, by contrast, the colonists had been told, were far less orderly. Superficially well organized, they tended to scatter and move about with considerably less regard for the effective organization of the whole. Life in their hives frequently bordered on the anarchic. Somehow, out of confusion and turmoil, they had succeeded in raising a civilization.

She determined to resolve the contradictions that were boiling within her. The very next off-period, she identified the location of the hive's subsidiary food preparation facility and headed in its direction, following the directions provided by her scri!ber. As she entered unfamiliar parts of the colony she paused from time to time to converse with thranx never before encountered, and they with her. No one questioned her presence. While out of the ordinary, there was nothing unlawful about it.

She spent some time talking with sanitation workers who supervised the hive's other waste terminus. The colony had been designed with at least two of everything in mind. If a critical component broke down, there was no hailing a neighboring hive for repairs or replacements. The nearest supplies lay parsecs away, and support could not be provided as soon as it might be needed. Between their incompatible technology and the restrictions placed on their movements, the hive's allied humans could provide only limited help. Of necessity, the colony had to be as self-sufficient as possible.

Despite diversions both enjoyable and educational, she eventually found herself in the auxiliary kitchen area. From there it was a simple matter to obtain permission to visit food preparation. What she saw there was a duplicate of the station where Desvenbapur had worked previously, identical down to the individual appliances and utensils manipulated by its work force. At present they were engaged in cleaning and treating a variety of native plants, rendering them suitable for thranx consumption. Without the ability to digest terrestrial vegetation, the rapid growth of the colony would have been greatly reduced.

She chatted amiably and casually with members of the staff, who were curious as to the presence in their midst of an unfamiliar representative of the sanitation division. No, an assistant preparator named Desvenbapur was not currently a member of their team. In fact, none of them had ever heard of him. Perhaps he worked exclusively on the night shift.

She knew she ought to make the journey back to her cubicle so she could get some rest before she had to report for the new day's work. She was being foolish, letting an incidental interest grow into a dangerous fixation. Hadn't Desvenbapur told her that he would be too busy establishing himself in a new zone and a new routine to welcome casual social contact? Hadn't he told her that as soon as he was settled in and comfortable with his work in the new sector that he would return to visit her? He had specifically asked her to terminate contact until such time as he felt ready to take pleasure from it again. Despite that, here she was, forcing the issue, trying to initiate intercourse he had requested she avoid. What was the matter with her?

She started to leave, to return to her own sector. Certainly if he had any reciprocal feelings for her he would be in touch as soon as he felt at ease with his new surroundings. It might well be counterproductive, even damaging, to their relationship for her to pursue the matter so vigorously. Did they *have* a relationship? She knew that *she* desired one, and she thought that he did as well. A demonstration of excessive inquisitiveness on her part might spoil everything.

She considered her options. There was a way to at least partially satisfy her interest without much risk of damaging relations. Locating a private information terminal, she plugged her scri!ber in and ran a search. Relief was palpable when his name appeared on the roster of workers assigned to this zone, food preparation division.

That should have been enough to satisfy her. Instead, adding to her distress and confusion, it only made her that much more anxious to see him again. She stood before the terminal until a polite whistle roused her to the realization that two

other hive members were standing behind her, waiting to
make use of it themselves. Restless and preoccupied, she
wandered off.

She would wait until the night shift, she resolved. Not
to speak with Desvenbapur, but to assure herself that all
was well with him. This she could do by speaking briefly
with others who worked in his department. Even deprived of
sleep, she was confident she could perform her duties tomorrow adequately, if not commendably.

She passed the remaining portion of the day shift exploring
the immediate vicinity, finding it, as expected, a veritable duplicate of her own. As shifts began their switch, she made her
way back to the kitchen area and lingered in its vicinity, randomly querying those arriving to begin work. None knew
of an assistant food preparator who went by the name of
Desvenbapur.

By the time the last worker had arrived she found herself
growing concerned. What if the transfer had not worked out
and he was ill? A check of medical records for the entire
colony took only an instant. It did not show a Desvenbapur
listed as being among the unwell.

This was senseless, she told herself. Obviously, today was
an off-period, a rest time for her friend. He would return to
work tomorrow. And she could not wait around and eschew
her own labor simply to assure herself that he was all right.

But why hadn't she been able to find at least one coworker
who recognized his name? He had been assigned to this
sector long enough to have established, if not intimate friend-
ships, at least casual acquaintances. From what she knew and
had seen of his work, an assistant food preparator did not
function in a vacuum.

Perplexed, she waited until the terminal was free to again
call up the rostering for food preparation in this zone. There
was his name on the list, bold and unmistakable. Not being
assigned herself to the kitchen division, she could not access
individual shift assignments. But she *could* locate anyone's
place of habitation. This she proceeded to do.

There it was: Desvenbapur, habitat level three, cell quadrant six, cubicle eighty-two. She contemplated the readout for

a long moment, wavering. Then, antennae set determinedly
forward, she strode off along the appropriate corridor.

It did not take long to locate the living quarters in question.
A pass with her scri!ber over the door ident revealed the
occupant to be one Desvenbapur, assistant food preparator. Proof enough of his residence—but not of his health.
Still, she hesitated. Request admittance, and she risked jeop-
ardizing their consanguinity. Depart now, and she would
preserve it, but without having achieved any personal satisfaction after having come all this way and spent all this time.

Perhaps she had acquired some of her friend's intermittent
hints of irrationality. Perhaps she was simply stubborn. In any
event, she resolved to wait for him.

The following day shift passed without any sign of her
quarry. By now her own shift supervisor would have marked
her as absent and initiated a routine search to ascertain her location, health, and status. Her unauthorized absence would
go down on her permanent work record, she knew, inhibiting
opportunity for advancement and commendation. She did
not care. The second night shift arrived, and still the door to
cubicle eighty-two remained sealed.

What if he was inside, having suffered some serious harm?
A dual coronary arrhythmia, perhaps, with both hearts beating out of cadence. Or a severe intestinal blockage. Curiosity
turned to concern, which begat fear. Rising from the resting
position in which she had been settled for more than a day,
she struggled on stiffened legs to the nearest general accessway and called for a domicile supervisor.

The female responsible for this section of living quarters
responded promptly, listened to Jhywinhuran's weary concerns, and agreed that the situation she was describing demanded some sort of resolution. Accordingly, permission
was obtained to make an unauthorized entry into private
quarters. As she followed the supervisor down the corridor,
Jhywinhuran was beset with conflicting emotions. If something grave had happened to Desvenbapur, she would be severely depressed. If, on the other truhand, there was nothing
wrong, she would undoubtedly find herself on the receiving
end of a well-deserved stream of imprecation.

She discovered that she could hardly breathe as the supervisor utilized an override to break the seal on the cubicle and slide back the door. They entered together. The interior of the compact living space was neat, clean, spotless; from the rest and relaxation chamber to the smaller area reserved for the carrying out of individual hygiene. In fact, it was more than spotless.

It had not been lived in for some time.

"There must be some mistake." Her gestures were clumsy, her words hesitant as she surveyed the immaculate, obviously untouched quarters. "His ident is on the door."

The supervisor checked her own scri!ber. Reflexively gesturing confusion, she checked it again. And a third time. When she looked up, the commingled movements of her limbs and antennae indicated more than simple puzzlement.

"You are right. There *is* a mistake. This living cubicle is unassigned."

Mandibles moving slowly against one another, Jhywinhuran stared at the senior female. "But his full ident is imprinted on the entrance."

"It certainly is. Be assured that I am no less curious than you to find out how and why it is there."

Jointly, they ran detailed searches. No assistant food preparator of any name had been placed in cubicle eighty-two by residential assignment. Yes, one named Desvenbapur had been transferred to the subsidiary kitchens. No, he could not be located. Perhaps his scri!ber was turned off or had run down without being noticed. Follow-up queries of every single worker assigned to food preparation in this sector revealed no knowledge of a Desvenbapur. Nor could anyone by that name be located *anywhere*, in any sector.

"Something is very wrong here," declared the supervisor as she concluded her searching.

Jhywinhuran was still working her scri!ber. "I agree, but what? He told me, told everyone he worked with, that he was being transferred to food preparation in this sector. His name is on the work roster."

"Just as his name is on the door to these quarters." The two females considered the situation. "Let me run one more search."

Jhywinhuran waited while the senior female waltzed the delicate fingers of her truhands over her unit. Moments later she looked up again, her antennae aimed directly at her visitor. "There is no record of a transfer to this sector being authorized for anyone in food preparation, or specifically, anyone named Desvenbapur."

"Then . . . he lied." Jhywinhuran could barely muster the appropriate clicks to underscore her reply.

"So it would seem. But why? Why would this friend of yours, or any thranx, lie about being shifted from one part of the hive to another?"

"I do not know." The sanitation worker stridulated softly. "But if he isn't here, and he isn't there, then where is he? And why is he wherever he is?"

"I do not know either, but unless something emerges to indicate otherwise, what we have here is unequivocal evidence of antisocial behavior. I am sure it will all become clear when he is located."

When he was not, something akin to alarm set in not only among those thranx charged with locating the errant assistant food preparator, but among their human associates as well.

Jhywinhuran found herself waiting in an empty interrogation chamber. It was of modest size and in no way remarkable except for the presence among the usual resting benches of a trio of very peculiar sculptures whose purpose she was unable to divine. They looked like tiny benches, much too small to provide surcease and comfort to even a juvenile thranx. Instead of being open and easily accessed, one side of each of the squarish objects was raised above the rest, so that even if you tried to settle your abdomen across it, the stiff raised portions would make it next to impossible.

The hive had been turned upside down in the search for the missing assistant food preparator. When it was determined to a specific degree of assurance that not only was he no longer present in the hive, but that his body could not be found, a startled Jhywinhuran had found herself called away from her labor and ordered to this room. There she sat, and waited, and wondered what in the name of the lowest level of the supreme hive was going on.

She did not have to wait long.

Four people filed into the chamber. Two of them between them had only as many limbs as she did. She had seen humans around the hive before, but not often. They did not frequent the section of the colony where she worked, and she had had no actual contact with them herself. From her predeparture studies she was able to discern that both genders were represented. As was common among humans, their skin and single-lensed eye color varied markedly. These and other superficial physical variations she expected. She also was not surprised when they sat down in two of the peculiar constructs whose function had so puzzled her. She winced inwardly, unable to see how any being, even one as flexible as a human, could call "relaxing" a posture that required the body to almost fold itself in half.

But she was startled when conversation commenced, and the humans participated—speaking not in their own language but in a crude, unsophisticated, yet impressively intelligible rendition of Low Thranx.

"How long have you known the assistant food preparator who calls himself Desvenbapur?" The human female blundered slightly over the correct pronunciation of the title.

Jhywinhuran hesitated, taken aback by both the nature of the question and its source. She looked to the two thranx present for advice, only to have the eldest gesture compliance. Not politely, either. Clearly, something serious was afoot.

"I met him on the *Zenruloim* on the journey out from Willow-Wane. He was pleasant company, and as there were only four of us bound for this world, we naturally struck up an acquaintance. I also met and became friends with the engineers Awlvirmubak and Durcenhofex."

"They do not concern us and are not involved in this matter," the eldest thranx explained, "because they are not only where they are, but they are who they are."

She gestured bewilderment. "I don't understand."

"Neither do we," the elder responded. "That is one of the purposes of this meeting: to reach understanding." His antennae bobbed restlessly as he spoke, indicating no especial sentiment: only a continuing unease. "Your friend has gone missing."

"I know. I helped to file the report."

"No, you don't know," the elder corrected her. "I do not mean that he has gone missing in the accepted sense. I mean that he is nowhere to be found anywhere in the hive."

"Nor," added the male human somewhat melodramatically, "is his corpse."

"The inescapable conclusion," the younger of the two thranx told her, "is that he has gone outside."

"Outside?" Jhywinhuran's confusion gave way to disbelief. "You mean, he has left the colony? Voluntarily?"

The elder genuflected sadness mixed with concurrence. "So it must be assumed."

"But *why*?" Acknowledging her acceptance of the human's presence, she included them in her question as well as the pair of somber supervisors. "Why would he do such a thing? Why would any member of the colony?"

The female human crossed one leg completely over another, an intriguing gesture no thranx could emulate half so fluidly. Jhywinhuran wondered at its hidden meanings. "We were really hoping you could shed some light on that, Jhywinhuran."

Hearing her name emerge from an alien throat, complete to the appropriate whistle-and-click accentuation, was a novelty the sanitation worker did not have time to enjoy. "I assure you all I have no idea."

"Think," the elder prodded her. "This is important beyond anything you can imagine. We are already, with the aid of our human friends, searching the surface above and around the colony for this absent individual, but it would be of considerable use to know who and what we are searching for."

"You keep speaking of Desvenbapur as though he doesn't exist." Something deep inside her felt bound to rise, however feebly or ineffectively, to the defense of an acquaintance who had brazenly lied to her.

The two thranx exchanged gestures. It was left to the younger to explain. "He doesn't. *Crrik,* the individual you know as Desvenbapur certainly does, but that is not his identity. When your report was filed and it was determined that the individual was no longer residing within the colony, a thorough background check was run on him in the hopes of learning or at least obtaining some clue as to what might have

prompted him to engage in such intemperate behavior. Given
the seriousness of his apparent transgression, the check was
correspondingly detailed.

"It included a search, via a surreptitious space-minus relay
operated by our human friends, of records that extend all the
way back to Willow-Wane—not only professional records
but personal ones as well. A portion of the finished report was
so extraordinary that despite the difficulty and expense a
recheck was demanded. It only confirmed that which had preceded it."

"What did you find out?" The two humans were temporarily forgotten.

The younger supervisor continued the story. "Something
this serious activates, as one of multiple automatic searches,
a full family background check. The records of the Hive
Ba show no mention of a Desvenbapur living or recently
deceased."

None of the four thranx mandibles were capable of dropping, in the human sense, but Jhywinhuran succeeded in conveying her astonishment at this astounding announcement by
means of a simple truhand gesture. "Then who is he?"

"We think we know," the elder told her. "He is very clever,
this individual, far more resourceful than one would expect
of an assistant food preparator."

"I always thought him so." Her horizontal mandibles
clicked softly while the verticals remained motionless. She
was more than a little dazed by this latest revelation.

"It all fits together." The younger supervisor was gesturing corroboration. "Tell me, Jhywinhuran: Did your absent
friend at any time ever express a more-than-passing interest
in the composition of poetry?"

This time she could only stare at her interrogators in stu-
pefied silence. It did not matter. Her hush was sufficiently
eloquent.

The senior supervisor continued, his mandibles moving
methodically. "On Willow-Wane there was no Desvenbapur.
Or Desvenhapur or Desvenkapur. Background investigation
discovered a Desventapur, an elderly and well-known electronics mapper who lives in the Hive Wevk. Also a Desven-

qapur, a harvester drone residing in Upper Hierxex." He shifted his abdomen on his resting bench.

"There is also a Desvengapur who is not only the right age, but also shows an interest in formal composition for purpose of performance."

"Is that the real person, the one we are talking about?" a shaky Jhywinhuran heard herself asking.

The supervisor gestured negativity. "Desvengapur is a mid-age female."

The younger of the pair took over, his speech becoming harsh and accusatory, the clicks sharper, his whistles shriller. "No living representative of the Hive Ba bears the name Desvenbapur. But on Willow-Wane there *was* an aspiring young poet sufficiently accomplished to be assigned the designation of soother. He managed to have himself appointed to the human outpost at Geswixt."

The human male chipped in. "Apparently this individual, for reasons we still do not know, desired contact with my kind."

"His name," the supervisor continued, "was Desvendapur. A real, existing person, according to all personnel background checks and official records."

A poet, she found herself thinking. A designated soother. No wonder her friend's "amateur" efforts had struck her as so wonderfully accomplished. There had been nothing amateurish about them, or about him, she reflected bleakly.

"He changed his name and his records." Her voice was dull, methodical, the words rising without difficulty to her mandibles. "He falsified his history and learned the trade of assistant food preparator. But why?"

"Apparently, in hopes of gaining assignment to the colony there," the female human responded. "Why he did this we still don't know. We'd certainly like to."

"Truly," declared the senior supervisor, "an explanation of his motivation would be most welcome. This Desvendapur is an individual who has been driven to take extreme measures."

Jhywinhuran indicated assent. "To make up a false identity, to equivocate repeatedly . . ." A sudden thought made her hesitate. "Wait. I can see how he could remake himself as an assistant food preparator named Desvenbapur, but what about his original self? Wouldn't it be missed, not only at Geswixt but elsewhere?"

"This Desvendapur's cleverness extends well beyond a talent for concocting agreeable phrases." The supervisor's tone was dark. "He participated in a short but unauthorized flight from Geswixt to the project outpost on Willow-Wane. On the return flight, the lifter that had conveyed him crashed in the mountains. It was presumed that everyone aboard perished in the fiery crash. Shortly thereafter, the name of one Desvenbapur appeared on the work rolls of the human outpost as an assistant food preparator."

She gestured astonishment. "How fortunate he was. That must have been a remarkable stroke of luck for him and for his plans, for I assume based on what you have told me that he must have been intending something like that for a long time."

"Certainly he was," the other supervisor readily agreed, "however there is now some question as to how 'lucky' he might have been."

"What are you implying, Venerable?" she stammered.

"The crash of his transportation on its return journey to Geswixt, leaving him an illegal and therefore unrecognized presence in the project outpost, is simply too convenient to be any longer considered a coincidence. Though much time has passed since this incident occurred, the appropriate authorities are even now reviewing the relevant records." He gestured with all four hands. "It is considered a distinct possibility that your friend contrived the crash of his transportation on its return flight to Geswixt in order to obliterate his old identity while providing an opportunity for him to create and adopt a new one."

While she was digesting this inconceivable volley of information, the female human commented, in that terse, tactless fashion for which humans were both famed and notorious, "What Eirmhenqibus is saying is that your absent friend, in addition to putting in jeopardy everything we have worked to achieve here, may also be a murderer." She had some difficulty with the appropriate accents for the thranx term for "one who kills its own kind," but Jhywinhuran had no trouble comprehending what had been said.

"I . . . I find that hard to believe."

"Then you are in good company in this room," the senior supervisor assured her. "Murder, falsification of identity, illegal assignation of profession, and now escapement. This Desvendapur has much to answer for."

"It is not something I would have expected of a soother." The other supervisor was quietly incredulous. "Your friend must be found, and quickly."

Both humans nodded assent. "This part of Earth was chosen for the colony not only because the climate is conducive to your kind," the female said, "but because it represents one of the last and largest regions on the planet in which the imprint of humankind has not been heavy. Very few people come here, and those that do travel about under strict supervision or professional guidance. But if anyone should see this Desvendapur, engaged in whatever purpose he is bent upon, he will immediately be recognized for what he is: an alien wandering about on a part of the Earth's surface where no alien is supposed to be."

"I do not think I need remind you," the male roughly told her, "about the delicate nature of the ongoing negotiations between your species and ours. Your . . . appearance . . . unfortunately, is off-putting to those of our kind who have not yet learned how to look beyond shape in the course of establishing relations. The great mass of humanity is still not entirely comfortable with the realization that there are other intelligent species, nor the possibility that some may be more intelligent than themselves. There exists a historical racial paranoia that is only slowly being eroded by contact with such as the thranx.

"The revelation that an illegal colony has been established here, in a part of the world where an alien presence is not officially authorized, could cast a serious pall on future as well as current relations between our respective species. In another ten or fifteen years, when the population of Earth has had a reasonable period of time in which to become used to your existence and appearance, the long-term existence of the colony will officially be made public. Realizing that your kind has lived among us in harmony and without friction for a studied length of time should, our psychologists tell us, greatly facilitate the formalizing of relations."

"But not yet," the female concluded. Jhywinhuran thought she looked tired, as if she had not slept in several days. "It is too soon—much too soon. The consequences that could result from premature disclosure are alarming."

The sanitation worker did not hesitate. In spite of any personal feelings she might retain for the engaging individual whose true name it appeared was Desvendapur, she was a dutiful and conscientious member of a hive. As such, she knew that the security and integrity of the community could not be compromised.

"I understand that he must be found and brought back before his existence is discovered by any passing humans. I will help in any way I can." She gestured sharply with a truhand. "Knowing him and being somewhat familiar with his nature, I can say that having gone to the trouble and extremes you have described, he may prove reluctant to comply."

It would have been better had one of the supervisors responded, but with the abruptness for which they were noted, it was the male human who replied first.

"If that proves to be the case, then of course we'll have to kill him."

19

An irritated Cheelo was about to respond to the alien's question, but before he could, a muted hum began to tickle his ears. Scanning the surrounding rain forest, he found his gaze being drawn to the tributary from which the striking anaconda had erupted. Ignoring the thranx's queries, he walked to the water's edge and squinted upstream. The hum grew no louder, but neither did it disappear.

"What are you doing?" Putting tentative pressure on his splinted middle leg, Desvendapur eyed the silent human curiously. "If you think after all this time that you're now going to persuade me that you are a naturalist by pretending to be engaged in some kind of profound observational behavior of the local fauna, you are—"

"Shut up!" Cheelo snapped. His tone more than the curt human words induced the poet to hold his peace. Or perhaps it was the hand gesture that accompanied the admonition; a sharp, downward chopping motion that Desvendapur had not encountered before.

The poet waited until he could stand the continuing silence no longer. Mindful of the human's warning, he kept his voice low as he moved forward to stand alongside the biped. The human's aspect and attitude were indicative of a sudden wariness.

"What's going on?"

"Don't you hear it? That vibrating sound?"

Desvendapur gestured affirmatively, then remembered to nod. "Certainly. While our sense of hearing is not as acute as yours, it is perfectly adequate." He tested the air with his antennae, seeking some radical new aroma, but caught nothing. "Some local animal, a forest dweller."

"Like hell it is." Putting out a hand, Cheelo urged the alien back into the undergrowth. Together they concealed themselves as best they could behind and beneath houseplants that here in their natural habitat grew to the size of small trees.

Wordlessly, he pointed at the eagle as it came gliding down the creek, its head panning slowly from side to side. Putting aside the queasiness that arose as a consequence of contact with soft, flexible mammalian flesh, Desvendapur indicated that he understood the situation. Only when he was certain that the eagle had passed well out of sight did Cheelo emerge from the brush and indicate that the thranx could do likewise.

"I do not understand." Antennae dipped and weaved balletically as Desvendapur gazed down the streambed, then turned back to the still-watchful human. "That was a particularly dangerous creature? Poisonous, perhaps, or stronger than it appeared?"

"That wasn't no damn bird at all. Eagles *scream*. They don't hum." Single-lensed brown eyes regarded the alien. "It was a machine. I've seen it before, or another one like it. I'm hoping it was nothing more than a routine, preprogrammed forest service overflight. I don't know what their inspection and censusing schedule is like. Didn't realize until I came here that the forest service used such sophisticated scanners. I guess they disguise them like the local critters so as not to alarm the fauna."

"This forest service you speak of may in fact not do that." Desvendapur eyed his human companion evenly.

Cheelo frowned. "Bug, is there something you're not telling me?"

Truhands crocheted the atmosphere. "There might be. Just as there is something you are not telling me. If I explain myself, will you reciprocate?"

"*Ay.* Yeah, sure." Still listening for any indication that the camouflaged scanner might be returning, Cheelo crossed his arms over his narrow chest and settled himself back against a tree.

"I suspect that cloaked device does not belong to any recognized human agency."

The perplexed human's expression contorted. "What do you mean, 'recognized'?"

"I think I know why it was so well disguised. It was not meant to be identified by your local authorities. It was designed to blend in with the local life-forms. And I think it was looking for *me*."

"For *you*?" Cheelo hesitated, then nodded knowingly. "Oh, right. Your fellow expedition members are looking for you. What is it? Past time for you to rejoin them?" Though still hopeful of finding some way of making money off the alien, Cheelo remained ambivalent about its presence and realized he wouldn't exactly be averse to its departure, either. It was slowing him down.

"Truly. But it has been time for me to rejoin them ever since I left."

The human shook his head impatiently. Explanations were not supposed to further confuse. "I don't get it."

"I am not supposed to be here."

"What? You snuck off on your own?" Cheelo chuckled softly. "How about that? A bug with balls."

"Since I have yet to master your extensive catalog of colloquialisms I will not comment on that observation. What I am saying is that I am not supposed to be here at all. In this place. On this planet."

This time Cheelo did not laugh. He stood away from the tree, his expression turning serious. "You mean your research expedition is an illegal one?"

Desvendapur hesitated only briefly. "How much can I trust you, Cheelo Montoya?"

"Completely." Expression blank, the human waited patiently.

"There is no research expedition." Turning his upper body slightly, the poet pointed eastward. "With the aid of certain select representatives of your own kind, a colony has been established in this part of your world."

"Colony? Of *bugs*?" Cheelo digested this, then shook his head sharply. "That's crazy! Even in a place as isolated as the Reserva Amazonia something like that would've been spotted before it got started."

Desvendapur begged to disagree. "Everything was done below the surface. Research, design, excavation, construction: everything. The colony's human sponsors provided and continue to provide the necessary cover to maintain our seclusion. Once the initial excavating was completed, expansion was not difficult. Or so the history that I studied of the colony declaims. I was assigned here. Unauthorized egress from the hive is strictly forbidden."

"This 'colony' of yours . . ." Cheelo hesitated uncertainly. This was bigger than he'd suspected. Much bigger. "It hasn't been authorized by the government, then? I mean, I don't exactly scan the media every day, but the big things, the major stories, you hear about them from other people. I've heard about your kind, but never anything about a bug colony."

"It is not authorized by your *visible* government," Desvendapur admitted readily. "Apparently only a few individuals from certain departments are involved. They have moved forward with this project on their own."

Like a child's building blocks, a crude but recognizable structure was assembling itself in Cheelo's brain. "So if this colony's been planted here on the sly, and nobody's supposed to know about it, and nobody from inside is supposed to go outside, then you're illegitimate twice over."

"That is correct."

Cheelo stood stunned, gaping at the calm, composed alien. Here he thought *he* was the one who had to be wary of discovery, and all along he had been traveling in the company of someone who had committed an offense beside which Cheelo Montoya's entire lifetime of minor misdeeds and infractions paled into insignificance. Every felony the part-time resident of Gatun and Golfito had committed had been provincial in nature, even the accidental killing in San José. Standing quietly before him was malfeasance on an interstellar scale.

He frowned. "Why're you telling *me* this?"

"To observe your reaction. I collect reactions." The thranx shifted on its trulegs, trying to spread his weight away from the injured, splinted limb. "I am not a researcher any more than you are a naturalist. I am a poet who seeks inspiration. I arranged to come here, to your world, in search of it. I illegally exited the colony in search of it." Like accusatory fingers, twin antennae were pointed directly at the biped. "It was in hopes of finding it that I went in search of humans who had not had prior contact with my kind."

Cheelo's thoughts swirled and collided. All the time the bug had been tagging along, it hadn't been studying the forest—it had been studying *him*. Not for scientific purposes, either. His bug was a goddamn artist, all right.

In his comparatively short lifetime Cheelo had thought of himself, envisioned himself, imagined himself as many things. A source of poetic inspiration was not one of them.

"What'll they do to you if they find you out here?" he asked pointedly.

"Take me back to the hive, to the colony. Debrief me. Ship me offworld as soon as proves feasible. Punishment will follow. Unless . . ."

"Unless what?"

"Unless my unauthorized sojourn here results in composition the likes of which has never been beheld before. I do not know how it is among humans, but among my kind great art excuses a multitude of transgressions. Additionally, all eminent artists are presumed to be at least partly mentally deranged."

Cheelo nodded. "Ay, I can see similarities." His expression darkened. "Just a minute. If nobody except these covert friends of your colony are supposed to know about its existence, and you've just told me all about it, then I'm compromised. You've compromised me." His eyes widened. "Shit, what'll they do to *me* if they find me in your company? I ain't going off to no bug world with you!"

"Obviously not. I imagine that either my people or yours will have to kill you to ensure your silence on the matter."

"My silence on the . . . ?" At that moment Cheelo wanted to reach out and choke the alien, except that constricting its neck would not result in a reduction in the supply of air to its lungs. It might be subject to suffocation in the coils of an anaconda, but not by any human. He could, however, by exerting diligence and all his strength, possibly break its neck. "Why'd you have to tell me all this? *Why?*"

"You deserved to know. If that disguised scanner had discovered us and we had been picked up, you wouldn't have known the reason for it. Now you do. I did not have to tell you about the colony to compromise you. Simply being found in my company by searchers from the hive would be enough to doom you."

The biped stiffened. "Who's doomed? Not Cheelo Montoya! I've been hiding from searchers all my life! I've slipped safely in and out of places nobody else would go near. Unless I want them to, no bunch of goddamned illegal sweet-stinking bugs is going to find me, either!"

A thranx could only smile inwardly. "An intriguingly aggressive response for a self-proclaimed naturalist."

Cheelo started to shout something more, only to find himself strangling in mid-declaration. His lower jaw closed and his voice changed to a dangerous, angry mix of accusation and admiration. "Why you ugly, burrowing, big-eyed, tooth-less bug bastard. You think you're pretty clever, don't you?"

"That is a proven fact, not hypothesis," the thranx replied calmly. "Why not tell me what *you* are, man?"

"Sure. Ay, sure, why not? It doesn't matter. You can't exactly walk into the nearest police depot and turn me in, can you? Sure, I'll tell you." He gestured at the alien's thorax pouch. "Why don't you get out that scri!ber of yours and take it all down? You might get a goddamn poem or two out of it."

Oblivious to the human's sarcasm, an excited Desvendapur hurried to comply. Holding the compact instrument out toward the biped, the poet waited eagerly.

"I take things from people," Cheelo told him pugnaciously. "I was born without anything, I saw my mother die without anything, and I had a baby brother who died before he had a chance to know anything. I grew up learning that if you want anything in this world you've got to go out and get it, because nobody's going to give it to you. This is a pretty advanced planet. Lots of nice new technology, good medicine, easy to get around, a lot cleaner than it used to be. That much I learned from history. I do read, you know."

"I never doubted it." Desvendapur was absorbing not only the human's words, but his attitude, his posture, his wonder-fully distorted facial expressions. Truly, the biped's ranting was a veritable fount of inspiration.

"Humankind's managed to get rid of a lot of things, a lot of the old troubles. But poverty isn't one of them. Not so far, not yet. I hear the sociologists argue about it a lot: whether there'll always be poor people no matter how rich the species becomes. Somebody always has to be on the bottom, no matter how high you raise the top." He shook his head sharply. "Me, I ain't going to stay on the bottom. When I found out I'd never be able to rise any other way, I started figuring out methods to take what I needed to lift me up. I'm not the only one, not by a flicker, but I'm better at it than some. That's why I'm standing here talking to you right now instead of licking my hospital dressings waiting to go in for a court-ordered selective mindwipe." There was something deeply gratifying about spilling his guts, even if only to an alien bug. Feeling more than a little reckless, he plunged on.

"I'm here right now because I killed somebody."

Desvendapur felt a thrill run through him. This was more than he could have hoped for: inspiration taken to and beyond a degree he could not have imagined in his wildest dreams. "You murdered another of your own kind?"

"It wasn't intentional," Cheelo protested. "I never meant to hurt nobody. Killing's bad for business. It just—happened. I needed the money. So I had to get away, to someplace where I could lose myself for a while." He gestured at the wild, all-enveloping rain forest. "This is a good place for that. Or it was, until I ran into you."

"You are still 'lost,'" Desvendapur assured him. "I will not give you away."

"You don't have to 'give me away.'" Cheelo's tone was accusing. "Like you said, all your brother bugs and their human friends have to do is find me with you and I'm history. Don't matter anyway. I was on my way out when you found me. I got an appointment. And you ain't helping me make it." Quietly, his hand strayed toward his gun.

"One more day." The thranx glanced skyward. "They haven't found me yet. I don't think they will, if I choose to continue hiding, but all I ask for is one more day in your company."

Cheelo's fingers hovered. Why wait? he told himself. Kill it now and move on. They'll find the body or they won't. Either way, he wouldn't be connected to it. As far as this unauthorized colony and its allies were concerned, he'd be just another solitary wanderer in the vast reaches of the rain forest.

But there was something in the alien's manner—an unrestrained eagerness, a desperation to learn, a need to achieve—that appealed strongly to something deep inside Cheelo Montoya. It wasn't that they were in any way alike: That was an absurd thought. Cheelo had never had a poetic or artistic impulse in his life, unless one counted the skill with which he relieved the unsuspecting and the unlucky of their valuables.

The camouflaged scanner had already passed this way. It was unlikely a second would be following it. Surely the resources of this secret colony were limited and any search it instituted, however frantic, must necessarily be circumspect. Otherwise it would attract the attention of the Reserva rangers or their own automatic monitoring devices. If he and the bug kept moving in the direction the eagle scanner had come from, they ought to be free of observation and safe from detection for quite a while.

Without really knowing why, he heard himself saying, "One day?"

The thranx nodded. Cheelo no longer thought the familiar gesture strange when executed by the alien. "One day. So that I may finish my note taking and observations and round them off smoothly and completely."

"I'm not sure I know what the hell you're talking about. I don't owe you nothing."

"No, you do not. Even though we are, in a way, spiritually of the same clan."

Cheelo frowned. "What are you babbling about?"

The thranx's tone did not change. "We are both outcasts, antisocials. And takers of life. I too am responsible for the death of another. All because I wish to compose something of importance."

There it was. This alien, this grossly oversized bug from another world, wanted to do something big, just like Cheelo Montoya.

No, he thought angrily, refusing to accept the analogy. We don't have anything in common! Not me and a goddamn bug! He said nothing aloud. What was there to say? He knew nothing of thranx society, of what it considered acceptable and what it did not, though he felt he could be certain of one thing: Surely among any intelligent species, the murder of one's fellows was considered inappropriate. He was wrong, but correct where the thranx were concerned.

"And if at the end of that time you remain tormented by uncertainties," Desvendapur was saying, "you can still kill me."

Cheelo started, his eyes widening slightly. "What makes you think I'd want to kill you?"

"It would be the logical thing to do." Two hands gestured in the direction of the human's holstered pistol. "I've seen your hands moving, up and down, back and forth in the direction of your concealed weapon, your gestures reflective of your changing mood. You have been thinking about it ever since we met. You could do it at any time."

"You're mighty confident I won't."

"No, I'm not." Antennae bobbed in a complex pattern. "I have been monitoring your pheromones. The levels rise and fall according to your state of mind. I know when you're thinking about killing me, and when you are not."

"You're reading my mind?" Cheelo gazed unblinkingly at the thranx.

"No. I'm reading your body odor. As I mentioned before, it is very strong. Even it is a source of suggestion to me." The heart-shaped head dipped slightly. "One more day."

"And then I can kill you? You just said yourself it would be the logical thing to do."

Again the alien nodded. "Very much so. But I don't think you will do it. If I did I would already have slipped away during the night."

Cheelo's tone was challenging. "What makes you so sure I won't do it?"

"Because you haven't already. And because doing the illogical thing, the unexpected, is what separates the exceptional individual from the great mass of the hive. Sometimes that individuality is not well regarded. In both our societies, iconoclasts and eccentrics are viewed with great suspicion."

"Well, I've sure as hell always been viewed with suspicion. One day." He considered. "All right. Tomorrow afternoon you go your way and I go mine."

"Agreed." The thranx gestured with both his scri!ber and

with a foothand. "I already have enough material to nourish composition for several years. It wants only some framing, some greater context. If you would consent in the time we have remaining to us to answer a few questions, I will depart your company tomorrow very much content."

"Yeah, sure. But right now let's concentrate on getting away from *here*, okay?" Raising a hand, he pointed upstream. "Let's put some more distance between us and that airborne scanner."

Falling in alongside the human, Desvendapur held his scri!ber out, the better to pick up the biped's voice more clearly. "Please tell me: When you killed your fellow human, what did it feel like?"

Cheelo glanced over sharply, wishing he could read those compound eyes. But they only stared back, glittering in the light that filtered down through the canopy, siliceous gems set in blue-green chitin.

"What the hell kind of question is that?"

"A difficult one," the alien replied. "Easy answers make for weak poetry."

The interrogation, as Cheelo came to think of it, was relentless, continuing all through the remainder of the day and on into the night. What the thranx gained in response to queries that Cheelo felt waned from the irrelevant to the inane he could not imagine, but the alien seemed pleased by every reply, be it fleeting or lengthy. Cheelo endured it all, not really understanding the purpose, knowing that tomorrow he would be free of questions and questioner alike. Free to make the appointment in Golfito that would forever change his life.

He was awakened not by the sun or the chorusing of monkeys, not by demonstrative macaws or buzzing insects, but by a gentle prod to the shoulder.

"Later," he grumbled. "It's too early."

"I agree," came a familiar, soft, gently modulated voice, "but it is necessary. I do not think we are alone any longer."

Cheelo sat up fast, throwing off the blanket, instantly awake. "Your friends, come looking for you?"

"That is the peculiar thing. I see only evidence of passing, and it is not of the sort that traveling thranx would leave behind."

Cheelo frowned. "What sort of evidence?"

"Come and look."

Following the alien into the undergrowth, Cheelo was brought up short by a sight as expected as it was shocking. The pelts had been neatly stretched and hung to dry on racks fashioned of trimmed poles bound together with vine. There were signs of recent cooking as well as places where the soil had been compacted by repeated bootprints. No biologist, he still recognized the skin of the jaguar and the two margays. There was also a lightweight container that, on inspection, proved to be full of feathers plucked from dozens of macaws and other exotic rain forest birds.

Lowering the lid on the container, he found himself scanning the surrounding jungle anxiously.

"What strange human activity is this? Some peculiar ritual the local officials are required to perform?"

"It's a ritual, all right." Cheelo was already backing carefully out of the small, cramped clearing. "But it has nothing to do with local officials. Just the opposite." He nodded toward the forlorn skins drying in the heat of early morning. "This is a poacher camp."

"That is a term I am not familiar with." Scri!ber out, Desvendapur paralleled the human's retreat. He could not keep from turning to look back at the hollow-eyed skins hanging forlornly from their crudely rigged racks.

Cheelo's eyes darted from side to side, tree to bush, as he nervously scrutinized the surrounding forest. "Poachers slip into places like the Reserva to steal whatever they can sell. Rare flowers for orchid collectors, rare bugs for insect collectors, exotic woods for furniture makers, mineral specimens, live birds and monkeys for the underground pet trade." He gestured at the covert encampment. "Bird feathers for decoration, skins for clothing."

"Clothing?" Desvendapur lowered his scri!ber as he looked back once more. "You mean, these people kill animals and strip off their skin so that humans can put them on?"

"That's about right." Alert for ants, snakes, and saw-jawed beetles, Cheelo pushed through a dense overlay of bright green leaves.

"But humans already have skin of their own. Beyond that,

you manufacture what appears to be perfectly adequate artificial outerwear to protect your soft, sensitive exteriors from the elements. Why would anyone choose to wrap themselves in the skin of another living creature? Does the act involve some religious significance?"

"Some people might look at it that way." His mouth widened in a humorless grin. "I've seen rich folk who treat fashion like a religion."

"And they eat the flesh of the dead animal, too." Desvendapur struggled to convey his distaste but was not yet fluent enough to do so, having to resort to gestures to properly express his feelings on the matter.

"No. These people throw the rest of the animal away."

"So each creature is killed only for its epidermis?"

"Right. Unless they sell the teeth and claws, too. You getting enough inspiration out of this?"

"It all sounds vile and primitive. This mystifying mix of the sophisticated and the primal is all part of what marks you as a very peculiar species."

"You won't get no argument from me."

Though Desvendapur had no trouble keeping up, and in fact even with his broken middle leg moved more supplely and easily through the forest than did the biped, he wondered aloud at the human's sudden desire for speed.

"The people running that camp would shoot you just as casually as they would a representative of an endangered species. Poaching in the Reserva is punishable by extensive mindwipe and a program of enforced social correctness. That's something I wouldn't ever submit to, and neither will whoever's smuggling out macaw feathers and cat pelts. We've already got your people looking for us. That's enough."

"Not quite enough."

Cheelo sucked in his breath. He could have kept going, could have tried to go around the muzzle of the weapon pointed in his direction, but that probably would have resulted in a journey of very brief duration.

There were two of them: very short men with very big guns. Their skin was the hue of burnished gold, their long black hair was tied unfashionably back, and they wore jungle mimic suits that allowed them to blend almost seamlessly

into the landscape of bush and vine and tree. The tip of one
rifle hovered uncomfortably close to Cheelo's nose.

He might have tried ducking, or slapping the barrel aside
or grabbing it, or pulling his pistol if his antagonist had been
operating alone. Unfortunately, he was not. His companion
stood nearby but too far away to tackle, his own weapon
held at the ready. Cheelo's fingers fell in the direction of
his concealed holster. The poacher holding the rifle on him
did not smile, did not speak. Only shook his head slowly,
twice. Cheelo's hand drifted prominently away from his own
weapon.

The other poacher stepped forward. After removing the
pistol from its hiding place, he proceeded to pat the stranger
down and remove his pack. Slinging Cheelo's belongings
over one shoulder, he stepped aside to regard the thranx.

"What the hell is this, *cabrón*?"

Cheelo dropped his hands to his sides as the point of the
rifle lowered from his nose to his chest. "That's an alien. A
thranx. Don't you *ninlocos* watch the tridee?"

"Yeah, man." The other poacher laughed once, curtly. "And
we have our own sensalude emporium here, too."

"It's a lonely life," the poacher shouldering Cheelo's backpack told him. "But it was good enough for my ancestors.
Hapec and I do okay." The man's gaze darkened. "As long as
nosybodies leave us alone to do our work." Dropping the
backpack, he knelt and began going through its contents.
After a while he looked up at his companion. "Not a ranger.
Not a scientist, either." He eyed Cheelo speculatively as he
rose. "He's a *pesadito*, a nobody."

"Good." His companion gestured with his rifle. "That
means nobody'll miss him." The man's hard, unyielding gaze
searched beyond the edgy Cheelo. "What do we do with the
big bug?" Using the muzzle of the rifle he prodded Cheelo
ungently in the stomach. "Where'd you get it, man, and what
good is it?"

"Yeah," added his comrade. "What's an ugly alien thing
like that doing in the Reserva, anyway? Does it speak
Terranglo?"

Keeping a careful eye on the rifles, alert for any opportunity, Cheelo thought fast. "No, it doesn't. Something that

looks like that? Are you kidding? It doesn't understand a word we're saying." Turning, he stared daggers at Desvendapur. "Its kind communicate by gestures. See, watch this." Raising both hands, he contorted his fingers strenuously at the thranx.The poet eyed the human's wiggling fingers askance. While he was not entirely sure of the newcomers' intentions, the fact that they were pointing weapons at Cheelo was something other than a testament to peaceful intentions. Their comments about his appearance did not trouble him, but their words, which despite Cheelo's ingenuous denial he understood with considerable faculty, caused him more than a little concern. The human's expressions he still could not read, but his companion's intent was clear enough: It might prove useful for one of them to feign ignorance of ongoing conversation. This he proceeded to do, replying to Cheelo's aimless manipulations with contrastingly eloquent gestures of his own. None of the humans had a clue what he was elucidating, but that was not the point. All that mattered was that they believed he and Cheelo were communicating.

"What did it say?" the nearer of the two poachers demanded to know.

Cheelo turned back to them. "It wants to know your intentions. I'd like to know myself."

"Sure," responded the other poacher agreeably. "First we're going to kill you, and then we're going to kill it, and then we're going to dump you both in the river." The muzzle of the second rifle shifted to point at the silent poet.

"You don't want to do that." Cheelo fought to keep his voice from shaking. He'd never begged anyone for anything before and he wasn't about to start now, but he wasn't ready to die, either.

The nearer poacher glanced over at his colleague and smiled unpleasantly. "Hear that, Hapec? Now he's telling us what we want." The rifle in his hands hummed softly with barely contained death. "We know what we want, man."

"I'm on my way up to Golfito, Costa Rica, to see Rudolf Ehrenhardt," Cheelo declared importantly. "He's expecting me on a matter of real importance."

"Too bad," responded the other poacher mirthlessly. "You're not going to make it."

He had wanted to lose himself, Cheelo reflected, and had done so. If these *ninlocos* didn't recognize the name of Rudolf Ehrenhardt, then he was in the middle of nowhere indeed. In a city, that name would have meant something, would have carried weight. Here, in the vast expanse of the Reserva, it was just a name. Of course, Ehrenhardt could not give a fig whether a hardscrabble lowlife like Cheelo Montoya lived or died. It was nothing to him. The cherished franchise promised to Cheelo would go to someone else. Since this pair did not know the name, it didn't matter anyway.

"Let us go," Cheelo pleaded. The second rifle was now pointed at the thranx, but he doubted he could wrestle the first away from its owner before his companion adjusted his aim and got off a shot. "We won't tell anyone you're around. What you're doing here is nothing to us." He spread his hands imploringly. "You don't understand. I *got* to make this appointment! It's my whole life, man."

"Sure." The poacher opposite laughed darkly. "We'll just trust you. That's how come Hapec and I have managed to bring this off for the past ten years: by trusting people. Now Hapec, he'd just off and shoot you right now. But me, I'm kind of a traditionalist. So I'll let you have any last words." He squinted past the thief, swatting away a hovering botfly. "You can ask the bug if it has any last gestures."

"You *can't* kill me!" Cheelo argued. "If you do, I won't be able to make my appointment!"

"Boy, that's tough. I'm all weepy inside." A finger nudged a trigger booster, and the hum from the rifle rose audibly.

Cheelo thought frantically. "Also, you'll have no way to communicate with the thranx."

The poacher shrugged. "Why would I worry about communicating with a dead alien body?"

"Because—because it's valuable. Probably valuable dead, but a lot more valuable alive."

The two wiry forest pillagers exchanged a glance. "Okay, *cabrón*. Talk. What's valuable about it?"

"You guys collect for the underground animal trade." He jerked a thumb in Desvendapur's direction. "Here's a specimen *nobody's* got, not even your richest, most private collector.

If they'll buy a spotted tapir or a black jaguar, think what they'd pay for a live alien."

"Hey," declared the other poacher, "we know a couple of guys who got a number of aliens in their private zoos, but none of them are intelligent. That'd be pushing the limit."

"Who's going to know?"

On the verge of personal and financial triumph for the first time in his life, Cheelo was not to be denied now. He reasoned with all the skill at his command. Somehow, some way, he was going to make it back to Golfito in time to present the payment to Ehrenhardt. As for the thranx, he had ceased to think of it as a person, as a living, intelligent being like himself. It was a commodity, nothing more. He was bargaining with that commodity for his life.

"The bug doesn't talk, so it can't object. Nobody but your buyer and whoever he trusts will ever see it again. It can survive on terrestrial plants and stuff, so food's no problem. Come on, guys, you're not thinking *big* enough. Imagine what your top buyers would pay for something like this!"

It was evident from his expression that the nearest poacher was giving this heretofore unconsidered prospect careful consideration. Cheelo tried not to give him time to think it through.

"And if nobody bites on the offer, you can still kill us both later."

"We can kill you right now, man." Again the rifle bobbed. "We sell it, we don't need you."

"Sure you do. Because I'm the only one who can communicate with it. If you want it to come along peacefully, you need me to convince it to do so. You could try and catch it, roll it up in a net, fight with it, but it might get injured. Isn't an undamaged specimen always more valuable?"

"You stay right where you are," the poacher warned him. "You move, you try to run, you cross your eyes funny, you're dead. Understand?" Retreating slightly, he and his comrade entered into a conversation marked by intense whispering. Cheelo listened hard but could not make out what they were saying.

Eventually the discussion concluded, and the first poacher

resumed his previous stance. "You still haven't told us what it's doing here."

"It's a naturalist," Cheelo informed them without hesitation. "Part of a small survey and study mission. But it's not authorized. So if this one turns up missing, the others can't go public for help. They're probably searching for him right now."

The other poacher reflexively glanced skyward. "If it's part of some alien science project, why would it come along quietly with us?"

Cheelo took a deep breath. "Because it wants to learn about humans. It trusts me. If I tell it we're going to go someplace where it can learn a lot about humankind, it'll take my word for it. Its cooperation will spare you a lot of trouble. By the time it catches on to what's going on, you'll already have it sold, crated, and shipped. Then it won't matter what it thinks."

Desvendapur listened to this exchange in silence. It was clear that his human companion was making up his story to forestall these two exceedingly antisocial types from shooting them. In this he so far appeared to be succeeding admirably. Meanwhile the poet kept silent and, as Cheelo had explained to the poachers, devoted himself to learning about humankind, a subject that was at present forcefully on display. He did not have to worry about either of the antisocials interpreting his hand movements because they were wholly unfamiliar with their meaning. As for them reading an expression, the inflexibly faced thranx had none to give away his true feelings.

"Why are you offering to be so helpful, *cabrón*?" The nearest poacher was studying him shrewdly. "What makes you think we won't kill you after we've sold the bug?"

Cheelo did his best to affect an air of disinterest. "I'd rather live for as long as possible. Besides, maybe whoever buys it will want to talk to it. That'd mean including me as part of the deal."

"You'd go along with that?" The other poacher was openly dubious.

"Sure, why not? The police are after me anyway."

"No shit? What'd you do, man?"

"Killed a tourist I was skragging. Bad luck, but that's not much of a defense in court. So you see, I'm probably on more wanted lists than you guys."

"And you think that maybe makes us some kind of brothers or something?" the nearer poacher asked.

Cheelo eyed him coldly. "No. If you thought that, I'd think you were pretty stupid."

For the first time, the poacher's expression softened. "You're okay, man. Twitch the wrong way and I'll still blow your stinking head off, but you're okay. All right. Explain to the bug that we're, um, collectors authorized to cull certain Reserva species that have bred to excess. We're carrying weapons to protect ourselves from dangerous forest predators. Tell the bug that we sympathize with its aims, that we've no love for the Reserva rangers who sometimes interfere with our work, and that we're going to take him to a museum." He glanced over at his colleague and chuckled. "A museum where he can learn a *lot* more about humans. Explain that it'll be well looked-after, and that you're coming along to translate. Tell it that after a couple of days we'll bring it back here so it can rejoin its colleagues. It'll have lots of swell stories to tell." He gestured with the rifle. "*Tell* it."

Turning, Cheelo stared into those expressionless compound eyes and began making snaky motions with his fingers. Would the bug understand? It had heard everything, but would it comprehend the need to keep silent and go along with the story? If not, at least one of them wasn't going to leave this patch of rain forest alive, and it would in all likelihood be the one with the fewest appendages.

He need not have worried. Desvendapur understood the situation quite well. He had no intention of speaking out. Clearly his human acquaintance had something in mind, a plan that would result in their salvation from these two virulently antisocial representatives of his own species. What that might be he did not know and could not imagine, unfamiliar as he was with the myriad mysterious workings of the human mind. Meanwhile he was delighted to observe and to listen. Already the experience had generated raw material enough for an entirely new suite, one that he would hopefully live long enough to render.

After several minutes of aimless, meaningless writhing, Cheelo turned around to confront their captors. "It has accepted my explanation and wants to know when we're going to leave."

"Tonight, man." The poacher gestured at his companion. Setting his rifle aside, Hapec moved off into the undergrowth. "I'm not going to tie you up because that might give your bug friend the wrong idea. Just don't do anything stupid."

Cheelo raised both hands, palms facing the poacher. "We've got an arrangement. Why should I risk it? If you can get me out of this hemisphere I'll be better off than I would if we'd never met." His gaze wandered to the patch of forest that had swallowed the other poacher. "We're going to walk at night? A GPS will show you the right way, but it won't light it for you."

The poacher hesitated uncertainly, then laughed anew. "You think we're going to walk? Man, if we had to rely on our feet the rangers would've caught us *years* ago. We've got an airtruck back in the trees. Mesyler two-ton carrying capacity, stealth construction, heat-signature-masked engine. Paid for, too. Not many people know this country like Hapec and me or how to get around the Reserva security net. We're *good*, man. We'll *fly* out. In an hour we'll be at a little place we keep just outside the Reserva boundary. You get to rest there while we put the word out to our regular people that we've got something special for sale." He grinned again. "You didn't think we were going to march you into Cuzco and stick you in a street stall with a price tag on your forehead, did you?"

Cheelo shrugged, trying to appear neither too smart nor unreasonably ignorant. "I don't know you *vatos*. I don't know how you operate. I wasn't assuming anything."

"Good, that's good." Extracting a smokeless stimstick from a shirt pocket, the poacher waited for it to ignite before slipping the aromatic mouthpiece between his lips. "Just don't assume that I won't fry your head the first time you piss me off."

20

While the poacher named Hapec busied himself breaking down the camp and carefully obliterating any memory of its existence, his colleague, whose name was Maruco, kept a watchful eye on their two prisoners. He concentrated his attention on the fidgety Cheelo, allowing Desvendapur to roam freely through the evaporating encampment. Whenever it looked as if the thranx might be wandering too far afield, Maruco directed his human prisoner to "call" the alien back. This Cheelo proceeded to do with much meaningless flailing of fingers. Desvendapur continued to fulfill his part in the masque by waiting for Cheelo to finish each charade before complying, not with the human's gestures, but with the directives the poet had already perfectly comprehended.

In this manner the two poachers remained ignorant of the alien's cognizance. Had Desvendapur possessed a weapon, he could simply have shot both of them. But all he had was the small cutting tool in his improvised survival kit. Granted complete surprise, he might have employed it successfully to incapacitate one of the two antisocials, but not both of them. They were too lively, too alert, too attuned to a life of imminent threat and danger. Additionally, while not directly suspicious of the alien in their midst, neither were they especially comfortable in the thranx's presence. Consequently, he was never able to get within a few meters of either of them before they began acting uneasy.

One such experimental advance caused Maruco to comment. "Tell the bug to keep its distance, man. God, but it's repulsive! Smells good, though. Myself, I think you're personally bent, but your suggestion is straight: Somebody *will* pay plenty for it." He shrugged, holding his rifle casually—

though not casually enough. "Me, I wouldn't keep another intelligence in captivity, but I never understood the people who do keep animals. Hapec and I, we don't even keep monkeys."

"Why do you guys stick with this?" Cheelo was genuinely curious. His attention wandered without ever entirely ignoring the poacher's weapon. Given a reasonable chance of success, he'd make a grab for it. Such an opportunity had not yet presented itself. "Rangers and security scanners must be all over the Reserva. Is poaching a few skins and feathers that profitable?"

"Hapec and me, we do all right. But it's more than that. Our ancestors lived free here, hunting and fishing all over this country. They took what they wanted, when they needed it. When the Reserva was drawn up and its boundaries formalized, everybody who lived here was kicked out and resettled on the borders of their former homelands. All in the name of preserving a lousy bunch of plants and animals and a natural CO_2 exchanger for the atmosphere. Like the planet was going to run short on oxygen, anyway." His tone was bitter. "This is Hapec's and my way of getting a little back, of reasserting our ancestral claims to this land."

Cheelo nodded somberly. "I can understand that." Privately he thought the poacher's explanation was a facile rationalization heavily layered with pretentious bullshit. Their two captors kept slipping into the Reserva not to honor their ancestors but because they were making a nice, cushy, illicit living, and for no other reason. Taking revenge for some long-forgotten, sketchily remembered great-grandpa had nothing to do with it. He'd known small-time *ninlocos* like Hapec and Maruco all his life, had grown up with them. Maybe it made them feel a little better to conduct their miserable, self-serving offenses under the cover of an agreeable fiction. Cheelo Montoya didn't buy it for a minute. What the ingenuous insectile in his company thought of the situation he couldn't imagine. Nor could he find out if he wanted to, at least not for a while. To ensure that Cheelo's captors kept him alive it was necessary for the bug to continue to play mute.

Rustling noises rose from behind the encampment, back among the denser undergrowth. Cheelo strained to see. "So, this little place of yours: Where is it?"

"You'll see soon enough." As Maruco spoke, his partner began to remove from their stretchers and carefully fold the partially cured jaguar and margay pelts. When he had finished with that, he resumed breaking camp, reducing everything to a pile of poles, bindings, and disparate organic waste. This was then scattered among the concealing brush, to decay and disintegrate, along with any indication that people had ever spent any time at this particular spot.

"Must be rough." Cheelo was under no illusion that his attempts at casual conversation would ingratiate him with their captors, but in lieu of any alternative activity, it would have to suffice. "Having to tear down and make a new camp every time you come into the Reserva."

Maruco was dismissive. "Gets easier with practice. You learn what trees make the best hide stretchers, what vines are the most supple and easiest to work. Why do you give a damn?" He grinned nastily. "Thinking of going into competition?"

"Not me." Cheelo shook his head. "I'm a city boy."

"I figured. You skin different game."

As soon as the airtruck was loaded, the two captives were herded on board. Cheelo found nothing exceptional about the vehicle. He'd seen camouflaged stealth transport before. But Desvendapur was fascinated. It was the first complex piece of purely human technology he had encountered in person, and every facet of it, from the layout of the instrumentation to the design of the climate-controlled interior, was new to him. There was, of course, no place for him to sit down. For thranx purposes, the floor was more accommodating than the seats designed for humans. He chose to stand, balancing himself as the vehicle lifted in virtual silence from its hiding place to rise into the canopy.

Though it took four times as long as a straight flight would have, Maruco followed a course that kept them below spreading crests of the forest emergents, utilizing the canopy for cover whenever possible and only rising above it when the airtruck threatened to leave too expansive a path of destruction in the form of broken branches and snapped lianas in its wake. From time to time the closely entangled rain forest gave way to meandering streams and the occasional *cocha* that allowed him to fly low at higher speeds without leaving a trail behind.

Only when the first foothills hove into view among the mists and low-hanging clouds was Cheelo moved to comment. "I thought you said this place of yours was just outside the Reserva?"

"It is." Maruco spoke without turning while his partner kept a watchful eye and the muzzle of a rifle trained on their human captive. "If you're familiar with the area, then you know the western border of the Reserva runs right up this side of the Andes."

Cheelo watched the foothills give way rapidly to steep, green-shrouded slopes. "I know. I just assumed your place would be down low, where you could hide it in the trees."

Maruco smiled knowingly as the airtruck, following a gorge, commenced a steady climb. "That's what any rangers patrolling the fringes would think. So we set ourselves up right out in the open, up where it's barren and cold and uncomfortable. What stupid *chingóns* would stick themselves out on a treeless ridge for everybody to see? Not anybody running a poaching operation, right?"

"We've never had any trouble," Hapec chipped in. "Nobody checks on us or our little shack." He revealed a mouthful of gleaming, artificial, ceramic teeth. Light gold was currently a fashionable dental tint. "Anybody asks, we tell 'em we're running a private bird-watching operation."

"It's not a whole lie." Maruco was in a jovial mood. "We do watch birds. And if they're rare enough, we also snare and sell 'em."

As the airtruck entered the zone of cloud forest and the permanent mists that cloaked the mountainsides in lugubriously wandering blankets of gray and white, the poacher switched from manual to instrument driving. Earlier, the dehumidifier had shut down and the vehicle's internal climate control had switched over from cool to heat. Meanwhile Cheelo continued the meaningless banter that fooled no one. If provoked, either of the two poachers would as soon shoot him as spit on him. He knew it, and he knew they knew he knew it. But it was better than dead silence or trading insults. At least he might learn something.

Desvendapur certainly was. Not only the journey but the edgy conversation taking place between the three humans continued to provide him with an unbridled flow of suggestion, stimulation, and inspiration. Unable to freely utilize his scri!ber for fear that their captors might appropriate it, he concentrated on observing and remembering all that he could. Tenseness and barely concealed agitation were racial characteristics his kind had abandoned in favor of polite communion hundreds of years ago. In a highly organized society that chose to dwell underground in eternally close quarters, courtesy and politeness were not merely encouraged, they were an absolute necessity.

Humans, apparently, fought and argued at the slightest provocation. The energy they expended in such recurrent confrontations was breathtaking to behold: wasteful, but fascinating. It seemed they had stamina to spare. The most excitable thranx was more circumspect and conservative. The knowledge that they intended to sell him into some kind of captivity did not engage him half so much as their constant bickering. Captivity, if it occurred, would not be so bad. It would allow him to continue studying humankind at close quarters. He doubted, however, that his troubled human companion felt similarly.

It was him these antisocial humans wanted, not Cheelo Montoya. Neither did the poet have further need for the self-confessed thief. More than once Desvendapur thought about speaking up, revealing to the two poachers his fluency in their language. The only reason he did not was because he knew it would mean the death of his companion. While that would be, based on what he knew of Cheelo and what the man had told him, small loss to the species, it contravened any number of thranx rules of conduct. Recreant that he was, Desvendapur was not prepared to break with custom and culture to that extent. At least, not yet. For the moment it was more amusing to play the game, to listen to the new humans make comments about him convinced that he understood nothing of what they were saying.

After a substantial interval the airtruck rose out of the clouds and into sunshine so bright and unfiltered it was painful. In the pure, cerulean distance rose peaks that effortlessly crested five thousand meters. Just ahead, a stony, intermittently green plateau rolled off to the west: hills standing atop mountains. The only signs of habitation were a few detached farmhouses and long stretches of mountainside covered with phototropic sheeting to protect the potatoes and other crops thriving beneath.

On the eastern edge of a high ridge stood a modest, unspectacular domicile attached by a pedestrian corridor to a slightly larger structure. A roll-up door retracted as the airtruck approached. Guiding the vehicle in manually—use of its automatic docking system ran the risk of sending out faint but detectable signals curious rangers might pick up—Maruco brought it to a stop in the exact center of the garage when the appropriate telltale on the truck's console turned green. A flip of one switch and the vehicle settled gently to the smooth, impervious floor. The door rolled noisily shut behind them as the structure's internal heating panels roared to life.

Flanking their captives, the poachers led them through the access corridor to the main building, which was sparsely but comfortably furnished. Halfway there Hapec frowned at the alien.

"What's the matter with it?" He nodded pointedly.

Cheelo, who had been paying little attention to the thranx as he tried to memorize every detail of their prison, now turned to see that the bug was quivering. It took him only a moment to realize what was happening.

"He's cold."

"Cold?" Maruco let out a snort of disbelief as they passed a wall readout. "It's twenty-three in here."

"That's too cold for thranx. It told me it found the rain forest brisk. And it's much too dry in here. It needs at least ninety percent humidity and more like thirty-three, thirty-four degrees to be really comfortable."

"Shit!" Hapec muttered. "*I'll* die."

"No you won't. But it's liable to."

Grumbling under his breath, the other poacher addressed the house system, directing it to ratchet the interior climate up to something approaching the reported thranx minimum level of comfort.

"Maruco!" His companion protested as both the humidity and the temperature began to climb.

"Quit your bitching," the smaller of the two poachers snapped. "It's only for a little while. Couple of days, until we can finalize a deal. Shouldn't take any longer, not for something as special as this." He smiled fatuously at Desvendapur. "You're going to make us rich, you sickening pile of legs and feelers. So be comfortable for a while. We'll live with it." The poet regarded the antisocial human blankly and with perfect comprehension.

"And now you," the poacher informed his other captive coldly, "get tied up."

"You can't do that," Cheelo protested. "It'll . . . it will upset the alien. It's convinced you two are friendlies. Necklace me and you'll unsettle it."

"So let it be unsettled. If we have to, we'll tie it up as well." Hapec was already removing fasteners from a drawer.

"You could lose it. It could hurt itself struggling to get free, or even choke to death."

"We'll take the chance." Both poachers were moving toward the apprehensive Cheelo, Maruco with a rifle still aimed at him. "If it protests, we can always untie you. Don't make this hard for us, or for you."

"Yeah," Hapec warned him. "Consider yourself lucky. By rights, the ants ought to be scooping out the last of your eyeballs right now."

Having no choice in the matter, Cheelo submitted to having the plastic restraints secured around his wrists and ankles. When the poachers judged them tight enough, Maruco removed the safety strips and the plastic sealed itself, melt-welding shut at the joints. Glancing behind him, the poacher noted the alien's lack of reaction.

"Doesn't look like your bug buddy is too upset. Make it easy on yourself. Tell it this is all part of some weird human welcoming ritual."

"Tell it yourself," Cheelo spat, his anger making him thoughtless.

Hapec's hand started to come up, but he was restrained by his companion. "Don't give him any excuses. And we really don't want to upset our prize pretty if we can avoid it." Leaning close, Maruco stared hard into the snugly manacled thief's eyes. "You, on the other hand, I don't mind upsetting. Behave yourself, and you'll end up with a nice, free, private suborbital ride. Make trouble and we'll just have to sell the bug without an interpreter." Straightening, he turned to regard the thranx, which was presently engaged in a detailed examination of the kitchen facilities.

"What does it eat? Is it hungry?"

Subdued and unhappy, Cheelo replied in a reluctant mumble. "It's strictly vegetarian: hates the sight of meat. It can digest a lot of terrestrial plants. I don't know what kind are the most nourishing. I'll have to ask it." He held up his bound wrists. "Of course, I can't talk to it with my hands tied."

Maruco's expression twisted. It was clear neither poacher had thought of that when they'd secured him. With a knife, he slit the wrist bindings. "Okay, but as soon as you get the answers we need, you get tied up again. And no tricks."

Cheelo spread his palms wide. "What am I going to do? Tell it to call the rangers? Remember, it's here covertly, too." Turning his attention to Desvendapur, he began an elaborate wiggling and twisting of his fingers.

The poet paid dutiful attention to these meaningless gestures before replying with truhand and foothand gesticulations of his own. What he said with his hands was that Cheelo was a *pontik*, a particularly slow and stupid kind of grub. The two antisocials were *pepontiks*, or *pre-pontiks*, an even lower class of intelligence not bright enough to be classified as stupid. None of the three humans had the slightest idea what his complex gestures meant, of course, but it amused him to respond so.

Determining how best to reply not to Cheelo's meaningless inquiry but to the antisocial's actual query was a bigger problem. Since he could not speak, he would have to establish his dietary requirements in some other fashion. Turning away, he embarked on an up-close examination of the sink, leaving Cheelo to fend for explanations himself.

Deprived of support, Montoya improvised. "It's not hungry right now, and when it's not hungry it doesn't like to talk about food."

Maruco grunted. "We'll thaw out a selection of fruits and

vegetables. It can pick out what it wants or needs. Meanwhile, I've got a sale to advertise. Hapec, you unload the truck." His partner nodded and headed for the access corridor that linked the two main buildings. The other poacher's gaze narrowed as he considered his one bound prisoner. "You bounce around enough to make me think you're trying to slip out of those seals, and I'll put a couple of 'em over your face." His smirk widened. "You can tell the bug it's part of the ritual." He glanced in Desvendapur's direction.

"I'm not going to check its pack, or container, or whatever that thing is riding on its back, because I don't want to upset it. I know it's not carrying any weapons because if it was it would have tried using them by now."

Cheelo nodded. "Like I told you: It was doing research. That's why it has cooperated so far. It's not armed." This, insofar as Cheelo knew, was the actual truth.

"Fine. We'll leave it at that—for now, anyway." Reaching down, the poacher slapped another self-sealing strap on the other man's wrists. In seconds they were tightly bound again. "That's so you can't 'talk' to it behind my back while I'm working."

Turning, he walked to a desk near the rear of the room and settled himself into a chair. Within minutes he was communicating with faraway places and the representatives of an orderly succession of individuals whose ethics were as impoverished as their bank accounts were expansive.

While a helpless Cheelo sat and fumed silently, the ever-inquisitive Desvendapur continued his exploration of the poachers' quarters. The temperature and humidity had risen to levels the poet found tolerable, if not entirely comfortable, and he was thoroughly enjoying a respite that he knew could not last. As he continued his examination of the room and its contents, Cheelo's expression underwent an extraordinary succession of contortions. None of them held any meaning for the poet, though it was clear by their frequency and urgency that the human was urging him to do something.

Desvendapur could not let himself be sold, of course. If no alternative presented itself, he was convinced that he could survive and even thrive in human captivity. But it was not the preferred option for the future. In human captivity, his performances would not be properly appreciated. He needed a thranx audience. Therefore, if possible, he had to find a way to return to the colony. Unable to see a way clear to doing that himself, he realized he would need Cheelo's assistance. That did not mean it was necessary to rush matters, and he had no intention of doing so. While the two antisocial humans desired to profit from his existence, Desvendapur suspected they would not hesitate to kill him if they felt sufficiently threatened. Surely Cheelo understood that.

Hapec soon returned from unloading and stabilizing the airtruck. Establishing himself in the kitchen area while his partner continued his steady stream of secured-transmission intercontinental conversation, the other poacher began meal preparations. For the moment, both captives found themselves largely, though never entirely, ignored.

Faced with a situation for which a lifetime of study and learning had not prepared him, Desvendapur was compelled to fall back on that one aspect of his personality that had never failed him: his imagination. As he pursued his examination of the domicile, he proceeded to lay out in his mind a sequence of actions in much the same way he would design an extended recitation, complete with appropriate revisions and adjustments.

None of this was apparent to the anxious Cheelo, who grew progressively more distraught in his bonds. Thanks to some fast thinking he had managed to buy some time, but, unlike a new communicator or tridee subscription, it was not guaranteed: There was no return policy in place in the event of dissatisfaction. The two poachers were not deep thinkers. Any little thing, any irritation of the moment or insignificant occurrence, might set them off. In that event he knew they might cast careful consideration and practicalities to the tepid wind that seeped upward from the cloud forest below, and blow his head off. He knew this because he and they were of a kind, representatives of that same subspecies of humanity that tends to *react* to awkward circumstance as opposed to thinking about it. Maruco and Hapec were too much like him for him to be comfortable around them. The devil he knew was himself.

Convinced he was at least not in imminent danger of being

executed, he switched from watching them to tracking the movements of the thranx. It was impossible to know what the alien was thinking since he could not talk to it without giving away the fact that it understood Terranglo. He had to content himself with imagining. What did it make of all this? Did it care what happened to him? Cheelo knew he didn't care what happened to *it*, but right now his future prospects rested entirely with the many-legged insectoid. His life was in the bug's hands—all four of them.

If it forgot the scenario, if it deviated from the play and spoke aloud, then the poachers would quickly realize that they had no need of a translator. He would be rendered instantly extraneous. There were many steep precipices just east of the prefab abode into which a body could be thrown to be swallowed forever by rain forest, gully, and cloud. Silently he importuned the thranx to keep silent. Even if they found themselves sold, at least they would still be alive. Future prospects seemed considerably more promising when viewed from a perspective of abiding survival. Who could tell? With luck he might be able to persuade their buyers to make a brief stopover in Golfito.

He tried to cheer himself up. If the poachers and the bug just kept their heads this wouldn't turn out so bad. Didn't he need to hide out for a while? Wasn't that what he was doing down in the untrammeled rain forest in the first place? What better place to lie low—after he had finalized arrangements for his future with Ehrenhardt, of course—than the private zoo or collection of some incredibly rich patron who had just made a very expensive and very illegitimate purchase? As he had so many times in his desperate, frenetic life, he set about trying to mentally arrange events to his advantage. Even the bug was cooperating, maintaining silence while pretending to examine every object within the building.

He was giving Desvendapur too much credit. The thranx was not pretending. While the poachers ignored him, he took the time to study each individual example of human manufacture in great detail, paying particular attention to how the two humans operated their manifold devices. Once, the one called Hapec caught the thranx peering over his shoulder as he ran the cooker. The human gestured clumsily and ordered him to step farther back. Maintaining the fiction that he could not understand the man's speech, the poet obediently interpreted the gestures and moved away.

By mealtime Cheelo, though still nervous and worried about the poachers' state of mind, had resigned himself to his captivity. He cooperated while Hapec fed him listlessly, and he watched with as much interest as the poachers while Desvendapur picked through the assortment of rehydrated fruits and vegetables he was offered. When their prize captive seemed satisfied, the two men sat down to their own meal. Dinnertime conversation on their part consisted of coarse jokes, inconsequential natterings, and an impassioned discussion of how much money they were going to clear for selling the only representative of a recently contacted intelligent species into involuntary captivity. While salt, pepper, and hot sauce played a part in their dining, their conversation was seasoned by neither ethics nor morals.

When Desvendapur had eaten his fill, he stepped back from the exotic but nutritious banquet his captors had laid out before him, ambled over to a far corner, and casually picked up one of their rifles, cradling the lethal device in his right truhand and foothand. It took a moment before Hapec noticed the alien aiming the muzzle of the weapon at him.

"Hey. Uh, hey, Maruco!" The human's lower jaw descended, and his mouth remained open to no apparent purpose.

"Shit!" His eyes darting rapidly back and forth between his two prisoners, the other poacher pushed carefully away from the table. "Cheelo! Man, you tell the bug to put that *down*. It's holding a full charge, and the safety is off. Tell it it's liable to hurt itself. What's it doing, anyway? We're its friends, helping it to see and study more of our world. Go on, man: Remind it!"

"I can't tell him anything," Cheelo replied tersely. "My hands, remember?"

This time Maruco didn't hesitate. Rising slowly from his chair and keeping his eyes on the enigmatic thranx, he nervously edged his way over to where his other prisoner was secured. Using his knife, he once again released the captive's arms.

A relieved Cheelo promptly began rubbing circulation back into his wrists. "Hey, what about my legs?"

"What about your legs?" the poacher growled. "You don't talk to it with your feet."

"Free his legs." Desvendapur gestured with the rifle. Designed for thicker-digited, clumsier human hands, the weapon felt light in his arms. Manipulation and activation would be a simple matter.

"Sure, just be careful with that . . ." Maruco paused, the knife halting in midswipe, as he stared wide-eyed at the alien. *"Son-of-a-bitch-whore!"*

"You can talk!" Both poachers were gazing in open-mouthed disbelief at the suddenly voluble alien in their midst.

"Not very well, but my fluency is improving with practice. His legs?" Again the rifle moved.

Slowly, the poacher knelt and ran the blade across the restraining plastic. With a curt gasp of relief, Cheelo kicked his feet apart.

A thranx did not need to look out of the corner of its eyes to see action transpiring off to one side. Multiple lenses scanned a much wider field than human eyes could see, allowing for considerably greater peripheral vision. He shifted the tip of the weapon significantly in the direction of the larger human, who had risen and taken a step in the direction of the other gun.

"Although I am not familiar with the kind of result it produces, I believe I know how this weapon operates. I also believe that you should move the other way and stand alongside your friend."

"It's bluffing." Maruco began edging away from Cheelo, who had risen from the chair where he had been imprisoned and was now stomping about in an attempt to get circulation flowing to his feet again. "It doesn't know how to fire the gun."

"Yeah?" Keeping his hands in plain sight, Hapec slowly and carefully came around behind the table to join his colleague. "Then *you* go pick the other one up."

As he studied the weapon-wielding bug, Maruco spread his hands innocently wide, ignorant of the fact that the sub-

ject of his supplication did not know the meaning of the
gesture.

"Okay, so you can talk. There's no need for this. We mean
you no harm." Smiling ingratiatingly, he nodded at the now-
standing Cheelo. "Our tying him up is just part of a special
greeting and guest ritual."

"No it isn't," Desvendapur responded in his whispery but
increasingly articulate Terranglo. "You forget that while I did
not speak, I could listen. I have heard and understood everything that has been said since you first appeared before us in
the forest. I know that you meant to kill us until Cheelo convinced you to sell us instead." He did not need to be familiar
with the extraordinary diversity of human facial expression
to interpret the one that now dominated the muscles of the
poachers' countenances.

Still rubbing his wrists and flicking out his feet to stimulate
the long-restrained muscles, Cheelo walked over to his alien
companion. Having resigned himself to being sold as part of
a package deal, he now found himself in a position he thought
not to experience again for some time.

"You're full of surprises, bug."

The heart-shaped head and its great golden eyes turned
toward him. "My name is Desvendapur."

"Ay, right." He reached out with both hands. "I'll take that
now. Not that I don't think you can use it, but I'm probably a
better shot than you." As the poet complaisantly handed over
the weapon, Cheelo added by way of afterthought, "You *do*
know how to use it, don't you? You weren't bluffing?"

"Oh, I'm sure I could have activated it. The firing mechanism is simple, and although the weapon is designed for
human arms and hands, it fits well enough in mine. I would
never have done so, of course."

"What's that?" Maruco strained to make certain he had
heard properly.

"Although we have had to fight to defend ourselves in the
past, and have evolved from primitive ancestors who battled
constantly among themselves, we have become a peaceful
species." Antennae bobbed elaborately. "I could never have
shot you unless my life was directly threatened."

"It was threatened!" Cheelo reminded him.

The thranx shook its head, further surprising the poachers by its mastery and utilization of a common human gesture. "My freedom of movement was at risk, not my life. Although my preference is to return to the colony, I could have tolerated being transported to another part of your planet, could have lost myself in exposure to an entirely new environment and surroundings."

Maruco blinked. "Then why did you pick up the gun in the first place?"

"As I said, because for many reasons I would prefer to return to the hive. Also because my life and freedom of movement were not the only ones at stake." Both antennae dipped in Cheelo's direction.

A welter of conflicting emotion surged to the fore within the thief as the thranx's words sank in. It didn't object to being sold. It had picked up the rifle for his sake as much as for its own. Confronted by the rara avis of actual, genuine emotion, he had no idea how to respond, did not know what to say.

Screw it.

"Come on, Deswhel—Desvencrapur. We're outta here." With the rifle, he gestured at Maruco. "I want the airtruck. I told you, I've got an appointment to keep. If coaxed right, I think that truck'll make it all the way up to the isthmus."

Keeping his hands in plain sight, the angry poacher nodded in the direction of the accessway that connected the ridge-top living quarters to the shop and garage. "You'll leave us marooned here."

"Bullshit." Cheelo laughed, enjoying the turn of events fully. "Your buyers are going to come running, and they'll be bringing their own transportation." He grinned broadly. "Of course, they're not gonna be real happy with you when they find out that the prize you offered them decided not to hang around. Now, what about that truck?"

"It's an open design," Hapec told him. "Take it. I just have to unlock the navigation system."

"Like hell. All you have to do is activate the cencomp. You think I'm gonna give you a chance to program the engine for self-destruct? D'you think I was born dumb, like you two?" Maruco's expression tightened, but the poacher said nothing.

"Let's go." Cheelo gestured with the muzzle. "Despindo—Des, you follow me. We'll get as close to this colony of yours as you think we safely can, and I'll drop you there."

"Colony?" Maruco's small black eyes blinked. "What colony?"

Cheelo ignored him, waiting for the thranx's reply.

"Among my people I am guilty of the most egregious antisocial activity. They would confine me until I could be sent offworld for more formal punishment. So if you do not object, Cheelo Montoya, I would rather continue to travel in your company. For a little while longer, at least."

"No can do, big-eyes. This boy's jungle jaunt is over. I got to fly a long ways now, or I'm gonna be late for the dance. Besides, don't you have your poems, your compositions, to perform for your fellow bugs?"

The blue-green head swayed gently from side to side. "Insufficiently mitigating circumstances, I am afraid. I would far rather continue my ruminations, would much prefer to seek additional inspiration. Some day, of course, I will reveal them to all the hives. But not yet." Overhead lighting sparkled in his eyes, imparting to the multiple lenses a muted crystalline gleam. "There is still so much more I wish to do."

"Have it your way." An indifferent Cheelo gestured again with the rifle. Plenty of time to decide what to do with the bug once they were safely back down in the rain forest. As the two poachers stumbled off ahead of him, Maruco looked back over his shoulder.

"What were you saying about a colony? There's a whole colony of 'em here on Earth? Down in the Reserva? I never heard nothing about anything like that."

"Shut your face and keep moving. I know the truck's coded, so you're going to start it for me."

"Then it's true! There's an alien outpost in the Reserva that's being kept from the public." Rising excitement dominated the poacher's voice. "And you didn't say outpost; you said colony." He looked over at his partner. "This might be the biggest secret on the planet. Any one of the fifty big media groups would pay a lifetime annuity for that kind of information. It's worth a helluva lot more than one live bug." Once more he looked back at the stony-faced Cheelo.

"What do you say, *vato*? We've got the facilities here for communicating worldwide while hiding the source of the signal. We sell the information to the highest bidder and split it three ways. Nobody gets sold; nobody gets hurt. Plenty credit for everybody." When Cheelo failed to respond, Maruco's agitation increased. "Hell, we don't need *you* to sell it. But the Reserva's a big place, and this colony or base or whatever it is must be really well hid. Hapec and I are down there a lot, and we've sure never suspected anything like this was there. *You* know where it is. Whatever media group buys in ain't going to want to go hunting for the place. They'll want to set down right on top of it, before some competitor gets wind of what's going on." His voice fell slightly. "You *do* know where it is?"

"Pretty much," Cheelo lied. "Close enough so that anybody interested could find it within a week."

"Well come on then, man! Don't waft this off. We can be partners. All of us, we'll be rich."

"First you were going to kill me," Cheelo reminded him, his tone chilly. "Then you were going to sell me as a talking accessory to a bug."

"Heyyy," the poacher demurred, "it was nothing *personal*." They were approaching the garage. "That was just business. You're a businessman, *chingón*. That was business then; this is business now. You need our business contacts; we need what you know."

Cheelo found himself growing confused. The poacher's insinuating spiel was beguiling. "What about the bu—about Des. He may be an outcast among his own people, but he'd never agree to the premature exposure of the colony."

"*Chinga* the bug," Maruco snapped. "If it has a problem with this, blow its stinking guts out. We don't need it no more. What do you care? It's just a big, ugly, alien *bug*."

"It's intelligent. Probably more so than either of you two. Probably . . . probably more than me. It's . . . it's an artist."

Maruco laughed madly as they entered the garage. The airtruck rested where it had been parked, sleek and silent, its propulsion system fully recharged and awaiting only coded reactivation. With it at his disposal Cheelo knew he could reach Golfito. Or at least Gatun, where he had friends and could safely refuel.

His finger tightened imperceptibly on the rifle's trigger. "It's not funny. I used to think it was, but I've changed my mind. So now what the hell am I supposed to do? Trust you?"

"Yeah, you can trust us. Can't he, Hapec?"

"Sure. Why should we do anything? We need you to show the site to whoever buys the story," the other poacher observed. As he spoke, he was drifting to his left, toward a wall lined with tools.

"Don't even think about it." The muzzle of the rifle flicked sideways so that it was aimed straight at the bigger man's back. As soon as it shifted away from him, Maruco whirled. A compact, high-strung bundle of muscle and furious energy, he threw himself at Cheelo.

21

As he tried to bring the rifle around to bear on his attacker, Cheelo's finger contracted reflexively on the trigger. A tiny, very intense, and highly localized sonic boom echoed through the building. Hapec gazed down in disbelief at the small but lethal hole that the sonic burst had punched through him from stomach to spine. Even as he clasped both hands over the perforation, blood began to gush forth between his fingers. Mouth gaping in a silent "O" of surprise, he staggered toward the two combatants before sinking to his knees and then toppling languidly forward, like a brown iceberg calving from the face of a glacier, to the floor of the garage.

Maruco managed to grab the muzzle of the rifle before Cheelo could bring it around for a second shot. They struggled violently and in complete silence for possession of the weapon—until a second boom rattled the diminutive one-way windows that lined the walls of the enclosure.

Thorax pumping, Desvendapur pressed back against the airtruck and contemplated the bloody panorama spread out before him. Two humans lay dead on the floor, their body fluids leaking from their ruptured circulatory systems. Only one remained standing, the weapon dangling loosely from a hand. Heart pounding, chest heaving, Cheelo stood staring down at the body of Maruco lying at his feet like a broken doll.

Desvendapur had of course read of such violence, and he knew of it from the evidence of his own family history. Here was the sort of confrontation that harked back to the time when the AAnn had attacked Paszex and wiped out most of his ancestors. But despite holding the weapon earlier himself he had not really expected to have to use it. This was the first time he had ever witnessed such savagery in person. "This—this is barbaric! A terrible thing!" Wonderful new phrases were already evolving unbidden in his brain, refusing to be ignored.

Cheelo took a deep breath. "It sure is. Now we'll never learn the activation code for the truck. We're stuck."

The poet's eyes rose to fix the surviving biped in their multilenticular stare. "I don't mean that. I mean that two sapient beings are dead."

Cheelo pushed out his lower lip. "Nothing terrible about that. Not as far as I'm concerned." His voice rose in protest. "Hey, you think I *wanted* to shoot them?" Desvendapur took a wary step in the direction of the accessway. "Take it easy. The conversation got kind of tense, I got a little confused, and they tried to jump me." When the alien did not respond, Cheelo became upset. "Look, I'm telling you the truth. They thought I was going to shoot them after they activated the truck. I wasn't going to. Sure, I *wanted* to, but I was going to leave them alive. All I wanted was out of here so I could get to my meeting. And before you go getting all bent out of joint, remember that they'd figured it out, about your being from a colony and all. If they'd been left here they still could've sold that information. Look at it like this: I had to shoot them to protect your people down in the Reserva."

"They might have tried to persuade others to go looking for the hive, but without specific coordinates they would never have found it. Never." Desvendapur continued to eye the biped accusingly, or at least in a manner that the defensive Cheelo continued to interpret as accusing.

"It doesn't matter," Cheelo finally declared curtly. "They're dead and we're not. Believe me, it's no loss to the species."

"The death of any sapient is a loss."

His human companion uttered several sharply intoned words whose meaning the thranx did not recognize. "I don't know about species wide, but there are sure some variations in our individual values." With the muzzle of the rifle he roughly nudged the corpse at his feet. Maruco the poacher did not move and would not poach again.

Walking over to the tool rack, Cheelo snapped the rifle into an empty charging cradle and turned to ponder the silent airtruck. "I can try to start this big bastard up, but unless these guys were completely confident in their isolation here, or were total idiots, there are probably about two million possible key codes." His gaze rose to the nearest of the one-way windows. "You saw the country around here on the way in. This place is really isolated. There's nothing nearby but some automated farming projects. We can try for one."

"I do not think so." Desvendapur argued.

"Why not?" His respiration slowly returning to normal, Cheelo stared at the thranx.

"While you were fighting with our captors I was hearing voices from their communicator. Someone with an especially authoritative voice was demanding to know where the one called Maruco had gone. When no response was forthcoming, the transmission was terminated with the words 'See you soon you little shit.' While I do not interpret that to mean that the speaker's appearance is imminent, it struck me as a promise to arrive in a finite period of time."

"You're right. Dammit!" Cheelo thought furiously. "I forgot about their bug buyers. We'd better not be around when they show up." A look of distaste on his face, he calmly contemplated the human debris staining the floor. "Help me with these two." Moving off, he searched for the manual door opener he knew had to exist.

"What are we going to do? Carry out some kind of formal burial ritual?" Despite his dismay at the carnage that had occurred, it would not prevent the poet from recording the details of what promised to be a particularly fascinating human rite.

"More like an informal one." Locating a control panel, Cheelo brushed touchplates, activating lights, servos, and an automatic washer before finding the one that operated the garage door. Cold, intensely dry air swept in from outside as the barrier rattled upward.

Working together, they hauled the bodies of the two poachers one at a time to the rim of the nearest obliging precipice and shoved them over the edge, watching as each limp lump of dead meat rolled and bumped its way into cloud-swathed oblivion. Desvendapur was disappointed by the lack of ceremony, having anticipated a certain amount of exotic alien chanting or dancing. But the biped who had become his companion mouthed only a few words, and none of them struck the poet as especially complimentary to or respectful of the deceased.

That onerous duty done, they returned to the deserted outpost where Desvendapur did his best to assist the human in cleansing the garage floor of blood. When he was satisfied, Cheelo stepped back to survey their work, wiping sweat from his forehead. Though the exudation of clear fluid by the biped's body as a means of maintaining its internal temperature was a process Desvendapur had already observed in the forest, he never ceased to be captivated by it.

"There!" Cheelo sighed tiredly. "When their buyers arrive, they won't know where their favorite *ninlocos* have hopped off to. They'll see that the airtruck is still here—we can't do anything about that—but that won't automatically lead them to assume that something's happened to them. They'll start a search, but one that's considered and unhurried. By the time they find the bodies, *if* they find the bodies, and figure out that maybe they ought to be looking for somebody like us—or like me, anyway—we'll both be safe and out of sight back down in the Reserva. I know if I follow the river it'll take me into Sintuya, where I can book a flight back to Lima. I still have enough time to make it to Golfito." Walking back to the wall, he yanked the sonic rifle free from the charging bracket.

"Expensive little toy, this." He rotated the sophisticated weapon in his hands. "So our trip up here wasn't a total loss. Let's help ourselves to the pantry and get out of here before nanny shows up."

"I cannot."

Cheelo blinked at the alien. "What d'you mean, 'you cannot'? You sure as hell can't stay here." He indicated a window that revealed the barren plateau outside. "Whoever comes looking for those two *ninlocos* won't hesitate about shoving you in a cage." Nobody'd make any money off it, either, he reflected.

"I will explain matters to them. That I wish to study them." Antennae bobbed. "Perhaps a mutual accommodation can be reached."

"You can take your goddamn studying for inspiration

and . . . !" Cheelo calmed himself, remembering that the visibly flinching thranx was sensitive to the volume of the booming human voice. "You don't understand, Des. These people who are coming, they're gonna be nervous and on edge because they're unable to contact their two guys here. They'll come in fast and quiet, and if the first thing they see is a giant, big-eyed bug wandering around loose instead of properly caged up, they might not stop to smell the roses—or the alien that smells like one. They're liable to blast you into half a dozen pieces before you get the chance to 'explain matters' to them."

"They might not shoot first," Desvendapur argued.

"No, that's right. They might not." He pushed past the thranx, striding toward the corridor that led to the outpost's living quarters. "I'm going to start packing. You want to stay here and put your life in the hands of a bunch of senior *ninlocos* who aren't exactly experienced in the formalities of unanticipated interspecies contact, you go right ahead. Me, I'd rather put my trust in the monkeys. I'm heading down into the forest."

Left behind in the garage to meditate on his limited options, Desvendapur soon turned to follow the biped into the other part of the station.

"You don't understand, Cheelo Montoya. It is not that I *want* to remain here. The fact is that I have little choice in the matter."

Cheelo did not look up from where he was stuffing handfuls of concentrates from the outpost's food locker into his backpack. "Ay? Why's that?"

"Did you not notice that I was barely able to help you remove and dispose of the two cadavers? It was not because their weight was excessive. It was because the air here is far too dry for my kind. More importantly, the temperature is borderline freezing."

Pausing in his scavenging, Cheelo turned to regard the alien. "Okay, I can see where that could be a problem. But from here it's all downhill into the Reserva. The lower we go, the hotter and more humid it'll become and the better you'll feel."

The heart-shaped head slowly nodded acquiescence while

truhands and antennae bobbed understandingly. "I know that is so. The difficult, and critical, question is: Will it become hot and humid enough soon enough?"

"I can't answer that," the human responded evenly. "I don't know what your tolerances are."

"I cannot answer it myself. But I fear to try it. By the wings that no longer fly, I do."

From hidden, long-unvisited depths Cheelo dragged up what little compassion remained in him. "Maybe we can rig you some kind of cold-weather gear. I'm no tailor, and I don't see an autogarb in this dump, but I suppose we could cut up some blankets or something. Your only alternatives are to wait here and hope you can talk faster than the people who are coming can shoot, or to strike out across this plateau and try and find another place far enough away that they won't search it."

The thranx indicated negativity. "If I am to walk, better to aim for a more accommodating climate than one I already know to be hostile." Turning, he gestured at the terrain beyond a window. "I would not make it across the first valley before my joints began to stiffen from the cold. And remember: I have one bad leg."

"And five good ones. Well, you think about it." Cheelo returned to his foraging. "Whatever you decide to do, I'll help you if I can—provided it doesn't cost me any more time."

In the end, Desvendapur decided that despite his increasing mastery of the human's language, he was neither confident nor fluent enough to risk an encounter with the dead poachers' customers. Already he had experience of the volatile nature of human response and its reaction to unforeseen events. Not knowing what to expect within the outpost that now failed to respond to their queries, whoever was coming in search of the absent poachers might well unload a rush of lethality in his direction before he could explain himself.

Whatever the chastisement meted out to him upon his return to the colony, it would not include summary execution. The question was, could he make it all the way down to the salubrious surroundings of the lowland rain forest? It seemed he had no choice but to try. Certainly the biped thought so.

Having made the decision, the poet fell to scrounging supplies of his own from the outpost's stores, relying on the human to elucidate the contents of the bewildering variety of multihued food packages and containers.

When their respective packs were bulging with supplies, human and thranx turned their attention to the question of how to insulate someone whose anatomy did not remotely resemble that of an upright mammal. Utilizing the clothing of the deceased proved impossible: None of it would fit over Desvendapur's head or around his body. They settled for wrapping his thorax and abdomen as best they could in several of the high-altitude, lightweight blankets that covered two of the station's beds. Unfortunately, these relied for their generous heating properties on picking up waved energy from a broadcast coil located in the floor of the single bedroom. Outside the buildings and beyond the coil's limited range, the caloric elements woven into the blankets would go inert.

"That's the best I can do," an impatient Cheelo assured his chitinous companion. "There's nothing else here that'd work any better. It's all tech stuff. Stands to reason they'd bring in the most basic of everything they'd need. In a town we could probably find some old-style, heavier wrappings." He nodded curtly toward the nearest window. "No telling how far it is to the nearest village. I know I didn't see one on the way here."

"Nor did I," conceded Desvendapur. Wrapped in the blankets that the human had clumsily cinched around him with cord, the thranx knew he must present a highly incongruous sight. Contemplating himself in a reflective surface, he removed his scri!ber from the thorax pouch that was now hidden beneath the artificial covering and began to recite.

Cheelo looked on in disgust as he tightened a strap on his own pack. "Don't you ever take a break from that composing?"

Winding up a stanza that oozed systemic emotion, the thranx paused the instrument. "For someone like myself, to stop composing would be to start to die."

The human grunted, one of its more primitive sounds, and activated the doorplate. The composite barrier began to roll upward. Cold, searingly dry air rushed hungrily into the insulated structure, overwhelming any warmth before it. Desvendapur's mandibles clacked shut to prevent the deadly cold from entering his system via his mouth. At such times it was useful not to have to open one's jaws to breathe. The biped had cut two long, narrow slits in the blanket that covered the poet's thorax, allowing his spicules access to the air. Internally, his lungs constricted at the intrusion of the frigid atmosphere. Trying not to shudder, he took a hesitant step forward.

"Let's go. The sooner we start downward, the sooner the air will start to warm and to thicken with moisture."

Cheelo said nothing, nodding curtly as he followed him out of the garage.

There was a path, of sorts, made by what animal or animals Cheelo did not know. It was just wide enough for them to proceed along it in single file. Possibly the poachers themselves had enlarged it to allow access to the cloud forest and the rare creatures that dwelled in the little-visited ecosystem lying between plateau and jungle. Llamas would not have made such a track, but far-ranging carnivores like jaguars or the spectacled bear might have tramped back and forth along the same route for enough generations to have worn a path through the unrelenting greenery.

Far more comfortable in the cool mountain air than his companion, Cheelo would have quickly outdistanced him but for the fact that the thranx, utilizing all six legs, was much more sure-footed on the narrow path. Where the thief was forced to take extra care before negotiating an awkward dip or steep drop, Desvendapur simply ambled on, so that the distance between them never became too great.

At midday they paused to eat beside a miniature waterfall. Huge butterflies fluttered on wings of metallic hue, skating the edge of the spray, while mosquitoes danced among the lush ferns that framed the musical cataract. Cheelo was feeling fit and expansive, but it was plain that his many-legged companion was not doing nearly as well.

"C'mon, pick your antennae up," he urged the thranx. "We're doing good." Chewing a strip of reconstituted meat, he nodded at the clouds scudding along mournfully below them. "We'll be down to where it's revoltingly hot and sticky before you know it."

"That is what I am afraid of." Desvendapur huddled as best he could beneath the thin blankets that hung all too loosely around him. "That it will happen before I know of it."

"Is pessimism a common thranx characteristic?" Cheelo chided him playfully.

Without much success, the poet tried to tuck his exposed, unprotected limbs more tightly beneath him. "The human ability to adapt to extremes of climate is one we do not share. I find it difficult to believe that you are comfortable in these surroundings."

"Oh, it's on the brisk side; make no mistake about that. But now that we're off the high plateau and down in cloud forest there ought to be enough moisture in the air for you."

"Truly, the weight of the air is improving," Desvendapur admitted. "But it's still cold, so cold!"

"Eat your vegetables," he advised the thranx. How many times as a child had his mother admonished him to do just that? He smiled to himself at the remembrance. The smile did not last. She had told him things like that when she wasn't hitting him or bringing home a different visiting "uncle" every week or so. His expression darkened as he rose.

"C'mon, get up. We'll push it until you start feeling better." Gratefully, the poet struggled to his six feet, taking care not to shrug off any of the inadequate blankets or put too much pressure on the splinted middle limb.

But he did not start feeling better. Cheelo could not believe how rapidly the thranx's condition deteriorated. Within a short while after their meal the alien began to experience difficulty in walking.

"I . . . I am all right," Desvendapur replied in response to the human's query. "I just need to rest for a time-part."

"No." Cheelo was unbending. "No resting. Not here." Even as the thranx started to sink down onto its abdomen, Cheelo was reaching out to grab the bug and pull it back to its feet. The smooth, unyielding chitin of an upper arm was shockingly icy to the touch. "Shit, you're as cold as these rocks!"

Golden-hued compound eyes peered up at him. "My system is concentrating its body heat internally to protect vital organs. I can still walk. I just need to rest first, to gather my strength."

Cheelo's reply was grim. "You 'rest' for very long and you won't have to worry about gathering any strength." Why was he so concerned? What did it matter to him if the bug died? He could kick the body over the side of the narrow trail and into the gorge where the rich friends of the dead *ninlocos* would never find it. Continuing on alone, he would make better time. Soon he'd find himself down by the river, and then back in the outpost of civilization called Sintuya. Climate-controlled hotel rooms, real food, insect screens, and a quick flight to Lima or Iquitos, then on to Golfito and his appointment with Ehrenhardt. After a rapid electronic transfer of credit, his own franchise. Money, importance, fine clothes, sloe gin, and fast women. *Respect,* for Cheelo Montoya.

It had been promised to him and was all there for the taking. With all that in prospect, why should he exert himself on behalf of a bug, even an oversized, intelligent one? The thranx had brought him nothing but trouble. Oh sure, maybe it had saved his life up on the ridge, but if he'd never met it, he would never have found himself in that life-threatening situation. As if that wasn't reason enough, the insectoid was a criminal, an antisocial, among its own kind! It wasn't like he would be extending himself to help rescue some alien saint or important diplomat.

Des's limbs folded up against his abdomen and thorax as he sank down and huddled beneath the blankets. Even his up-standing antennae folded up, collapsing into tight curls to minimize heat loss. Cheelo stared. Ahead, the trail beckoned: a slender, rutted, dirt-and-mud track leading to one paved with gold. With luck—and if the trail held—he'd be down by nightfall and in Sintuya the following evening. He felt good, and as he went lower, the increasing amount of oxygen gave an additional boost to his spirits.

He took a couple of steps down the trail, turning to look back over a shoulder. "Come on. We can't stop here if we want to get out of the mountains by nightfall."

"A moment, just a moment," the thranx pleaded. Its voice was even wispier than usual.

Cheelo Montoya waited irritably as he gazed at the impenetrable, eternal clouds crawling up the green-clad slopes. "Ah, hell." Turning, he walked back to where the alien had slumped to the ground, all blue-green glaze and crumpled legs. Swinging his pack around so that it rested not against his spine and shoulders but across his chest, he turned his back to the poet, crouched, and bent forward.

"Come on. Get up and walk. It's downhill. Let one leg fall in front of the other."

"Fall?" The barely perceptible, protective transparent eye membrane trembled. "I do not follow your meaning."

"Hurry up!" Annoyed, impatient, and angry at himself, Cheelo had no time for stupid questions. "Put your upper limbs over my shoulders, here." He tapped himself. "Hang on tight. I'll carry you for a while. It'll warm up quick as we go down, and soon you'll be able to walk on your own again. You'll see."

"You—you would carry me?"

"Not if you squat there clicking and hissing! Stand up, dammit, before I have any more time to think about how dumb this is and change my mind."

It was an eerie, chilling sensation, the touch of hard, cold limbs against his shoulders, as if a gigantic crab were scrambling up his back. By utilizing all four front limbs the thranx was able to obtain a secure grip on the human's upper torso. Glancing down, Cheelo could see the gripping digits locked together across his chest beneath pack and straps. All sixteen of them. The embrace was secure without being constricting. The thranx was solidly built, but not unbearably heavy. He decided he could manage it for a while, especially since it was downhill all the way. The biggest danger would come from stumbling or tripping, not from collapsing beneath the moderate alien weight.

Twisting to look around and down, he saw the other four alien limbs hanging loose, two on either side of his legs and hips. Exquisite alien body scent filled his nostrils. Enveloped by perfume, he resumed the descent.

"Just hang on," he snapped irritably at his motionless burden. "You'll feel better as soon as it's warmer."

"Yes." Sensing the four alien mandibles moving against

the flesh of his shoulder, Cheelo tried not to shudder. "As soon as it is warmer. I do not know how to thank you." The exotic alien syllables echoed eerily against his ear.

"Try shutting up for a while," his human bearer suggested. The poet obediently lapsed into silence.

The more relaxed beneath the extra weight he became, the faster Cheelo found he could move. By afternoon the pace of their descent had increased markedly. True to his word, the thranx maintained a merciful muteness, not even requesting that they stop for a meal. The alien's silent acquiescence suited Cheelo just fine.

By the time the shrouded sun had commenced its swift plunge behind the Andes in search of the distant Pacific, Cheelo estimated that they had descended almost halfway to the rain forest below. Tomorrow noontime would see them enter the outskirts of the lowlands, where the temperature and the humidity would reach levels uncomfortable to Cheelo but complaisant for the thranx.

"Time to get off," he told his passenger. Reacting slowly and with deliberation, the thranx released its hold on the human's torso and dropped to the ground.

"I could not have come this far without your aid." Clutching tightly at the blankets with both tru- and foothands, the poet singled out a log on which to spend the coming night, painfully straddling it with all four trulegs. The dead wood was damp and chilly against his exposed abdomen.

"Ay, you have to be feeling better." Without knowing why he bothered, Cheelo tried to cheer his companion. "It's warmer here, so you ought to be more comfortable."

"It is warmer," the thranx admitted. "But not so warm that I am comfortable."

"Tomorrow," Cheelo promised him. Kneeling beside his own pack, he searched for one of the smokeless fire sticks he had appropriated from the poacher outpost. The stick was intended to help start a blaze, but in the absence of any dry fuel he would just have to burn one stick after another until they made their own tiny campfire. They were as likely to find dry wood lying on the floor of a cloud forest as orchids sprouting on tundra.

As he prepared his simple meal Cheelo noticed that the thranx was not moving. "Aren't you going to eat?"

"Not hungry. Too cold." Antennae uncurled halfway but no further.

Shaking his head, Cheelo rose and walked over to examine the contents of the alien's pack. "For a space-traversing species you're not very adaptable."

"We evolved and still prefer to live underground." Even the thranx's usually elegant, graceful gestures were subdued. "It is difficult to adjust to extremes of climate when you do not experience them."

Cheelo shrugged as he rehydrated an assortment of dried fruit. At least water for food rehydration was not a problem in the cloud forest. With the onset of evening it was already beginning to precipitate out on his skin and clothing. Blankets or not, they would be compelled to endure at least one chill, moist night on the steep mountainside. Hot food and drink would help to minimize its effects.

Despite its obvious disinterest in the food, the thranx ate, albeit slowly and with care. Scarfing down his own meal, Cheelo watched the alien closely.

"Feel better?" he asked when both had finished. As always, it was fascinating to watch the bug clean its mandibles with its truhands. It put Cheelo in mind of a praying mantis gleaning the last bits of prey from its razor-sharp jaws.

"Yes, I do." A foothand traced a discreet pattern in the air while the two truhands continued their hygiene, causing Cheelo to reflect on the usefulness of possessing two sets of hands. "This gesture I am making is one of more than moderate thanks."

"Like this?" Cheelo's arm and hand contorted in an ungainly try at mimicry.

The alien did not laugh at or criticize the clumsy attempt. "You have the upper portion of the movement correct, but the lower should go this way." He demonstrated. Once again, Cheelo did his best to imitate the comparatively simple gesture.

"Better," declared Desvendapur. "Try it again."

"I'm doing the best I can." Muttering, Cheelo adjusted his

arm. "Between shoulder and wrist I've only got three joints to your four."

"Near enough." The foothand extended and pulled back at a particular angle. "This is the gesture for agreement."

"So now I'm supposed to learn how to nod with my arm?" Cheelo smiled thinly.

The lesson was an improvement over charades. In this manner they passed the time until total darkness. They had to keep the lesson simple. Not because Cheelo was insufficiently flexible to approximate the thranx's gestures, but because there was no getting around the fact that the more elaborate ones required the use of two pairs of upper appendages. Despite his desire to learn, the thief could not see himself lying down and writhing all four limbs in the air like a beetle trapped on its back.

Morning arrived on the underside of a cloud, crisp and moist. Yawning, Cheelo turned over in his bedroll. The night had been clammy and cold, but not intolerably so. The temperature had stayed well above that common to the plateau high above.

He stretched as he sat up, letting his blanket tumble from his shoulders to bunch up around his waist. Glancing to his right, he saw that his alien companion was still asleep, huddled beneath its makeshift cold-weather gear, all eight limbs contracted tightly beneath its thorax and abdomen.

"Time to move," he announced unsympathetically. Rising, he scratched at himself. "Come on. If we get a good start we'll be all the way down by evening. I'll rehydrate some broccoli or some other green shit for you." Among the litany of terrestrial fruits and vegetables it had sampled, the thranx had proven particularly fond of broccoli. As far as Cheelo was concerned, this only reinforced the differences between their respective species.

When no response was forthcoming, either verbally or in the form of the by-now-familiar elegant gestures, Cheelo walked over and nudged the blue-green torso with a foot. "Rise and shine, Des. Not that you don't shine all the time."

To look at the thranx was to see nothing wrong. The same brushed, metallic blue-green sheen gleamed from wing cases and limbs, head and neck. The multiple lenses of the eyes, each as big as a human fist, threw back the early morning light in cascades of gold. But something was missing. It took Cheelo a long moment before it struck him.

It was an absence of fragrance.

There was no smell. The delicate, flowery miasma that was the thranx's signature perfume had vanished entirely. Bending over, he inhaled deeply of nothing but fresh mountain air. Then he saw that along with the enthralling alien scent something else had departed. Leaning forward, he gave an uncertain shove with both hands.

Stiff as if frozen, the thranx fell over onto its side, scavenged blankets fluttering briefly like dark wings. They had become a funereal shroud. Rigid legs and arms remained fixed in the positions in which they had last been held, folded tight and close to the body.

"Des? C'mon, I got no time to coddle bugs. Get up." Kneeling, he tentatively grasped one upper limb and tugged gently. It did not flex, and there was no reaction. Using both hands, he pulled harder.

A sharp, splintery crack split the air, and the uppermost joint, together with the truhand, came away in his startled fingers. Blood, dark red tinged with green, began to seep from the maimed limb. A shocked Cheelo straightened and threw the amputated length of alien appendage aside. The dismemberment had provoked neither reaction nor response. Stunned, Cheelo realized that Desvendapur was beyond both.

Sitting down hard, indifferent to the damp vegetation and the cold clamminess of the ground, a disbelieving Cheelo could only stare. The bug was dead. No, he corrected himself. No. The poet was dead. Desmelper . . . Dreshenwn . . .

Christ, he cursed silently. He still couldn't pronounce the alien's name. Now it was possible he never would, because the owner of that appellation could no longer lecture him on the fine points of thranx enunciation. He found himself wishing he'd paid more attention when the alien had talked about himself. He found himself wishing he'd paid more attention to a lot of things.

Well, it was too bad, but it wasn't his fault. Unpredictable destiny served as every sentient's copilot. Just because the thranx had met his here on a cold, wet mountainside in the

central Andes didn't mean Cheelo Montoya had any obligation to follow its lead. *His* fate still lay somewhere in the future, first in Golfito and then in the remunerative flesh pits of
Monterrey. His conscience was clear.

As for the bug, he owed it nothing. Hell, it didn't even belong on his *world*! The consequences it had suffered were the
consummation of its own unforced, willful actions. No guilt
concerning the final outcome attached to Cheelo or, for that
matter, to anyone else. It was dead; things hadn't worked out;
and Cheelo had seen it all before, albeit only among his own
kind. No big deal. No big deal at all.

Then why did he feel so goddamn lousy?

This is ridiculous, he told himself. He'd done his best by
the alien, just as it had by him. Neither of them had anything
to be sorry for. If called before a court of judgment, both
could have honestly proclaimed the verity of their conduct
while traveling in each other's company. Besides, if the situation were reversed, if he, Cheelo Montoya, had been the one
lying dead and motionless among the undergrowth, what
would the thranx have done? Returned to its own people, for
sure, and left him to rot forlorn and forgotten on the surface
of the sodden earth.

Of course, Cheelo Montoya had nothing to leave behind.

He wavered. There was no one to coerce him, no accusatory visages staring at him from the depths of the cloud
forest. Whatever urgency he felt came entirely from within,
though from where within he could not have said. It made no
sense, and he was nothing if not a sensible man. Everything
he had ever learned, every ounce of self, all that there was
that went to make him what was known as "him," shouted at
him to pick up his gear and be on his way. Head down, get
going, abandon the no-longer-needed campsite by the little
waterfall. Seek out a comfortable room in beckoning Sintuya, arrange his flight, and claim the franchise that had been
promised to him. His life had been one long litany of misery
and failure. Until now.

Tightening his jaw, he rolled the body, blankets and all,
into a dense mass of dark green brush. There it would lie
hidden from above until the cloud forest claimed it. Not that

the perpetual clouds needed any help in concealing objects on the ground from above.

Snatching up his backpack with a violent grab, he swung it onto his shoulders, checked the seals, and started resolutely down the trail. As he did so, he stumbled over something unyielding. Snapping off a muttered curse, he started to kick aside the piece of broken branch, only to see that the obstacle that had momentarily interrupted the resumption of his determined descent was not made of wood. It was the upper joint and hand he had unexpectedly wrenched from the thranx's body.

Divorced from the rest of the arm, it had assumed an air of artificiality. Surely those stiff, delicate digits were detached from some calcareous sculpture and not a living being. Sublime in its design, sleek and functional, it was of no use to its former owner anymore, and certainly not to him. Bending to pick it up, he examined it closely for a moment before tossing it indifferently over his shoulder and resuming his descent.

Down among the next line of vegetation he halted. Cloud forest trees bloomed intermittently year-round. Ahead rose one that was like a roaring blaze among green stone, an umbrella of brilliant crimson blossoms. Sunbirds sipped drunkenly at the bounteous nectar while giant electric blue morpho butterflies flitted among the branches like the scoured scales of some fantastic cerulean fish. Cheelo stood gazing at the breathtakingly beautiful sight for a long time. Then, without really knowing why, he turned around and began to retrace his steps.

22

Shannon didn't much care for her new posting, but it was a step up from covering tourism and reforestation projects. At least Iquitos had facilities, something to do at night, and climate-controlled shopping where city dwellers could escape from the oppressive heat and humidity. It could have been worse, she knew. The company might have assigned her to report on tropical research. That would have meant weeks at a time living out in the jungle with scientists who would condescend to her questions while resenting the imposition on their time, the access her presence provided to general media notwithstanding. Being assigned to the district office in Iquitos was better, much better.

It also offered the opportunity to do more than just report news. Hard to descry in the rain forest, traditional human-interest stories were plentiful in the city and its enjungled suburbs. Like the one that had presented itself this morning, for example. Plenty of reprobates and lowlifes tried to lose themselves in the vast reaches of the Reserva, but sooner or later their presence was detected by automatic monitoring devices and they found themselves a guest of the rangers.

The only thing different about this one was that instead of petty misappropriation of credit or common vandalism or illegal entry or poaching, the subject had been booked on a charge of murder. Iquitos could be a rough town, but homicide was uncommon. Advanced law-enforcement technology coupled with the threat of general instead of selective mindwipe was usually enough to forestall most killings.

That was not what made this particular case intriguing, however. What made it interesting from a general media standpoint was that its progenitor had "a story." She was mildly curious to see if the teller was as crazy as his tale.

A guard was stationed outside the interview room; not surprising considering that the one incarcerated within stood accused of a capital crime. Having already been scanned for possession of weapons and other forbidden items, she identified herself to the sentry's satisfaction and was granted admittance. As the door slid into the wall he stood aside to let her enter.

The aspect of the solitary figure seated on the other side of the interview table was not promising, and she found herself worrying that she might well be wasting her time. Not that there was any especial demand on it at the moment. Pulling out and activating her recorder, she checked to make sure that the protective cover had retracted and that the lens was clean. Treated to repel dirt and grime, it flickered briefly in the subdued overhead light.

The brief flash caught the attention of the prisoner. When he lifted his head, she was able to get a better look at him. It did not improve her opinion. Neither did the way he looked at her, used to it as she was.

"I was expecting a reporter, not a treat." He leered unpleasantly. "How about we get the monkey cop to opaque the window?" He nodded toward the doorway.

"How about you keep your mouth and your eyes to yourself and you answer my questions?" she retorted flatly. "Otherwise, I'll waft and you can play with yourself until the official interrogators land on you again. They won't listen to your lunatic stories, either."

His macho bravado instantly deflated, the prisoner looked away. Fingers working uneasily against one another as if he didn't know what to do with them, he muttered a reply. "First you got to get me my personal belongings."

Her dyed and striped brows drew together. "What personal belongings? The report on you said you were picked up out in the forest with only the clothes on your back."

Leaning forward, he lowered his voice to a conspiratorial whisper. "When I saw that the rangers had me referenced, I buried my pack. Without what's in it you won't believe a word I say."

"I doubt I'll believe a word you say anyway, so what's the big deal? What's in your miserable pack that you had to hide from the rangers? Illegal narcotics? Gemstones?"

He grinned, this time knowingly. "Proof. Of my story."

Shaking her head sadly, she turned off the recorder. No point in wasting the cell. "There *is* no proof of your 'story.' Not in some mysterious buried backpack or anywhere else. Because your story's crazy. It makes no sense."

The smile tightened but did not disappear entirely. "Then why are *you* here?"

She shrugged diffidently. "Because it sounded different from the usual run-of-the mill rubbish we use for backscreen fillers. Because I thought you might be good for a new angle or two on how some miscreants try to mask themselves from the attentions of the legal process. So far I'm just annoyed, not enlightened."

"Go dig up my pack and I'll enlighten the hell out of you. The contents will enlighten you."

She sighed heavily. "I skimmed the report. There are *no* thranx in the Reserva. There are no thranx in this hemisphere. Their presence on Earth, like that of all representatives of newly contacted sentient species, is restricted to the one orbital station that's been equipped with proper diplomatic facilities. We have occasional closely supervised visits by especially important individuals holding the rank of eint or higher, but they are not allowed outside the official boundaries of Lombok or Geneva. Even if one somehow managed to end up here, it couldn't survive."

Inclining toward her again, he dropped his voice so low that she had to lean forward to make out the words. She did not relish the proximity. Despite the treatment accorded any incoming prisoner, he still stank strongly of his time spent in the Reserva and of his own disagreeable self.

"You're right. 'One' couldn't survive. But a properly prepared and equipped landing party could."

She rolled her eyes and looked away. She'd had just about enough of this homicidal *ninloco* and his pathetic fantasies. "Now you're trying to tell me that there's not one, but a whole landing party of thranx bashing around undetected inside the Reserva? What kind of moron do you take me for, Montoya?

If the rangers can run down one human like yourself who's trying his damnedest to avoid them, don't you think they'd find something as alien as a thranx? Much less a whole landing party?"

"Not if it stayed underground and had human help," he shot back. "And I wasn't trying to avoid the rangers. Not anymore. I wanted to be picked up."

She frowned uncertainly, her irritation diminishing just enough for her to sustain a modicum of interest. "Underground? You're trying to tell me that there's an illegal thranx landing party operating inside the Reserva and underground?"

His countenance subsided into a complacent smirk. "Not a landing party. A hive. A colony." His tone had become insolent. "There aren't a dozen or so thranx in the Reserva—there are hundreds. And they're not peeking at plants or collecting butterflies—they're living there. And breeding."

She stared hard at him, at this slender, vainglorious *madrino* who sat with arms crossed and smile smug. He did not look away. She wanted to, but could not. Not quite yet.

"So what's in this pack of yours that would prove a claim as outrageous as that?"

"Then my 'crazy' story might be a little newsworthy?" He was taunting her now. She wouldn't let him get away with it.

"Give me the coordinates for this pack of yours and we'll see what's in it. If anything. If it exists."

"Oh, it exists all right." He glanced briefly toward the doorway. "But first we need to come to some kind of agreement. Officially recorded and witnessed."

"Agreement?" Shannon was not pleased. Her bureau's discretionary expense file was in proportion to her assignment. Iquitos wasn't Paris. "What kind of agreement?"

For the first time since she had entered the interview room he appeared to relax. "You don't think I'm going to give away the story of the century out of the goodness of my heart, do you?" For a moment, his eyes took on a faraway look and his voice fell to a whisper. "I *have* to get something back, because I've already missed my appointment. I forfeited the franchise. For this." He shook his head slowly, his tone disbelieving. "I *must* be crazy. One other thing: We tell it my way. I want editorial input."

She started to laugh, but then she saw that he was serious. "So now in addition to being a murderer you want to be a journalist?"

His eyes lowered. "That killing up in San José was unfortunate. An accident. It'll all come out at my hearing." The smile returned, sly and knowing. "It'll be a sealed hearing, you'll see. I know too much, and the government doesn't like people who know too much to run around loose babbling what they know. But it'll be worth it to you. I promise."

She sat up straight and turned her recorder back on. "Never mind all that other nonsense: What makes you think you know anything about telling a story?"

Pursing his lips, he blew her a kiss. She recoiled distastefully. "You just bought mine, didn't you?"

The pack was there, surprisingly far to the south, buried in a shallow pit between two gnarled strangler figs. Right where he'd said it would be. That in itself meant nothing. The presence of an identifiable, functioning thranx device inside was likewise conclusive of nothing except the owner's ability to obtain contraband through channels with which he was clearly familiar. The section of thranx arm, however, was another matter. It was sufficiently fresh and well-enough wrapped so that it had not yet begun to decompose, even under the relentless assault of the opportunistic rain forest. Taken together, they lent veracity if not proof to the prisoner's story.

The next time Shannon visited Montoya, she had company. Not rangers, but a pair of commentators from her company and one wizened, white-haired senior editor.

The prisoner eyed them with an amiable wariness. On the table between them lay the section of alien limb and the device that had been removed from the buried backpack. Neither appeared to have been touched, though in fact both had been carefully examined with a view toward verifying their authenticity. This had been done. Now it remained for the exceedingly curious media representatives to find out how these unlikely objects had come to be in the possession of a minor criminal whose erstwhile home lay far to the north on the American isthmus.

One of the reporters pushed the device across the table in

Cheelo's direction. "We know that this is of alien manufacture, but we don't know what it does."

"I do. It's a scri!ber. I told you—Des was a poet. That
means he did more than just put words together. Among the
thranx, poetry is a performance art. I know: He performed
a couple of times for me." A gaunt, regretful smile split
his features. "I didn't get much out of it. Didn't understand
the words or the gestures. There was a lot of clicking and
whistling, too. But God, it was beautiful."

The reporter who had asked the question was about to
laugh, but her companion put a restraining hand on her arm.
Leaning forward, he spoke understandingly. "I'm Rodrigo
Monteverde, from the parliament district. I haven't seen
the kind of performance you're referring to myself, but I've
talked to those who have. Your description fits."

"These thranx have performed for ranking officials. A
couple have been on the tridee." The senior editor did not stir
as he spoke. "He could have seen a recording."

Shannon gingerly pushed the length of amputated limb
toward the prisoner. "What about this? What's this?"

Montoya lowered his gaze to the blue-green fingers. His
insides knotted and a sharp pain shot through his gut, but to
all outward appearances he was unaffected. "That? That was
my friend." He looked up, smiling at Shannon before shifting
his attention to the gray-hair who obviously called the shots.

"I'm offering you the biggest story of the last hundred
years. You want it, or should I put out the word that I'm ready
to talk to another media conglomerate?"

The senior editor retained his unshakable composure, but a
hint of a smile toyed with one corner of his mouth. "We want
it—if there's anything more to it. The question is, what do *you*
want?" He nodded in the reporter's direction. "Ms. Shannon
here has apprised me of your petition but did not supply any
details."

All eyes were on him, components of expectant expressions. He reveled in the attention. It made him feel . . . big.
"That's better! First, I want all charges pending or planning to
be filed against me dropped."

"I understand you committed a murder." Shannon's tone
was dry as dust. She didn't like him, Cheelo knew. That did

not matter. What was vital was that she saw the opportunity to work on a big story. He was not the only one to whom the word was important. Much of the world still worked that way. "It was accidental, like I told you. The idiot had to go macho and grab the gun and there was a struggle. Nobody could prove premeditation. Scan the wife and you'll see that I'm telling the truth."

"Nevertheless," declared the senior editor inexorably, "you left an innocent man for dead."

"Fix it." Cheelo's tone was harsh and uncompromising. "I know what the media can do. After all charges are dropped, I want my permanent record expunged. I'd like to start over, clean."

"So you can fill it up again?" The editor sighed. "What you ask is doable. Expensive and awkward, but doable. Especially if what you say about scanning the wife holds up. What else?"

"Some credit in my account. I haven't settled on a sum yet. We can work that out together." His tone turned wistful. "You probably won't believe me, but by letting myself get picked up I sacrificed a lot more money than you can imagine. More than that, I gave up a career."

"How noble of you." As the editor spoke, all three reporters were taking notes. *Notes,* Cheelo thought silently. That's all any of us are: a bundle of somebody else's notes. When we die, we're all dependent on the notes made by others. Unless we take the time to make some ourselves.

"One more thing." He pushed the alien scri!ber toward Shannon. "I want everything that's on here published. I don't know what that means in this case, or how you'd go about doing it, because it's not like human poetry. But I want it *done*. I want it all published and disseminated. Among the thranx as well as here on Earth."

" 'Disseminated'?" Shannon eyed him archly.

"Hey, I'm poor, not stupid. I want Des's art—out there. For everybody to see."

"It won't mean anything to us, to humans," the second reporter pointed out.

"Maybe not, but the thranx are going to be exposed to it whether they like it or not. Once disclosed, they won't be able to ignore it. It's great stuff, important work. *Big* work." He squeezed his eyelids together. Hard. "Bigger than anything *I'll* ever do."

For the first time, the open hostility and contempt Shannon had been feeling began to give way to incertitude. "How do you know that, if you couldn't understand any of it?"

"I know because of the way Des believed in it, the way he talked about it, the way he showed it to me—even if I didn't understand much of it. I know because he gave up everything to try and achieve something important. I'm no artist—I can't sculpt, or paint, or weave light, or write real well. But I know passion when I see it." He brightened. "Yeah, that's what it was about Des. He was passionate." He tapped the scri!ber's protective casing. "This gadget is full of passion, and I want it splashed out there for everybody to see."

For the first time, the senior editor showed some animation. "Why? Why should you care what happens to the work of some obscure alien artist? The art means nothing to you. *He* meant nothing to you."

"I'm not sure. Maybe—maybe it's because I've always felt that everybody should stand for something, even if the rest of society doesn't agree on what that is, and that nobody should die for nothing. I've seen too many people die for nothing. I don't want it to happen to me, and I don't want it to happen to Des." With a shrug, he looked away, toward the single window that was too small for a prisoner to crawl through. Outside lay the city and beyond, the rain forest.

"It'll probably happen to me anyway. I'm not anything special. Never was and probably never will be. But I'm going to see to it that it doesn't happen to him."

While the reporters waited respectfully, the editor considered the prisoner's words. Eventually he looked back up at Cheelo. "All right. We agree to your terms. All of them. *Provided* there's something significant and real at the end of this alien rainbow of yours."

A mollified Cheelo leaned back in his chair. Despite the backpack, despite its unarguably alien contents, he was not sure until the very end that the media people would go for it. Unless he was very much mistaken, he would soon be walking the streets again. A dead thranx poet had cost him a career but bought him his freedom.

What the consequences of that freedom would be he could not have foreseen. He expected to be free. He did not expect to be famous.

Searching only within the section of rain forest specified by the thief allowed the reporters and their staff to locate the hive within a few weeks of Cheelo supplying them with coordinates. Worldwide revelation followed and outrage ensued. Exposed and confronted, the representatives of the colony and their covert human allies pleaded a case which for them could have only one outcome.

Their careful, cautious diplomacy undone, human and thranx emissaries scrambled to salvage what they could of a shattered process of prudent negotiation. Forced to advance all interspecies colloquy and bring forward proposals that were barely in the preliminary stages of synthesis, they hastened to compose and then sign the first formal treaties between humans and thranx some twenty to forty years before they were ready. Both species would simply have to deal with the unpredictable consequences. The alternative was a formal break in relations coupled with the possibility of open hostilities.

As for the Amazonian colony, it was allowed to remain only because humans were hastily granted reciprocal colonization privileges on the thranx homeworld of Hivehom in addition to the much smaller installation on Willow-Wane. A site was selected on what the bipeds soon came to call the Mediterranea Plateau, a dominion too bleak and cold and dry for the thranx to settle. Forced together by the circumstance of revelation, human and thranx rapidly discovered that they complemented one another in ways that could not have been predicted by formal diplomacy. The first tentative steps were taken to overcome each species' abhorrence of the hideous appearance of the other.

As for Cheelo Montoya, who only wanted to sink back into the backstreet society in which he had grown up, albeit with a bit more money, he found himself transformed from petty, remorseless street hustler into a paragon of interspecies first contact. It was a celebrity he did not seek and did not want, but once his part in the business was revealed he no longer had any choice in the matter. Eagerly sought out for interviews, thrust beneath world-spanning tridee pickups, he was repeatedly reminded of his personal inadequacies by questions he could not answer and requests for opinions that were beneath his ability to formulate. With his face thrust relentlessly before an inquisitive world, he lost any semblance of personal privacy. Poked, prodded, queried, challenged, the object of rumor and the subject of speculation, before long he found himself regretting that he had ever tried to make a single credit off his unsought relationship with the dead alien poet. Harried and harassed by a pitiless media and a bastard-loving populace, he died sooner than he should have, ennobled by a public whose historical appetite for falsely inculcated minor deities verged on the unbounded. His funeral was a sumptuous, splendid affair, trideed all over the planet as well as to all human and thranx-settled worlds. He would have decried the waste of money.

The monument they placed above his coffin, at least, was something big.

The thranx were less ingenuous. Forced by its exposure to accept on its merits the work of a monstrously antisocial artist who normally would have been resolutely ignored, the highly conservative thranx performance establishment proved unable to repudiate its worth. The power and passion with which the deceased Desvendapur had endowed his compositions would not be denied.

So it was that Cheelo Montoya, who did not want it, was forced to endure the fame that the renegade poet Desvendapur had sought. Offered a shocking amount for his memoirs, he had laboriously transcribed them for the media with the help of a small army of ghost writers. As he told it, the tale of his encounter and relationship with the renegade thranx artist took on a glamorous, heroic mien. Poetic, even, so that while later generations knew that a murderer and a poet were responsible for the forced, accelerated pace of human-thranx contact, the line became blurred as to who was which.

With tentative, cultivated, ceremonial contact shattered by the unscheduled revelations, relations between the species were advanced by perhaps half a century in spite of, and not because of, the exertions of well-meaning, hard-working, professional emissaries. There was precedent. History is often fashioned by insignificant individuals intent on matters of petty personal concern who have motives entirely irrelevant to carefully planned posterity. It was just as well.

Had humankind contacted the next intelligent race they encountered prior to formalizing relations with the thranx, the Commonwealth might very well never have come into existence. As for the duplicitous AAnn, their upset verged on outrage as they saw their traditional competitors for habitable worlds forge an ever-deepening relationship with the militarily strong but mentally unpredictable humans. Bereft of stratagems for countering the seemingly inevitable alliance, the government of the emperor sought the advice of any who might have an efficacious solution to propound.

As it happened, Lord Huudra Ap and Baron Keekil YN stood ready to supply one.

NEXT—DIRGE

Don't miss the second book in the
Founding of the Commonwealth series:

DIRGE
by Alan Dean Foster

Published by Del Rey books in hardcover.
Look for it at your local bookstore.

*For an exciting preview
please read on . . . .*

Surrounded by members of the *Chagos*'s staff, Burgess was staring intently at the tridee. Magnification was visual, not schematic, so he was able to observe the craft that had just joined them in orbit in all its alien glory. It was an impressive ship, at least twice the size of the *Chagos*. While the prevalent configuration was similar to that of the *Chagos* and all other vessels equipped with the universal variant of the KK-drive, its design and execution differed in a multitude of significant respects.

"Not ours," one of the techs seated nearby murmured unnecessarily.

"Not thranx, either," the first officer added. "Unless they've been hiding something from us. Could it be one of those AAnn ships the thranx are always trying to warn us about?"

Burgess looked doubtful. "I've seen the AAnn schematics the thranx have provided. This design is much too sleek. Could it be Quillp?" Burgess longed for expertise in an area his crew, through no fault of their own, did not possess.

"I don't think so, Captain." Though far from positive, the first officer felt secure in hazarding a guess. If he was proved wrong, he would be delighted to admit the mistake. He hoped he was wrong. The inherent pacificity of the Quillp was well known.

Looking sharply to his left, Burgess snapped a question. "Any response to our queries, Tambri?"

The diminutive communications officer glanced over at him and shook her head. Her dark eyes were very wide. "Nothing, sir. I'm trying everything, from Terranglo through High and Low Thranx to straight mathematical theorems.

They're chattering noisily among themselves—I can pick up the wash—but they're not talking to us."

"They will. Keep trying." Burgess turned back to the three-dimensional image floating in the air of the ship's bridge. "Who are they and what the blazes do they want here?"

"Maybe they've already claimed this world." The observation no one had wanted to voice come from the back of the command section. "Maybe they're here to inform us of a claim of prior rights."

"If that's the case," declared the first officer, "they've been mighty subtle about advertising any prior presence here. There isn't so much as an artifact on the planet, much less an orbital transmitter. There's nothing on either of the two small moons, or anywhere else in the system."

"That we've found yet, you mean." Having stated a contention, the dissenter felt bound to defend it. "We've only been here a couple of months."

"Okay, okay," Burgess muttered. "Let's everybody keep calm. Whatever the situation, we'll deal with it. We didn't expect to encounter sapience here, much less evidence of another space-traversing species. They're probably taking our measure as carefully as we are theirs." *But I wish they'd respond to our communications,* he thought tensely.

"Look there!" someone in the growing crowd pointed.

A second, much smaller vessel was emerging from the side of the first. Winged and ported, obviously designed for atmospheric travel, it began to recede swiftly from the flank of its parent vessel. Its immediate purpose was self-evident. Anything else those aboard might intend could not be divined from tracking its progress.

"Get on to Pranchavit and the rest of the landing party," Burgess barked at the communications officer. "Tell them they're probably going to have company."

Once again the officer looked up from her instrumentation. "They'll want to know what kind of company, sir."

Burgess glanced over at the tridee holo. "Maybe they can tell us."

By the time Kairuna and his companions arrived at the camp, it was alive with questions and concerns, anxiety and confusion. No one seemed to know what was going on, including those who had recognized the audible signal for what it was. Now they troubled themselves with unsupported inferences and paranoid suppositions. In such company, Alwyn was in his element.

Pushing and shoving their way into an already crowded mess hall, the three late arrivals found themselves confined to the narrow remaining open space next to the rear wall. Up by the service door that led to the main stockroom, Jalen Maroto was waving his arms for quiet. When that didn't work, he put a compact amplifier to his lips and simply shouted everybody down.

"Shut up! If you'll just shut up, I'll tell you what's going on." As the crowd noise subsided he added apologetically, "Or at least, what we know."

"I know!" Shy as always, Alwyn was not afraid to proclaim theories where others were hesitant to venture facts. "Something local's finally showed up to cause trouble. What is it?" he demanded to know. "A herd of predators? A fast-mutating plague?"

"There's a plague, all right," the team leader declared through the amplifier, "but it's one we brought along with us." Delighted to take advantage of the emotional release, a number of the assembled turned their laughter in the specialist's direction. Unrepentant but temporarily subdued, he tried to meet the ridicule of each and every one of them with a defiant glare of his own.

" A ship has gone into orbit near the *Chagos*," Maroto informed scientists and support personnel alike. "We don't know where it's from, what species built it, or what their intentions are. So far nobody on the *Chagos*, including the people who are supposed to know about such things, has been able to pull a fact out of a big basket of ignorance."

"They're not thranx?" someone in the crowd wondered loudly, referring to the intelligent insectoid race with whom humankind had been cautiously developing relations over the past thirty years.

"We don't know who or what they are," Maroto replied, "because they're not responding to the *Chagos*'s repeated queries to identify themselves. If they're thranx, they're being mighty close-mouthed about it."

"The bugs may be ugly, but I've never heard of them going mute," Idar murmured softly.

"I know what they are." When no one reacted to his latest assertion of certitude, Alwyn assumed a plaintive tone. "Well? Doesn't anyone want to know what I know?"

"Nobody wants to know what you know, Alwyn, because you never know half of what you claim to know." Unlike his companions Kairuna had the advantage of being able to see over the heads of just about everyone in the crowd.

"Go ahead and mock." Alwyn was confident as ever. "These are the hostile, rampaging, bloodthirsty aliens we've always feared encountering as we extend our sphere of influence."

"I thought the AAnn were supposed to be the hostile aliens," Idar pointed out.

"That's what the thranx claim, but so far we've only the bugs' word for AAnn hostility. No, these are something new. New and hostile," he concluded with an assurance that regrettably was not born of proof.

"If they're hostile," a contrary Kairuna argued, "why are we still standing here talking? Why haven't they turned this site and all of us to dust?"

"Just you wait." Secure in his latent mistrust, the specialist glanced knowingly skyward.

Aside from the fact that scattering into the trees could be misinterpreted by those aboard the rapidly descending alien shuttle as a hostile gesture, there was (the feelings of a certain suspicious support specialist aside) no overwhelming reason to do so. The parent ship continued to swing in low orbit within viewing distance of the *Chagos*, moving neither toward nor away from the human vessel, its communicators silent, the identity of its occupants still a mystery. No one on board the *Chagos* was surprised when the alien shuttle braked atmosphere and began a swift, calculated curve that would put it on the surface directly in the midst of the survey team's encampment. Indeed, given the on-going proximity of the two KK-drive craft, Burgess and his fellow staff officers would have been perplexed had the alien shuttle chosen to set down anywhere else.

At first nothing more than a distant point of light sifting

down through an azure sky, the alien landing craft grew rapidly in size and dimension until its descending silhouette differentiated sharply from the framing clouds. Assembled between field and forest, fewer than a hundred human faces strained to make out the lines and design of the unknown vessel.

The landing was smooth and almost silent, as if the pilots had been practicing on similar open fields for years. As the whine of multiple engines became tolerable, hands fell from ears to shade eyes as the craft turned to approach the crowd. There being no need for ceremony while engaged in survey, Pranchavit and Morobe were reduced to greeting the visitors in clean duty clothes. Kairuna smiled to himself. The prim head of the Argus scientific team, at least, was no doubt regretting the absence of his fancy dress uniform.

There was a stirring as the landing craft maintained speed during its turn, and a few of those gathered in front found themselves wondering if perhaps their desire for a good view of the proceedings might not be misplaced. But the many-winged alien lander pivoted neatly on its double set of nose wheels and lined up parallel to the crowd. Those in front relaxed. Nothing of an overtly offensive nature was in evidence. Kairuna knew of several researchers and techs who had armed themselves in defiance of directives. Pistols remained concealed by multiple layers of cold-weather clothing and bulky jackets.

Eagerness filled the air like a cool fog. What would the aliens look like? Would they be atavistically alarming like the thranx? Elegantly handsome and yet vaguely sinister like the AAnn? Or quaintly charming like the Quillp? Humankind had yet to voyage sufficiently far, had still to encounter enough intelligent species, to be blasé at the prospect of meeting still another.

Perhaps they would look like nothing the smooth-skinned simians in their glistening new KK-drive starships had yet met. They might be towering horrors, or diminutive pacifists. Or diminutive horrors or towering pacifists. No one knew. Kairuna and the rest of the survey team would be the first to gaze upon these new, previously unencountered alien countenances. He and his associates were acutely conscious of the singular privilege that was being accorded them.

Everyone had been thoroughly, if hastily, briefed. No matter what the aliens looked like, no matter how repulsive, or absurd, or disconcerting, or surprising, all reaction was to be kept to a minimum. There was to be no cheering lest sudden noises upset the visitors. No wrinkling of faces, no distorted expressions that might be misinterpreted in the event the visitors communicated by similar means. No expansive gestures in case they asserted themselves in a manner akin to the highly gesticulatory thranx. Response to any overtures and all expressions of greeting would be made by Pranchavit and Morobe. Everyone else was welcome to watch, but in stillness and silence.

That did not prevent Idar from nudging Kairuna in the side as an opaque cylinder slowly and silently descended from the belly of the alien craft. It looked as if a particularly sleek bird was laying an oblong egg. Nearby, a grim-faced Alwyn patted his side.

"Not to worry. I'm carrying a regulation sideshot with a full clip."

"It won't be much use to you in the brig," Idar hissed at him.

"Both of you, be quiet." Kairuna nodded. "They're coming out. Or something is." The possibility that the aliens might choose to make first contact through intermediaries such as mechanicals could not be discounted.

There were no mechanicals, however. The aliens had chosen to greet the tightly packed crowd of anxious bipeds in person. There were three of them. Nitrox breathers themselves, they were clad only in lightweight clothing of some unfamiliar fabric that shimmered in the bright, cold air, and no helmets or other headgear whatsoever.

The reaction to their appearance was a uniform gasp on the part of the assembled humans. Kairuna was unaware that his lower jaw dropped slightly, leaving him standing in full defiance of orders with a mock-stupid expression on his face. Idar stood wide-eyed but with more presence of mind as well as person. Alwyn, whose left hand had been hovering in the vicinity of his concealed weapon, was moved to comment, but mindful of the general directive to keep quiet, held his peace.

It was a good thing he had the forbearance to keep from drawing the gun. The aliens might not have reacted immediately to its emergence, but his erstwhile fellow humans surely would have. It was not that his naturally suspicious nature was in any way mollified by the aliens' utterly unexpected and novel appearance. Only that he was for once, no less shocked than his companions.

DIRGE
by Alan Dean Foster

Available at bookstores everywhere.

To find out more about the Commonwealth
and other worlds of Alan Dean Foster visit
www.alandeanfoster.com